SEMPER FI

SEMPER FI

WITHOUT COMPROMISE

J.W. MINTON

BALBOA.
PRESS
A DIVISION OF HAY HOUSE

Balboa Press books may be ordered through booksellers or by contacting:

Balboa Press
A Division of Hay House
1663 Liberty Drive
Bloomington, IN 47403
www.balboapress.com
1-(877) 407-4847

ISBN: 978-1-4525-7361-8 (sc)
ISBN: 978-1-4525-7363-2 (hc)
ISBN: 978-1-4525-7362-5 (e)

Library of Congress Control Number: 2013907792

Printed in the United States of America.

Balboa Press rev. date: 06/10/2013

MANY ARE CALLED TO NOBLE WORK OF THE GREAT COMMISSION, ENTRUSTED TO TEACH ALL NATIONS BY WORD AND DEED, AND EACH SAINT IS HELD TO ACCOUNT. THE GOOD STEWARD IS REQUIRED TO BE FAITHFUL, TO BE HOLY AND LET THE LIGHT SHINE, TO BE SEPARATED FROM THE WORLD. BUT SO OFTEN AS SOME SET HAND TO THE PLOW THEY SEEM TO LOSE THEIR GRIP, DISTRACTED AWAY FROM HARVEST GOALS BRIEFLY OR ALTOGETHER. BLEMISHES AND SHREDS DEVELOP IN THE TATTERED UNTENDED TAPESTRY OF HOLINESS, THE LAMP DIMS OR FLICKERS AWAY. COMMITMENT TO THE GRAND MISSION IS BETRAYED AS WEAK, SPORADIC, OR ABANDONED IN WHOLE OR PART. THE FACE ONCE SET LIKE A FLINT IS TURNED ASIDE.

ON THE ROAD OF LIFE THERE IS NO CUSTOMARY COURSE OF MORAL OR SPIRITUAL EROSION, NO INESCAPABLE PATH TO PERDITION, AND THE FIASCO OF FAILURE IS NOT ALWAYS A FREE-FALL, BUT OFTEN JUST SEEMINGLY INSIGNIFICANT SIMPLE SINS OF GREED OR CLANDESTINE CARNAL EXCURSIONS. NOT ALWAYS A CHOICE OF COMMON CRIMES OR MAMMOTH MALEVOLENT MISCHIEF, MERELY THOSE TRIFLING DEPARTURES FROM CONVENTIONAL RULES OF MODESTY AND VIRTUE, POSSIBLY JUST A FEW LITTLE WHITE LIES OR OTHER DECEPTIONS THAT BETRAY A LACK OF HONESTY AND INTEGRITY. SLIGHT SECRET SINS. BUT BEWARE THOSE TINY TURPITUDES WILL BE FOUND OUT, AND RESULTING REWARD FOR THE ERROR GREAT OR SMALL CAN BE TERRIBLY SHAMEFUL, EMBARRASSING, SO HUMILIATING, AND PACKED WITH PERSONAL PAIN, ANGUISH, GRIEF AND REGRET.

YET THERE IS HOPE FOR ONE THAT HAS STUMBLED. IN SPITE OF THE ERROR THERE CAN BE RESTORATION. OUR GOD CAN MAKE SWEET LEMONADE OUT OF EVEN THE SOUREST LEMONS, AND AT A TIME OF FAILURE CAN STILL PROVIDE A WAY, AS THINGS CAN NONETHELESS BE WORKED OUT TO EVENTUAL GOOD FOR THOSE THAT LOVE THE LORD AND ARE CALLED ACCORDING TO HIS PURPOSE. THE GOALS ARE STILL WITHIN REACH AS THE RIGHTEOUS RECIDIVIST STUMBLES AND RISES AGAIN WITH RENEWED RESOLVE TO PRESS ON WITH MIND FOCUSED ON HIM, AND HE WILL DIRECT THE PATH TO THE PRIZE OF OUR HIGH CALLING.

WHY?

JESUS LOVES ME.

TABLE OF CONTENTS

PROLOGUE

All throughout life in the human condition there are encountered questions for which there seems no responsible answer or situations where the questions in principle should simply never be asked. Some things are whispered which amount to nothing more than idle gossip. Some things are shouted for the amusement of those that have nothing productive to contribute. Some remarkably stupid people become celebrities, and as celebrities their opinions are sought and highly revered. By law or social convention society impinges upon our ability to apply a satisfactory remedy to some impossible situations, or restraints inflicted by vague religious ideologies wherever they might have come from. There are sentiments imposed by perceived parameters of honor and decency, or standards of morality and ethics. Occasionally, honor and decency codes are in conflict with those standards of morality and ethics. These rules are often levied no matter what the nature and extent of harm done to innocent individuals or groups. Some of the rules enacted really do not benefit any individual or group in our society, they are simply enforced because the culture requires it, and often just because that's the way it has been done founded upon history and established order. This is the stuff that wars and other human struggles are made of.

This tale that follows is based upon actual facts, and one particular situation that had no acceptable resolution at the time of occurrence and were the same facts to arise again in this present day there would still be no universally acceptable solution. The names of individuals and places have been changed but the persons involved and their many friends and relatives will easily recognize who the story is about, and will likely find great humor in the way the full account is told, and some of the details disclosed will provide links that might enlighten folks that were curious about particulars and why things happened as they did. There are foundational features throughout the story that are very important in understanding the outcomes in the latter part of the tale. We give you the facts; then you can raise your own questions and answer them however you might please.

You should conclude that there is no responsible counselor that would orchestrate any particular outcome for the underlying circumstances related in this tale. If you might encounter any individual or individuals caught up in similar situations you would be well advised to remain silent and not encourage anyone to choose one solution over another. This might leave your friends or relatives standing alone without your astute counsel, but you should first consider that even though things worked out quite well for the stars of our story, your friends or relatives might not be so fortunate, and you surely would not want to be blamed in whole or in part for their lifetime of ostracism, isolation and resultant misery.

J.W. MINTON

CHAPTER 1

SEMPER FI

Semper Fi. Semper fidelis: A phrase from the early Latin language, meaning Always Faithful. Always loyal.

Semper Fi. It's a standard adopted or informally claimed in ancient and modern times by several institutions and military organizations around the world, but is now generally accepted as the official motto of the United States Marine Corps. It's the comforting state of mind that makes a universal remedy to be applied to so many of the hurts of the human condition. Almost any question you might ask of any US Marine, it should be his first thought to preface any answer.

Semper Fi. It's in the blood of every US Marine. It seems to cause an enduring sentiment for those of like mind, a permanent condition known as 'Frater Aeterni', which simply means 'brothers forever'. It's not an ointment that you can see, but its generous application results in remarkable changes in those that are immersed in its ambience. It turns a boy into a man. It turns a man into a patriot and a hero. It gives that man real character and a way of life. It provides for him a peculiar pride in his identity with the few, the proud, the Marines. 'Honor-Valor-Fidelity'. Ooh Rah! Oooooh Raaaah!

Semper Fi. So often it has been seen, how a pipsqueak kid of lesser height signs up for a tour with the United States Marine Corps. Almost from the moment his signature hits the line, he is exposed to Semper Fi. It may be that his brief stature and his regular weight of about 100 pounds dripping wet, his horn-rimmed glasses and hesitant personal presentation, his unkempt hair, a wimpy voice along with the sloppy posture and drooping shoulders suggests he might be a sissy. He probably never had to make his own bed or clean his own room, his loafers are dull and loose fitting, sloppiness and irrelevance are in his way of life. Oh, dear reader, be assured that there are new recruits for the Marines that are giants, and there are those that are physically really much less than giants. The Drill Sergeant just loves to get hold of all kinds, and when those kids get through a few months of training and indoctrination, they're all about six-foot ten, and have bulging muscles and impressive dimensions. Well, you know that's not really altogether true, but don't tell that to any recent graduate of Parris Island or MCRD San Diego.

QUESTION: Well, just how is it that they can build a Marine from the ranks of youngsters?

ANSWER: Boot Camp

In the USMC Boot Camp, they grind up those kids, crush them down, rip them apart, and build a real man, a real Marine from those used parts. They teach them honor and courage and commitment. While they have them all shredded well, they seize the youthful heart and on that precious pump they tattoo the words 'Death before Dishonor', and over every USMC Boot Camp door you'll find emblazoned the words 'Semper Fi'.

Consider this: when that young Marine recruit swaggers out of Boot Camp, he now walks tall and straight. His hair is cut short. His uniform is neat and well pressed, his military issue dress shoes are shined to a glistening sparkle or his boots neatly laced. Maybe he still wears those horn-rimmed glasses, but see now the confident look in his eyes to match the poised stature and assertive manner. He'll likely want to go home to Little Rock or Memphis or Albany or Portland, or whatever other place, where he will offer a smart salute and courteous bow from the waist as he respectfully greets his father with a handshake that could crush the knuckles, and a proper "Yes, sir. No, sir"; then an affectionate hug for his mother and grandmother, and surely that same gentlemanly courteous recital of "Yes, Ma'am. No Ma'am" that was never before part of his conversation. If they still have his room available upstairs, he will likely later leave it in the most orderly and tidy condition, as never before it was. He will probably not show his mother his new Marine Insignia tattoo, and he will not be heard to openly recite the jokes heard in his barracks, lest he receive a remonstrative smack from Gramma.

Semper Fi: It is a fellowship of like minds. Semper Fi unashamedly signifies the dedication the Marine has for the Corps and the country, and to fellow Marines. For instance, should you visit the old soldiers' home in your town, please note that the Army guys will pal around with anyone. The Sailors like to sit and quote from their Dictionary of Navy Slang. The Air Force guys walk around gazing at the clouds and thinking of former days of glory up in the wild blue yonder. The Coast Guard guys seem to be always reading the newspaper, no matter how old it might be. But, if there are at least two or more Marines, they will be sitting over there together, since they are the only ones that really understand and fully appreciate each other and what it means to be a US Marine.

Semper Fi. It's a way of life. It's not negotiable. It is not relative. It is durable and without compromise, and is so very absolute.

Unfortunately, in the human condition, in even the most intimate and personal relationships, intrusion by outside influences can erode the sincerity of a person who has made pledges of love and commitment, so that one's vision and reason are obscured, promises made seem to be no longer worthwhile, honor and integrity are jaded and faded, unclear and unreal, and alluring temptations draw otherwise faithful hearts into a foreign abysmal abyss from which there seems no escape. It begins with just a little compromise. A tiny concession to relieve a sudden moment of greed or passion. Sometimes a generous application of stubborn Semper Fi can do wonders to defeat or divert those influences before the damage of compromise is done. Semper Fi is not just a military watchword for victory in battle. It can be a tremendously powerful dynamism to bolster the heart and mind in the face of what might appear to some to be superior and indefeasible force and really impossible circumstances. Oh, what tangled webs we weave when first we practice to deceive. A liberal dose of Semper Fi can keep one free of that tangled web.

Unfortunately, there are a few bad apples in every barrel. We find that some individuals simply cannot or will not meet the standard of excellence required of a US Marine, and they fade away quietly, or they get drummed out of the Corps. Among those departing souls you will find anguish and resentment for their failures as they try to assuage their irritation in suggesting that the standard they failed to meet is artificial or unattainable. There are many ways to ethically respond to that acrimonious rancor such as simply pointing to the white crosses to be found at Arlington or Point Loma National Cemeteries, and so many other places across the nation and around the world marking the resting places of honorable young men who did meet standards of Semper Fi.

Semper Fi: One of the most interesting features of the Boot Camp graduate is the strong respect for the flag of the United States, Old Glory, the Stars and Stripes. Why is there so much regard for a piece of cloth, when there is no such peculiar esteem for the Union Jack, the Rising Sun and so many other battle flags and identity garlands? Give this some thought: The Monarch of Great Britain is still on the throne. The Emperor of Japan is still the Monarch of Japan. When the United States threw off foreign rule of the king of England, they adopted instead a flag. The subjects of the King of Great Britain pledge allegiance to their sovereign. The subjects of the Emperor of Japan pledge their allegiance to their highly regarded Emperor. The citizens of the United States pledge allegiance to the flag. We don't have a king of our republic.

In England they do not allow any spitting on their sovereign. They don't allow anyone to set fire to the king. They have no tolerance for those that would publicly insult the king or queen. What would happen in Tokyo to anyone that tosses stones and insults at the Emperor? Why is it that in the US so often in the past we have tolerated draft dodgers to burn the US Flag?

Semper Fi: It's nice that many Christian societies have adopted the symbolism of the Christian flag. It's like the Union Jack. It identifies our Old Ship of Zion. But our King is still on His throne. He has not abdicated. He still rules and reigns and we shall be with Him for eternity. We pledge allegiance to our King. We should not pledge allegiance to the man-made battle flag that identifies the community of Christians.

Semper Fi: The Holy Bible is overflowing with promotion of spiritual Semper Fi, admonitions for the saints to keep on keepin' on, enduring to the end, and the likelihood that your faithfulness might aid some weaker saint to carry on and on. And if you do carry on to the end, where does that get you?

May we respectfully invite your attention to some very interesting informative words of St. Paul as he stated in his most incisive letters to the saints, found in his second letter to Timothy at Chapter Four and in Ephesians Chapter Six, where he demonstrates a great respect for Semper Fi:

Now just imagine that Field Marshall Five-Star General Paul the Apostle, in full military regalia with a whole chest full of campaign ribbons, swagger stick in hand, is addressing a vast army of dedicated saints standing at attention, soldiers of the Lord having put on the whole armor of God, listening to every word in the order of battle:

"I charge you therefore before God, and the Lord Jesus Christ, who shall judge the quick and the dead at His appearing and His kingdom: Preach the Word; be instant in season and out of season; reprove, rebuke, exhort with all long suffering and doctrine. But watch in all things, endure afflictions, do the work of an evangelist, make full proof of your ministry. Put on the whole armour of God that you may be able to stand against the wiles of the devil. For we wrestle not against flesh and blood, but against the rulers of the darkness of this world, against spiritual wickedness in high places. Wherefore take unto you the whole armour of God that you may be able to withstand in the evil day, and having done all to stand. Stand therefore, having your loins girt about with truth, and having on the breastplate of righteousness, and your feet shod with the preparation of the Gospel of Peace; above all, taking the shield of faith, wherewith you shall be able to quench all the fiery darts of the wicked; and take the helmet of salvation and the sword of the Spirit, which is the Word of God; praying always with all prayer and supplication in the Spirit, and watching thereunto with all perseverance and supplication for all saints. For I am now ready to be offered, and the time of my departure is at hand. I have fought a good fight. I have finished my course. I have kept the faith. Henceforth there is laid up for me a crown of righteousness, which the Lord the righteous judge shall give me at that day; and not to me only, but unto all them also that love his appearing."

That's sounds like 'Semper Fi' ***Ooooh Raaah!***

CHAPTER 2

TRADITION

Over many generations since the early 1800's the Cole family has had a tradition that identifies the clan with the United States Marine Corps. Within that history have been ordinary enlisted men, non-commissioned officers, general officers and field ranks, lieutenants and captains, and high-ranking officers. Some have served short enlistments, and some have been career Marines. Some have been wounded in battle; some died in the conflicts into which they were called. Historically, every single one of the Cole clan that so served did so honorably, with a noble commitment to Semper Fi, and an excellent record. There were only a few years when there was none of the family on active duty somewhere in the United States Marine Corps.

Captain Richard C. Cole served in the Corps early in the Twentieth Century, fought honorably in the First World War, wounded at Belleau Woods, and eventually retired after more than twenty years of honorable service. His son, Major Richard C. Cole, Jr., was a career Marine, already a Captain at the commencement of World War II, and was wounded twice in heated battles in Europe and in the Pacific. His injuries at Iwo Jima were so severe as to cause his retirement from the service. His son, Captain Richard C. Cole III, lost most of one foot in the Korean conflict, and he was likewise then forced into retirement.

Richard C. Cole III and wife Shirley had three sons: Richard C. 'Rick' Cole IV, Charles Edmund Cole, and Lawrence Emmet Cole. The family moved to Springfield, Missouri, where all three of the boys attended public schools, and all graduated from Hillcrest High. The father was in Springfield employed by the Gospel Printing Company, and Shirley was a pool stenographer for the business offices of their denominational church society. They all regularly attended their fundamentalist Christian church, and the boys took part in just about every church youth activity. Their lives were immersed in fellowship of the saints. They all had their teenage romances with girls from their church and other Pentecostal and Baptist groups around this Bible Belt community.

Charley Cole married young at age 19, and went off to Arkansas to work with his in-laws at one or another of their hardware stores, and that solid marriage produced a couple of little girls that charmed all the grandparents.

Rick Cole didn't have much luck at marriage. At age 20 he wed a Methodist girl of about 17 years of age, but that immature teenage bride left him a couple of months later to run off with an old boyfriend, so that marriage was annulled. He married again about a year later, to a pretty blond from Kansas, but that union wound up in divorce after less than a year of wedded bliss. Single again, Rick moved back home with his folks and matriculated at Missouri State University, which was then still known as Southwest Missouri State College, where in his sophomore year he finally noticed and married Sharon, a young lady that had admired him for years. She was already a senior and graduated with her BA that same year, and they continued to live with Rick's parents, while he kept up with his college studies, and managed to graduate with a bachelor's degree in less than four years. His young wife had a baby during this stay, and when she got pregnant a second time the little family moved out on their own. Rick got a job with a Springfield Public Utilities company, and the second little boy was born. Sharon's family insisted that they be allowed to name both children. Sharon got a job with one of the grammar schools in Greene County, while a babysitter took care of the two kids. Sharon got interested in the principal at her school, and that was the end of the marriage. Rick continued at SMS for a while, and then at expense of his parents he attended graduate school at the University of Missouri in Columbia, where he got a Master's Degree in Education. He worked part-time at various jobs in order to keep up with the child support. Not long after graduation with his M.Ed. degree he was offered a job as Superintendent of a small school district in Illinois, even though he had no teaching experience. This three-time loser never even dated any ladies after his third marriage failed. Neither Charley nor Rick showed even the slightest interest in joining the US Marine Corps.

Lawrence 'Larry' Cole was the youngest kid in the family and had an entirely different life. He was about 6'3" and very handsome, with wavy dark brown hair and dark brown eyes, and had a perfect muscular physique. He dated the pretty girls, but never showed a lot of serious interest. He was a scholarly student, got excellent grades, and was from all appearances the most dedicated Christian in the family. He took a leadership role in all the youth activities at their church and sang in the choir. He started with piano lessons when he was in second grade and kept up with his music all the way through high school. He played the piano for congregational singing at his home church and filled in at several other churches around town when the regular piano person was away on vacation or whatever. He played and sang with a teenager Gospel Quartet, loved to quote tons of scripture from the Old and New Testaments, and occasionally would take over the pulpit to preach some fiery sermons that were of great satisfaction to his proud parents. When Larry played the piano for the quartets he could really get goin' on the keyboard, and had an amusing habit common to Gospel Quartet piano players: Larry had 'happy feet' that bounced about while he spanked those piano keys with quick fingers, and when he really got excited he'd lift his chin and toss his head from side to side in a most amusing way, glancing at the audience from time to time with a huge happy grin. When he was sixteen years old, he was baptized in water at his home church in the tank by the choir loft, and gave a marvelous witness for the whole congregation to hear, in which he proclaimed his commitment to the Christian life and the mission of the Great Commission, sprinkling his testimony with more quotations from Holy Writ. His mother took down every word of that testimony in shorthand on the flyleaf of her King James Bible. His parents were so full of pride in their little baby boy. The congregation was impressed with his robust commitment and the strength of profession in the Word.

Larry Cole graduated from Hillcrest High at age 17. He could have immediately enrolled in one or another of the colleges around Springfield, schools of academic excellence, but his folks thought that this youngest of their brood ought to enroll with a university of greater esteem, grander prestige, superior recognition, such as an Ivy League school. And so it was that Larry Cole matriculated at Princeton University, all the way up in New Jersey, away from the mundane world of the Ozarks. His folks were on that campus for only two occasions: to deliver Larry to his dorm and to be present a few years later at his graduation.

Larry took with him to Princeton all the hopes and dreams shared with his parents, but within the first few months of this high-caliber institutional exposure, those dreams seemed to fade. With the onset of compromise,

Larry Cole became a backslider. He was pledged to a national fraternity; his dormitory room-mates all claimed to be atheists; several of his professors ridiculed organized religion and mocked the thought that anyone could be raised from the dead, laughing at foolish Christian traditions and ethics. He met several students from the seminary that probably should not have been labeled as ministerial candidates. Surely they were not good examples of the fine student body in religious studies, because their behavior was not as it should have been, considering that these particular guys put away at least as much booze as Larry's fraternity colleagues.

During that first year at Princeton, starting with little tiny bits of compromise that grew into greater neglect of principle and commitment to Christian character, Larry simply abandoned all that testimony stuff, took up the alcohol habit, drinking beer and all the exotic liquors offered to him, did a few drugs, smoked pot and popped pills, and his language became atrocious. The young socialite girls at the school spotted him early on, and he had many trysts over his tenure at Princeton. The church where Larry attended all his younger life was extremely conservative, with disdain for ballroom and other recreational dancing, and his first real dancing experiences were with the young socialites of the Ivy League, and Larry became a fair terpsichorean. He did one unusual thing at that school that he never had done before: Larry went out for soccer, and became the best kicker on the team. He had tremendously powerful legs, and could launch that soccer ball into the net from the furthest spots on the field if nobody got in his way. He could do something more that nobody else could do: Larry could easily kick a 15 kilogram medicine ball through a second floor window or over a parked car. Try that sometime!

Notwithstanding the distractions, Larry Cole got excellent grades, and was academically very competitive all through his years at Princeton, never once missed any of his classes or a soccer game, and had some very encouraging endorsements from the faculty. He usually did summer studies to accumulate more graduation units, so to abbreviate his stay at the school, and returned home to Springfield only for about two weeks at the end of the summer, and for about ten days over the Christmas holidays. On these sojourn moments at home with his family and friends he assumed his former religious manner, sanctimoniously prayed over breakfast and dinner, spouted scripture like an itinerant evangelist, and would sometimes address the young people's group gathered for weekly events at the church, and doing so in a most sober and humble way. However, upon his return to the university dorm his manner quickly changed back to the vulgar and intemperate charlatan known well by his college companions, and his façade of faith was discarded. His little compromises had resulted in the entrenchment of real hypocrisy.

One faculty member suggested to Larry that he should consider becoming involved in the military ROTC program, but Larry would only consider the US Marine Corps, rather than the Navy and Army regimens. He could have undertaken Navy ROTC with some sort of Marine Corps stipulation, but preferred to wait until his senior year to become committed. And so he did, receiving a commission as a Second Lieutenant at the time of graduation with his BA, plus a USMC tattoo on his chest, and he was off to MCB Quantico to absorb the Marine Corps régime, and for the first time in his life he had his hair cut short in a crew style. These things that now identified Larry with the USMC family tradition pleased his folks so much, and they were very proud of him, except that his Mom was annoyed with that 'Semper Fi' tattoo. Larry chided his Dad about the tattoo, since it was exactly like the one that was inked on the father's chest.

Upon arrival at Marine Corps Base Quantico, things changed again. 2nd Lt. Larry met a Chaplain there by name of Captain Stanford E. Linzey, who was filling in there for a few months for the regular chaplains who were on other assignments. He had served with the 3rd Marine Division on Okinawa and 1st Marine Division at Camp Pendleton for years but also ministered to the newly commissioned officers from all over the East Coast. Chaplain Linzey cornered Lt. Larry at the Officer's Mess, asked if he was the son of Richard Cole of Springfield, and on confirming that he was he informed Larry that his Dad had asked Brother Linzey to watch over him while in Quantico. Now, Brother Linzey was one of those Pentecostal preachers, and in all his ways he promoted the kind of devoted Christian lifestyle that Larry had so hastily abandoned in his first few weeks and months of the Princeton Experience. But Larry had also become something of a phony guy in his college days, and merely put on his Christian hat and uttered all the Christian buzz-words to impress the good Chaplain. It didn't work with Brother Linzey, and this fine brother did not mince words with Lt. Larry, telling him that he oughta 'pray through' and get right with God. And, so he did. He then immediately tossed out the cigarettes and other bad stuff hidden in his duffel bag, and after shedding a few tears of further redemptive restoration, Larry seemed to once again have a grasp on his Christian commitment, and he really did intend to thereafter lead a pristine Christian life. Chaplain Linzey returned to San Diego to serve at the Marine Corps Recruit Depot, trying to give proper guidance to young recruits. Larry finished at MCB Quantico, and then went on to active duty in San Diego with the Third Marine Aircraft Wing at Marine Corps Air Station Miramar nearby. Larry Cole was a genuine Marine Corps Pilot, then before long he was promoted to 1st Lieutenant and expected to soon be deployed to the Far East.

In that time after leaving MCB Quantico and before assignment to the war zone, almost from the moment of his arrival at MCAS Miramar, Larry started backsliding once more. He never did take up the tobacco habit again, never again smoked pot, never more did he do the illegal drugs. But he would often go with his buddies to get hammered on beer and liquor at the pubs around San Diego, and had a lot of sinful flirtations with floozies that frequent those places.

Lt. Larry would be living loosely from day to day, and then Chaplain Linzey would somehow appear at odd times and irregular intervals, walking up behind him unannounced or hailing him from across the way, or be standing there when Larry got out of his plane to walk toward the lockers. Now, some of these preacher types often inquire "How is God treating you?" but Chaplain Linzey would always ask Larry "How are you treating God?" and Larry learned long ago that Brother Linzey was a man that you could not bamboozle with buzz-words or empty testimony. Chaplain Linzey would invite Larry to go with him to some secluded corner and have a few moments of prayer. At intervals, Larry would go get 'saved' again at one or another of the local evangelical churches, or maybe we should say that he often had to get 'reclaimed' and 'recommitted', but within a couple of weeks he'd be back boozing and carousing. Larry was becoming a habitual backslider. He really tried to do better. He really was sincere. But Larry seemed to lack spiritual maturity. And then Chaplain Linzey would show up again at the most inopportune times, boldly abandoning that secluded private corner idea, and praying with Larry right out on the flight line tarmac, and in other public places with people passing to and fro, with a hand on Larry's shoulder as the two of them would bow in prayer. Chaplain Stan Linzey would pray with anyone, anywhere, anytime, whether in a secluded private place or on any street corner or lobby of the bank. During the Vietnam War he was seen more than once praying alone in the hallway outside one or another of the surgical operating rooms at Balboa Naval Hospital San Diego.

Lt. Larry took intensive training in the fixed-wing Douglas A-1 Skyraider attack fighter-bomber aircraft, which was a propeller driven single-seater anachronism at the time, and soon found himself sightseeing in Asia at government expense, in some quaint little land known as Vietnam. He had two successive tours in Vietnam, and was wounded twice in the second deployment. Six Skyraiders were on a low level close air support assignment over enemy territory when Larry's craft was riddled on both sides by ground fire. The armor plate around the cockpit protected the pilot from small arms fire and most heavy machine gun bullets, but the intensity of the peppering was unnerving. Running low on fuel and out of ammunition after completing his run, he banked sharply and pulled upward to return to his base, and as he turned his aircraft a fusillade of firepower tore through the left side of the cockpit and several of those bullets ripped through to strike the escaping pilot in his upper thigh and in the small of his back. Blood spurted everywhere, filled his flying suit and began to flow out of the places where the bullets entered. Lt. Larry was immediately aware of the searing penetration pain of those projectile intrusions, and his entire lower body became numb and very weak. The agony was unbearable. With the general numbness he could hardly move his legs and feet to work the steering of the plane. He managed to complete the turn and pull up above the clouds to head back to camp, and radioed the wing commander to tell of his plight. A couple of his fellow pilots along in their own Skyraiders chose to escort him to base. They maintained radio contact all the while, but Lt. Larry didn't hear much of their encouraging chatter. He was too busy trying to put together a deal, praying that God would somehow find it in His grace to forgive Larry the Backslider just one more time, and maybe cast some sort of blessing on this shredded aircraft in order to limp back to a safe landing, or in the alternative to send some instruction over to the keeper of the Pearly Gates to allow Larry to enter and maybe give him at least some humble assignment swabbing the streets of gold or polishing the walls of jasper. Larry offered the Lord all kinds of concessions in this regard, promising God that if he would step in to help Larry the Unworthy Servant in this hour of great need then Larry the Habitual Backslider would change his evil ways, clean up his act, and become a truly righteous person of pristine Christian character. So Larry renewed his commitment to the Lord and the Mission of the Great Commission, promised to never again touch that filthy tobacco or any kind of booze, and declared that he would never ever touch any more illicit drugs or blow pot, and most importantly he vowed to never again utter a profane word or tell any naughty fibs.

Lt. Larry managed to maneuver his bullet-riddled airplane into the general area of his base landing field, but the tremendous loss of blood together with the paralyzing wounds suggested that he might be better off to simply bail out and ditch the plane. He could sense that he was gonna black out, as his vision became blurred and he was so dizzy and lightheaded he could hardly see his gauges and could not focus on anything outside the cockpit. His companions in escort started yelling at him on the radio to tell him that he just overshot the field and to turn back and when there was no response from Lt. Larry, one of his buddies simply buzzed right over him not more than fifteen feet away, and the tremendous noise and backwash woke up the fading Lt. Larry at least sufficient so that he could wrestle enough to turn his plane around and bring it down closer to the ground to try to land it on the field going in the wrong direction. He was unable any more to work his legs and feet, and he was so far gone that he could not stay conscious anymore. Fortunately, his engine went dead when the plane ran completely out of fuel a short distance from the end of the landing field, and to a casual observer it would have appeared that Lt. Larry managed a perfect three-point dead-stick landing, but in truth that pilot slept through the whole landing episode, and with the extra-long runway surface designed for larger aircraft, his plane managed to coast to a stop about twenty feet short of the very end. He was later told that his parachute was also damaged in the hail of bullets, and would probably not have carried him safely out of the sky.

The ground crew gently removed the limp figure of this wounded warrior from his place of slumber there in what was left of that lovely Skyraider, took him immediately for emergency medical attention, where they pumped a lot of blood back into his body and did a few temporary repairs, but it was obvious that the neurological damage to his lower back was such that he needed more professional attention than local clinics could provide. One of the surgeons came to his bedside to bid farewell, and handed Larry one of the bullets that they had removed from the area around his spine, just a small trophy to memorialize the visit. Within a few hours he was on a transport plane taking him over the Pacific Ocean to Balboa Naval Hospital in San Diego. He was riding on a gurney when he arrived at the airfield in San

Diego and was greeted at the gate by Chaplain Stan Linzey, who accompanied him in the ambulance to Balboa Naval Hospital and directly to the surgical theatre, praying with Larry all the way. When Larry awakened from the induced sleep of anesthetic Chaplain Linzey was holding his hand. Larry spent a couple of months recovering from his wounds, including recovery therapy to restore full use of his lower limbs, and most of his doctors assured him that there might be no lingering problems resulting from the damage caused by his encounter with Viet Cong bullets. When he was better able to ambulate without assistance, he was ordered to what was then still the El Toro Marine Corps air facility near Irvine, California. For the rest of his military service days he never again returned to the conflicts in Vietnam. At this time, Lt. Larry Cole was almost 26 years old; with about five years' service time, and he intended then to remain as a career officer with USMC, whether or not in flying service. He already had a chest full of medals that were so very impressive when he wore his fancy dress uniform, and expected to be elevated soon to the rank of Captain.

Lt. Larry was under continuous evaluation by the medical people at Balboa Naval Hospital, and no decision had yet been made about his physical fitness to continue on active duty. Pending final determination he was given an assignment that required him to work in the two places: MCAS Miramar near San Diego and MCAS El Toro near Santa Ana. He usually drove back and forth in his old Toyota sedan. He was no longer interested in the propeller-driven planes, and was training in jet aircraft, with instruction taking place between the two USMC facilities. Even if the medical folks approved of his continuing on active duty, the nature of his Vietnam wounds brought into question whether or not he could be a realistic candidate for advanced training and eventual service in the newer jet-powered craft.

CHAPTER 3

<u>GENERATIONS</u>

The scriptures suggest that we are each part of another, and are inextricably identified with generations past, and for those that are interested in the study of genealogy there are many interesting things to discover about our forebears.

The Carillo family of Southern Mexico was fairly wealthy, with a long history of land ownership going back to the earliest days of Spanish rule. Osvaldo Carillo as a young man left the comforts of that family to seek his own fortune, to experience adventure, to learn the meaning of life, and simply get a job. He became a roustabout in a traveling circus that toured through Southern Mexico in the late 1800's. As in most circuses he had to do many different jobs. He was about sixteen when he first joined the troupe, and learned various crafts as he went along. He could read very well, was skilled with numbers, had a marvelous memory for detail, and an especially good recall for names of individuals and places. He did all the lighting and electrical work for the employer, such as there was in those early days. His most important circus assignment was that of wheelwright and blacksmith. The traveling circus moved on those old wooden-spoke wheels with wagons pulled by mules and horses. For longer trips they would put the wagons up onto railcars to be transported. Osvaldo had to build spokes and repair the wheels, and those wheels had metal straps for treads before the advent of rubber tires, axles that had to be repaired or replaced, greased and otherwise serviced, the wagon tongues kept in working order, and the draft animals had to have new horseshoes on all hoofs from time to time. The eighteen or so wagons had to be kept in good repair on roofs and carriages, for traveling residential quarters, animal transport and equipment storage and moving. The circus folks lived in and under those wagons throughout the seasons. Even the newcomer to the circus has many roles, putting up and taking down the tents and performance arenas, working the booths, feeding the animals, and most important of all to be some sort of performer to amuse the paying guests. Osvaldo's most favorite assignment was to be a clown. He had an unusual talent: his vast repertoire of facial expressions. Osvaldo could carry on such long and elaborate conversations without speaking a word, but just smiling or frowning, wiggling his eyebrows, grinning in a very funny way, feigning pain or expressing pleasure, and his eyes could laugh or cry on demand. To meet Osvaldo was a lingering memorable delight. Lazy folks don't last long in a traveling circus, and about every minute has to be in some way productive. Osvaldo tended the horses and mules, but he did not drive them. As a passenger during relocation, he would have other performers teach him how to play the guitar, the accordion, how to beat the drums and toot the horns. Being busy was a way of life.

Unfortunately, at the turn of the century the bigger circuses became more mechanized, both in operation of the events and in motorized transport, and Osvaldo's circus operator owners could not be competitive. Their wagons were old and needing replacement, their performers were likewise growing old and there were no replacements, so the owners of that little traveling circus simply sold everything, graciously divided up the meager proceeds among the remaining employees, and everyone went their separate ways. Osvaldo ended up in a blacksmith shop in Tijuana, Mexico, and was from there recruited by a little old lady in Los Angeles to come work with her Studebaker Wagons and Electric Cars, doing the repairs and such. He stayed on with her until her death, and she simply gave him the whole store when she passed away. Osvaldo continued the business thereafter, and with the arrival of gasoline-powered Studebaker trucks and cars, he did fairly well, until the outbreak of the Great Depression of the 1930's.

Periodically, Osvaldo would return to Mexico City to visit with his family, and when he was in his middle 30's there met and married Ximena Vazquez and they had one daughter named Ximena, born and raised in East Los Angeles. 'Most everyone called her 'Shimi'. When she grew up, this young Mexican lass was mucho good lookin', kinda short at about 5'3", with a slender frame, and the most beautiful dark eyes ever. She was such a happy little girl, happy all the way through school, and the happiest of all when at about age seventeen she met Stewart Remington, a then-recent graduate of the University of Southern California, whose family owned a couple of Buick dealerships in Los Angeles County and a Chevrolet agency in the Riverside area. In the midst of the Great Depression these happy young people were married at the Catholic Church in Los Angeles and began to live happily ever after. It wasn't much later that young Stewart inherited all the family auto dealerships and related businesses, and Shimi sorta inherited her father's Studebaker sales agency when her Dad got too decrepit to carry on the business. Deeper and deeper into the depression many car dealers went broke, and bankruptcy was the only way out for dozens of failed agencies. The Remington group just barely managed to hang on for all those lean years.

It was in the summer of 1941 that a most unusual thing happened to cause both a lot of good and a little bit of consternation. An alliance of GM dealers had put together a central parts and supplies operation under a separate corporation, located near the City of Long Beach, California, and there they had monstrous warehouses packed to the ceilings with merchandise. When so many of those participating dealerships closed their doors permanently, that parts corporation filed bankruptcy, and the Referee in Bankruptcy ordered an auction to sell off the merchandise, with the proceeds to pay claims of creditors. The sale was properly advertised, the auctioneer had all his tables set up and a crew of assistants on hand to help in what he expected to be a two or three day auction. Stewart Remington went to the auction with one of his Buick salesmen, and they turned out to be the only bidders to show up. The auctioneer in frustration accepted the one bid to purchase everything en masse, banged his gavel and 'knocked down' that one bid for Ten Dollars, which Stewart Remington immediately paid in cash on the spot. However, being the only successful bidder created a colossal problem: all of everything in those two particular buildings had to be removed within thirty days. Stew Remington had no place to store all those things that were packed to the ceilings and wall to wall, and didn't have any money to pay movers to relocate the stuff, anyway. The next morning he started his search for space. He had three fairly large buildings used by dealerships under his control, but nowhere near enough room for all the things to be moved. On the next Tuesday afternoon, he received a phone call from a gentleman with the Vultee Aircraft Company, the new tenant for two of the buildings to be vacated, and because of urgency in the need for that space he was willing to work a deal. Vultee would provide all the workers and all the trucks for transportation of everything to be moved. The only thing Stewart had to do was to tell 'em where to deliver it all. Vultee agreed to pay all costs related to the move. A huge vacant warehouse was rented for a pittance in Riverside, and another in San Bernardino, and they managed to get that entire inventory moved out of those two huge buildings in less than one week, which made

Vultee happy, and made Stewart Remington rich. It took them several weeks to inventory all that stuff, and found that there were hundreds of brand-new engines, radiators, radios, headlights and lenses, windshields and other glass, seats and interior things, fenders and all kinds of body parts and whatever else it would take to repair and refurbish anything made by General Motors, including trucks and automobiles for models for the last twelve to fifteen years and through the coming 1942 model year.

Several weeks later, as the people were finishing their inventory of merchandise recovered from those two large warehouse buildings, the auctioneer phoned to ask when Stewart Remington would be coming to get the rest of his stuff included in the auction, pointing out that there was another building about two blocks away from the two that Stewart originally thought were the only ones involved, and that other building was also huge and packed tight with more and more parts and auto supplies that were included in the purchase, but these parts were mostly stacked wall-to-wall and to the ceilings, separated on shelves and in thousands of drawers and various containers of differing dimensions, so many different tools and mechanical devices. These smaller things were at least as important as any other of the materials purchased for that Ten Dollar procurement price. This third building was not attractive to Vultee, so their earlier generosity was no longer available for this massive move. Stewart Remington had to ask the bank to advance him enough money to pay for men and transportation equipment required for moving all that treasure to a place he rented in Pomona. When WWII started it became impossible to buy a new car, and older models needed repairs and parts. Stewart Remington was about the only one in Southern California that could forthwith provide most of those parts, and his GM agencies flourished accordingly, all throughout the war years. Many more car dealers failed between 1940 and 1945, and Remington bought up for small change a number of franchises, located all over Southern California. After the war, the Remington's probably owned more car dealerships than any other one family in the state. When the custom car and hot rod craze came in the '50's' and '60's' those older parts were much in demand, and Remington had a lot of equipment then still available.

Stewart and Shimi Remington had four children, one boy and three girls. The boy Reuben Carillo Remington was the first to arrive, born in California, and so very welcome in that home. Then almost five years later came little Ximena Debra Carillo Remington, who was a very pretty little girl that loved to dance. About four years after Debra and last to arrive were the identical twins, Ximena Teresa Carillo Remington and Ximena Antonia Carillo Remington, exact look-alikes with dark hair and lovely brown eyes, and happy smiles on every occasion. The three girls were born in Mexico City, and in keeping with family tradition all four of the Remington children were baptized as infants at the great Catholic Church in that capitol city. None of these kids were any trouble in school, got good grades and had a very normal life, except for the fact that their mother sheltered them, and was constantly hovering over each one. Momma Shimi lived for her family. She shared every joy and every tear, every pain and every disappointment. These kids were her life blood. She had somewhere been infused with a massive dose of motherly love.

Momma Remington did something that all mothers should do: she talked with her kids and she listened to her kids, asking questions and answering questions. If she didn't have what she considered a good answer for any particular query, she would with her children trap Stew Remington as soon as he got through the front door in the evening, and if they were in a hurry for an answer they'd phone him at work. If Dad didn't have what he felt was an adequate response, he'd look in the books, maybe bring the books home with him and the whole family together would do a little research. Those kids could page through the dictionary quicker'n anybody else.

The back yard at the Remington place looked like a school playground with all the equipment: slides, teeter-totters, rings and Jungle-Gyms, and a really nice playhouse. The kids rode up and down the streets and sidewalks on bicycles and tricycles, and little pedal-powered cars. Nobody ever asked for a pony, or they would have had one or more of those, too.

Summertime, when school was out, the Remington's would all pile into the station wagon and go to some exotic vacation places, like Big Sur, the Redwoods, Yosemite, the Cascades, Zion, and have a great family time together. When Disneyland opened they were among the first to have season passes. The kids seemed to know all the names of the wild animals at the San Diego Zoo. They went many times to check out the displays at the Monterey Aquarium, and traveled through Chinatown San Francisco several times. Throughout the summer all the Remington kids would play on the beaches nearby, and all got fried in the warm sun. For two or three weeks each summer they would visit relatives in Mexico City. All these things they did as a family. A happy family.

Reuben was the only Remington child born in the US. When young Reuben was just a little guy, he loved to be held and his Mommy liked to humor him, every time she could get hold of him. He was not a screamy child, and by the time he was almost a year old you could reason with him to be quiet. When he started walking and wandering about, his Mom would always be there to catch him should he trip on something or wander too far. A little older and he discovered how much fun it was to make noise. When he would go through the house beating on his drum, his mother would grab an old pot and a wooden spoon and they'd go around making noise together. Most of us would have thumped the noisy little brat on the head and tell him to cut out the racket. No. No. Momma Remington put in a lot of time wearing out her wooden spoons and denting those old pots, and had to buy several more drums for her leader, until little Reuben was distracted to other things.

There is an old adage 'Spare the rod and spoil the child' and the Holy Bible is often cited as the source of that admonition, but you will be hard pressed to find it there. If you might want to look it up, may we suggest that you consult the works of poet Samuel Butler, and his work 'Hudibras'. The Holy Bible does have reference to the use of the rod to chasten occasionally, but some authorities advise that the rod referred to is the Shepherd's rod with a crook at the end to pull in the wandering sheep, and not simply for crackin' a kid in the head. 'Thy rod and thy staff they comfort me!' The temperament of Reuben Remington was so quiet and cooperative that there were few occasions when he got his head thumped or an ear twisted. His folks never yelled at him or frightened him in any way. The scriptures repeat it so many times 'fear not', and it would seem a violation of that constraint to threaten a child with a physical drubbing punishment so to arouse fears and emotional apprehensions, anxieties and erosion of tranquility. Reuben got kissed on the top of his head at least a thousand times more often than his contemporaries.

Reuben was but four years old when his folks told him that he had a little sister or brother coming in a few months, and they admonished him of his responsibility to help welcome that child and to teach him or her all the rules around the house. By the time little Debbie arrived Reuben was well informed, and was frustrated early on when the little diaper-clad sister was unable to talk with him or follow his instruction, but he was the first to feed her with a spoon, always willing to hold her bottle while she slurped away. He would sing to her to help her drop off to sleep, and as she grew older he became her guardian and able assistant in everything. She was recruited to help in the drum beating and pot banging parades, as he taught her how to play the kazoo and the toy piano. Reuben never became angry with the little sister, never yelled at her, and always held her hand whenever the family would go on walks. He was her example to follow.

Little Debbie was also a very serene child, and even as an infant was fairly peaceful. Sure, she'd scream for attention, but was easily calmed just by the touch or the glugging on her bottle or chewing on a pacifier. She would follow Reuben anywhere and would respectfully listen to just about anything he had to say. They would watch cartoons on TV as Reuben patiently explained to her the humor, and she honored him by pretending to understand. In all her childhood little Debbie was not spanked even once, she never heard any threats ever in her happy home, and the only yelling and screaming that took place there was when Reuben and Debbie were playing between themselves or when they had troops of other youngsters visiting and tearing up the back yard.

When Reuben was about nine years old and sister Debbie not yet four, they were told that Momma was soon to bring them some little sisters to play with. Reuben was old enough then to comprehend most of this, but Debbie wanted to know where these little ones would be coming from, and "Can they speak Spanish?" And then the precious pair did arrive on time. Reuben and Debbie were delighted beyond description, and were amazed to watch those two squirming little ladies. They were so thrilled to be able to hold them, and would trade off from time to time. Such excitement it was for them to be able to hold their bottles and pat them on the rump to put them to sleep. They would hover over them and sing little children's songs, and each would have a lap full of sister as they watched the cartoons on TV, and wondered why the little ones didn't laugh at the humor on the screen. Reuben and Debbie were thrilled to help the twins learn to navigate and walk around the tables. By the time they were old enough to beat drums and march around the house Reuben was too old and mature to take part in such childish noise making, but he would applaud the way the twins 'phzzzzz-d' their kazoo's. As with their two older children, the Remington's never had to spank these twins, never had to threaten them with corporal punishment, never yelled at them or did anything to arouse fear or apprehensions. Actually, these two little girls would cringe with fear when anyone yelled at them or threatened either in any way. They were the two most happy and well behaved young ladies that anyone could ever hope for.

Momma Remington was often caught up in undeclared pillow fighting wars, usually at bedtime, surrounded by the belligerents and suffering blitzkrieg from all sides. Momma was never the winner. Surrender was so much easier to help quell the riots and get the warriors into their beds.

CHAPTER 4

EVOLUTION

Momma Shimi Remington invested more than 100% of herself in her children, constantly encouraging each and every one, indulging all of them, taking them to every amusement park in Southern California, sitting in the floor with them to play board games, splashing about in the kitchen to amuse them as they learned culinary skills, taking them about any place they could think of to go. She was especially pleased to show them off to her clan in Mexico City. The entire family was bilingual, as fluent in Spanish as in English. Momma was so proud of her kids, so delighted with them as they grew from toddlers to teens and beyond. When the twins were less than a year old, Momma thought that a happy day was when she could push the double deck stroller down the sidewalk while the older kids danced about. She loved to parade her clutch through Montgomery-Wards and Sears and on visits to the car dealership offices. It really boosted her ego when strangers would stop and make nice comments about her kids. Stewart Remington was an encouraging bystander in all of this pampering, and enjoyed watching his busy wife hastening and shuffling about to tend to the whims of her little brood. The Remington house was a very contented home. As the years passed by, as the children grew older, changes were taking place, particularly as the kids matured physically and otherwise, but Momma seemed to be locked into another fairytale time and perception, in such a way that she continued to hover over her brood, and tried to share each and every event of their waking day.

Momma still viewed her children as just her little kids, all sorta like playground youngsters, and took little notice that Reuben had grown taller, and had to shave sometimes twice a day to scrape off that heavy dark brown growth of beard. After he learned to drive and got his license, she took little note of his frequent absences, nor his weekend trips with friends. He didn't have a job, but Momma gave him all the money he needed, almost on demand as one might feed a hungry infant. Reuben was extremely handsome and virile. Momma wanted Reuben to enjoy his young life. After he graduated from high school, he immediately enrolled in summer college courses to aggressively accumulate more units toward graduation. At the end of that summer he enrolled at University of Southern California, and became a fraternity person, with a long list of friends and colleagues, both male and female, some of whom came from very affluent homes. He would always run with the fast crowd and felt most comfortable holding a cocktail glass and slurping caviar with them. He didn't use tobacco in any form, and never did the drugs. He liked to hold a martini cocktail in his hand just for effect as he moved about in a reveling crowd, but he seldom actually took in any alcohol. When the occasion called for it he would light up a cigar, but would never smoke it as he fondled it with flare. He simply assumed the posture and appearance of the upper crust.

Reuben was busy, busy, busy, and was always working to gain some undeserved advantage, to find the easy way, scheming some sort of an arrangement to make the easy profit or benefit, and this materialistic young man continued with this avarice through high school and on into college. At USC he joined a number of greedy young men of like mind to form their own little wealth-generating cartel in Reuben's sophomore year, and these young guys proved to be very resourceful and shrewd in their investments and promotions. Reuben graduated from USC with a business degree at age 20, and his folks wanted to give him a new Buick as a graduation gift. He informed them that he preferred a Bentley or Rolls-Royce to better impress his business partners and prospective clients, but he had to be content with the new Buick Roadmaster. After graduation, he and his colleagues rented an office on Wilshire Boulevard, and somehow got control of a seat on the Stock Exchange, dealing with all kinds of stock trades and new issues. They actually did quite well for several years, and Reuben bought a huge swanky house in Beverly Hills. All this while still in his twenties. His parents were dazzled by all the apparent wealth accumulation, and very proud of his success and accomplishments. They actually knew nothing about his dealings, and when he explained some petty matters to them he seemed to blab nothingness.

Debbie Remington grew up to be about the same size and physical makeup of her mother, a little over 5'2" and fairly slender, but kinda buxom in appearance. She was very popular in grammar school and junior high and all the way through graduation from her high school, especially in her little clusters of Spanish-speaking admirers that had their own high school cliques. She had an excellent reputation for modesty and decorum. She was always nicely dressed and with only enough cosmetic enhancement as to display her unusual physical loveliness. Debbie started going out with young men before she was sixteen, and had long lines of male admirers asking for dates. She graduated with honors from high school, and then enrolled part-time at Santa Ana College, a two-year community college. It took her three years to get her A.A. degree. While attending that school she worked part time for her father at one of the Buick sales agencies. She was provided with a new red Pontiac sedan for her own personal use. At age 20, she was intent on attending Long Beach State, and had actually been formally accepted when her attentions were diverted by romance. She fell in love with an older student at Santa Ana College by name of Pedro Verdugo, who wanted everyone to call him 'King Pete'. It turned out that even though the average age of a community college student might be younger, this guy was around 27. Debbie told her parents that this young man was a football hero. The fact turned out to be that he was on the team his first semester, and played about one minute of one game. His academic failings got him booted off the team. His academic record in his second semester got him booted out of school. This guy looked like a real thug, resembling a street gangster from the darker alleys of East LA. His long dark hair hung down to his shoulders. He wore a heavy 'Fu-Manchu' moustache and unkempt sideburns. This Pachuco wannabe was well-built, with strong arms and beefy chest. He liked to wear a sleeveless black leather jacket to better show off the ugly and profane tattoos on those muscular arms. He wasn't short but wasn't tall, standing about 5'11".

One of the really negative things that did not sit well with Debbie's parents was when King Pete asked Stewart Remington for a loan of $50.00, to be repaid from his next paycheck. He claimed to be an executive with a company called WM Corporation, which turned out to actually be true. He was a garage service man for garbage trucks. He kept that job for about six weeks, got fired for some sort of insubordination and the fifty bucks never did get repaid at any time. Debbie's parents told her to ditch this creep, but at age twenty she ran off to Las Vegas and married King Pete Verdugo without consulting her parents. She never did then nor thereafter receive an engagement ring or wedding band. She dropped out of college, started working full time for her Dad's new car sales agency, and from the time of the marriage she was the only one of these two newlyweds to have regular honest employment. The folks bought for them a little house over in Tustin, about eight miles from the Santa Ana auto agency where Debbie worked for her Dad, but the parents weren't stupid enough to give over the legal title to the place. Mr. Verdugo's old Ford collapsed on some side street up in Los Angeles, so Debbie convinced her Dad that he should be charitable to her new husband and provide him with a car from the loaner fleet of the dealerships, and he did. The folks also provided all the furnishings for the Honeymoon cottage. Remington's kept the legal title to the cars and everything else, somehow knowing that this marriage would not last long.

All through high school and through the first two years of her Santa Ana College career, Debbie was always neat and well dressed, at all times well groomed and modest in appearance, with a little bit of makeup to embellish her natural beauty. With the advent of romance with King Pete, Debbie began to wear less modest attire to please him; she would splash on heavy fragrances; she smeared her face with thick coats of cosmetics and wore heavy false eyelashes. She had her ears pierced at several places on each ear, and wore numerous earrings and other gold and silver adornments there. She had gold and silver charms and multi-color bracelets half-way up both arms and gold chains on each ankle. She wore several heavy chains about her neck. Her modest wardrobe was abandoned in favor of more provocative garments. She was no longer the lovely maiden of her youth, but chose an appearance that looked like she had just got out on bail. Debbie began to smoke cigarettes openly, and her refrigerator was filled with beer and liquor bottles. At her home the coffee table and nightstands were cluttered with her husband's girlie magazines and other pornographic materials. After Mom and Dad Remington saw this stuff in Debbie's house, they chose not to visit there anymore. She was welcome to come to their home any time she wanted, but they asked her not to bring Mr. Verdugo. She did continue to frequently visit her family, and on several occasions Momma Remington noticed the bruises on Debbie's face which she tried to cover with heavy makeup. The bruising and redness on her lower arms and legs were not so easy to hide. When Momma first noticed these blemishes she inquired of the source of misery, and Debbie brushed off the questions with the suggestion that she tripped and fell off the porch. But it seemed that Debbie too often fell off that porch. This marriage of Debbie seemed to be without matrimonial harmony, but unexplainably continued. Precious Debbie had joined ranks with social cranks. This concerned both her parents, but mostly was Momma Remington troubled, deeply distressed, greatly saddened at the obvious loss of something precious.

One further feature that set Mr., Verdugo apart from his contemporaries: He had a wide mouth gracing his strong jaw line, and his front teeth were well aligned, but just a bit larger than average size. He had a firm smile accentuating his confident manner and displaying those handsome choppers. But King Pete wanted to have something more to display with each sardonic smile, so he had some dental aggrandizement on his maxillary margins. His upper right lateral incisor was covered with a full gold crown. On his upper left canine tooth he had a fairly large diamond implanted into the tooth. He had such a large enough stone that it was buried right into the body of the tooth, not just glued to the surface. Very gaudy but also very distinctive. Question: Why would a responsible dentist invade into the surface structure of a healthy tooth just to plant a big diamond?

When one by one the older two Remington kids left the shelter of her arms to establish their own separate households, Momma was disappointed with their departures, preferring rather that somehow they could remain with her forever in their happy home and under her umbrella of security. It can be a very emotional matter to let go of something you love so. But, being unable to keep them in diapers, she simply redirected her concern and watchful care to the twins. She joyfully observed and encouraged their evolution from little kids to become big kids, and rejoiced when her teenager twins became beautiful young ladies. Remarkably beautiful young ladies.

The twins Teri and Toni were an altogether different story from the day they were born. These two seemed to be exactly alike in every physical way. They were beautiful as infants, and got lovelier with the passing of time. Identical twins draw attention anyway, but these two were so pleasant and filled with constant overflowing joy that seemed contagious, so that their glee would create a happy place wherever they might be, and this unusual manner began before they could even walk. They amused one another constantly, laughed and sang together incessantly, giggled and jumped, cackled and skipped about, would dance and spin around by the hour, and were such a delight to watch. They were never unpleasant. They never had a bad day. They were never known to pout or throw tantrums. They never had a disagreement between themselves about anything. Never. For that matter, they never seemed to have disagreements with anyone, whether individually or as a team.

The twins were reading very well in English and in Spanish before they even started kindergarten. They had their little friends at school and visiting in their home, but they were happiest when amusing one another. In attendance at the public school starting in the first grade, the principal announced that siblings should grow up apart, rather than to be dependent upon one another, in order to establish independence and proper development, so he placed these girls in separate classes. Momma Remington was incensed to hear of this arbitrary action, and went immediately to demand that the girls be kept together. The dispute escalated when the school principal refused to comply, stating that it was a policy established by order of the school board, based upon the sound advice of the school psychologist. In order to avoid open conflict with the principal and an imperious school board, the Remington's simply removed the twins from the public school and placed them in the nearby Catholic education program, where the nuns and priest administrators were more sympathetic. The girls thrived. The other two Remington children remained in the public school and had an altogether different social conditioning.

The Remington twins had an unusual trait. They would happily engage in conversation with each other while both were talking over the other, chattering and chortling, clucking and giggling with the humor of each other's comments. They did this from the time they were in diapers. To a casual observer it would seem impossible that anything was being communicated between them, a cacophony of pleasant chatter. They could listen and absorb each other's prattle while rendering simultaneous discourse. It was especially amusing to listen to them doing teenager talk, both talking at the same time, one in English and the other in Spanish. After protracted banter each could tell just about everything covered in the exchanges. Amazing.

These charming twins had another clever communication talent: From the time they were just little kids, as they might be sitting at the breakfast table or on opposite sides of the room, or separated by a noisy crowd, and without saying even one word could communicate a complete conversation with silent exchange of facial expressions, humorous smiles or frowns, winks and blinks, nods and shakes, grins and pouts, and funny wobbling eyebrows.

When the twins were twelve years old they were fitted with orthodontic braces, and after two years of suffering for the sake of beauty, those braces were removed on their fourteenth birthday. The result was absolutely perfect, and their sparkling white teeth complemented further their natural loveliness. These two were a couple of precious dolls.

The twins returned to public school in tenth grade, and there was no problem with rules requiring separation, so all their classes were together. They continued to thrive, and were very popular. The boys became more than just a little interested in these lovely specimens of feminine pulchritude, but Momma Remington insisted that there will be no dating until age sixteen. When the girls did turn sixteen years of age they had apparently reached their optimum height of a tad over 5'6" and that was about 4 inches taller than their sister Debbie.

While all the kids were out of the house attending their respective schools, Mrs. Ximena Carillo Remington got involved in the charity programs of three Catholic churches: at the big Catholic Church in Santa Ana, and the smaller churches in Costa Mesa and Capistrano. She was tremendously popular with all the dozens of ladies in each group, and each such group would meet for lunch at least once a month. The Remington dealerships gave generously to promote the good work of each such cluster of lovely people.

CHAPTER 5

QUANDARY WITHOUT RESOLVE

Debbie Remington had been wed to Mr. Verdugo for just a few weeks when he began to noticeably change in manners and temperament, and over the next several months she accumulated life experiences that no caring Mother would wish onto anyone's child. King Pete was harsh, abrasive and abusive, and physically violent in his frequent tirades. Notwithstanding his oppressive behavior toward his young wife and just about anyone else that got in his way, Debbie remained irresolute and tolerant, weak and submissive, with a meekness never seen in her younger days. She would probably be the poster child for the battered wife syndrome, and her parents were forced to stand by and anxiously watch as their baby girl devoted her life to this cruel tyrant she chose for a husband.

Debbie continued to work for her Dad's car dealership in Santa Ana, but one early spring day she failed to show up for the customary exchange of greetings with other employees. It was almost 9:00 that morning when a phone call came for Stewart Remington, and the operator recognized the voice of Debbie. Stewart Remington's little baby girl was crying and almost hysterical, and difficult to understand. Her Dad listened patiently for a minute or so to allow for the weeping to subside, and then she managed to tell enough for him to realize that Debbie had been arrested and was in the Orange County Jail, not too far distant from where he was then seated. He told her to hold on for a short while, and he'd arrive with a bail bondsman or a lawyer.

An experienced bail bondsman is a good friend to have. Most people have no intention to ever need such a friend, but really now, don't you think it would still be a good idea to drop by your nearest bail bondsman's office and get acquainted? Maybe you could take him a few dozen doughnuts or a box of chocolates. Or maybe if you are a car dealer you might want to sell him a real bargain. Who knows but what some day you might need a nice bail bondsman.

Stewart Remington had at one time or another sold a car or cars to every bail bondsman in Orange County, and was on a first name basis with each and every one of them. He simply chose the first bondsman he could think of, one Wally Bernstein who also happened to be located a couple of blocks away, and they went together to retrieve Debbie from the clutches of that guy from Nottingham. The bondsman person is allowed more freedom in moving about the jail and mingling with the hapless prisoners. A respected bondsman can work miracles for folks when he wants to, or when he has a huge commission to be earned on a transaction. Apparently, the women's jail was working slowly that day, and Debbie was still being processed when the bondsman arrived, but the Matron in charge remembered that lovely box of See's Candies that Wally had given her last Christmas as a token of his appreciation for her many favors over the years. His request to expedite the matter of Debbie Verdugo was so honored that they had the bond fixed at a minimal amount and Debbie was out the door in less than fifteen minutes, looking disheveled and weary, with eye shadow smudges and smears caused by the torrents of tears, and she was carrying her bulging property bag.

As they were processing the frightened Debbie through the exit desk, the Duty Sergeant asked if there would a bail bond also for her husband 'King Pete', and Stewart Remington with a scowl replied "Let that !@#$%^&* rot right where he is", whereupon he placed loving arms around his little baby girl, kissed her atop her head, and took her to his home. She wept inconsolably the entire way along the road to that residence. Otherwise the ride home was quiet, though the atmosphere was charged.

Arriving at the Remington home, they found that only Momma Remington was on site, Reuben was moved out to Beverly Hills and likely digging for gold somewhere, and the twins were off to school. They sat their little girl down on the couch, and Momma retrieved some damp cloths with which to wipe away the flowing tears and soothe the troubled brow. It took a while for Debbie to really settle down enough to tell so much of her tale as she was willing to divulge, but that was enough to completely alarm her folks.

As for the early morning events of this particular day: Mr. Verdugo had been 'gone on business' with his foul-mouthed friends for about the past six weeks.

Debbie had just awakened, showered, and got dressed for work in her flashy questionable manner, with the heavy lipstick and eye shadow generously swabbed onto her face, and the strong fragrance of some malodorous French perfume liberally applied. Her blouse was tight fitting and provocative in design, to match the short skirt she wore. This is the way her husband likes for her to look and smell. She was walking into the kitchen area when she heard Mr. Verdugo just arriving home after his night of carousing with his favorite gangster cronies from East LA. He had been standing in the kitchen for a few minutes loudly demanding fresh coffee when the cops came knocking at the rear door. Mr. Verdugo shot through the nearest exit and toward the back bedroom, while Debbie reached for the door. She had not even yet touched that doorknob when the entire door came crashing down in a hail of splinters, and several noisy men quickly ran into the room shouting and shoving, some in uniform and some looking like they could dress better for these occasions. They were followed by several more stern looking men, all of them dressed in nice suits and looking like they were ready for work at the nearest bank. These guys must have been really impressed with this bedizened woman that looked like she was a Lady Clown from the traveling circus. They firmly pushed Debbie to one side and ran in every direction. One of them went quickly to the front door and opened it for easy entry of several more uniformed officers. They were not gentle at all in the way they ushered Debbie into the front room, and when she asked what was happening they rudely told her to "shut up and sit down here. Don't move or you might get shot!" Well, that harsh sort of greeting should get someone's attention, and Debbie was becoming very distressed. She immediately sat down on her couch, watching intently everything going on around her, and with each word she hears and with each thing she then saw happen it just threw her deeper into shock. She could hear the riot racket coming from the back bedroom as the officers wrestled the resisting Mr. Verdugo to the floor and placed him in handcuffs, and then had to fight him every inch of the way from down the hall, finally dragging him into the area where Debbie was seated and then she was starting to really come unglued. The cops roughly deposited their unhappy captive on the floor, as he continued screaming epithets and unkind threats. Back in the 60's they did not yet have cans of spray mace or electric shock tazer stun guns, or Mr. Loudmouth would have been a really great candidate for that kind of constable blessing. Without trying to reason with him or inform him of the cause for his sudden popularity, after consulting among themselves in an isolated corner, the uniformed officers picked up the recalcitrant prisoner and shoved him along and through the front door, depositing him into a police cruiser there waiting, as he continued loudly screaming vulgarities. At the same time, they hauled Debbie to her feet, callously turned her about and placed her in handcuffs without any explanation other than to say that she is now 'under arrest'. They were only a little more gentle than they had been with King Pete. She was placed in a cage in the rear seat of another police cruiser, and it took off down the street. She very courteously inquired of the uniformed driver what this whole thing is all about, and that driver was a lot more calm and polite in telling her that he did not really know all the facts, but heard that there had been a shooting in Los Angeles, and that someone might have died, and the driver of the car in her driveway was observed departing the scene.

When the officers delivered Debbie to the Orange County Jail, she arrived there before 8 O'clock, and she had to have all her ornaments removed so that she could be fingerprinted and have her 'mug shot'. They tried to put all that jewelry, trinkets and rings in a regular size 'property bag', but it would not all fit. So Debbie's stuff was given a special big property bag, bulging with her tasteless ornaments. They don't usually have female prisoners change into the jailhouse jumpsuit right away, especially if it looks like they might make immediate bail. But Debbie's garments were such that it was the more responsible thing to do in getting her out of those 'streetwalker' clothes, and so they did. After the mug shot she politely asked to use the phone for a local call, while waiting for the next part of the booking process. They don't usually do things out of order like this, but they did allow Debbie to make her one allotted phone call, to let her Dad know where she was.

Well, you can imagine the emotional roller coaster that Momma Remington had to deal with when she heard these things. Bear in mind that Momma had been in despair ever since her little girl first got involved with this street gang thug, and had managed to keep her sentiments locked up inside her breaking heart now for the many days, weeks and months since that little girl ran off to Las Vegas to actually marry that moral misfit. It is reasonable to imagine that this particular devoted mother had beautiful plans for her baby, probably from the day she was born, to have her grow up to be a lovely bride, maybe to have a big wedding with all the trappings, and all that 'happily ever after' as part of her life with a handsome and reliable husband, and maybe someday to bring home many little squirming grandchildren. Perhaps Momma Remington had some tiny shred of hope that Mr. Wonderful would somehow become with the passing of time a more responsible and mature person, maybe become respectable and more conventional. Surely there must have been at least the most remote possibility that he could change. Well, knowing the strong sentiments of Mrs. Remington, she was more likely hoping that lightning would strike down this slimy creep, and then her precious baby girl could again assume her virtuous identity and all would be forgiven.

Upon hearing that her child had been arrested, and that there could be the threat of prison, Momma Remington took a deep breath, and went into the bathroom to get more damp cloths to dab on Debbie's brow, then she sat with Debbie's head in her lap for the rest of the day, and all was quiet. All was silent.

Dad Remington got on the phone and called his favorite Criminal Defense attorney in Santa Ana, whom we shall facetiously identify as 'Clarence Darrow II' (since he would not allow us the use of his true name), and recruited him to the defense of this baby girl. That lawyer told him that it would be unethical for him to represent the Mr. Verdugo, and would only be able to work for Debbie. Stewart Remington then spewed out some profane epithets that are not fit to be repeated here, suggesting that Mr. Verdugo could and should rot in prison (and likewise burn forever in some other place). Well, that little commentary also served the purpose of informing the lawyer that Mr. Verdugo didn't have much hope of the Remington family helping with his bail.

Mr. Darrow did not straightaway demand a written retainer, but did immediately launch a probe into the Orange County prosecutor's office to see what he could find out about the facts of the problem. He was told that this matter was a Los Angeles case, and he'd have to deal with the LA District Attorney's office. A call to the Los Angeles County DA's office did not at first get a lot of information. They promised to call back as soon as a Deputy DA could be assigned. Not willing to wait, Mr. Darrow contacted the top honcho at the LA County Sheriff's Department, and got an almost immediate response to tell important details of the case, and so then was told that:

Mr. Verdugo has been for about two years on the watch list for illicit drugs and marijuana transporters. He was parked in his own car about a block away from an undercover transaction, in which the cop got shot in the leg, and the guys involved immediately in the buy managed to get to their car and race away, with several LA Police cars in hot pursuit. When the chasers and the chasees passed by where Verdugo was quietly parked, he quickly fired up his car and raced away in the opposite direction. Another unmarked car with federal agents in it followed Verdugo from a safe distance at posted speeds, all the way from East LA and into Orange County. They by radio alerted the Los Angeles law enforcement people of their location, and asked for Orange County backup. They saw Verdugo go into the residence, and when both the plainclothes and uniformed officers arrived, these federal guys joined in on the fun of breaking down doors and harassing the occupants of that house.

It turned out that the undercover officer only suffered a superficial gunshot wound that was not life-threatening. Stop! Hold on right here. That gunshot wound might not be life-threatening, but those bullets tearing into the flesh and underlying tissue and ripping up the muscles beneath, that really hurts! Next time you hear about a cop that got just a trivial little 'superficial wound', don't ignore the immediate pain and continuing discomfort that police officer is suffering for your sake.

The LA Sheriff people also informed Darrow that at that very moment the federal people were tearing apart Debbie's house, under a proper search warrant issued that same morning by an Orange County Superior Court judge, looking for contraband much like that for which Mr. Verdugo was well known to be dealing in.

Clarence Darrow II said that he could not provide a very encouraging opinion based only on what he was told on the phone. If the search of the house did not turn up any incriminating evidence, it seemed to him that there was no great likelihood that Debbie would even be charged. He was right.

Debbie went to her place to pick up some things and to rescue her red car, and was instructed that she should not answer the telephone there, mostly because should Mr. Verdugo call to demand someone come down and go his bail, or whatever else he might demand or discuss, the jail telephones are monitored and calls recorded, and any unfortunate comment or statement made by or to Debbie could have negative impact on her defense. When Debbie got inside the front room of her home she found a disaster area that looked like a bomb had gone off. Everything was torn apart and tipped over, and those investigators from law enforcement were not the least bit neat and orderly in their search for contraband or other incriminating things. They did not bother to clean up after themselves.

Debbie stayed with her folks for a couple of weeks, and after a few days started back to work. The newspapers in Santa Ana and Los Angeles carried the descriptions of the crime and the arrests on the front page, noting that 'Gang Warfare has come to Tustin', including the names of the drug kingpin by name of Pedro Verdugo and his wife Debra Verdugo. They included King Pete's really ugly mug shot with the articles. The Television Evening news featured the story for a few days, and Momma Remington was terribly embarrassed. Actually, she was humiliated. She was truly ashamed. She was crushed, devastated and emotionally destroyed. She kept everything inside until the immediate pressure let up, and then in the quiet of evening she wept uncontrollably, and sobbed through the night. She several times wondered aloud if any of her church groups friends would figure out that the 'Debra' in the news reports was a Remington. This whole thing was an unbearable disgrace to the Remington family.

King Pete was transferred to the LA County Jail, and bail was set much too high for him to pay the bond premium out of his pocket change. He was told that his wife had made bail, so he phoned his house several times to prod Debbie into bamboozling her Dad to help with his bail. He was unable to make contact by phoning home, so he assumed that Debbie might be with her folks. He phoned the Remington house, and Momma Remington recognized his voice with just a couple of words spoken, she slammed down the phone and uttered a long string of naughty descriptive words as part of that exercise.

Well, Clarence Darrow II was right. The Los Angeles County DA did not even file a formal criminal complaint against Verdugo or Debbie, and Mr. Verdugo was released without further adieu two weeks after his arrest. Mr. Darrow was informed of the non-filing, and advised the Remington household accordingly. Mr. Wonderful had one of his gangster pals come to pick him up from the jail and deliver him to the home in Tustin. The news media made no mention of charges being dropped.

Debbie decided to go home to console her beloved, to stroke his woeful brow and comfort him for all the terrible treatment he had received, to confirm she just knew that King Pete could never do the bad things that he had been so wrongfully accused of. Mr. Verdugo began to drink all his beer and liquor from the well-stocked refrigerator to celebrate his freedom, and stayed tanked up for the rest of the week. The guys that got in the squabble with the undercover agent were not so fortunate. The judge 'threw the book' at them, and they were sent off to a few years of free room and board at expense of the taxpayers. King Pete had to find some new partners in crime, and did so rather quickly from the abundance of malefactors running loose on the streets of East LA.

Momma Remington begged and pleaded with Debbie to stay with Mom and Dad, and not to go back to that scum that brought about all this public disgrace, but Mr. Verdugo seemed to have some strange hold on her heart and soul. Within a short time Debbie put on again her surfeit of jewelry and all that other excess of ornamentation, painted up her face as before, put on her skimpy garments, and returned to work at her Dad's dealership. Can you imagine what her fellow employees thought of all these things, and the whispering that echoed around the dealerships? Stewart Remington staunchly ignored the past, and hoped for better days.

Without explanation and not so much as a courteous farewell to Debbie, Mr. Verdugo disappeared after a few days had passed, and was not seen again for a couple of months. During his absence he did not phone or send any sort of postcard or other remembrance. He was driving one of the loaner cars from the Remington dealership loaner pool, and all of the parking tickets written against that car were received at the desk of Debbie Verdugo, and the dealership paid for all those reminders of how careless and inconsiderate King Pete was. But those parking tickets were coming in from locations on the southern border of Texas and Arizona, so Debbie knew the general area where her King Pete was wandering about. During most of the time when King Pete was gone Debbie would stay with her folks in her old room at the Remington place.

CHAPTER 6

<u>HOPES AND DREAMS</u>

About two months after Debbie Verdugo had her humiliating problems with the law, her brother encountered disaster of his own foolish making, which almost eclipsed everything bad that had ever happened in the life of Momma Ximena Remington.

During his college days Reuben Remington was caught up in petty schemes to generate revenue. Almost from the very day that he graduated from the University of Southern California, he was totally immersed in more heavy duty intrigues that promised to make him rich. He joined with his collaborating colleagues from USC to work the investment and bond markets throughout California, and he was the youngest participant in the plans, more than a mere follower, he was deeply involved. They formed corporations in California, Nevada and Delaware, all to use in conducting their business affairs. Then they filed a number of stock corporations under assumed names, as part of their many various ruses. They each obtained the necessary personal and corporate licenses and permits from the California Corporations Commission and the United States Securities and Exchange Commission, to add to the appearance of legitimacy and propriety.

Apparently, at the outset all these stock and bond transactions were perfectly legal, and the amount of legitimate revenue these young fellows managed to generate among themselves was amazing. Their several alliances proved to be very profitable. But Reuben and his cohorts were not content with a whole lot of money that didn't come in fast enough, and they began to put together deals that promised big bucks quickly. Some of their outrageous sales pitches were so unbelievable that a cautious informed investor would surely laugh at them. No. No. Not so. Many of their mercenary financiers appeared to be knowledgeable and very experienced in national and international money matters.

Reuben and his cronies continued for several years in their corporation ventures and phony investment scams, and the revenue numbers were astronomical.

Investors were flocking to their front doors, and scrambling atop one another to hand over millions of investment dollars in elaborate schemes. Some of their claims of offshore tax avoiding investment programs were so ridiculous that not even the most stupid person would put down ten cents to own a part of such a house of cards. The money came in by the ton, and greedy investors promised to bring more of their own money and to bring friends and business acquaintances to share in generating the easy money and great wealth. Reuben Remington was a prime promoter in this criminal enterprise. He was among these participants the most skilled in accounting and reading the financials. He could really 'cook the books', and could hide foul deeds better than others; and conversely he could spot flaws and blunders in the records generated by other crooked 'experts'. It takes one to know one, and he was really good at this.

From his share of early revenue, Reuben Remington used his own trunk full of cash to pay off completely his beautiful big home in Beverly Hills, with an eight-car garage and a swimming pool of huge dimension. The architecture was magnificent. The landscaping was spectacular. The location was in the best part of the most affluent neighborhood. The neighbors were rich and famous. He traded in his Buick that his folks had given him years ago, and got a white Bentley Convertible to fill one of those garages. His success was such that he was accompanied by the most beautiful movie starlet wannabes in his going about the popular watering holes in Hollywood and Beverly Hills. He was almost daily mentioned in the celebrity worshiping columns of the newspapers in Southern California. He had himself become one of those rich and famous persons he admired so much. Those celebrities like to mingle with money moguls, and Reuben had attained that lofty status. His parents were dazzled by his success, but apprehensive of the manner in which the wealth was rapidly coming in. Stewart and Shimi Remington were careful never to be photographed at any of Reuben's many receptions, and had nothing to do with his business affairs, directly or indirectly. Some of Reuben's colleagues encouraged the Remington's to throw in a chunk of money and just watch it grow and grow. They invested not one cent, and never suggested that anyone else should so invest.

Wealth and fame can be fleeting, and the adoration of those folks that want the infusion of wealth to continue on and on forever can be turned to scorn and disgust when the gold stops flowing. And so it was with young Reuben

Remington when he was still in his 20's as his house of cards collapsed, his phony ploys dried up, his fraud was betrayed by one of his trusted colleagues in a deal made with the federal prosecutors, and most of the other partners in crime seemed to disappear into the woodwork or wander off into the mist, and simply took what they could quickly drain out of the company bank accounts, which the prosecutor claimed to be in the multiplied millions of dollars' worth of draining, and those erstwhile friends must have ended up on some tropic isle beyond the reach of the Justice Department.

Reuben Remington was the goat, the scapegoat, the guy that didn't get away, and the whole terrible load of civil and criminal liability fell right on his head. He was arrested by FBI agents as he entertained a large crowd of admiring Hollywood types sipping cocktails around the grand pool at his swanky Beverly Hills home. He was still wearing his tuxedo when they took his mug shots at the jail, and the resulting photos were actually sorta glamorous. He retained some very expensive Beverly Hills attorneys to represent him in these matters, and their legal fees charged up front and paid in advance were outrageous, so much as to almost empty Reuben's coffers.

In the criminal matter: The scowling federal prosecutor slammed his fist on the counsel table, accusing Reuben Remington of being a cruel and unrepentant crook, and a shameless fraud that fed on the ignorance of the poor innocent investor, a hardened criminal still in his 20's, an uncommon thief that should be punished to the fullest extent of the law, and the jury agreed with that merciless growling prosecutor, finding Reuben guilty on all felony counts. The sneering old District Court judge sentenced him to a long federal prison term.

In the civil matters: Dozens of lawsuits were filed against the phony corporations and their scheming executives, but the only one they were able to actually serve with process was Reuben Remington, and he was easy to find because he was locked up in the Federal Detention Center. Money judgments were rendered one after another against Reuben and the holders of those judgments were trying to go against all his properties, including that swanky home and all his cars, the expensive furniture, and several hundred dollars yet remaining in his very last bank account. Some concerned creditors forced an involuntary bankruptcy, so that all the aggrieved losers could share proportionately in equitable division of all and everything that Reuben had remaining. Reuben almost cried when they told him that the nasty ol' Trustee in Bankruptcy had seized his beautiful white Bentley Convertible and sold it at auction.

Reuben really did have the very best and most expensive criminal defense lawyers in all Southern California, the kind with swanky offices on Wilshire Boulevard. They actually did the best job possible to try to get their hapless client free of those clutches of the law. Well, what do you know about criminal lawyers? Some folks think that all those shyster attorneys are crooks. It might seem that way at times, but those dedicated barristers are by nature of their business known to be mercenary, and as mercenaries their allegiance and concern for client welfare is limited to availability of financial resources to pay their fees. When his lawyers lost Reuben's case they recommended appeal to a higher court, but by that time they had used up all of Reuben's money and the Bankruptcy Court took all other available assets to cover debts to the creditors. Reuben was broke. His devoted legal team abandoned him. He had become penniless and could probably have enlisted the services of the Public Defender at public expense to advance the appeal but Reuben had too much pride to stoop low seeking such charity. He asked his folks to foot the tab for an appeal, but the Remington family attorneys reviewed the record and determined that the evidence was so strong that it would be a waste of money to pursue the matter any further in the appellate courts. There was no appeal of that District Court criminal judgment and sentence.

As one might expect, all this stuff really hit the fan. The newspapers and trade journals had something to pound the drum over for month after month, and all the related editorials agreed that Reuben Remington was a liar, fraud, cheat, and a thief. The ultimate image portrayed showed Reuben Remington was stupid.

And the tremendous impact on Momma Remington was so sad to see, as she crumbled beneath the burden of embarrassment, humiliation and shame. This once proud mother that loved her babies so much was crushed under a terrible load of mental and emotional anguish. She felt that all her friends and church acquaintances had abandoned her. They no longer phoned or came to visit, and she couldn't bring herself to even go out into the light of day. Her husband and the twins had to do the shopping because Momma was afraid she might be recognized by former friends or maybe some stranger that had read the newspapers. No amount of coaxing could get her to come out of her shell of grief and despair.

Reuben ended up in the United States Penitentiary at Lompoc, California, which is a medium security lockup for prisoners that don't offer much risk of running. At least two from the family went to visit him two or three times each month, and after a while they were able to get Momma to go also to see her little baby boy. At that first visit, the family was seated at the visitors' table, and Momma completely broke down when Reuben walked in wearing the standard prison garb. She grabbed him and would not let go for the full time allowed for visiting that day, all the while weeping uncontrollably. At the end of the visiting session, as Reuben said goodbye and disappeared beyond the door, Momma completely collapsed into a pile of weeping lamentations. They had to call for a wheelchair to get her back out to the parking lot. She cried softly all the way home. Her agonizing grief was real and painful.

The drive from Orange County to Lompoc is a long distance, so after the first few visits to see Reuben the family would stopover to see relatives in Oxnard whenever they passed by, because it was about half way between Lompoc and the Remington home, just to break up the long trip. On the way home from Momma's first visit she could not stop weeping, but they stopped off to see the relatives in Oxnard anyway, and Momma continued her weeping all through the visit. The Oxnard relatives acted like they didn't notice, and didn't ask about the tears. Momma got to where she could go to Lompoc without disintegrating in dismay. The Oxnard relatives never mentioned Reuben nor did they ask where he might be.

CHAPTER 7

COMFORTING WORDS

The individual and concert tragedies suffered by the Remington family in such quick succession, together with the resulting anguish and despair felt by everyone concerned, particularly the grief and humiliation felt by Momma Remington, were just unbearable. It affected all of them.

Reuben was at a distance from all the grief and sorrow brought on by his schemes and the ugly publicity he garnered in the process. The newspapers and other media had a field day with him and his money-making machines, and seemed to take perverse delight with the prosecution and sentencing articles to amuse the reading public. The family had to live through all this, but Reuben was more concerned with his personal plight and at first seemed to be oblivious and unexposed to most of the diatribes against him. Sure, he was aware of some of this raging that went on, but he seemed to be essentially unconcerned that those arrows of insult wounded his mother so deeply. Maybe it was simply a lot easier for him to look the other way.

Debbie was not at a long distance from the heartache she caused with her arrest and the horrid publicity generated in the newspapers and media, but that did not work to alter her behavior. Almost as bad, she seemed unaware that the way she chose to dress and parade around like a *fille de joie pouffiase* was itself an embarrassment to her family and former friends. Debbie was very much aware of her mother's continuing depression, but chose to believe that her Mom was so reclusive and withdrawn mostly because of Reuben's behavior. Debbie was actually making matters worse by her choice to remain with the drug lord King Pete Verdugo. She contended that her husband had not been convicted or even charged with any crime, and those naughty cops were just harassing him.

One of the incidental problems that erupted as Momma's depression continued and deepened was the effect that it had on the twins Teri and Toni. They held up socially OK at school, even though it was embarrassing to have a few people ask about the newspaper reports, to which they responded that they really knew nothing. On the other hand, the twins not only had sympathy for Mom, they had real empathy, and the three began to show signs of clinical depression. All three of them had trouble sleeping, and could not concentrate on tasks at hand. There were lingering feelings of hopelessness and helplessness. The twins' school grades were affected accordingly.

Momma Remington continued in her sorrow and painful grief, to the point that the priests at her three chosen Catholic churches came to pray with her one early morning. Two of these priests were participant in the new Charismatic renewal that was then sweeping through Catholic societies, and they were so inspiring and encouraging in their sincere prayers and well wishes. These guys were different. Two days later, these two Charismatic priests came again, but this time they brought with them a protestant pastor of a little independent evangelical church in San Clemente, a Texas transplant by name of Brother Russell DeWitt, whose prayers seemed to shake the walls. These three praying ministers laid hands on the lady and prayed and prayed that she might somehow be delivered of the burden of depression and grief that troubled her so. Well, she claimed to be feeling better for all their efforts to touch the throne of God on her behalf, but in truth she was not much better. She did like the Pastor DeWitt and his lively presentations with the strong southern drawl and humility of a true gentleman, and smiled at his easy-going manners. The following Sunday she drove by herself the twelve or fifteen miles to attend morning services at his church, where nobody knew anything about her or the grief she had recently known. She went again the next Sunday, and took the twins with her. The young men in attendance took note of the new teener girls. Just going to church in a place where she and her problems were not known seemed to have a restorative effect on Momma Remington, and the girls seemed to be happier, too. When Debbie began to spend more time with her family, she would also go to church with the rest of them. She was a sight to be seen there, but it was for her a great environment.

At insistence of her husband and concurrence of the three ministers that advised her, Ximena Remington went to talk with a Christian psychologist counselor in Santa Ana, and he in turn introduced her to a Christian psychiatrist by name of Ray Bowie, MD, who specialized in treating depression and could provide her with prescription medications to help her rest more comfortably. This great Christian counselor prayed with Shimi Remington, and told her that rather than to spend her afternoons in emotional collapse, she should practice the power of prayer and in her prayers to follow the scriptural admonition to focus on the needs of others, even to pray for politicians and enemies; to pray without ceasing until the light shines through. Just watching the TV news and reading the newspaper would lead any intelligent person to conclude that praying for politicians is wasted time, but she did it anyway, because God is the source of miracles. Dr. Bowie's very practical advice was far better than any pills or other narcotic medicine, and his efforts did help considerably. Shimi continued to counsel with both of these Christian counselors for a long while. This season of better sentiments went on for several more months.

The Remington family had the good fortune to have great lawyers and excellent counselors. Others have not been so fortunate. The Book of Psalms starts right off with an admonition that suggests we should not seek counsel of ungodly persons, and in the Book of Proverbs is the suggestion that there is greater comfort in a multitude of counselors. If a proper diagnosis is not forthcoming it might be well to continue seeking help from more professionals, but when the problem and its source is identified it really doesn't help to hear confirming opinions of an abundance of professionals, as sometimes their diagnoses and prognoses don't agree with one another and we're faced with making more difficult choices.

The practicing Christian has as many problems as anyone else. Remember: The rain falls on the just and the unjust. Being a Christian does not exempt anyone from the afflictions of mankind, and the salvation experience does not by itself entitle anyone to live for two hundred glorious robust years in this life. Read it for yourself, it's in the Book: read the part about threescore and ten. People of faith seem to die regularly. Read the Obituaries! But to be sure, our God is a healing God; our God is the source of miracles; our God is anxious to do great things for you and through you. Our emphasis should be on spiritual things, but it is very difficult to stay spiritually focused when disaster strikes or disease runs rampant. Prayer changes things. But if you don't seem to have an immediate answer for your urgent personal and intercessory petitions, be assured that there is nothing in the human condition that can occur without the consent of God. His eye is on the sparrow.

The practicing Christian that suffers mental or emotional problems ought to seek out the counselor that holds common spiritual ideals and maybe more than one counselor just to be sure. But 'Christian Counselors' come in a variety of disciplines, sizes, types, shapes and forms, with varying intensities of commitment to Christian principles. A psychologist, psychiatrist, marriage counselor, family counselor, juvenile counselor or whatever that bills himself or herself as being a Christian counselor can provide therapy and prescribed treatments, but if he or she neglects to prescribe prayer then you might have some concern for that counselor's perception of himself or herself and what the goals of the practice might be. If they're not willing to pray with you and pray for you that should tell a whole lot about their mercenary or missionary goals. The objective of any such Christian counselor should be to promote mental and emotional health, to encourage peace and spiritual comfort. Otherwise, may we respectfully suggest that you once again read Psalm 1:1. Where would be a better resource for these things than the Greatest Counselor of all, the Prince of Peace, whose name is Wonderful, the Mighty God is He. Prayer is the most effective prescription. ℞: **Prayer**

Any counselor should know his or her limits. This rule applies to lawyers and doctors, psychologists and psychiatrists, ministers and missionaries, and even extends to family and helpful friends. When encountering a problem beyond the limits, that counselee should be referred to a therapist with appropriate skills. Some of the drivel that unqualified counselors put out with is terribly harmful. For instance: marriage between a man and a woman is symbolic of the relationship between Christ and His church. Anything that comes between Christ and His church or any individual or group within the church, we call that sin. If it separates a person from God, it is sin, and you might as well apply that proper label. Any counselor that recommends sin to soothe the soul is a crackpot, and when your counselor recommends divorce as a solution to marital problems it raises huge red flags reflecting on his or her credentials as a 'Christian Counselor'.

Lawyers are the worst offenders in this matter of personal or family counseling. So many good marriages could be saved were it not for stupid mercenaries that destroy all hope of reconciliation, and that can include so many little petty disputes, so much pouting and sulking over meaningless disagreements. It might well be that the battered bride should dodge the pain and grief in the best way she can, but her decision to dump her perceived oppressor by legal means ought to be her decision and her 'Christian Counselor' should not impinge on that prerogative. A certain lawyer in Sacramento, California, used to specialize in handling divorces for marriage counselors. That should tell you something about the lawyer, but even more about the people that want the whole world to know how brilliant they are as 'counselors', and you will understand this better by applying the teachings of Jesus in the Book of Matthew and the Book of Luke, where he expresses His scorn for the 'Blind leading the blind'.

Remember: The good counselor is one that recognizes the problem. The good lawyer is one that recognizes the question. It is not required always that the counselor have a ready answer, since he or she can go find the answer. If they don't recognize the question then how can they artfully apply any answer? As for the lawyers that recognize the question, they can go to the books and find a good answer. If that brilliant advocate is any good at all in legal research, and if he cannot find the right answer, then he should be astute enough to make up a good answer, since one that is fabricated by an accomplished attorney ought to be at least as good as the answer that cannot be found. It ends up as a matter of persuasive oratory.

Then arises the question: How does one find a good lawyer? How can one recognize a good lawyer?

Good question. Even the most stupid lawyer in town has a great education, and his conversation can be powerfully persuasive with absurd arguments that impress the unenlightened. Maybe if you have a few hours to spare on any given day, you should visit your County Courthouse, go to the 'Law and Motion Department', and see how much respect the judge there has for lawyers in general and individuals in particular. These proceedings are open to the public. Take along a sack lunch for the noon break, but do get back in time for the commencement of the afternoon calendar. This can be very entertaining, especially in the more populous counties with a greater case load.

By the way: in this age of electronic communication online, most State Bar Associations have public access to some of the State Bar records. If you have a lawyer demand some up-front fees and costs from you for some civil or criminal matter, you might want to consult with those online records before you pay anyone anything. Then you might want to go down to the courthouse and check the record to see how many times that attorney has been sued for malpractice or mishandling cases. You might even be so bold as to ask that attorney about any disputes he or she in the past has had with clients, and his or her reaction should be noted.

As for other professional counselors, most states keep public access records, but some of their records are considered very confidential until an official negative finding, and even then the information available might be very limited, but even 'very limited' can be enough to raise suspicions.

CHAPTER 8

TERROR

Time or eternity, places and events, participants and observers, rewards and results, payments and penalties, injury and pain, suffering and seeking, hope and despair, elation and disappointment, faith and doubt, strength and weakness. And the list goes on and on to describe encounters in the human condition. Some of these things are of our own making, and some are imposed by circumstances over which we have no control. Some foster great disappointment and some bring boundless delight. Some events and circumstances might seem to create unbearable burdens, but a fortunate turn of events might magically appear to make for an altogether different and unexpected peace. And then there might come even more difficult trials and tribulations, disasters and defeats. Where does one turn for escape?

In the midst of calamity a person might want some word of encouragement suggesting that the troubles and misfortunes may soon subside. There just has to be an end to the hard times, some relief from the anguish and pain. And then there is that sanctimonious comforter that comes up with the profound observation that some other person is suffering from something even worse. Well, that's a great relief, isn't it? Your finger is ripped to shreds in the gears, and the other guy has a bad case of acne. How does that relieve the pain in your finger? How does that save your hand? Maybe Mr. Comforter could simply turn off the power switch, or at least give you a nice Band-Aid. Do you remember Job's comforters? They are still around and they'll be calling on you when you need comfort, and they'll give you the same advice they gave him.

Whatever recommendation one might receive from well-meaning counselors, it might be better to consult the writings of the Apostle Paul, found at Romans 8:28, where he suggests that all occurrences can work together for good to those who are called according to His purpose. Many astute preachers have designed long sermons protesting the proper application of these precious words of scripture, often in such a way as to wholly neutralize the verse and its reasonable implication, including the purpose of imparting hope to the believer. Hopefulness is what the entire Book of Romans is all about.

Then it often seems that troubles come in relentless waves, one problem following another and often more than one difficulty at a time. So it was within the Remington family.

Momma Remington was almost eighteen years old when she married husband Stewart, and after a year or so she gave birth to first child Reuben. Stewart Remington was several years older than his wife. Their marriage commenced at a time when the US was caught up in a great depression and war clouds were gathering over Europe and the threat of hostilities was in the air around the world.

For the first seventeen years of his life, Reuben Remington was a happy fella, got good grades in school, had a lot of affluent friends, had an excellent relationship with his doting parents, and got along super well with his three sisters. His worst problems began when he left home to go away to college, and was drawn into schemes of his avaricious companions. He wasn't the victim of alcohol or drugs. He wasn't stolen away by sexual assignations. He was not drawn into political intrigue. He was enchanted with wealth and all the things that money could buy. He wanted the money muscles. These dreams of mammon multiplied throughout his college years and became his downfall when at a very young age he went to prison for his choices gone awry.

For the first twenty years of her life, Debbie Remington was a happy young lady, remarkably beautiful, popular and respected for her modesty and integrity, got top grades all the way through high school, and was well on her way to gaining a great university education. Her parents were so proud of her, indulged her every whim and she got along well with everyone in her family. Somewhere along the way, a force beyond her control seemed to take over her judgment, and she ended up married to a real creep. The news media was filled with reports of her arrest. She was drawn into a society of dark and foreboding lifestyle, and her appearance changed substantially from modesty to something else.

For the first sixteen years of their lives, Teri and Toni Remington lived in a happy and contented world. They were perfectly beautiful from the day they were born, and they were the greatest blessing ever to their folks.

They were happy and filled with joy that was contagious to everyone they encountered.

Then came that really bad season for the Remington family. Their daughter ran off with that drug-dealing street gang thug and made other choices that caused so much anguish for her parents. Their only son was convicted of heavy duty crimes in federal court and was sent to prison. The publicity was so humiliating. While the Remington family was falling apart, their businesses seemed to be thriving. But the worst was then yet to come, adding greatly to the grief.

Debbie lived with her gangster husband in her own home in Tustin, about twenty miles north of where the Remington family residence was located in Southern Orange County, but she seemed to spend more and more time staying at the family home than she did in her own place. It was almost as though she had no real household apart from the family. She would spend probably three weekends each month with her family, and probably four or five nights during the week, staying in her old bedroom still maintained for her use. Except for her chosen dark lifestyle and poor taste in clothing and cosmetic appearance, her manner was pleasant, and her conversation was always agreeable. But when Debbie departed to return to her Tustin residence, the twins would look at each other and to their mother, and shrug their shoulders as they were all wondering whatever will become of Debbie?

Even when Debbie went home, she would often live alone while 'King Pete' was off to some undisclosed destination conducting his private business. Recall that when she first inquired of these absences she got a smack for her curiosity along with the admonition that his business is none of her business. Mr. Verdugo often had big wads of money in his pockets, although he never shared it with Debbie. She worked every day for her Dad, and her income was enough to handle all the household expenses. She suspected that her husband was doing drugs, and knew that he engaged regularly in drinking binges that would empty their fridge. His gangster friends would often join him in all night drug and drinking sprees, and the morning after would be sprawled around the house on the furniture and the floor. When those ruffians showed up, Debbie would lock herself in the back room, or make her way out to her car and go spend the night with her folks. Things worsened over time, and when Debbie had been married less than a year, there was a tremendous disaster.

On a Saturday morning in early October, Debbie was working in her office at the car agency in Santa Ana, Momma Remington and daughter Toni were off shopping, and Teri was alone in the family home puttering. About Ten O'clock or so, without knocking first or otherwise announcing his arrival, 'King Pete' let himself in at the back door near the kitchen. Teri was in the front room but responded to the yelling in the kitchen, only to be confronted by the noisy intruder, who seemed to be in an angry drug-induced stupor. What happened next is too horrible to describe. When Mr. Verdugo finally departed the place, he left Teri bruised and bleeding, slumped on the floor in the library, hysterically weeping and screaming.

The shoppers returned home about noon, carried a few bags of groceries through the kitchen door, heard the screaming and weeping noises coming from the library, and immediately went there to find Teri in an uncontrollable condition. They picked her up and took her into the bedroom, and tried to comfort her, but her frantic screaming continued, and her words were slurred and unintelligible. The bruising was already within the welts, and wounds about the eyes were inflamed and swollen. In between her incoherent shrieks she seemed to be repeating "Pete. Pete."

They straightaway phoned Dad Remington and told him of these things. He was predisposed to then immediately call the Orange County Sheriff to report these things, and he did so before leaving the office to go directly home. There were three squad cars in his driveway upon his arrival there, along with an unmarked police cruiser. He found three uniformed officers and a lady plainclothes investigator inside trying to get some coherent statement from Teri, but she was so stressed that there was no understandable statement then available. There was no doubt that Mr. Verdugo was the source of the grief, and an all-points bulletin was quickly arranged. All agreed that Teri should be taken immediately to the nearest emergency room for diagnosis and treatment. Mr. Verdugo was nowhere to be found.

It was necessary to employ a strong sedative to quiet Teri's hysterical screaming and uncontrollable weeping. She was admitted to the hospital, and did not awaken until the next dawn, to find her Mom and sister Toni sitting faithfully by her bedside, as silent sentinels in this time of stress. The ladies had been instructed to refrain from eliciting any conversation relating to the previous day's assault, but to immediately call the Sheriff's Investigator when Teri stirred from her long sleep. When that Investigator arrived, she had a scholarly-looking lady with her then introduced as a psychiatrist that helps in the investigation of rape cases where the victim is demonstrating extreme hysteria. They asked Momma Remington and Toni to remain in the room, but at a short distance only, so that Teri could see them and be somewhat comforted by their familiar presence. The investigation commenced and continued at a very slow pace, but when it became necessary to describe the previous day's encounter, Teri exploded into uncontrollable weeping and hysterical shrieking. The good doctor tried every kind of reasoning and soothing words, but once Teri started crying and screaming they couldn't get her to stop. When the doctor and the investigator turned and walked over to where Mom Remington and Toni were trembling in the corner of the room, in just that moment when nobody was there to restrain, Teri leaped out of the bed and ran into the bathroom and would not come out. She locked the door, but ran through the opposite door into the neighboring room that shared the facilities, and hid in the closet as the patient in that room wondered what could be happening. Following the screams, they managed to locate Teri cowering and shrieking in that closet, and gently guided her back to her own bed. Not able to get her settled down, they administered more sedative, and Teri slumbered again through the night, while family members stayed in her room, seated in comfortable leather chairs, taking turns watching over her as she slept. The psychiatrist suggested that someone from the family should be there at all such times in event Teri should awaken, needing the comfort that might come from seeing a familiar face.

The next day, Teri seemed to be more calm and collected, ate a light breakfast, and was a little more at ease. For about two hours she seemed to be in a tranquil mood, but volunteered nothing about the problem that brought her to that place. Then through the door walked sister Debbie, and that was all it took to end the tranquility, as Teri completely fell apart, shrieking and pointing at Debbie, telling her in so many words that Debbie's life was in danger because of terrible threats, then jumping out of the bed, she grabbed Debbie by the sleeve and tried to drag her into the bathroom for such protection as that place of refuge might afford. The lingering effects of the trauma suffered seemed to bring about a loss of contact with reality. As Toni was witness to these things, she too began to break up, and they ended up having to give her a light sedative. Momma Remington managed to keep her own emotions bottled up inside, but her heart was wounded and weeping.

Every time the investigators tried to prompt information from Teri it would trigger the hysterical weeping and screaming, and it was impossible to get any sort of statement that would support the charges of sexual assault. But if they could locate Mr. Verdugo, it would be entirely possible that he might offer a confession. They sent Teri home with a supply of medication, and instruction for all the family to limit their conversations with her to petty family chatter, and not risk the explosion of hysteria that could cause permanent emotional damage and unpredictable behavior.

Mr. Verdugo showed up about two weeks later, went down to the Sheriff's Office and gave a statement denying ever even being in Orange County at the time of Teri's incident, and he provided two stalwart lads from some nice neighborhood in East Los Angeles to verify under oath that King Pete was at their YMCA swim club meeting in Compton all that day instructing neighborhood children on how to do backstrokes and dog-paddling. The one director in charge at YMCA that day by telephone verified their statements. In the 1960's there was not the sophistication in forensic science in such matters as there has developed in more recent times.

The psychiatrist dealing with Teri on behalf of the Sheriff's Department asked Stewart Remington to recruit at least two other qualified psychiatrists of his choosing to collaborate in making a diagnosis and recommendations on how to deal with Teri's disjointed displays, particularly to determine if there was any way on the near horizon where she could reveal details of her experience. The Criminal Law attorney friend in Santa Ana recommended a psychiatrist from Pasadena, and that doctor recommended a list of reliable professionals from which list Dad Remington selected a third doctor and that doctor happened to be Ray Bowie, MD, who had counseled Momma Remington on several earlier occasions, and the family had great confidence in him.

After considerable testing and professional counseling, all three of these psychiatrists agreed that it would cause permanent mental and emotional damage for Teri to have her relive the details of the assault, and she would surely be unable to stand up to the rigors of a trial in which her indicting testimony would be required. The doctors agreed and recommended that this matter be drawn now to a hasty conclusion, and that Teri should be sheltered away from any mention of the traumatic events of that now distant day. As part of their evaluation, these doctors also dealt with what seemed to be an emotional collapse of twin sister Toni, who had no direct exposure to the trauma of Teri's event. These doctors all agreed that there was an unusually strong emotional bond between these young ladies, and not simply a clinical display of empathy. In other words, Teri should not be considered for treatment apart from Toni.

Dr. Bowie's advice to the family was a little different from the other professionals. He felt that both Teri and Toni should continue to see their personal needs as in great part spiritual, and to bask in an environment that would be conducive to spiritual development. In other words, once in a while go to church for worship, but don't get socially involved; continue to pray without ceasing, and to focus on the needs of others. This was good counsel, but simple advice that was not strong enough to immediately deal with the depth of trauma.

The County DA's office declined to file formal charges against Verdugo, saying that without a statement from the complaining witness it would be hard enough to simply rely on the medical evidence of forensic science of that time, but in the face of sworn statements of the two young friends and the more reliable declarations of the YMCA director, it would be next to impossible to gain a conviction of King Pete Verdugo. He was however warned against ever being found anywhere near the Remington home. Debbie Verdugo seemed to believe everything her husband says, and particularly to respect the sworn statements of his reliable friends, and the marriage of Debbie and King Pete went on for many more months, strained at best.

The Remington family was not at all pleased with the DA, and continued to hold their grievance against King Pete for his ruining the life of their precious Teri. And when Teri was so affected, it caused a similar depreciation in the effervescent personality of her twin. These were the only remaining babies in her care, and with their emotional storms, it likewise had a terrible negative impact on Momma Remington. A pallor of gloom settled over the Remington home, and it seemed that all the happy times had now vanished; the sparkling smiles were seldom seen again. Even Stewart Remington seemed to have lost his old zest and vigor, both in the home and in his businesses. He used to stay late and work with salesmen and customers, but now he tired of the daily grind and would often arrive home around Two O'clock in the afternoon. The long chats he used to have with his bride were a thing of the past. When he went to look for her in the back rooms, he knew he could find her in the twins' bedroom, sitting quietly moving back and forth in the old rocking chair, and the room suffered with the silence.

The Remington home was no longer a happy place.

CHAPTER 9

ENCOURAGING SIGNS

All of us have some good days and some otherwise. Some awaken with the dawn and breathe in the new morn, stretch arms toward the sky, then bounce up to confidently meet the challenges of the day. Some grousers don't want to face anything, but would much rather sleep for a few more hours, or at least a few more minutes. And there are those unfortunates with burdens and disappointments that trouble them night and day, and they endure restless sleep with hopeless darkness and despair as constant companions. Even those disposed to bliss and the happy life might encounter occasional troubles and grief to displace rest and joy, but those folks seem to have a storehouse of hope to carry them across and beyond the chasm of mental and emotional discomforts. But, for Shimi Remington it seemed that there was now no hope, no abiding confidence in eventual relief. Her hopes and dreams were by circumstances destroyed. She could not see light at the end of her tunnel of grief.

It was bad enough for Momma Remington to have to deal with the heavy emotions involved in the problems of her two oldest children, though with help of Christian counselors and the prayers of priest and preacher she had over the past months almost come to grips with her grief. But now the added heartache brought on by the October incident tipped the scales so far the other way. This new gloominess continued for some time. It was terribly harmful for Momma Remington, and ordinarily one would expect that a strong woman would rise to the occasion and accept that it is her maternal duty to turn aside her own sentiments and try to lift the family out of the community of gloom. That's easy to say, but the wounds were so deep and jagged. It helped her spiritually to have the priests and the Texas preacher come regularly to pray with the family, and she did seem to enjoy the down-home southern style of Brother DeWitt. Shimi Remington became a regular at DeWitt's church, and one or more of her three girls would occasionally go with her for Sunday morning worship services. She got to where she really looked forward to those inspiring Sunday Sermons, and didn't want to miss a one of them. Both of the twins seemed to continue having a paranoia reaction to crowds, and the professionals advised that the girls just stay away from large gatherings for a while to avoid anything that might trigger again the panic of the past.

It was decided that Teri's fragile emotional condition was such that she should not return to high school for the rest of this first semester of her junior year, and would be tutored at home for a while. Toni stayed home with her twin for a couple of weeks, and things seemed to become more stable. Then Toni started back to school on a Monday, and lasted about half a day when she started to crack. She began to quiver and quake, and became very upset, and couldn't say why. She felt a great sense of detachment, and went to the nurse's office to try to work through it. She was aware of her disquieted demeanor being so obvious, but she got more and more panicky, and kept muttering about Teri being alone and needing her. They called home and told Momma Remington to come get her little girl before she shivers apart.

By the time Toni got home, she had settled down. She was a bit embarrassed by what she described as her infantile conduct. She tried several times to explain her odd behavior but words seemed to fail and in truth she did not understand it all herself. Momma and her babies sorta chuckled at how these emotions seemed to be contagious among them, but could not deny the strength of their identity with each other.

The Psychiatrist Dr. Bowie made a house call late that afternoon, and the ladies thought he'd be amused to hear that Toni had a sentimental twin fit so strong that she had to come home from school that morning. He quizzed both girls about the whole scene, then told all three ladies that it might appear humorous to all of them and to all casual observers that there is such an attachment between these girls, but it appeared to be a serious matter, a genuine separation anxiety syndrome, and the unusual interdependence in this twinship shared so for these many years has probably resulted in a genuine constitutional attachment that would be difficult now to pull apart. When the three doctors had done their earlier evaluation, they took note of this matter and at that time had casually mentioned the unusual attachment each twin had for the other. The separation anxiety disorder in the books is usually found in much younger children, and can be treated by many methods. But in adults it is much more difficult to mitigate. Dr. Bowie left after an hour or so to return to his office, and there immediately phoned those other psychologists to further discuss this matter with them, and all agreed that Teri and Toni seem so uniquely bound emotionally and otherwise that it would not be wise to separate them at all anytime soon. For so long as they are embarked upon a common enterprise things will be fine, but society imposes constraints on these things and somewhere along the way these girls will have to learn some independence. In other words, just leave things as they are for now and maybe with the onset of years and greater emotional maturity things might change. Not likely to change but at least possible.

Dr. Bowie suggested that it might be best to have Toni stay with Teri and do the school studies at home for the rest of the semester, and maybe both of them can return to school in the spring. He also suggested that they both avoid the confusion encountered in large crowds and social congestion, lest Teri have a relapse of hysteria. The twins heard all the doctor's comments, and even though they were amused with the dilemma posed by their cooperative attachment, they smiled and took it all in, and talked about it for a couple of hours that evening, planning to get some books and articles to read up on how they are joined at the hip. When a person suffers from a real mental or emotional condition, it might help that person to be more comfortable if he or she can understand the root of the problem and the cause and effect, but if the problem is genuine then just to understand is not necessarily to cure.

Come the next Sunday morning, Momma Remington told her twins that they could sit at home and watch some evangelists on TV, or whatever, but she was gonna go to church to hear her now favorite Texan expound on scripture and social conundrum. As she finished puttering and painting her face and straightening her frock, she was startled to have her husband sneak up behind her and reach out to tickle her in the ribs, noting that his bride was in an unusually good mood today, and he couldn't risk some handsome stranger flirting with her at church while her spirits are so elevated, so he decided to go with her to protect his own interests. And he did.

Momma Remington did settle down over the next few months, but regressed somewhat each time she recalled the reality of her son in a real prison fashioned by the law of the land and her baby girl in a virtual prison of her own making. She had recurring periods of emotional depression and mental stress.

Over the Christmas holidays, Teri decided that she would go with Toni and try to mingle with the congregation for Midnight Mass at the small Catholic Church a few miles distant, and everything seemed to work out alright. Then there was a singing event at the Calvary Chapel in Costa Mesa, where there were a lot of people jammed into a large sanctuary. That worked out fine, too. On the first Sunday of the New Year both Teri and Toni attended another Sunday morning service at Pastor DeWitt's church, and were comfortable in the morning services so that they went together to the young people's rally there that evening. One of the handsome young men worked up enough nerve to invite the girls to go with him to a cupcake party at the home of one of the families from the church, and Teri became very anxious and jittery with unexplained fright, so they declined saying "maybe some other time". As they were driving home together, just the two of them, Teri blubbered that she almost exploded in fright when that young man approached her, then added "Maybe I'm not so settled down as I thought."

When the high school spring semester began, Teri and Toni went back to school for the rest of their junior year and tried to act like nothing had ever happened, but they could feel a little tension in the air, and Teri began to have thoughts that some of these kids might have heard what had happened. She several times silently thought "Maybe they are all whispering behind my back." Both girls managed to suppress negative thoughts, but by the end of the day they decided that they might better wait a few more weeks to return to school. They called Dr. Bowie and asked if they could discuss with him this fear of whispering, and they did manage to deal with the matter in such a way that the issue didn't come up again that school year. Even though they both managed to cope with the crowds, neither of the girls seemed to recover their former effervescence. Ever since they were in diapers and all the way up to their sixteenth birthday they were fizzy with frolic and happy as clams, skipping and prancing about, just perfectly situated kids. But since the trauma of the incident they were no longer sparkling and bubbly. They never laughed much anymore. Gone was their 'cheerful chatter'. They seldom smiled other than the forced courtesy smiles, and they avoided socializing with school chums. Nobody at school ever said anything about the incident in October, and it was extremely unlikely that anyone knew anything about it. Any observer would have to conclude that these beautiful girls had become terribly dull. They managed to get better grades in all their classes, but scored zero points on the social calendar.

At the end of their junior year, both the twins took on employment with two separate Remington car dealerships, in Costa Mesa and Laguna Beach. Dr. Bowie felt that this arrangement would probably not dissolve or even weaken the fear of separation problem, but it would help them to be comfortable in different environments where they would encounter dissimilar people and situations, which would help to advance individuality and confidence. Any need to be with one another or with their Mom could be humored by being together in the evening, and if they find some sudden urge to hear one another's voice there would be the telephone, and in any high intensity panic they would be close enough to drive to have lunch or share a malt together. Having their father as their work supervisor was a blessing under these circumstances. Things worked out really well until one of the car salesmen that thought he was God's gift to women tried to push serious flirtations with Teri, and became obnoxious. It didn't help his cause for him to then also be a married man. She became very anxious and upset, and had a little mini-relapse, and opted to take off early that afternoon and go home. When Toni found out that Teri was distraught enough to leave work she took off also to care for her needy sister. They both went back to their own jobs the next day, and apparently someone got the word to that narcissistic salesman so that he stayed away from Teri's office area after that.

The social conditioning engendered by circulating freely in the workplace, having pleasant contacts with co-workers and customers, seemed to help further stabilize both girls emotionally throughout the next couple of months or so, but they still lacked their former gleeful manner. In any event they commenced that senior year in high school at the end of a warm summer, and had no major incidents at all that final year. They rode together in their own car to school, coped with traffic and the perils of the road, and did smile more often. They didn't wear flashy clothes or paint up to draw attention to themselves, and kinda faded into the background.

The twins were age 18 in their senior year, and youngsters that age should be enjoying their last year in high school, with all the football games and rallies and such. But these young ladies did not go to football games or any other school sporting events and social functions. They did not appear to be reclusive or anti-social, but they simply did not function well in crowds. Either or both would go visit brother Reuben at his vacation villa in Lompoc and otherwise attended church regularly on Sundays throughout the year, but seldom participated in any church group social activities. They graduated from high school the next spring, and went to work again at Dad's dealerships for the summer. Teri again worked in Costa Mesa and Toni toiled in Laguna Beach. Their plans for the coming school year were undefined, but they did not want to move away from home to attend college. Cal-State Fullerton appeared to be at that time the closest major school to where they lived, and they sorta thought they'd go there.

CHAPTER 10

MEETINGS AND INTRODUCTIONS

More than a year and a half had passed since the unfortunate October incident, and everything seemed to be more stable at the Remington home. At least two of the family would drive up to the Lompoc Federal Penitentiary to visit with Reuben the Guest of the Government, two or three times each month. Debbie continued to spend more time with her family than she did living in her own home, and nothing was mentioned about what had happened to Teri, and she would frequently ride along to visit the lockup where her hapless brother's body was being held against his will. When Debbie rode along going to Lompoc she wore her atrocious costumes and all that gold and silver jewelry, amounts of makeup and foul-smelling French perfume. At the prison visiting room, many of the prisoners there ogled Debbie and just knew that she was one of their own kind, but Debbie snubbed the flirtations. A couple of Sundays each month she'd go with her Mom and sisters to hear the family's favorite Texan preach the Word and charm the troops at his church in San Clemente. Unfortunately, she then dressed like she was visiting the prison. On more than one occasion, some proud parishioner seeing Debbie's outrageous costumes would cast a critical eye or disapproving scowl that Momma Remington could see, but she got used to it, and when it would happen she'd sorta chuckle and roll her eyes, never letting Debbie see her so joining in ridicule of these outrageous fashion choices.

Both Teri and Toni were still in doldrums resulting from the October incident, and really had bland and less than happy dispositions. They were definitely not moody or in deep depression, but it seemed that something was missing; life was still out of tune. Not really gloomy, but not bright either. The family had been counseling regularly with Dr. Bowie and Pastor DeWitt for some time. The twins took quite seriously all the pulpit ministry, and together they pored over the scriptures and so much of the literature available on this matter of salvation in Jesus Christ, and they accepted innocently all those scriptures they read. They memorized tons of sacred writ and tested each other on details, and would consult with the writings of various experts on their meaning. They would pray together and with their Mom every morning and every evening. For them there was no exploding revelation, no sudden surge of conviction, just a gradual infusion of the Holy Spirit and divine inspiration. They discussed the matter with their parents and their counselors, and firmly decided that they should follow up their Christian experience with baptism in water. On a Sunday morning in April of their senior year of high school they got dunked by the good Pastor DeWitt. That single experience seemed to bring some spiritual release, adding a transcendent tempo to their existence. They still had an anxiety that haunted them as a vestige of trauma from the October episode, but this one response to scriptural admonition gave them a healthy shot in the arm. Their folks were pleased and proud to see them take this step, and sister Debbie wanted to hear more about it.

At the time of graduation from high school the twins were 18 years old, immediately went to work full-time for their Dad, and since age 16 each one of them already had a car from the 'loaner' pool so they could drive to and from work, and to get around to wherever else might be a destination. Teri's work assignment was still to the dealership in Costa Mesa, and there was some highway driving to get there from home. Toni continued working in Laguna Beach, about the same distance from home.

On the Sunday following graduation from High School, Teri and her Mom went to church in San Clemente while Toni and Debbie went with their Dad to Lompoc. Precious Teri didn't usually spend a lot of time with makeup, lipstick and eye shadow, but this particular morning she was very careful to look perfect, applied a very modest amount of cosmetic, and upon checking with the mirror she tossed herself an approving wink and a happy smile. She chose to wear a nice dark brown pantsuit with a flattering jacket, over a white blouse that had a distinctive lace collar. Teri was driving the old loaner car and Momma was ridin' shotgun. On arrival at the church parking lot, as Teri steered the vehicle into the first available space, she noticed at the front entry the Pastor DeWitt shaking hands with a tall dark-haired young man with a crew-cut. He was essentially dressed in black, with black shoes, black pants, a black turtleneck sweater, and a really nice white sports jacket. Even from a distance, as soon as Teri spotted this guy her world was instantly changed. The brightest sun suddenly burst onto the morning sky. She could hear little birds singing in the breeze. The ocean air was crisp and refreshing, but she sorta lost her breath anyway, and she could almost hear strumming of harps and tinkling of wind chimes in the background. She gave not the least thought to the possibility that this handsome young man might belong to someone else. Teri was dazzled and really had no particular thoughts. Her Mom noticed immediately that Teri now sported an impish smile such as she had not seen her wear anytime recently. They exited the vehicle, and as they walked toward the front door of the church the young man disappeared into the foyer. Teri wanted to ask the Pastor DeWitt just who was that young man, but conventional modesty imposed silence, and Teri let her mother offer greetings to the pastor as Teri hurried inside to see what might have come of the handsome stranger, but she couldn't spot him. Teri and her Mom entered the sanctuary through the double doors leading to the right side of the auditorium and sat down on a pew about eight rows from the front, nearest that far right aisle. Momma Remington noticed that Teri was just a little anxious as she glanced about the room, which was most unusual for Teri who for going on two years now had not shown the least bit of interest in her environment or any of the people in it.

Diminutive ol' Sister Bowman was playin' the piano as the little church orchestra cranked up a few hymns to accompany the choir singing when the congregation stood to join in, and Teri's line of sight was obscured so that she couldn't see much in any direction. But after a brief opening prayer, everyone was invited to be seated, and Teri got a quick glimpse of the man in black sitting down on the front row over to the far left, by the altar. Momma watched with amusement as Teri was searching among the throng of faces, and noted that when she spotted what she was looking for Teri spontaneously broke into a happy smile, the kind of smile where you don't show the teeth, the eyes burst into an uncontrollable sparkle, and an impish grin can be almost detected. They call this a display of subdued glee.

All during the church service, with the stand-up sit-down stand-up sit-down drills so common to the regimen of these evangelical societies, whenever she could get even the slightest view of the man in black, Teri's eyes would be glued to that figure, and when somebody's head got in the way so that it again obscured her vision, Teri would innocently turn aside and silently anticipate the next stand-up sit-down exercise when her head would automatically turn to catch another glimpse of this handsome new arrival. Brother DeWitt made the announcements from the pulpit, and after enlightening the troops, he waved his hand over to his right to where the man in black was seated, and told the congregation that they had a special guest today. He went on to say that "Most of you know that I at one time pastored a church in Springfield, Missouri, and gathered many wonderful friends there. Out in the foyer there is a desk where anyone can pick up this week's editions of church literature, and one of my dearest friends is in great part responsible for putting that work together at the Gospel Printing Company in Springfield, and that good friend's son is visiting with us here today, and his name is Larry Cole. Let's all show him that he is welcome". He then motioned for Larry to stand, and the audience courteously applauded him. Teri gleefully clapped her hands together like she had not done for a long time. Now she even knew the name of the man in black.

Well, the good Pastor DeWitt delivered his powerfully persuasive sermon, and as is common in Pentecostal societies he concluded by offering the altar call invitation for sinners to come down and give their hearts to the Lord, then added that if anyone needed prayer for any human affliction they would be welcome to come on down and have the elders of the church lay hands on them so that they might be healed or otherwise delivered of any noisome problem, and then opened the altars to anyone that wanted to have a moment of private personal prayer and "touch the hem of His garment." Well now, even though Teri had never ever before responded to such an invitation, she did this time. Now ya gotta get this picture: the congregation is still in an attitude of respectful prayer, and in this sort of church that can be kinda noisy; sinners were down near the altar talking with the pastor; people in need of prayer were solemnly holding hands with one or more of the elders; and the man in black was kneeling at his seat near the far left aisle. Momma Remington shook her head in disbelief as she watched her baby girl boldly stroll down that far right aisle, across in front of the altars, and over to that far left side, down near the front, where she took up a righteous pose with eyes reverently closed, and then she slowly opened one eye to get another peep at the man in black, who was still busy on his knees. From her vantage point she could see that this young fellow was not wearing any rings, and more particularly of interest to this young lady was the fact that he was not wearing a wedding band. Teri glanced up and over to the other side of the room where her Mom was standing near the wall and watching her with much amusement, and as she caught her eye Momma smiled and made that little signal with the two index fingers, where one finger strokes the other as if to silently say 'naughty, naughty'. Teri just dropped her jaw in a joyful way and wiggled her eyebrows, and was embarrassed that her Mom caught her in the act.

Consider that this mother had been troubled for years about her progeny in general, and for more than a year and a half last past has been concerned for this formerly morose little baby girl in particular, and Momma was now tickled pink to have that child suddenly erupt into joy over some guy that she has never met. Then consider that this 18 year old young lady, surely at that age at least a little bit mature, who has never kissed a boy, who has never been out on a date with a guy, who until now has never shown even the slightest interest in any fella, who until now has had a terrible dread of strangers and morbid fear of men in particular, betrays in this childish way an interest in the man in black. Wouldn't you think that a responsible parent would urge caution? Momma was pleased.

The altar party was breaking up, and Teri managed to make it to the front door before the pastor got there to greet all the parishioners. She had to wait for Momma to catch up, and as fortune would have it Momma came strolling up right alongside the man in black, the two of them chatting away. Rather than to wait for the good pastor to properly introduce her to this obviously perfect young gentleman, Teri walked over to where her Mom and Mr. Perfect were still chatting, and as she approached, this most marvelous fellow turned to greet her, and when she heard his voice for the first time she almost melted. Even his masculine baritone voice was perfect, and his manners so suave and amiable. Standing right next to him he looked even taller and more flawless. Teri was so enchanted and so busy looking at him that she didn't hear him ask her name, but Momma came to the rescue to say "This my daughter Teri". He reached out to clasp her hand in greeting, and Teri almost fainted with delight. She stammered at first, but quickly recovered her poise to say "I am so pleased to meet you." About that time the pastor leaned over to intrude on this introductory tête-à-tête, saying: "Well, I see you folks have met. Where is the rest of the family?"

Well, the crowd dispersed about then, the pastor wanted to introduce the special guest to other parishioners before they all left, and Teri reluctantly allowed her Mom to drag her out to the car. Glancing back several times to get a parting peep at the man in black, she exclaimed to her Mom "Yeah, Mom,

I know I've just made a big fool of myself. You and everybody watching must think I'm really stupid. Well, I feel really stupid. I don't know what came over me. Honestly, I have never ever felt this way in my whole life. That guy is just so handsome, so perfect, and so dreamy. Well…I really don't know what to say. Now I'm starting to really feel stupid. I hope he doesn't think I'm weird. He must think that girls at this church are all weird and wacky." Teri then fell silent, but on down the road she interrupted the silence with the observation that "Oh, he is so handsome. Just wait 'til Toni sees this guy. She's gonna flip." Then a long silent pause, punctuated with "Wow, he is so perfect" and "Did you see he wasn't wearing any rings?" Momma chuckled and shook her head in relief to consider that the long dark night might be ended, a thing of the past.

Teri and her Mom went directly home, had some soup, turned on the TV and didn't watch anything. Teri sat in the overstuffed chair quietly for a while, then got up and wandered aimlessly around, muttering something about how she wished Toni would get home soon, so's she could hear about the tall dark stranger. Well, Toni did not get back soon and would not likely be home until late, so when Mom asked if Teri might want to go to church this evening, the response was immediate without a word spoken, as Teri just winked real big and tossed her Mom the sign 'Thumbs Up!' Evening services at the church were such that the congregation would start to gather about 5:45 or so. When Momma indicated that it was about time to leave for the long drive to the church, Teri bounced out the door, and her Mom could see through the kitchen window that Teri was skipping happily all the way out to the car, then opened the door and got behind the steering wheel, started the engine and commenced to blow the horn to hurry her passenger to get in and let's get going. Hardly anyone was there when they arrived, but Teri and her closest confidant (maybe we should say one of her two closest confidants), were happily chatting as they awaited arrival of the rest of the parishioners, and more particularly to so await one specific tall dark-haired guest. Well, he didn't show up at all that night.

You'd think that the disappointment and frustration brought on by the 'no-show' that evening would have caused some despair and disappointment, grief and sorrow, etc., but these Remington girls are actually very strong and resilient, and can be very patient and persevering. It is true that Teri came unglued under the strain of terror and great fright in the October incident, but she had her feminine supremacy in reserve for such a time as this. Well, what next? Oh, now is the time for the secret weapon*: **_prayer_**

During the drive home that evening Teri sheepishly enlisted her Mom to help her pray, and on arrival at the home they spent a few minutes puttering, then they knelt together and reached out to touch the Throne of God, in an acknowledgment that He is the Creator and Ruler of the Universe, expressing gratitude for His mercies that endure forever, thanking Him for His many gifts and graces, particularly giving thanks for salvation full and free in Jesus Christ, and without being too presumptuous about today's events, very sweetly and almost timidly to thank the Lord for the gift of fellowship of the saints, and especially one particular saint of recent acquaintance. Then Teri without the least shame humbly added a special request: "***Please send him back to us again!*** Amen and amen!!"

When Teri and her Mom finished with their brief season of prayer, and while they were yet kneeling across from one another, Teri looked her Mother right in the eye, and was silent for several seconds, then smiled and diffidently said "Do you feel as silly as I do?" Mom grinned and said nothing.

Teri then kissed her Mom goodnight and left her to watch the TV late news, then retreated to her bedroom, got into her sleeping garments, turned off the lights leaving only the little night light for a dim luminescence, crawled up onto the center of her bed to await the return of her twin, and took advantage of the wait to continue in prayer.

When Toni got home about midnight the two of them chatted happily for a couple of hours, and couldn't sleep anyway. Toni received a full report. A very joyful report.

The next morning Teri was the first to get up and do all the bathroom puttering and preparation for her day, singing and humming and fully expecting that sometime soon the Lord would answer her current urgent prayers. Toni came prancing in and asked "Is he here yet?"

Teri had a very happy time at work, and left at the end of her day. As she drove jauntily down the highway, her old Ford loaner car started to sputter and lost power. She pulled over to the side of the road, got out and stood behind the back bumper looking lost, hoping that a CHP cruiser might happen along. The unsympathetic fellow travelers sped right on by, but she actually had to stand there only about half a minute when she heard the screech of tires about fifty yards ahead of where she was stalled, and an old Toyota was backing up to stop right in front of her place of predicament. The driver side door opens and a tall guy in a khaki uniform gets out and tosses a big smile her way. Teri almost went into paroxysms of boundless delight and could hardly contain the glee mixed with great amusement to see her handsome man in black now outfitted in military garb, and all she could do was laugh and jokingly say "Help! Help! My car is busted down and I need help!" His response was to flash her that perfect masculine smile and say "I thought it was you. Wow, this is my lucky day!"

Mr. Perfect told Teri the needy traveler to hop into his old clunk and he would take her to a telephone so's she could call a tow truck. Then came the dilemma: As much as she would like to accept the offer of a rescue ride, she just could not get in a car alone with a stranger. Not even a stranger that is not really a stranger. Not even this very special stranger. With emotions bordering on consternation, Teri managed to say that they have a rule at her house that disallows riding alone with a man, and adding "Maybe we should both stop and pray for a nun and a priest to come along to act as chaperones". He responded to say "Well, in that case you can take my car to wherever you want and I'll wait here to guard your vehicle until you return. OK?" With that, he offered her the keys to his car. She actually had no alternatives other than to wait for the tardy arrival of the CHP guy or start walking. She elected to take the keys, and told him that she lived just a couple of miles away, and would be back shortly with help, then she drove off and kept smiling gleefully all the way for the few miles to her home.

When she drove into her driveway, she hopped and skipped all the way through the kitchen door. Meeting her Mom face to face, she blurted out "Mom. Mom. I found him! I found him! He was out on the freeway. I found him!" Her mother looked at her quizzically and asked "You found who?" to which she replied "That guy in the white jacket. The Mr. Perfect Person. My car broke down on the highway and he drove by and rescued me. He's waiting there now to guard my precious and most valuable old Ford. Let's call triple-A and order a tow truck, then you get spiffed up and we'll go down there and rescue him. Oh, Mom, he is so beautiful. He must be the most handsome guy in the entire universe. He's even nicer today than he seemed yesterday. Wow, God sure does answer prayer, and He works fast. Mom. You're not gonna believe this, but he is all dressed up in a soldier suit, and he must be some kinda General or Captain or something like that. You're gonna love the way he looks all dressed up in that uniform. Hurry up! We must not keep the General waiting."

Momma Remington was delighted to hear this good news. Teri quickly got on the phone to triple-A and gave the operator directions on where to find the disabled car, then she kept encouraging her mother to hasten, to quickly run back to the side of the road before some interloper comes to steal the prize that God surely intended for Teri. Mom told Teri that Toni went with her Dad to a Zone Managers' reception for some GM bigwigs and there was no way to guess how long that will take.

Teri and her Mom left the Toyota parked in the driveway, piled into the silver Mercedes sedan and sped off to 'rescue the General', and found him waiting patiently, seated atop the trunk lid of the broken-down Ford. He spotted Momma Remington and offered a courteous salute and called out "So we meet again." Now, bear in mind that this lady had met this young man only once, and that was just a fleeting occasion, but she took the liberty of giving him a big bear hug and said aloud "You are my hero. You have rescued my little baby girl!" He smiled his most modest smile. The triple-A tow truck pulled up in about three minutes, and they showed the membership card and gave delivery instructions to the driver on where to take the ailing Ford, and left the scene to get back to the Remington house.

Mr. Perfect was in the rear seat as they moved on down the road and all three exchanged idle chit-chat. In the course of that conversation Teri learned that her 'soldier' (her 'General') was a 1st Lieutenant in the United States Marines, a pilot stationed at Marine Corps Air Station El Toro nearby, but he did not at that time volunteer much more information about his military service. Arriving back at the house, they all went inside and sat around for a while, then Lt. Larry suggested that the three of them should go out to dinner together and get better acquainted. Momma declined, saying that she should stay home and await the return of her husband, but that Larry and Teri should go out for a leisurely dining experience and talk about politics and slaying dragons. As quickly as her mother had made that harmless suggestion Teri had a sudden fright pop up in the pit of her stomach. She did not know what to say or what to do….or whatever. She was simply stunned for that brief moment, and her Mom took note of the flicker of fright in her eyes. Momma patted her little girl on the hand and soothingly said that Teri should go with Lt. Larry, and gratuitously added that Larry was a big strong honorable man and would protect her with his life. She sort of made this comment as though to generate humor, but she leaned over and said to Larry where Teri could hear "You do promise to guard her with your life?" and Mr. Perfect flourished his brightest smile with the reply "I promise that she will not be harmed. I will protect her with my life." Somehow, when Teri heard him say this she suddenly felt very much at ease. Maybe it was the soothing sound of his voice. Maybe it was his cool manners. Maybe it was the accumulation of hopes piled up since yesterday morning. Anyway, Teri nodded her head in agreement and said "Sure. Where do you want to go?" Her confident mien suggested that she was an old hand at this dinner-dating protocol, and she then disappeared down the hall to freshen up before departure.

Teri retired to her powder room to check with her mirror, considered whether repairs and refurbishments might be needed, and chose to simply accentuate the lovely lips with a minuscule touch of lipstick, just a slight trace of eye shadow, a bantam sprit of carnation perfume, along with a healthy dose of happy smile. She brushed her teeth vigorously, brushed her hair lightly, decided that a change of garments would take too long and wasn't really necessary, and she was ready to meet the world. Once again she snapped off that confident wink at her mirror, and turned to exit the room. She reappeared at the place where her Mom and the General were chatting away, and seemed radiant in appearance and affable mood.

They chatted happily all the way out to the car, her General gallantly opened for her the door, and without the least reluctance she plopped into the passenger seat, waved at Momma who was observing from the window, and they were gone. As the car disappeared down the road, Momma Remington stood watching, and as the tears welled up in her eyes, she bowed her head and offered a prayer of sincere thanks for what she then perceived to be the work of God.

CHAPTER 11

FIRST DATE

As Teri and her military man went toolin' down the road, the first subject of conversation was to decide what the young lady would prefer for her evening repast and where to go to find it. Larry confessed that he was new to the area and didn't even know the location of towns and much less how to find the restaurants. So Teri suggested a little restaurant over off the highway in San Clemente, just a few miles away. She could feel herself getting the jitters sitting next to this handsome gift from God, and felt that her conversation was not making sense. Larry was so much more composed, and let this lovely angel carry on continuously about any and every topic that popped into her head. They got to the restaurant, sat at their assigned table, ordered whatever, then sat back and looked at each other. At this lull in the action, Teri just looked at her dream date and timidly said "I know you must be bored with my silly adolescent chatter. I've gotta tell you something, and I really don't know how to say it. This is the first time for me ever to go out on a date. I have never even wanted to be alone with a guy, and I am so nervous. I don't know what to say. I don't know how to act. I'm sorry."

With this harmless revelation, Larry told this angel person that he had been told she was 18 years old, and asked how it is that she over the years had escaped the army of young men that surely must pester her constantly. Rather than to be responsive to the question, Teri tilted her head to one side and innocently shrugged her shoulders. Then the waitress brought the appetizers, the grinning pair dabbled in their food, and somehow completed most of the meal. Every so often Larry would put down his fork, fold his hands and look across at the angel, and chuckle softly asking "Really? This is your first date? I feel so honored. I am so flattered. I feel like I must be one of God's most favorite persons to have the privilege of just being seen with you in public. I'm sure that all these people here are ogling you and admiring me for having such a beautiful companion. You must think that this is just some phony line, but I think you should know that I'm thrilled to be here with you. You are a dream come true." Her response: "I don't know what to say or how to say it. But that's what you get when you're dealing with amateurs."

As they departed the restaurant, Teri looked happily up at her newfound friend and asked "Would you like to go walk on the beach? It's just a block or so down this street." He replied: "OK. But I want to tell you something first. I have to make a confession. This is the first time I have ever been out walking with a beautiful girl on her first date. Furthermore, I have never been walking on the beach alone with a precious person like you. I want to make a really good impression, and don't wanna make any mistakes. If I say something wrong or do something that you don't like, or whatever, you gotta promise to kick me in the shins, OK?" Teri responded "Well now, it sounds to me like you're some kind of amateur too. So that sorta makes us even. Which shin do you prefer for planting the message?" and he says "Whichever one you find convenient. Now to get this party started, and just so I don't get kicked right at the beginning, I gotta know: Can I hold your hand? I have never held a girl's hand while walking on the beach." With that revelation, Teri stopped and looked him right in the eye and reached out slowly and tenderly and took his hand, with the further remark "I never imagined that a first date could be this much fun!" Then he boldly suggested "May I kiss your hand m'lady?", whereupon she giggled and placed the back of her hand on his lips, and he made a loud smooching noise, and said "You're right. I never imagined that your first date could be this much fun!"

The sun had gone down an hour ago, the beach was vacant of tourists and surfers were nowhere to be seen. The First Date Celebration Society kicked off the shoes and left them on a convenient mound of ice plant on a sandy dune, and strolled out onto the beach holding hands. About two hundred yards further down the way they turned to walk out into the surf, and all the while they were giggling and talking small talk, splashing and kicking the sand like little kids, and soaking their garments. But when Larry asked sports questions, his lovely companion told him she knew nothing about sports, and in the further course of conversation she indicated that she had not seen any games live since ninth grade. "You've never been to a professional baseball game?" and she shook her head and mumbled "No" and in further queries she informed that she had never been to any pro football or basketball games, no hockey games, and had never even been to any church league games. That seemed to negate any discussion of pro sports and even local athletic events.

Then he learned that she had not been about anywhere for the past two years. There wasn't much to talk about, but the opportunities appeared endless for places to take her from this point in her young life.

As they were splashing in the surf and admiring the full moon aloft, Larry casually inquired of the lass what has been her most recent big event, and Teri said that over the past year she has been studying the Bible, and a few months ago she got baptized, and that kinda lifted her into a different realm. That comment was all it took for these youngsters to launch into a scripture quoting exchange, and they happily tossed about their thoughts on the meaning of one verse and then another, covering various topics and applications to modern life. They got started on this Bible quoting back and forth and didn't notice how far they had sauntered along the coast. When they got to where their shoes were waiting it was getting late. They hastily grabbed their footwear and his socks and scurried off to get in the car and return to the Remington house.

Arriving in the driveway at her home, Teri remarked that her Dad's car was not there so the revelers probably have not returned from the business reception. Larry gallantly opened his lady's door, bowed and took her by the hand to assist her in alighting from the vehicle, and continued to hold her hand as they approached the kitchen door, which he politely opened for her and bowed again as she entered. Momma Remington was seated on the couch in the front room watching some comic on TV. Teri was feeling her oats again, and as the beach strolling team entered Larry released her hand. Teri immediately grabbed his hand again and called out to her Mom "Mom! Mom! We have a report for you. Look. Look here. See! This handsome gentleman has been holding my hand. And that's not all. He actually kissed me, right here on my hand. Aren't you proud of me?" Momma silently stared at these two for a moment and probably wondered "Is this guy really a smooth operator, or is he devoid of romantic skills?", and then calmly said "I'm glad you had a nice time".

After a few minutes of idle conversation, Lt. Larry excused himself and said he had to get back to the base. Momma stood up and moved toward her departing guest and barked "Hold on a minute, Mister. Haven't you forgotten something?", as she extended her hand in such a way as to suggest that he owed the hand a little goodbye kiss. This insignificant gesture caused a glow that filled the room, as this knight in shining armor bowed chivalrously and bestowed a most noble kiss on that lovely little dangling hand, and he then turned and disappeared into the night. As his taillights glowed on down the street, both Teri and her Mom watched until the newfound friend was altogether gone, and Momma turned to her little baby girl and said "He kissed my hand. Did you see that? He kissed my hand!" and that was all it took to get Teri to launch into a detailed account of every minute of her first date. She had been reciting for about ten minutes when Toni and her Dad got in, and not only did she have to start over about the first date, she had to start her recital from the point where her old Ford got stalled on the highway. They were there for a couple of hours rejoicing about all this happening. Stewart Remington listened intently for about fifteen minutes before he decided that this is all about girl stuff, so he left to go to bed. Teri confessed that the evening's events were the happiest time in all her life, and she was gonna pray without ceasing until he returns. She suddenly became silent and her face went blank as she mused "I don't think he has our phone number! Ah, well. God will work it out!"

As the departing swain drove down the highway toward the officers' quarters on base, he in his mind went over all of the events of the evening, and kept remembering that beautiful face, that lovely voice, the innocent admission about the first date, and all the other things that would now be permanently kept in his bank of pleasant memories, and he began immediately to plot his next move.

The next day, Lt. Larry the jet propulsion aircraft student was sent south to Miramar for some sort of education or practice, and was unable to give thought to working on Teri's second date. It then occurred to him that he didn't have her phone number, but remembered the name of the dealership where she worked in Costa Mesa. So the next following day, about 4:00 O'clock PM or so, he called Teri at that place. The operator buzzed her desk and said that some Marine General is asking for her on line four. It took a few seconds for Teri to catch her breath and blink her eyes and think silently to herself "Thank you dear Lord. I knew you could work it out!"

Larry was overcome with delight to have located the most beautiful girl in the world again, so pleased to hear her voice, and blurted out "I feel like a teenager again. I wanna take you out to some exotic entertainment, but haven't figured out just what to propose. Can you ice skate?" She replied "Well, to tell the truth, I haven't been on skates for a couple of years, but if you can keep me propped up,

I'm willing to try my best. When and where would you like to go?" He told her that this evening would be great, maybe first to go out for a bite to eat, and then she can choose the skating place. Then Teri suggested that her skating partner might just come by the dealership and pick her up, to save time.

Lt. Larry arrived at the car dealership within about fifteen minutes. Teri was really tittering by the time he arrived. She was so proud of her now favorite friend, and she wanted to introduce him to everybody in the office. The first person she came to was the supervisor lady, and Teri blurted out "Fran. I want you to meet the love of my life. This is Larry Cole, and he may not look like it in Levi's, but he is a commissioned officer in the US Marine Corps, and he is the pilot that has been hovering over this building, flying his jet plane for Uncle Sam." To which Miss Fran responded "Oh! You're a Marine Corps pilot?" He replied to inform her that he was indeed a Marine Corps pilot, and she further inquired if he had yet been deployed to Vietnam, and he told her that he had already served a couple of deployments there, but was now in training at El Toro for other types of aircraft. This was the first time that Teri had heard any mention of Lt. Larry flying in a war zone, and just the thought of it struck fear in her heart. She felt sorta odd. He touched her on the nose with his index finger and said "Love of my life?" and her face got red as she tilted her head and just smiled. She asked a few more questions about his Vietnam combat service, and he tried to avoid any mention of wounds or bullets flying about. The more he told the more alarmed she seemed to become. She thought to herself that she just within the past few days had found 'the love of my life' and it frightened her to think that he might have to disappear into the wars of some foreign place.

Well. Larry was really greatly amused and flattered to hear his angel that he had only recently met describing him as the love of her life. If she really felt that way, and is bold enough to tell others, it puts a lot of wind in the old sails. This abbreviates the courting and gets down to serious hand-holding.

Larry met about ten or more office staff and salesmen at the dealership, Teri phoned her Mom to tell her that she would not be home until late because she was going for ice skating lessons, and then winked at Larry and said "Let's go!", as she dragged him out to the parking area. She was just glowing as she grinned and asked what would be the itinerary this evening. At her suggestion, they drove north to a place called 'Belisle's Restaurant', and Teri warned him that the helpings were huge, so they ought to order but one plate to be shared. She added "Let's get the ground beef steak, with mushrooms and gravy. That's my favorite!" They sat in one of the booths in the farthest part of the dining room, and doodled with their food for hours, as they delightedly chatted about just anything and everything that young people can think of as they commence the serious dating regimen. The ice skating idea faded away. Larry worked up enough nerve to bring up recollection of her comment about him being 'The love of my life', and that he was elated to hear her describe him that way. Up until that moment she had felt like a silly teenager around this young military person, but now she assumed a more mature and responsible manner, and said in a serious tone "I'm sure it's just a strong case of juvenile infatuation, and it will soon blow away" She was tickled to hear his reply: "No. No. I don't want to spend another lifetime to find the perfect love. You should let your sentiments grow and grow, and we can live happily ever after." She grinned a bit and then flashed a huge smile to display those perfectly aligned teeth.

Larry drove the little angel back to pick up her car, then escorted her all the way to her home just in case the old Ford broke down on the highway. When she drove up her driveway, got out of her car and walked up to the kitchen entry door, he beeped his horn and waved, then drove away.

When Teri went inside the house she found Toni and her Mom hungry to hear the report, and Teri related a full account of every second of her evening's excursion, and tried to quote every word exchanged with 'The love of my life'. Toni almost swooned to hear all these wonderful things, and Momma Remington seemed to take special delight to hear that the daughters that have suffered terribly for the past couple of years have something that has brought such joy to their lives. Teri then sheepishly said: "You guys. I can't tell you how happy I am that this marvelous man has sorta dropped out of the skies and right into our lap. I prayed and prayed that God would send him back to us, and I really do believe He wants this guy to become part of our lives. Don't you think we should stop right now and maybe thank God for what He has done?" Toni responded to say "Well. Ya know? I haven't even met this guy yet. Maybe we should pray that he has a twin brother for me!" Those three ladies did then kneel down and thanked the Lord for His benevolence, and asked that God send some ministering angels to guide them in all they do, particularly to help them make intelligent decisions and especially to say the right things, and of course to sheepishly add "Thank you dear Lord for sending the General to brighten our lives, and please guide him back to our front door!" Amen and Amen.

CHAPTER 12

SERIOUS WOOING

Beyond the second date on that Wednesday evening, Lt. Larry Cole was preoccupied with his instruction and hands-on orientation for jet aircraft at the MCAS El Toro base on Thursday and Friday. But now having the little lady's home number and her shy request that he call her, the budding romance was continued by telephone, and tenuous arrangements were made for the flyboy to pick up the teenager on Friday evening for a loosely described date, for dinner together at some exotic restaurant and then to complete that ice skating exercise.

Larry arrived at about 7:00 O'clock that evening, and found his newly discovered treasure waiting anxiously, all bright eyed and bushy-tailed, in exceptionally good spirits. She was home alone, and indicated that all the rest of the family had gone in to Santa Ana for shopping. She sparkled. Her perfectly beautiful face was all done up so well, her long dark hair was in a really nicely fixed ponytail style, and her fingernail polish was lovely. Since this date was to include some ice skating, she wore a white outfit suitable for the occasion. The little lady was jittery with obvious delight as her knight in shining armor informed that her carriage awaits, and she pranced merrily out to the car, where he opened her door and took her by the hand to assist her entry into the passenger seat, and they went on down the road. Larry looked over at her and could see that this lass was radiating a joy so contagious. For about ten seconds as they pulled away from the stop sign she was watching the road, then redirected her gaze to just watch her chauffeur, and every time Larry turned to glance her way he could see those magnificently happy dark brown eyes glistening with that distinctive glee. He asked her where she'd like to go for dinner and her instant reply was "Let's go to Belisle's. I haven't been there for ages!" This didn't really track well with recollections of recent history, but these teenage types don't always have much contact with time and space realities, so Larry thought nothing of it.

They got to the restaurant OK, but the place was crowded on this Friday evening. They decided to put their names down on the list and patiently sit outside to wait their turn. As they were sitting on the concrete barrier there, a number of guys took note of the lucky dude with the really good-lookin' girl. They exchanged petty chit-chat for about thirty minutes, and then were escorted back to the same table as they had on the earlier occasion. The waitress handed each of them the standard menu, but the little princess curtailed the process with the observation "This place serves huge dinners, so we ought to get just one order." Larry mused again about his recent orientation on the size of the portions, and asked what she'd like to have this evening. She replied "Oh. I always prefer their fried chicken. It's the best." Larry blinked but said nothing about the fickle diner's preferred selections. Girls can be that way.

The blissful duo grinned at each other and yakked back and forth as they waited for the waitress to return with their food, and Larry was so taken by the amazing display of elation in this maiden's manner. She had this unusual way of pitching her head from side to side as she talked, and every measure of discourse was sprinkled with positive gems of pleasant observations. She was so cute! Everything about her was so perfect.

The fried chicken was really great, just as described and plenty. They took their time wading through all of it, and would have had a leisurely puttering over dessert, but there was a long line of hungry customers waiting for their table, and the pretty young thing was anxious to get to the skating palace. She suggested that the ice rink over in Anaheim was very nice, and so they went there to try it out. They had to rent the skates at the rink desk, and Larry sorta got a special thrill in lacing up her boots. He took note of her faultlessly designed feet, and her picture-perfect ankles, and as he patted her on the ankles, he added: "Please forgive my being so forward, but I gotta say that you are the prettiest girl in this world. If you can't tell it from the smile on my face, I want you to know how proud I am to be with you and for everyone to see us together." The little lady just grinned.

The attentive young swain grabbed the dainty hands of this lovely lass and pulled her to her feet, then as they stood there facing each other holding hands, she said "Y'wanna know sumthin'? I'm so happy. I am so happy!" Then he leaned over and timidly enquired "Is it OK if I hold your hand? Is it OK if I put my arm around your waist?" Her curious reply was to say: "Sure you can. Why would you even have to ask?" and he then told her: "Well, I didn't want you to kick me in the shins." And then she asked: "Why would I kick you in the shins?" Obviously, this young thing has a short memory.

Well, Larry was indeed dazzled by the most perfectly designed legs in all the known world, but he was really impressed with this girl's skating skills. They slid out onto the ice and into a group that was behind some slow moving old folks. The little skating person tugged on Larry's arm and actually forced him to speed up to pass the herd that was blocking their way, and as he thought they were gonna crash into those poke-along persons she nimbly maneuvered around all of them, first to the left and then to the right of anyone in the way, tugging his hand as she zipped and zoomed around the rink in a very confident display of skill and splendid balance as she swerved and swayed around and around the entire surface of that ice. Well, ya know? Up until this moment Larry thought he was pretty good at this ice-skating stuff, but this little angel was so skillful and obviously comfortable on the ice that he felt embarrassed with his less competitive display. As the little skating star sorta slowed down, she maneuvered over very close to him and hugged his arm, looked up at him and said "When are you gonna put your arm around my waist?" Then she flashed a rascally grin and squeezed his arm as they at her chosen speed passed all the folks that were leisurely gliding around the room. After they had swerved and swayed, weaved, bowed and turned, they slowed face to face holding hands and spun around in circles, smiling at each other and ignoring everyone else on the floor. To a casual observer it would appear that they had practiced this routine for years. Then the precious ice maiden tugged them together to a full stop, pulled both her hands loose and placed them on the sides of her handsome partner's face to pull him down closer to where she could whisper in his ear "Would it be OK if I kiss you in front of all these people?" He grinned his approval, and she did. Not a big slobbery kiss and not a slow romantic sort of smooch, but a serious sort of playful buss. When she completed the task, and with her hands still holding his face, she pulled his head down once more so that she could whisper: "I am so happy. I am so happy I'm gonna shiver apart!"

They continued their skating for a couple of hours, interrupted only by the several intermissions imposed by the rink management. Several young couples came up to them to ask if they were practicing for the Olympics or some sort of tournament. They chuckled and shook their heads, then when the music started they again slid out onto the ice. She continued to hold his left hand and he kept his right arm around her waist as they would swerve and weave, banking to the left and to the right in perfect unison as though they had been skating together forever. Larry was just a bit startled when the little ice princess let go of the arm hugging and placed her arm around his waist, and even more startled when she boldly gave him a big waist hug, and as she did so she looked up at him and said: "Is it OK if I hug you like that? I am so happy I just gotta squeeze you!" This time Mr. Larry could not contain his amusement and asked: "Well, then. Is it OK if I hug you anytime I want?" She chortled her reply "Sure, need you even have to ask?" And his response was to say "Well, I didn't want you to kick me in the shins." She looked at him with her curious expression. She snickered and sheepishly said "Ya wanna know sumthin'? I have never ever had any guy hug me before. I have never skated with a fella before. That's the first time I ever kissed a guy in my life. This is such fun! Did I tell you that I am so happy?" Larry timidly indicated that he had one more question; "While we're on the subject, I have one more question—Do I get to kiss you anytime and anywhere I want?" She reached up and with her index finger tapped him on the nose and said "Now you're pressin' your luck!" Without actually answering his question, she added "Well, do I get to kiss you anytime I want to?" and he told her "Be my guest!", so she kissed him on the back of his hand and they together raced around the rink until about 11:00 O'clock, took off the skating boots and exited the building. When they got outside, she grabbed his hand and his arm and started hugging tight again, and openly observed "Wow. We really covered a lot of territory tonight, didn't we?" They got into the car, cranked it up and headed for home, laughing and cackling all the way at every silly little thing. When they got to the house, apparently nobody else was there. Larry escorted his lady to the door, gave her a romantic little kiss on her forehead, offered a gallant salute and turned to leave, and got about twenty feet away when the lovely lady called out to say "This has been the nicest day of my whole life. Thank you for making it all so perfect."

When Larry got over to his car and reached to open the door, she once again called her stern order "You better call me, and don't wait so long next time." Lt. Larry felt totally effervescent all the way back to quarters.

As Lt. Larry disappeared beyond the boulevard stop sign, the ice queen closed the door, turned around to face her twin and just gushed with glee. Teri said that she had been anxiously watching that driveway for all these hours, knowing that Toni was having the time of her life doing whatever the evening offered, and demanded a complete report. The two of them skipped together down the hall and to their room, and giggled and chortled and laughed while they put on their sleeping garments, then in the subdued light of the room they sat cross-legged in the middle of one bed as Toni gave her the detailed report. First she gushed and babbled endlessly to say that everything Teri had told her was oh so true, confirming that this handsome newcomer was surely the most wonderful guy ever!

That next morning at about 10:00 O'clock, Teri was at Saturday morning work when she received a phone call from a guy that the receptionist described as a Marine General. Before she said anything, Teri took a deep breath and smiled as she collected her thoughts, then answered saying: "What took you so long to call? I've been patiently waiting to hear from you since 5:15 this morning." Well, Mr. Larry the General replied to say "I was probably awake at that time, 'cuz I just couldn't sleep. I had such a swell time skating with you, and holding your hand and exchanging hugs. I was so proud when you kissed me in front of all those people. And the way you dance so well on the ice really made both of us look like pros. It sounds so inane for me to say this, but you must believe me when I tell you that ever since I first met you I have just had the time of my life. Thank you so much. See ya later!" and without even giving her a chance to respond, he hung up. Teri really melted to hear this great news, but she would have preferred to chat a little longer.

Teri immediately phoned Toni at her Saturday morning work down in Laguna Beach, to give her an updated report, as she chortled and clucked about her phone call from the General. She tried to remember every part of a relatively short exchange of conversation, but it was the sentiment and simplicity of that phone call that left both of these ladies floating among the clouds. When they got home together later that day they went over the whole scene of the last evening's events and that morning phone call, and then went over all of it again and again for about an hour. About 4:00 O'clock that afternoon, their Mom came home with a couple of pepperoni pizza's, and the family sat around the kitchen table gabbing and passing the time of day, but the twins mentioned not a word to their folks about last night's events or this morning's phone call.

CHAPTER 13

DECEPTION

Saturday evening and the Remington family is gathered together under the umbrella on the patio, munching pizza. The incessant chatter springing from the enraptured heart of baby girl Teri is focused on this new fella she has met, and her father listens quietly as nobody else seems to be able to get a word in edgewise. Teri brightly describes every little detail involved in getting into church and out again, and every emotion while there in the same room with this marvelous gift from God who actually spoke to her then and out on that otherwise lonely roadway on Monday following. Now you'd expect a mature young lady would be reluctant to betray the intimate particulars of her feelings. She should know better. She shouldn't reveal her childish attraction to some stranger she has not even met. She should know that folks would see how foolish she is to drool over some new guy in church. Ah, but consider the precious innocence of a virtuous young lady that is pure of heart, with nothing to hide, experiencing new emotions for which she is entirely unprepared.

Even though it was evident that little Teri had simply fallen victim to childish infatuation, it was so much nicer than the bland spirit that has been hovering over the family for the past many months. This juvenile ebullience is a welcome relief. So just go ahead you silly girl, bare your soul, reveal the youthful fascinations that flood your heart, and show us what really innocent puppy love is like. This is an interesting display of glee that is not common for this lovely young lady, and that glee has displaced the gloom.

Teri had been babbling away for some time when sister Debbie arrived to share in the pizza, and came in somewhere at the middle of Teri's report. So Teri happily started all over again to tell of her adventures with the man of her dreams. While all this happy blathering continued, sister Toni sat quietly enjoying every little detail and anxious to interrupt to tell her own part of the tale, but she had to remain silent.

Early evening and Teri is still jabbering as the telephone rings. She screeched aloud and leaped up to run toward the ringing; all the while yelling "It's him. It's him. It's gotta be him!" and so it was. The General is calling, and anxious to inform his lovely little lady that if she is not otherwise committed for Sunday she might want to ride down to San Diego for a tour of the zoo. He went on to explain that his brother is arriving early Sunday morning to attend some sort of convention for school administrators to be held at a big San Diego hotel, and his plane gets into San Diego Lindbergh Field Airport about 8:00 AM. Maybe Teri could ride along, they could pick up brother Richard when his plane gets in, take him to his hotel and have breakfast there, leave the brother to work that convention while Larry and Teri spend the rest of the day trudging around the San Diego Zoo. Teri just melted on the spot. Agreeing to everything proposed, she said goodbye in the most pleasant way she could in words design, gently placed the phone on its base, and turned blissfully to confront her quiet audience with every eye glued on her and anxious to hear the plan. With a relaxed look of contentment, she slowly and silently returned to take her seat among her admirers, sat down leisurely and said "I'm gonna go to the zoo".

The next morning, before sunrise, the General pulled into the Remington driveway, where two figures were awaiting his arrival. When he stepped out of the car, those two figures approached. Teri introduced her sister Debbie, who was even at that early hour all painted up and equipped with her bangles, rings and beads, wearing those atrocious false eyelashes. Teri was yet unabashed as she introduced Debbie to her now most favorite person, and cordiality flowed all around. The happy pair departed and went toolin' on down the road. Momma Remington was not part of that welcoming and introductions committee, but as she thought the rest of the house was yet slumbering she was watching out the kitchen window with much amusement. When Debbie came into the house she found her Mom and sister Toni waiting to ask of her "Well, what did you think of Teri's first boyfriend?" and Debbie was quick to respond with "Wow! That is one really handsome guy. He is more even yet than what Teri told us! He's a smooth operator, a real gentleman".

Larry didn't even try to hide his elation at the thought of having his newfound treasure with him for the entire day, and the grin permanently glued to his face betrayed the fact that he was even yet just a little kid at heart. The trip to San Diego was pleasurable every inch of the way. They got there about a half-hour before the scheduled arrival time of brother Rick's flight, so they parked the car in the nearest open space and walked hand in hand over to the terminal, totally engrossed with each other. As they sauntered casually along, Larry noticed that on this outing the little lady held his hand palm to palm with their fingers clasped in a web, rather than the arm hugging that she did so well. Probably just the casual mood that these females are famous for.

They waited for Rick at the gate, and soon he appeared with smiles and back-patting, and Larry was so proud to introduce older brother to the perfect angel. Of course Rick was thoroughly captivated with her appearance, and was bold enough to say so. The little lady blushed and fluttered her eyelids so innocently. She made an excellent impression on him, and he audaciously announced that the first chance he gets he's gonna call Mom and Dad Cole to tell about how their baby boy Larry is dating a Hollywood movie starlet. More blushing and more eyelids fluttering. They chatted back and forth all the way out to the car, and exited the parking lot to go straight out to Mission Bay to get Rick registered at his hotel, then tossed his luggage into his room, and went to the dining area for their buffet breakfast, his being included in the cost of the room. The convention registration wasn't open until about 11:00 O'clock that morning, but Rick wanted to shower and shave and otherwise prepare for the program, but first they took about an hour playing with their eggs, bacon and waffles, guzzled gallons of coffee, and that hour was intermittently interrupted several times by Rick boldly leaning toward Teri and making his flirtatious comments, "You are the most beautiful girl in the world" and "Are there any more like this where you come from?" and "You have the most perfect eyes.", but when he said "You have the most perfect smile", she replied that she had braces when she was younger.

They left Rick in the lobby and went on to the zoo, and at that exotic place they wandered aimlessly in and out of the many avenues and corridors, along the pathways and trails, past the monkeys and apes, giraffes and elephants, rhinos and hippos, snakes and lizards, amazed by the many beautifully colored tropical birds, the flock of pink flamingoes, the parrots and parakeets, and all the many sights there to be seen. But they seemed to be most amused with each other, and Teri thrilled to touch her treasure's hand, and he thrilled to hold her hand so possessively, and in such a way as for everybody there, all those thousands of people passing to and fro, to see that this pretty girl belongs to Larry Cole. Now, Lt. Larry had only first met this precious thing a short while ago, but he was already feeling that she was becoming a permanent fixture in his heart.

They stayed on at the zoo until just before 6:00, and then returned to the hotel in Mission Bay, to chat some more with brother Rick, maybe have a cup of coffee and a cruller or two, before heading north. In the course of conversation, Rick said that his convention was scheduled to end on Wednesday, but that his hotel reservations would take him all the way to next Sunday morning, so he intends to rent a car and see some sights. Without first consulting with Larry the chauffeur, Teri volunteered "Great! We can drive down and ferry you back to the airport on Sunday morning!" Larry the chauffeur was amused to hear that his little princess was happy with (a) spending time with him on the road to and from San Diego, and (b) she seemed to approve of at least this part of his family. So they made it a date, left dear brother standing out by the little palm tree, and then the cheerful couple headed north.

Allowing for stops along the way they arrived at the Remington home about midnight, and Momma was waiting up for her baby to render her report. Everybody else in the household had already gone to bed. She met them at the front door, and cordially invited Larry to stay a while, but he indicated that he really should check in at the officers' quarters soon. He offered his little courtesy bow and salutes to both ladies, leaned over and kissed Teri on her forehead and started out the door. He was almost out onto the porch when he heard "Hold it Mister. Haven't you forgotten something?", he turned to find Momma's outreached arm with that pretty little hand dangling, and the message was clear. He bowed in a most chivalrous way, as though this were some Shakespearean drama, took her hand and kissed it so sweetly, and with a smile he looked up into her eyes and gave her a flirtatious wink. Then he was gone. Momma looked at Teri and said "Did you see that? He kissed my hand again!"

Teri and her Mom started the idle chatting about the day's events, then they were joined by sisters Debbie and Toni, and the four of them gossiped for another hour. Teri told of each and every little adventure for every minute she had been gone down south. Toni was vicariously thrilled to hear each tiny detail, all about the many places of interest they had explored, seeing the lions and tigers, and meeting Larry's brother Rick. It had been such a glorious time for Teri, and just as satisfying for this little audience. Nothing was said about the plan for that next Sunday to drive down there again.

When everyone retired for the rest of the night, Teri and Toni continued gabbing about the zoo trip, and that's when Teri said that their ruse needed another conspirator. In order for Toni to easily take part in the trip to San Diego for the next weekend, they'd have to get the rest of the family off to visit Reuben, with Toni left at home and free to roam, but Momma wouldn't want her baby girl to be left alone. Knowing that Debbie would enjoy the intrigue, they agreed to pull her into the plot. And so they did.

The next day, the twins phoned to encourage Debbie to come on out to the house again, so they could talk about something of interest. Then, while Momma was preoccupied in the kitchen the twins took Debbie to the back bedroom to disclose the details of their ruse and enlist her in the plot. This is known as skullduggery.

These schemers couldn't wait to trade places again, so Teri and Toni swapped work assignments for the day, to include trading the loaner cars that each drove and Toni had the General pick her up from the Costa Mesa dealership for a leisurely two-hour lunch at Balboa Island. Nobody was the wiser. To balance the scales, Teri and the handsome young gentleman went to the ice rink in Fullerton on Thursday evening.

The Thursday skating was an interesting event, and Larry felt that there was something different in the air. The precious person again altered the way she held his hand, without the hugging of the arm, and her demonstration of skating skills seemed to be curtailed. She wasn't pulling him into those dramatic banks and turns, and chose to leisurely move along with the throng rather than to rocket around the rink. When the traffic eased up, he stopped in the middle of the flow to place his cupped hands on her cheeks and lean over to give her a brief kiss on the lips. Her reaction was to smile and say "That was a nice surprise!"

Debbie and Toni worked at their dealerships all day Saturday, and Teri spent the day with Larry wandering around the amusements in Santa Monica. He was becoming more audacious in muttering romantic comments, and Teri was squeezing his hand harder and hugging him more often as her whispered comments were just short of any serious 'I love you'. Teri phoned home to let her mother know that they were going for dinner at some Italian restaurant, and would try roller skating for a while later in the evening. Then came the skating, hugging and exchange of more romantic whispers and muttering for several hours. It was after midnight when Larry delivered his little lady back to the care of her Mom, and as he made his exit there was the unabashed reminder that sounded like "Hey, mister. Haven't you forgotten something?" Momma got her hand kissed again.

Teri prodded the family to leave for Lompoc a little earlier than usual on the following Sunday morning, suggesting that they should stop and have breakfast at Pea Soup Andersen's along the way, and so they did. Debbie and Toni opted to stay home and go to church morning and night. The others had been gone not more than ten minutes when Larry's old Toyota came up the driveway, where the sisters greeted him noisily, and he loaded up his lady love and went toolin' on down the road. Debbie got dressed up in her most alluring frocks, ornaments and ointments, and went to church looking like she had spent the night in jail.

Once again the General was totally enthralled to be with his most favorite person. She was all dressed up in a really cute green pantsuit with stylish jacket and matching flat-heeled shoes. Her long hair was on this occasion just pulled away over her ears and allowed to tumble in long dark curls over the shoulders and down the back, making a beautiful frame for that flawless face. They yakked about anything and everything as they drove along and spent more time glancing at one another than looking at the road. When they got to the hotel, they went up to the front desk to have the clerk let Rick know that they were there, and while Larry was talking to the clerk Toni the Teri was happily standing there looking around. Rick walks up and stands in front of her and she just stares back. Rick tries to strike up a conversation but Toni the Teri sorta looks bewildered. Fortunately, Larry recognizes the voice and turns about as Toni realizes that she is supposed to be already acquainted with this handsome stranger, and breaks into a smile saying "It's early yet, and we've come a long way."

The travelers went with brother Rick to the hotel breakfast buffet, and enjoyed a superb refection of all kinds of typical breakfast items and fresh fruits. Rick didn't have to be at the airport until about 11:00 O'clock, so they all three leisurely gabbed until departure time. While seated there, Rick reached into his shoulder bag, pulled out a camera and started taking pictures, with the comment mostly directed at Toni "The folks are gonna want to see some pictures of you two. They will be so delighted to see how cute you are."

Rick got checked out of the hotel and got checked in at the airport, boarded the great silver bird and was gone. It took a little while for Toni to become adjusted to the name 'Teri', but she was sorta used to that confusion. They spent the rest of the morning and all afternoon wandering around 'Sea World', and Larry noticed that his pretty partner had taken to hugging his arm again and muttering "I'm so happy. I'm so happy". Right when they had meandered into the midst of a large group of people, Larry's little lady stopped, reached up with both hands to grab his face, pulled him down within range and planted a big smooch right on his lips while all those people were watching. Larry chortled and blinked his eyes.

Our hero splurged that evening to take his lady love to a really swanky dinner at the 'Mister A's' restaurant. She was impressed. It was the first time that Toni ever had steak and lobster.

The touring two made a few stops but got to the Remington place before midnight. The family had not yet returned from their visit up north, and Debbie greeted them at the door. Larry tried to leave quietly but his lovely lady grabbed his sleeve and tugged him back through the door, whispering "Haven't you forgotten something?" so he sheepishly gave her a little kiss on the forehead, to which she groused "Wow. Is that all I get for all my loyalty and genuine affection?" He looked at her tenderly as with her index finger she tapped her lips and winked a flirtatious eye. Larry quipped "I guess you've noticed that I am kinda shy." With that he put his arms around her and gave a big hug, then provided more adequate farewell osculation.

These young twins managed to carry on this frivolous ploy for eight or nine weeks before Momma Remington figured it all out. But before their amusing scheme was betrayed they actually managed dozens of furtive excursions and amusements, in which one or the other of the twins would accompany the General to various amusement parks and public events, the San Diego County Fair (twice in one week), a number of beach walks in the evening and several afternoon tours through one or another park, visits to several museums, and quite a number of dinner dates. Other than to notice the hand-holding styles and the different hugging habits, and maybe the difference in skating skills on occasion, Larry Cole did not suspect anything.

Momma Remington at first was greatly amused that her little girls had thought up this witty ruse to romance the handsome young man, sort of sharing the resources. Her aiding and abetting them in their deception lasted only about three weeks, when Stewart Remington discovered what they were doing. Up until this discovery Stew Remington had only met Larry twice and those occurrences were very brief. The three conspirators didn't actually see their plot in the same light as the father, and he demanded that they disclose the truth and apologize for duping the General. That same early evening, when Larry phoned to speak with Teri, she invited him to come over and share in a surprise. He said he'd be there by 8:00 O'clock, and he was.

When Larry arrived, he was greeted at the door by Stewart Remington, who invited him to just make himself comfortable and be prepared for a shock. Then Momma Remington calmly ambled in with a smile, and as she passed by the bewildered young man she leaned over and patted him on the hand, then sat down on the couch opposite where Larry was seated. This honored guest immediately knew from what Stew Remington had said and how Momma was acting so diffident that something was awry. They all three sat silently glancing at one another, when the twins marched in together and stood right in front of him. They said nothing, but just smiled at him. Whatever they might have expected of Larry they were wrong. He first turned almost green, then flushed almost white, then as the truth became more evident his face became flushed bright red. He was speechless. He was almost in a state of shock. When Momma saw his unexpected reaction, she tried to intervene to offer some sort of excuse at first, then as the girls observed in silence their mother tried to offer words of apology and expressions of regret if the ruse had offended him. Larry said nothing, but the chagrin shown on his face told a story that cast a gloom about the room. Larry was mortified with this disclosure that made of him a dupe, a sucker, a fool. He was instantly embarrassed, humiliated at his own behavior that would surely have been so very different if he had known of this unusual situation. The girls saw his consternation and the tears began to trickle down Toni's cheeks. It was evident that Teri was becoming very anxious, and she sat down beside her 'Love of my life' and tried to take his hand, but he pulled it back as he looked at her with a totally vacant stare. He stood up slowly, moved forward to where Toni was trembling and crying, placed his hand behind her head to pull her forward, then he kissed her on the forehead. He turned to where Teri was seated quietly looking up at him, and he knelt in front of her, placed his hand on her cheek and kissed her on the forehead, saying "Please forgive me. I am so ashamed of my behavior." he rose again and touched Toni on the arm, and spoke to her essentially the same words. He walked over to where Momma Remington was now standing, and repeated that same brief word of apology. Then he walked over to the door, and as he passed by Stewart Remington he reached out to shake his hand and say "I am so sorry. It will never happen again." With that Mr. Larry Cole strode swiftly out to his old Toyota sedan, and disappeared into the fog. This left Stewart Remington to by himself deal with three bawling women. Neither of these two parents felt that the ruse imposed on Larry was so great as to generate this kind of dramatic departure.

These three women just kept on weeping. They went nonstop for at least an hour there in the front room without saying much, but kept crying. Stewart Remington in his mind felt that this sort of display was altogether unnecessary. This is overreaction, totally uncalled for. Firstly, Larry should not have acted the way he did, and secondly, the ladies should not be so emotional. This whole stupid thing will blow over and we'll look back on this silliness and laugh it off. This drama has now ruined the whole evening. He kissed each of the ladies on the head, and kissed his wife also on the nose, patted them all on the hand, and went to bed.

Actually, each of these three women were experiencing completely separate though related emotions: Momma was concerned for the peace and hopes of her two favorite children, and only mildly disappointed with the departure of the General. Toni was weeping for Teri's loss of the love of her life. Teri was crying because her precious sister was unhappy. They were both bawling because Larry their General was gone out the door and they were both suddenly without the emotional support he provided, and they both felt embarrassed and depressed that they had offended this guy that had in such a short time become essential to their existence. There are many more ways to define and distinguish their joint and separate heartache, but all lumped together it was a very convoluted emotional puzzle.

CHAPTER 14

RECONCILIATION

The morning after the big breakup it seemed like the dawn of a new day failed to brighten the gloom of the passing night, and the ladies were still upset. Momma Remington was dismayed because her baby girls are both saddened in the departure of their knight in shining armor. Teri was falling apart for the complete collapse of her first and only romance. Toni was crushed because her precious sister was going through a devastating emotional experience, in which situation she too felt a tremendous loss and huge vacancy in her teenager heart. For Toni it was first a vicarious feeling of loss and then a very personal defeat. However it might be described it was a family disaster for Stewart Remington.

The twins impatiently waited and prayed that the Lord would send some special angel with great ameliorative skills to work some kind of magic and bring back their hero. Oh, we can find humor in the machinations of teenagers and the curious webs that they weave, and shake heads in wonderment at the outcome of their juvenile schemes. But when tragedy results from the botched plan in spite of good intentions, it really can cause painful scars. The heart of a young girl can be a very fragile piece of equipment.

The Remington girls didn't go to work that second day beyond the big breakup, but impatiently waited by the phone for the call they hoped and prayed would come, but the telephone remained silent. The tears continued to flow, and Momma joined them in those incessant prayers. Surely the Lord would take note of the sincerity and particularly of the urgency of their pleas. This was the scene that welcomed Stewart Remington when he returned that evening, and the gloom and sniffling continued into the late evening. After the family retired for the night he could still hear murmuring coming from the twins' bedroom. He just couldn't understand why this whole romance could be so blown out of rational proportion, and he was beginning to think that maybe that silly little childish ruse really wasn't all that bad, and considering how things have developed he wished he had kept his nose out of it.

On the third day, Debbie came to visit right in the midst of this debacle, and was probably more amused by the family drama openly exposed. Bear in mind that Debbie had endured the derision of her parents for her choice of lifestyle and selection of a husband, and the spectacle created by the stupid antics of her younger sisters should provide a veil to cover the bungles in Debbie's past. Even though Debbie had been recruited willingly in at least part of the underlying subterfuge, she no doubt took some perverse delight in knowing that the favored younger sisters had been so mischievous as to dupe the chump. Anyway, however callous Debbie might be, the whole scene was so pitiful that even the hardest heart would be touched. She dragged her Dad off into a quiet corner and asked "Dad. Can't you do something?"

These anxious moments continued for almost a week, and Stew Remington could see that the ladies of his household were not getting any better. He realized that the whole affair was now so serious that he had better do something or the result would be as bad as the terrible season of depression and hysteria that they endured two years ago. Hey, all this crying and disconsolate gloom has gotta stop. He decided to phone Larry and try to get together with him, maybe recruit his assistance at least temporarily, to get these sobbing women back on track until some miracle be sent from the Miracle Source. He made contact early that following day, and about 9:30 or so Larry showed up at the dealership, was ushered into Stew Remington's office, and instruction was given to hold all calls, cancel all appointments, and simply do not disturb.

The discussions began "Larry. I need your help. I am facing several situations that are beyond my control, and I believe that you are the only one this side of Heaven that can help. I don't really want to be telling you the things you are about to hear, and as I disclose some very intimate history maybe you would prefer not to be involved. If you want to just break and run, I won't hold that against you. Only a fool would be willing to get involved in this morass, and I am hoping that you are just that kind of fool." He went on to describe in detail his own happy relationship with his wife of more than thirty years, particularly to assure that she was until a couple of years ago the most stable and happy wife and mother on the planet, with a peculiar habit of pampering all of her children, wholly preoccupied with watching them grow from infants to young adulthood, looking forward to having a huge troop of grandchildren and living happily ever after. Shimi Remington was very active in a number of Catholic charities, and had highly visible social standing all over Southern California. Then came a series of tragedies that shattered her life. She was a strong woman before, but the weight of all the difficulties has almost destroyed her.

Stew Remington went into great detail to describe each and every one of his children, and all their separate features that delighted their parents from the cradle to young adulthood, and then to describe how with the passing of time and escape from childhood their choices were unfortunate and not at all in keeping with hopes and dreams of the parents.

Then Stew Remington went through the history of oldest daughter Debbie, how she was "such a beautiful child, maturing to be a modest and virtuous woman, but got sidetracked when she commenced a romance with a guy from the Los Angeles street gangs who changed her life completely to become what you see now." He told about the arrest and all the ugly publicity, and did dwell on what a scum he thought 'King Pete Verdugo' was, and how it seemed to be easier for Shimi Remington to blame King Pete with the imposed changes in the life of Debbie, rather than to blame her for error of her ways. That reasoning was in great part why Debbie is still welcomed at the Remington home, while Verdugo would likely get shot if he showed up there. The continuing saga of Debbie was described as trauma number one.

Then he asked Larry "Do you know anything about my son Reuben? The one that we go visit at his home in Lompoc?" Larry said that the only thing he had ever been told was that the brother Reuben lived in Lompoc, and nothing more. Stewart Remington then went on to tell about Reuben's financial frolics throughout college years, and how his very lawful business turned to a very questionable enterprise, and then on to a criminal career. "Lompoc is where they have the US Penitentiary, and my only son Reuben was convicted of numerous felonies involving fraud and embezzlement, and that got him a whole lotta years at Lompoc with free room and board at government expense. All through the trial the newspapers here featured daily snippets from the trial court records, resulting in Shimi's feeling of shame and family disgrace. This all happened a little more than two and a half years ago, and until you came on the scene my wife whimpered and cried about it quite a bit." The Reuben fiasco was trauma number two.

Then the story takes a few predictable turns, particularly where Momma Remington directed her motherly love and affection to her twins when her two older children disappeared into the mist, and how she became a sheltering and overly protective parent, hovering over them constantly so that no harm would ever come to them, no stranger could ever drag either of them away. There was an emphasis on the symbiosis of twinship that became constitutional with these particular girls, so that they should not be required to navigate apart from one another. There was the amusing observation that whatever impacted the one twin would be felt by the other, so that if one got sick they both had to go to the doctor. If the one be happy, they would both be happy. If the one was sad, they would both be sad. They didn't walk in lockstep, and each had separate groups of friends and altogether independent activities and amusing individual habits that are often difficult to detect. But they were most happy when they were together, and they never have had an argument among themselves or any sort of confrontational disagreement with anyone else. If a dispute might arise with a third party, they would go away and comfort one another rather than to endure uncomfortable friction.

With obvious great hesitation, Stewart then informed Lt. Larry that the most discomforting part of the Remington family tragedy was very difficult for him to tell, and that was trauma number three. He said that this part of history would have to be abbreviated for the sake of overwhelming emotion if for no other reason. He told of how at age sixteen during their junior year in public high school both girls were just doing so well, with school and social engagements, and so happy at home. Shimi Remington and one of the twins returned home from shopping to find the other twin screaming hysterically and collapsed on the floor in the library, completely bashed and broken. She had been cruelly raped and beaten. Then came the less than detailed explanation that the one responsible was King Pete Verdugo, Debbie's husband, and that he enlisted several of his LA Neighborhood friends to vouch for him and his being with them at the time of the assault. The psychiatrists advised that going through the rigors of a trial would be permanently damaging, and after weeks of sedation the little victim settled down, but had recurring nightmares that caused considerable fear and hysterical screaming. The DA chose not to prosecute. The emotions did settle down some, but the innocent manner of the girls faded away. The girls and their mother have lived under this pallor of gloom ever since. That is, until Larry Cole showed up at church one Sunday morning several months ago.

Dad Remington went on to tell how he and his wife had regrets about letting Debbie date younger and how they refused to allow the twins to start dating until they were sixteen, and then how the tragedy of the assault deprived them of their innocence when they should have been enjoying all the activities in high school and all that. "Larry. Believe me when I tell you that you are the only guy either one of these girls has ever dated. They've been afraid to even be alone with a boy, and when you showed up that Sunday morning everything changed for the girls, and because they have been so happy it has really pumped up Shimi's spirits. I don't know what these girls have told you, but through their tears they have both told me many times that they love only you. I don't know how that will work out, but you are the man of the hour, and my only hope of getting any rest tonight. Won't you at least try to help me stabilize this situation?"

"Larry. Can I talk you into coming back? I know you must be mad about the deception the ladies pulled on you, but you can forgive them just this once, can't you?" Larry the erstwhile hero shook his head and replied "I'm not angry with your wife or your girls. I'm terribly frustrated and disappointed with myself. If I had only known that I was dealing with two young ladies rather than just one, I wouldn't feel so bad. By the way, you didn't tell me which one of the girls was the victim, but I already know." Dad Remington asked just how he found out, who was it that revealed this family secret. Larry was slow to respond but said "I'm not gonna tell you how I know, and I hope you never find out what I'm talkin' about. Let's leave it at that."

Well, let's depart from this tale for a moment to consider several things so important to fully appreciate how ridiculous is this predicament, and weigh the facts:

Dad Stewart Remington has now revealed at least in essential part the facts that would lead a reasonable person to conclude that this is a truly troubled and fractured family, and at least at this point it would appear that Larry Cole is a perfectly innocent party. It is now disclosed that Momma Remington suffers from such terrible mental problems that she has repeatedly required psychiatric care and psychological therapy. It has been revealed that older sister Debbie is so dumb and unstable as to be married to a drug-dealing LA street gang person, has herself been arrested and spent a little while in jail on suspicion of criminal involvements, and Larry has already seen the physical appearance of that wayward sister. It has been divulged that avaricious older brother Reuben is a convicted criminal now doing time in federal prison for his felonious anti-social behavior. Further disclosures betray that these twin girls are mental and emotional cripples, their unusual interdependence creates a challenging convoluted confusion of mirrored personalities, and the two of them together seem to have a proclivity for plotting irrational subterfuge against innocent victims. Dad Remington has already suggested that it would not be unreasonable for Larry to turn aside and walk away from this bizarre situation, though all the while begging for him to stay on board for at least a little while to help him stabilize the vessel. Wouldn't it be wiser to simply move away from this poisonous situation as quickly as possible?

Well, fortunately Larry decided to listen to his heart, at least in part prompted by the fact that these two young ladies are the most beautiful creatures he has ever seen, and the inescapable feelings of genuine affection for both of these lovely young ladies.

Larry sheepishly told "There is another little problem that could really complicate things for us. I really do love both of these angels. I wouldn't want to hurt either of them." To which the father responded "Well, take 'em both, and at least for so long as it might take to work our way out of this crying crisis. I just know you're our only hope right now."

"Well, Larry. Whadda ya say? Will you help me?"

Larry smiled his most humble smile, stood up tall, and said "Sure. Are they at home now? I'll call them and maybe go to see 'em. Maybe this afternoon." It was already about noon, and no good reason to wait.

Stewart Remington rose up and shook Larry's hand and said "It's a deal. But don't let anybody know we talked today, and don't tell anyone what I said. If anyone wants to tell you anything, that's OK with me, but I would prefer that your phone call to them seem sorta spontaneous, all on your own after you gave the matter some thought. And by the way, maybe you could kiss my wife's hand again. She gets quite a thrill when you do. Wow, I feel so much better to get all this off my chest. What a relief. Now you can play it by ear!"

Larry asked to use the phone right there on the desk. He dialed the girls' number, and when Teri answered he coyly said "Hello, is this the prettiest girl in the world?" and her quick reply was "Well, one of 'em!" Then, with her cheery response he started feeling his oats enough to ask "Are you in love with anyone in particular today?" and she without hesitation said "Yes. I am hopelessly in love with a United States Marine, and I'm not really certain but I think he is a Major or a General, or maybe a corpuscle or something like that." He then felt confident enough to ask "Do you have a sister that might be interested in a friend of mine?" and she replied "No. She is already hopelessly in love with a United States Marine, and she says she is quite sure that he is a Captain or a Major or a General or whatever, and nobody else has a chance with her." He told them that if they wanted, he'd come visit this afternoon, and Teri said that they would be waiting at the curb.

Larry turned to salute the father of his favorite twins and was a little serious when he said "I know I'm sailing into perilous waters. But I just gotta go see my favorite twins. I think this will be a lotta fun."

Stewart Remington looked at him quietly for a moment, then motioned for him to come near for a little whispered message: "I really appreciate your helping us, so let me help you with something. Toni has almost no earlobes at all, and Teri has a flat brown mole under the left side of her jaw, not quite round and about the size of a dime and you can see it from across the room. Teri is serious and Toni is very sentimental."

Larry chuckled and noted: "I don't know how I'm gonna handle all this, but I promise you I'll try my best."

CHAPTER 15

PERIL OF COMPROMISE

Driving that distance from the dealership in Santa Ana to the Remington house, Larry recalled the last time he had been there. Now there is the really frustrating confusion in his mind as he recollected all the places he had been with this lovely girl, and now there are two of them and he doesn't know which one he might have been with at the church, at the beach, at the restaurants, at the skating rinks, at the fairgrounds, and all those other amusements over the past several months. And what about all those flirtatious comments, all those affectionate hugs, all that hand-holding and public smooching? He well remembered the beautiful face and features of the girl of his dreams, and now there are two of them, and he doesn't know which is which. Worse yet, he recalled how he felt when he realized that his behavior over those months was not respectful under these circumstances. His departure from the Remington home last time seemed to him now so trivial and indefensible. If all the things he was told by their father are true, or if even just a little bit true, his silly fit of pique now made him to appear petty and immature, and has caused a lot of unnecessary grief. He now felt like he had been pouting irresponsibly. Larry was building a mound of self-imposed embarrassment for his rash behavior, and as he drove along he wondered how he might gracefully deal with this when he gets to his destination.

As Larry wheeled his old Toyota around the corner, over to his left he could see the two figures standing at the curb by the Remington driveway. They stood quietly and composed until he got parked and exited the car, and then those two young ladies scurried over and stood silent and smiling like a couple of Cheshire cats. Teri was the first to speak "I love you and I missed you." Then Toni started crying and blubbering "I just love you so much, and I'm so pleased that you're here" Teri added "Well, it's your turn now. Aren't you gonna say how you love us with all your heart and promise never to leave us again?" Still trying to negotiate the best deal under these awkward circumstances, he thought to ask "Well OK then. Do I get to kiss you and hug you any time I want?" Both of them just smirked and nodded in the affirmative, and then they had a community hugging exercise. Toni continued to whimper and repeat "I am so happy! I am so happy!"

The girls each took an arm and clutched tightly, escorting their prize over to and through the front door, then to be seated on the couch. As their mother was looking on, each one took her place to sit right in front of him on the coffee table, and just stared at him with pleasant expressions. One would have to conclude that they were very, very happy to see him. Toni was still blubbering and blurted out "We don't even have a picture of you. Can we get a picture made?" And his reply "Sure, when would you like to do it?" Toni was quick to inform him that they have an appointment this afternoon at the portrait studio, and have only twenty minutes to get there.

Larry invited Momma to go with them to the picture-takin' place, but she said she was busy and for the three of them to have a good time. He told her that they shouldn't go anywhere without her. Not only was she needed to act as chaperone, but if she would just go along and sit in the front seat, then the girls could sit in the back and there would be no arguments about who gets to ride shotgun. Momma chuckled at the proposition, then told him: "Larry. Larry. Larry. You have a lot to learn about my little baby girls. First of all: they never argue. Never in all their lives have they ever had a disagreement. Secondly: We always let the girls decide just who gets what, and they always work this out on their own. My advice is to just let them decide. There won't be any problems." The one with the mole rode up front on the way to the portrait studio, and the one without earlobes got the favored place on the way back.

The girls got all polished up immediately when they earlier got the call that their hero was on the way, to wash away the red eyes and all the traces of morose weeping, getting all freshened up to see their champion and recapture his favor. Momma made the appointment with the photographer. When Larry finally arrived, the twins were wearing matching black sleeveless outfits with no jewelry, and their long dark coiffures were all carefully brushed into really impressive ponytails, with silver clasps. Larry was wearing green pants and a light green turtleneck shirt, with a dark green sports jacket. They together looked great for photos that afternoon.

The gentleman at the portrait studio welcomed them and inquired which of them would be first. The girls without hesitation in common chorus said: "All of us!" Up until then, Larry had not considered that there may be any problems on such preference, and he resolved the question in his mind by simply following the advice he had received just a few minutes ago and "Let them decide." And so they did. They had several shots made with Larry seated alone, several shots of Larry standing alone in a classic pose, tall and erect, proud and with a most confident smile, and several shots of Larry surrounded by his twins. There were no poses in which only one of the twins was photographed. Now Larry is not stupid. Larry is learning valuable lessons. The most important lesson is that these girls are always in synch, always in harmony, and like to be together without partiality. They treat one another with a remarkable deference.

The finished photos weren't ready for several days, and the first time Larry saw any of them was the next week as he walked in the front door to be facing a very large gold framed studio portrait hanging in what appeared to be a permanent place of honor in the entry hall of the Remington home. It was magnificent, with Larry Cole impressively standing tall and smiling assuredly, with his arms extended and hands touching the shoulders of the twins seated in front of him in regal manner. He looked like the king of Spain posed with the queen, except that here he had a pair of queens. Larry was instantly overjoyed to see what importance and respect was shown for him and his twins, but it seemed also to be a suggestion that the three of them had a certain togetherness. A short time later, as the girls were chopping lettuce and onions in the kitchen, Momma Remington motioned for Larry to follow her down the hallway, and stopped at an open bedroom door. She without saying anything just pointed into the bedroom and over each of the girls' beds was a framed portrait of Larry Cole. Different poses, but just the one subject. Larry was startled, shocked, pleased, delighted, sorta embarrassed, and did not know how he should react to what he considered a very flattering tribute. He just stood there for a brief moment looking at those pictures, didn't know what to say, and didn't know at all how to respond. So he reached down and took Momma's hand, gently pulled her toward himself, and kissed her on the back of that hand, as her husband has suggested he might do, and she melted, gushed and glowed. As for the large framed picture of the three of them together, he asked if they had a smaller copy for him to send to his parents, and they did have several for distribution. Larry didn't really think then about how he would explain these things to his family, but for the moment all was well. It wasn't until much later that he became concerned and curious as to why the parents would allow these silly girls to take over their home's entire entry way to display the picture of a boyfriend. Then as you might give it some further thought, you'd have to wonder how they explained this to friends, relatives and visiting strangers that might walk through that door to be confronted with such an image.

As for sending a copy of that picture to the folks in Springfield, the brother Rick has already paved the way. He had sent a couple of snapshots that he had taken in San Diego. Since the week following his introduction to Teri Remington, Larry had been giving his folks regular reports on how he was promoting the romance with the young lady that he described as the most beautiful girl in the world, a girl that goes to church and spouts scripture, a girl with perfect ankles and knees, a girl that could easily win Olympic gold for her ice skating, a girl that giggles and laughs and hugs his arm. Well, how now can he tell the folks that there are two of them and he doesn't know which is which?

With all this now out in the open, it really was more comfortable to visit the Remington house. Larry was getting more accustomed to the blatant way these two young ladies worshipped him, and how they would hug and kiss him brazenly in front of the parents. This was an entirely new emotion for the girls, and because of their innocent ignorance of conventional manners for promoting budding romance, they just let it fly. On several occasions when they were spontaneously squeezing his arms on each side or running fingers through his short-cropped hair, or with one in his lap and the other with arms about his neck, they would both at the same time be yelling their unrestrained accolades like "We love you!" and "You beautiful man!" and "Where have you been? We've been lonesome!" As Stewart Remington observed this previously unknown behavior of his little girls, he would shake his head in amazement, shrug his shoulders, and tell Larry "It's all your fault!"

Well, everything seemed to be going along very well for Lt. Larry Cole. He was quite certain that he would soon be promoted to rank of Captain in the United States Marine Corps, and everyone in his family would be so proud of him. His most unusual single romance with two beautiful young ladies at the same time was moving along nicely without regard to whatever complications might arise. His training with jet propulsion aircraft was moving ahead suitably, his operation of all the various items of intricate equipment and operation seemed to be doing well, and the people at MCAS Miramar and MCAS El Toro didn't have any open criticism of his work. The regular checkups at Balboa Naval Hospital didn't seem yet to result in any negative prognoses.

On a weekday at Miramar, a couple of young Marine flyers invited Larry to go to lunch at one of the local watering holes, and so he did. He rode along with them in a flashy Lincoln sedan, and they arrived at one of the grills where was offered every brand of beer, barbecued ribs and fried chicken, and all the waitresses wore provocative skimpy outfits. Larry had been here before, but as soon as he sat down and looked about, he became uncomfortable. One of the waitresses came to their table to get the orders, as she draped her arm over Larry's shoulder, placed her hand on the back of his neck with a massaging squeeze, and suddenly Larry Cole felt very ill at ease. He had the unexpected realization that he should not be in this place, and that waitress had no business touching in such an intimate way the neck that belongs to someone else. Make that some two else's. This was one of the first times he felt that he really did belong body and soul to those twins. He wanted to immediately get out before somebody saw him there and reported him to Momma Remington. Unfortunately, he had come with the friends in their car, and was now their prisoner. While the other guys ordered beer for everyone, Larry opted for tea. The others ordered piles of ribs. Larry said he was not really hungry, and would just sample the French fries from the other plates. He was so relieved to escape that place.

The two lovely ladies demanded that their hero phone them at least every day, and if he neglected to call, they had his number and would call him. If he didn't have a good excuse to do otherwise they would schedule amusements for the three of them every night of the week. They all rode to church together and those pretty girls were not the least bit reluctant to show their possessiveness for all the world to see as they clutched his arms and scrunched up close as they walked along, and sat as close to him as propriety would allow while worshiping in the sanctuary. On the first occasion when Pastor DeWitt saw this blatant display he looked Larry in the eye, silently pointed toward each of his clinging admirers, and raised his eyebrows with a very inquisitive expression. Larry grinned and shrugged his shoulders. 'Nuff said.

Applying conventional considerations to young love, or should we better come right out and identify the emotion as simple transitory infatuation, this silly three-way romance surely had no promise of satisfactory result, and really ought to cool down mercifully and quickly or create disastrous emotional ruin. These girls had already shown proclivity for hysteria and breakdown under stress. It would seem that Larry really was sailing into perilous waters. But it would soon be revealed that it was too late to simply sail away from all of this.

This unusual romantic excursion went on for about three weeks from the time that Stewart Remington had called Larry in for the long talk that led to the reconciliation of Larry Cole and his twins. He now had been gone for several days on a training flight that took him to a couple of military airfields in Oklahoma and Kansas, and had just returned late last evening. It was on that next day, early Wednesday morning, while on duty at El Toro in his flying suit and ready to take off again, a phone call came from Dad Remington, and his voice had an ominous tone as he said "Larry. We have a really big problem. I think we ought to treat it as an emergency. Can you come to my office right away?"

Larry got in touch with the CO, told him he had a family emergency, got relieved from the scheduled maneuvers, and went immediately to his quarters to change clothes and scoot on over to Santa Ana to find out what sort of emergency it could be. Knowing that Teri had a past history of emotional collapse, he was much concerned that some terrible relapse was threatening. Knowing that Toni got stirred up whenever Teri fell apart, he just knew that she must be wobbly. By the time he got to the Remington office, Larry was dreadfully worried. Once again as Larry sat down in the office, Stew Remington instructed his secretary to hold all calls, bar the door and do not disturb.

Dad Remington said "Larry. I don't really know how to start. We have a huge problem. It's something that I would never have expected. I am not angry, but I'm very disappointed. My wife is just crushed. My girls have been crying again for two days and two nights. The past couple of weeks have been the most jubilant days ever for the twins, and my wife has been beside herself with glee to watch her little babies having so much fun worshipping you and sitting in your lap, laughing and giggling, tickling you and each other, smooching and hugging you without the least reluctance. Both of them have your portrait proudly posted over their desks at the dealerships, and you have brought such joy to their hearts. This has been like Heaven on earth for the whole family since you came into our lives. Well, all that has changed. We found out on Monday this week that the girls are both pregnant, about six or seven weeks along. These things must have happened before you found out that they were twins. I think I now know what it was that you said you never wanted me to know. Now the entire world will know, and worst of all is that my wife knows. You now have in her eyes suddenly become a worthless scumbag."

Larry became very quiet. Very pensive. His silence seemed to make the entire room into a cold glacier, and all he could do was sit there staring at the floor and shaking his head.

Larry was no longer the proud General. He could no longer be the perfect answer to the girls' prayers. This news was the most disturbing revelation of his entire life. Those dinky little Viet Cong bullets that tore through his body were nothing compared to this terrible disclosure. He felt emotionally crippled, helpless and weak, stripped of pride, covered in guilt, naked and without a place to hide, and hopeless with no way of escape. This was easily the worst moment of his entire life. Now everyone is gonna know that he is just a phony. His testimony promoting purity, holiness, virtue, honor and integrity has this moment gone swirling down the tubes. All those righteous-sounding prayers and displays of devotion to morality and noble countenance now are indictments against his true character. Now these prayers are only transparent shields through which the true spirit of debauchery is betrayed. This is what can happen when a Christian yields to compromise. This was a very sobering moment.

Stewart Remington watched quietly as Larry the former hero sat there shaking his head, and that frozen silence filled the room for several silent minutes. Then Larry took a deep breath and looked up at the source of this terrible report, and asked "What am I to do? Wow! This is terribly embarrassing. Both of them? Oh, this is so awkward. The girls must be falling apart. I can imagine what your wife must feel like. Oh, wow! Is it safe for me to ever show up at your place again?"

Dad Remington told how he has had to deal helplessly with the weeping women for the past couple of days, and when his wife was taking time out from her tears he was able to discuss the catastrophe and possible cures in at least a little detail. "Now, Larry. This has been an ordeal for our family, and I know you are not pleased with this unwelcome news. You know our family is traditional Catholic, and there will be no talk about abortion. But, since there is really no way for us all to be at ease with any of this, there is no justification for making it worse by making bad decisions. If you want to just cut and run, just walk away from an impossible situation with no responsible solution, you ought to do so now. If you want to get up now and leave, we won't chase you, we won't be hiring any lawyers to harass you, there will be no requests for you to pay any expenses now or later, there'll be no demands for child support. You are now free to go your way and you'll likely never hear from any of us ever again."

Larry the former hero looked up at Stewart Remington and firmly responded "No. No. I can't leave the girls to go it alone. I'm responsible for what they're gonna have to go through, and if you folks will allow me to share the burdens, I want to stay with the ship."

Larry the former hero. Larry now the disconsolate rule breaker. Larry the steadfast leader in moral and spiritual conduct now by his own behavior is betrayed for the entire world to see that Larry has compromised his Christian testimony and the commitment to honorable comportment and exemplary manners. Now so obvious that Larry is still the habitual backslider, revealed in the most embarrassing and humiliating manner, and in such a way as to sully the honor of two innocent young ladies. That secret sin done in darkness is now exposed for all the whispering gossipers to share. Larry silently sat wistfully, wishing he were somewhere else, and hoping that this unpleasant news could just be part of a passing dream without consequence.

After a prolonged silence, Stewart Remington broke the ice to say "OK. The ladies know that you and I have talked about these things, and they are waiting now at home to hear how you have taken the news, and what sort of resolutions we might propose. I think the girls are especially anxious to find out what your reactions are to what I've told you. My wife is angry and not likely to cool off soon, but the girls will be pleased and proud to hear that you're not gonna cut and run."

Buoyed somewhat with what Dad Remington has now said, Larry asked "I feel like I ought to be with the girls right now, but do you think it's wise for me to go around your wife when she's so upset?"

Dad Remington felt that he ought to phone the house to let everyone there know how things have gone with the day's revelations, so he did, and this is what Larry could hear of the ensuing exchanges of conversation: "Helloo, Sweetheart. I've talked with Larry. He wants to know if it's safe to be within a hundred yards of a very angry mother of pregnant twins. How say you?"

Irate screaming and screeching could be heard coming from the other end of that phone line "You tell that scum to get his butt out here, and do it now. I gotta score to settle with him." And Dad's response was "Yes, dear. I will give him the message. You can expect us in just a short while. And while you are waiting, may I suggest a long cold shower?" You could hear a string of unladylike profanities shrieking as the phone was slammed down on the other end of the line. One could assume that Momma was furious, and not likely to be napping anytime soon.

Stewart Remington congratulated Larry the debauchee on his bravery, but was quick to warn him that on this trip he was entirely all alone to face a hostile Mexican who was very much like an angry mother bear protecting her cubs, adding "Hoping that you might want to take your chances, I called the girls aside this morning to warn them that you would be on your own, and for them to remain silent and not try to offer any sort of aid or assistance while you suffer with the storm. You're gonna take all responsibility for what's happened, and the girls cannot share any part of the blame. OK? I'll explain this better later. Can you handle it?"

The Dad's warning made Larry feel even more apprehensive, but he humbly answered "Well, I really deserve to get clobbered. But, believe me, if I had known all the little details before we would not be facing this unfortunate situation now. But, I won't run away. I have no idea how to work through this trouble, but the girls shouldn't have to deal with it alone. I'll stay with it 'til the bitter end." To which the Dad replied "Oh, yeah. While we're on the subject of the 'bitter end', you might be relieved to know that I hid my wife's gun and ammunition in the garage." Wow, that news must've been a great consolation.

Since it was entirely possible, if not entirely probable that Larry the scum might have to beat a hasty exit from the Remington house, it was decided that he should drive his own car and park it in a location and in the right direction so that he could escape more easily.

Upon arrival at the home, Larry followed Dad Remington through the front door and immediately noted that his portrait was no longer in its place of honor on the entry area wall, then spotted the remains of that portrait smashed on the floor on the farther side of the hall, apparently a victim of the occasional earthquake so common to California.

CHAPTER 16

MUSIC AND MEDICINE

Larry had taken about a half-dozen steps into the entry hall of the Remington residence when the storm broke and the screaming began. Adding to his misfortune was the fact that Momma Remington had been dealing with the horse flies that were usually in residence at the neighbor's barns but had recently invaded her place, and she had a can of fly spray in one hand and a flyswatter in the other. She caught Larry off guard as he entered and got him with both those weapons of mass destruction, all the while screaming things like 'hypocrite' and 'heartbreaker' and 'beast' along with several more epithets swathed in descriptive profanity. Larry's first subdued reaction as he tried to dodge the artillery was to silently think to himself that this is a lady that he first met in the aisles of an evangelical Christian church.

Whack. Whack. Pfffftt, pffftt, ppffffttt. He turned away as she continued her merciless onslaught, but she followed him right through the doorway and into the living room, where the young victims of his wrongdoing were seated and quietly observing the one-sided conflict that had turned that room into a war zone. When the fly spray ran out she threw the empty can, which bounced off Larry's head and hit the plate glass window. Trying to make a strategic retreat he carefully maneuvered his way over to a place where the table was between him and the mother bear, but she continued to shake her flyswatter menacingly and spewed out a sustained delivery of profane diatribes. She retreated into the hallway screaming threats all the way, and Dad Remington leaned over toward him to whisper "You deserved that. But you're doin' great. Try to stay out of the kitchen. She has a lotta butcher knives in there. She's gone to the bedroom, probably to get her double-barrel shotgun, but I know it's not there." Those reassuring words must have been a great comfort. *Shotgun?*

The twins sat apart quietly on opposite sides of the room, looking pitiful with their eyes all red from crying through the night, and their hair was sorta mussed up. All the pain and discomfort from the attack of Momma, along with all her descriptive insults, could not have hurt Larry more than to see these precious angels looking so sad. Teri was seated on a regular chair with her hands folded in her lap, and Toni was on the couch holding a large pillow and quietly whimpering. This was the scene as Momma came charging through the door again, saying: "Well, you creep. What do you have to say for yourself?" He lifted his hands in a gesture of placation and opened his mouth to speak saying "Well...I don't...." and that's all he managed to get out before she screamed "Sit down and shut up. You worthless jerk!" She got those words out as she reached for a vase full of flowers and heaved it at him from across the room. It missed the target but the flowers fell on his head and shoulders. Dad Remington motioned for Larry to sit on the vacant couch, across from Teri and with Toni over to the side, each about ten feet away from where Larry was nervously seated. He glanced up at Teri and saw that she was bland of expression as she sorta quivered in fright with all the yelling and screaming of insults. On guard against more missiles that might come his way, he glanced over at Toni, and she now had her face buried in the large pillow she was holding. Larry had a flood of conscience to think that he had caused these precious persons to suffer this way and look so pathetic.

Then Momma charged back into the affray and commenced again her tirades with the question "What are you gonna do now that you have ruined the lives of my little girls? You have destroyed their blameless lives, and you have shattered our home. I am devastated by what you have done. How could you be so cruel as to rip away the innocence of my precious little baby girls? You...you...you twerp." With that harangue yet incomplete, Momma sat down, grabbed for herself one of those pillows off the couch, covered her face with it and began to sob uncontrollably. Both of the girls left the places where they had been seated and went to Momma's side, knelt down and patted her on the shoulder and tried to cuddle with her. Toni turned toward Larry and tried to force a little smile, but she failed. Now Larry really felt bad, as he stood up and worked his way over nearer where the little angels were trying to console their weeping mother.

Dad Remington again went over to whisper so that only Larry could hear: "You deserved that also. But you're doing great. Keep it up. She can't carry on this way forever." Great words of inspiring reassurance!

When several minutes of sobbing were past, Momma looked up at her husband and with a pleading expression on her face said "Stewart. Can't you do something?" He calmly replied "Well, let me give this a try. Girls, you sit over here on the couch, and Larry can we have you sit over here in this chair?"

"Larry. There doesn't appear to be any way out of this jam. But, just in case you can come up with some miracle, we'd like to hear about it." Larry lifted his hands slightly as he shook his head dolefully, and looked over at the girls that were looking sadly back at him. Nothing more was said. The atmosphere was fully charged but woefully silent. The girls had said nothing during these anxious moments of supercharged emotion.

Momma Remington held her pillow in her lap and continued softly weeping, then laboring to hold back more tears, she said with a scowl "Estupido. Idioto. Tonto. You better come up with something or....or....or. Well, you can't just sit there. Say something!"

Larry took a deep breath, lifted both hands as though in surrender, and said "I will do anything you ask of me."

Then, with something only slightly less than a scowl, Momma Remington says "What do you mean that you will do anything we ask of you?"

And he calmly replied in such a way as to offer some sort of reassurance: "I promise you that I will do anything you ask of me. But I want to ask something of you first. I want you to promise me that there will be no abortion for anyone. Whatever happens, there must be no abortion."

To which Dad Remington replied "You got it, Larry. We promise you that there will be no abortion here for anyone, no matter what happens. Now will you further explain what you are trying to say?"

Larry went on: "I promise that I will do whatever you ask of me from here on out. I will pay all the expenses. I will pay child support. I will pay whatever amount of money you ask from me. I will do whatever you ask of me. Without reservation I promise to do anything you ask of me."

Momma interjected: "OK. You loser. Go shoot yourself!" To which suggestion her husband interposed: "No, Shimi. Let's be reasonable. Larry is trying to be fair and practical. Tell ya what, Larry. Why don't we give this matter a little time to cool off? Why don't we gather here again tomorrow at noon? That will give you some time to think, and Shimi and I can discuss things, and maybe we can consult with some other knowledgeable people to try and find a reasonable disposition. OK?"

With obvious relief at the suggestion that he could get out of there alive tonight, Larry replied: "Swell. Let's do that. Now, would it be alright if I talked with the girls?" To which suggestion Momma screamed "No. You cannot talk to my girls! You stay away from both of them! Do you understand me? You stay away from my little baby girls! Don't you touch my girls! You jerk!" And Dad Remington kinda saves the day, hoping to avoid any unnecessary friction, still hoping that Larry might say something to the girls to soothe their aching hearts, and said "Now, Shimi. It won't hurt to allow Larry to talk to them right while you and I are here to chaperone, and we'll be hearing each and every word. Surely, Larry wouldn't say or do anything to hurt either of them." With a half-snort she lifted that pillow off her lap, dabbed at her eyes with a little hanky, and with a grimace accompanied by an uneasy gesture of truce, she just waved her hand and gave up the resistance to Larry talking with the twins.

Larry went over and sat on the coffee table in front of where the little angels were seated, and said "A friend of mine suggested that I should not touch you, but apparently it's OK if I say 'I love you' and that means both of you, I really do love you with all my heart. I don't have the slightest notion of how all of this will play out, but I'm sure everything is gonna be OK. I promise both of you that I will not ignore my obligations, and I will never leave you stranded. I wish I could take both of you in my arms and just hold you tightly for the next ten hours or so, and maybe you could sleep quietly as I cuddle you both. Whatever happens, I want you both to know that I will love you forever, I will want to be with you forever, and I'm gonna pray real hard for God to send us some kind of solution for our little problem. Maybe that should be 'two little problems' if you please." and as he ended his little sermon there was that voice in the background that sarcastically said "You hypocrite. If you had spent your time praying instead of ruining my babies' lives, we wouldn't be having these problems!"

Larry then stood up and addressed Dad Remington: "I would rather spend the rest of the day trying to say something to encourage the girls, but maybe you folks would rather I just leave. But I want to offer my reassurances that I will do whatever you ask of me. Whatever it is, I promise I will do whatever you ask."

With that, Larry gave his little salute to the girls, turned and gave another salute to their mother who basically scowled and said "Pafoooff", and he then shook hands with Dad Remington who followed him out to his car, and along the way remarked "Wow, Larry. You really held up very well. I'm proud of you. That was truly a great little speech you delivered to the girls. I was very impressed, and in spite of the appearances and the jeering words of sarcasm you probably made an OK impression on my wife. We'll see you tomorrow. Maybe Shimi will change her mind about you shooting yourself and perhaps just ask you to hold your breath for an hour or so."

Another silent salute and Larry was gone.

All the way back to the base Larry felt totally depressed about the whole situation, but mostly disheartened for the looks of misery on the faces of his most favorite persons. He turned in early, and didn't sleep until the wee hours. Larry prayed a lot that evening, and was for a time fretful that God would just reject his prayers outright, because Larry had failed the Lord so many times. He felt that the world's worst habitual backslider should not receive any sort of divine compassion, but on the other hand these two precious young girls surely deserved much clemency and maybe a lot of miracle mercies in this hour of ridiculous trouble. Consistent with his promise, Larry asked that the Lord send ministering angels to soothe the hearts of the precious pair, and more particularly have angels stand guard so that nothing bad happens to those priceless passengers that are temporarily lodged with those girls.

At the Remington home, the atmosphere changed substantially after Larry was gone. It wasn't late at all, but the girls went to their bedroom, both took showers and spiffied up a bit, put on their nightgowns, then sat together facing each other on one of the beds, chatting quietly. No tears; just renewed hope. Their Mom came in a while later, much more calm than she was earlier, sat on the other bed and was quiet for several minutes, then said "You kids think I was too harsh on your young man, don't you? Well, maybe I was too noisy. Maybe I did put on too much of a show. But I'm sure he understands how I feel about the surprises he dropped on me. I just don't know what we're gonna do about all this. I thought last week we were the happiest clams on earth, and now all this disturbance and unbearable pressure pops up. Well, I want you to know that I'm gonna try to do better next time he comes around. Maybe we can find a way. Ya know what? He has convinced me that he really does love you kids, and before all this stuff blew up in my face, I was getting to where I liked him. Ah, well. I guess somehow we'll get this all worked out, and you'll be happy." With that she stood up and went over to hug and kiss her little baby girls, and disappeared out the door.

Teri looked at Toni, and Toni grinned, saying: "I think she's already startin' to crack. Now I really do think everything will somehow be worked out. I don't ever want to give him up." Teri agreed "Yep. She's going soft and everything is gonna be OK. And I agree with you that we should never give him up. I think we should stop right here and pray that God will somehow help us through all this", and so they did.

Meanwhile, Stewart and Shimi Remington were discussing things over in their bedroom, and agreed that they ought to consult more knowledgeable people to find a solution to this predicament.

Early the next morning Mom and Dad Remington were gone to seek counsel of their advisors and on other undisclosed missions.

CHAPTER 17

SOLUTIONS

As agreed, Larry the scoundrel was at the front door of the Remington house at noon that next day, and was greeted there by the Master of the House, which was somewhat of a relief for Larry, who was hoping that he would not be met by the mother bear. Stewart Remington was cordial, invited the guest to enter and as he did so he noted that the shattered picture frame and portrait had been removed from the entry hall. The former location of that portrait seemed even more bare as he passed by. They stood briefly together in the hallway as Mr. Remington whispered "Larry. Ya gotta follow the same rules as yesterday. I've already instructed the girls to stay out of it, and just be quiet. They can't take your side on anything, and they can't otherwise get involved in any squabbles. You're on your own. OK?" Larry the former hero nodded agreement as they both entered the front room. Seated on the overstuffed leather chair was a surly mother whose mood had not improved much from the day before, and seated together on the opposing couch were the twins, all scrubbed up and bright-eyed. The mood of the twins seemed unusually calm and light, which was a great improvement over yesterday.

Larry ambled over to a place near the pair of angels and smiled as he said loud enough for all to hear "I love you and you. I love you even more today than I did yesterday!" Both of them grinned and silently lifted their hands to make little mini-salutes. A few paces further and he took a seat where he had an excellent view of the entire room, and near enough to the exit to facilitate hasty departure as necessary. Dad Remington sat down on the end of the couch near the twins, then commenced the session by saying "Well, Larry. It looks like we've all made it safely through the night, with high hopes that we can likewise make it through this day. I know you've been thinking about all the circumstances that have brought us here at this time, and we'd like to hear whatever you might have as a solution." Larry answered to say that he had hardly slept all night worrying about how this surprise situation might be troubling to the twins and their folks. "I thought about how my family is gonna take it when they find out that their 'fair-haired boy' broke the cardinal

Christian rules that promote purity and modesty and honor. But, I really can't see any perfect solution to these things." Momma grunted.

Then having given Larry his opportunity to launch the first proposition, Dad Remington told Larry that he and his wife had deliberated the matter for hours among themselves, and augmented those discussions this morning in calls to gain the advice of others, including professionals in psychology and psychiatry that were already acquainted with some fragile situations within the family, and then had actually gone into Santa Ana to discuss the matter with an attorney, and had talked by phone with another lawyer in Los Angeles. Without then yet disclosing any of the advice received from these third parties, he went on to say "Larry. Do you stand by your promise to do whatever we ask of you?" And Larry quickly responded "I will do anything you ask. But, I would first want to tell you something, and ask of you something in particular. First: I truly love both of these girls, and not one more than the other. I don't want you to push any solution that might leave either of them on the outside looking in. What one gets, they should both get. Second: I ask for the privilege of treating them both the same, no bias. Otherwise, you still have my promise to do whatever you ask of me, and I promise that I will not change my mind."

The father nodded his head very seriously, then said "OK, Larry. We'll take you at your word, and accept your promise just as you have stated. Now, after careful consideration, we've made the decision that you should marry Teri, and give her child your name." Larry took a deep breath, turned white as a sheet, appeared troubled and distressed, and timidly responded "Yessir." The girls looked shocked, and Teri gestured in such a way as to suggest that she wanted to be heard. Her Dad raised his hand toward her sorta like a cop stopping traffic and raised his index finger to place it over his lips in a 'shushing' gesture, and added "And Larry. We'll accept your promise to do whatever we ask of you, and after careful consideration, we've made the decision that you should marry Toni, and give her child your name." Larry brightened up immediately, the twins commenced to smile uncontrollably and looked at each other blissfully, then everybody turned their eyes over to where Momma Remington was observing all this, and she finally nodded her head and then rolled her eyes toward the ceiling.

After the shock had dissipated, Larry turned to Momma Remington and said "OK. But you gotta promise to come visit when they throw me into San

Quentin for bigamy or polygamy or whatever." Momma glared at him and said "Don't joke about it."

Then Larry got quite serious to add "OK. But if my commanding officer gets wind of it, they'll have me up for court martial and slap me with a dishonorable discharge." To which observation Momma added: "Tough luck for you, Pal. You can go get a job pickin' lemons or choppin' cotton."

It was obvious that Momma had not abandoned her hostility, but Larry chose this moment to formalize the engagement, so he got up, stepped over and sat on the coffee table in front of the wide-eyed angels, dared to take the hand of each one, and boldly said "OK, ladies. You heard what they said." He looked over at their father seated close by and asked "Mr. Remington, sir. Do I have your consent to marry both these young ladies? That means that you consent to my marriage to Teri, and you consent to my marriage to Toni." And he without hesitation replied: "Yes, Larry, you have my consent to marry Teri, and you have my consent to marry Toni, that means that you have my consent and encouragement to be married to both of them at the same time." Then braving the wrath of the angry Mexican lady, he asked: "Now, Mrs. Remington, will you consent to my marriage to Teri and my marriage to Toni just as we have discussed here today?" Momma started grousing and it looked like she was very uncomfortable as she twisted in her chair, looking at the floor and then the ceiling and then the walls, nervously patting her foot on the floor rapidly, and then finally glaring at Larry, she barked "Yes. You have my consent!"

Now, with the customary parental consent matter out of the way, while still holding the girls each by a hand, Larry scooted the coffee table back to where he could get down on one knee in front of them, saying "I think I'm supposed to get down on my knee to do this. Teri, do you love me?" The giggling response was augmented by a finger pointing toward her sister and the words "I'm Toni. She's Teri." To which Larry blushed to a very red beet color and said "Sorry. I promise to work on it. I'll get it right in no time. I'm just kinda nervous. I've never done this before. OK. Toni, do you love me?" and she smiled real big, and only Larry was aware of the strong squeeze he got on his hand, as she responded "I love you so much. I love you with all my heart. I promise that I will always love you." Then he turned to the other twin and asked "Teri, do you love me?" and she quickly replied "Yes. Yes. Yes! I started loving you the first time I laid eyes on you. I am bubbling over with love for you, and I will love you forever!" Larry chuckled out loud and asked "Really?" and there then came back a chorus of "Yes.Yes. Yes! We love you" and they repeated this several times.

There came a gruff voice from over in that direction, saying "Hold on a minute, Mister. I suppose you have planned some kind of dramatic plea for the hands of these maidens. Well, you can stop right there and come with me." With that little interruption Momma Remington stood up and motioned for Larry to follow her into the hall. When they had gone the entire length of the hallway and into the master bedroom, she turned around and briskly asked whether Larry had the rings with him, and he responded to say that all this has happened so quickly that he just did not have time to go shopping. Then she scowled at him to ask "Are you aware that today is the girls' nineteenth birthday? Did you bring for them some nice gifts?" Larry turned all shades of red, flushed with embarrassment he admitted that not only did he forget this special day, he didn't even know when their birthday was. She shushed him and turned to retrieve from the top dresser drawer two small boxes, opened them up for Larry to see two identical sets of diamond engagement ring and wedding ring. Each engagement ring had a huge center stone that must have been larger than a couple of carats, and six smaller side stones of about a ⅓ carat each, with wedding band to match, all beautifully set in platinum. In keeping with common custom these rings were not cheap nor were they modest. These rings are the kind that people notice and young girls swoon for, but most importantly were they so very sparkly and beautiful so as to dazzle the families in Mexico City. As she closed the boxes and handed them to Larry she said "My girls deserve the best, and these are just that. The rings are your responsibility, so no gift from me is intended." Then she lifted her voice to a loud growl to say *"You'll have to pay back every dollar. You're gonna hafta pay every last dime!"* Then more quietly she suggested that he inform the girls that the rings should serve also as birthday presents, but she sternly warned "Don't you ever forget their birthday again!"

When the audience in the front room heard the menacing growl about "***You're gonna hafta pay every last dime***" Dad Remington leaned toward the girls and whispered "You're gonna love this!" as Momma returned with her solemn unsmiling grumpy look, and took her seat in that chair.

Returning to the front room, Larry pushed back the coffee table even more and knelt on one knee, turned to look at Momma Remington and tossed her an impish smile. Having heard the twins and their unabashed declarations of undying love, Larry pushed on with "Teri, I love you, will you marry me?" and she didn't even flinch as she gleefully replied "Yes, Yes!" and he turned to the other and asked "Toni, I love you, will you marry me?" and she sniffled as her chin began to quiver and replied "Yes. Yes!" and Larry pushed on just to be sure as he further inquired "That was individually, and now I ask you both together, Will you marry me?" and they both started to tremble saying together "Yes. Yes!"

Then Larry reached into his pocket and brought out those two boxes. He once again turned to toss a mischievous grin toward Momma, adding the wobbly eyebrows for effect, opened the boxes to reveal the contents to the newly betrothed twins, and they started to coo and coo. Another cute grin glowed as he volunteered out of context "Happy Birthday" He then said "One of my very best friends helped me select these for you. I think you'll like 'em" He placed the boxes on the table and withdrew those sparkly engagement rings both at the same time. Then he smiled at the girls as he wiggled his eyebrows and winked, telling them to raise their left hands and hold them closer together, and he placed the rings on each at the same time so that he could later boast that he showed no bias, and the girls just exploded with glee. Larry acted silly like a twelve year old child, rocking his head back and forth and hooting.

Now that the formalities were over, Larry with a bit more confidence glanced back and forth at his betrothed pair and said "Please understand that I am still under restrictions. I think I'm supposed to kiss you and give you a big hug to confirm these things, but there might be some objection from the gallery." And from behind he heard the castigating call to sarcastically say "How very cruel. You get these girls all worked up with your romantic blabber and those remarkably beautiful expensive perfect diamond rings, and then you can't even give them a little kiss? You're a real gentleman!" which comment suggested to all in that room that Momma might be getting soft but wasn't about to go along with everything Larry said or did. The girls were under no restrictions, so they converged on him from both sides and started squealing like two happy little piglets, planting kisses all over his head and neck, nose and ears, arms and hands. The cluster of lovebirds fell over on the floor, and Teri sat on his legs while Toni roosted on his chest, and both proceeded to tickle him, as the stoic matriarch looked on with feigned disgust. This was the first time in a coupla years that the girls engaged in their unusual simultaneous 'cheerful chatter', which seemed to delight everyone present, and it was the first time that Larry had heard either of the girls speak in Spanish. This happy scuffle went on for several minutes. The atmosphere in the room seemed to become vastly improved.

When the happy trio got through tussling, the girls propped Larry up against the couch, and the newly betrothed twins took up their posts on each arm as they curled up next to him, hugging and squeezing, squirming and cuddling, occasionally peppering his hands and face with cute little kisses. Larry appeared to be so very much at peace with the world. Teri leaned over to face her twin and exclaimed "I'm engaged to be married to the most wonderful man in the whole world! Do you want to see my new ring?" to which Toni responded "Yeah. Me too! Take a look at my new ring!"

Momma Remington just sat there and watched the whole scene, and when she could catch the eye of her husband, she smiled and winked at him. Dad Remington saw that little wink and exclaimed "Well, kids. I think this whole thing is gonna work out OK. Did you know that your mother has already ordered the Wedding Invitations?" Then Momma piped up to ask if the girls wanted to include with each mailed invitation a picture of the affianced pair, and they applauded the suggestion. That being agreed on, Momma looked sternly at Larry the Lieutenant, and ordered him to come this next Monday morning dressed in his most impressive formal Marine Officer uniform, with all those campaign ribbons and such, and have more pictures taken at the portrait place for insertion into the invitations.

Teri was curious to know when they were to be married. Toni wanted to know if they were to be wed both at the same time, and wondered just how that would work out. No matter how comfortable everyone here might be with the arrangements, the underlying circumstances required practical management. The lawyer in Santa Ana was a Mexican that had graduated from the prestigious University in Mexico City and was an abogado admitted to practice in Mexico, and also an experienced attorney practicing in California; and that Mexican lawyer consulted with another such lawyer in Los Angeles. These two lawyers consulted with several others versed in the international law and customs, one of which was a retired Superior Court judge. They all came up with the conclusion that if Remington's would follow detailed instruction it would be extremely unlikely that there could ever be any successful criminal prosecution of Larry or either of the girls for bigamy or polygamy. Likewise, they assured that there could be no civil liability to anyone and there could not under current law be any successful attack on the marriage of Larry and either or both of the girls.

The Mexican lawyer insisted that everyone follow his instructions to the letter. He personally went with Teri and Larry to apply for the California marriage license, to assure that the application forms contained the right information. According to that Mexican lawyer's instructions, Teri's wedding was to take place in two weeks at the Catholic Church in nearby Santa Ana, and Toni's wedding would be two weeks later at the great Catholic cathedral in Mexico City. Larry's family and all the California friends, neighbors and relatives would be invited to the California nuptials, and all the family in Mexico would be invited to the celebrations there. That lawyer would accompany them to Mexico City to personally oversee all the documentation relating to those ceremonies, and to obtain some peculiar legal documents.

Like two little kids, as they continued to hold their favorite prisoner, the girls immediately started planning their weddings. Teri demanded that Toni should be her maid of honor, and likewise Toni insisted that Teri be her maid of honor. That left them with the decision as to whether or not they wanted any bridesmaids, and they agreed that since they had very few acquaintances left, and of those there were no close friends, they opted to grab their older sister Debbie, rip off all her jewelry and clutter of bangles, scrub all that grease off her face, hide her fake eyelashes and black mesh hosiery, and have her be the only other bridesmaid at both weddings.

Larry asked if maybe he could make one further request for sake of propriety: "Would it be OK if I asked my parents to come out for another little family meeting to cover the same things we have done today? If it's OK with you, I'd like to see if they can come out right away." Being so agreed, he phoned his folks immediately. They agreed to come the very next day.

As all were then seated there in the front room, Larry felt uncomfortable even asking, but he managed to suggest that he would like to just sit and stare at his twin fiancées for the rest of the day. Mom Remington said nothing but just got up and went into the kitchen for some sort of task. Stew Remington shook his head and smiled, saying "Ya know? I think everything is gonna work out fine. I am so relieved to get this matter settled. I think this whole scenario is just gonna be OK, and everyone is gonna be happy. I gotta tell ya' that a great weight has been lifted off my shoulders. Larry, please consider that you are now already part of the family, and you can come to see your sweeties any time night or day, stay as late as you want, and take them out for a stroll, or out for a taco, or just sit and stare at them." Hearing this, Larry timidly asked if maybe Dad Remington could get his wife to agree to these things. Larry and the twins went out to sit on the patio. With Larry in the middle and a pretty girl on each side, they sat in the swinging lounge chair like three happy little puppies for several hours, as the newly betrothed twins compared matching engagement rings and wedding plans. These young ladies must have repeated at least a hundred times that they were so pleased with the outcome of the situation, and every time they said it one or the other or both of them would hug and kiss their hero. Toni cried several times and muttered over and over "I'm so happy! I am just so happy!"

Larry's folks did come that next day, landing at LAX at about mid-morning and both pairs of parents were to meet together with the happy trio that afternoon about 2:00 O'clock. Larry picked up his folks at the airport and hauled them with his trusty Toyota sedan. All that distance from LAX to the Remington place gave some time to talk. He started out asking what they thought of the picture with him and the twins, and they gushed to say that these girls were really so very pretty and appeared to be modest and virtuous young ladies, but which one of them would be the one that Larry is romantically involved with? And, of course he was quick to inform them that he was romantically involved with both of them. Then they asked just what was the surprise that had brought them all the way to California in such haste? Larry responded to say that he wanted their approval to get married, and that disclosure eventuated to the revelation that he intended to marry both of the girls. His mother said "Whooooop" and his father shook his head in disbelief, then said "Larry. That's illegal!" and Larry said that he had no choice in the matter because the girls were both pregnant, and that he had promised that he'd do anything the Remington's asked of him to repair the situation.

Well, as would be expected, both of the Cole parents began immediately to question not only the propriety of engaging in bigamy or polygamy, but how Larry could be sure that he is the father of these children, with the immoral California girls well known for their running up and down the beach romancing the boys, and how would you know that they are actually pregnant? Then began the uneasy discussion of how it might impact his career in the Marine Corps if anyone found out about his two wives. Then they managed another dozen or so good reasons why Larry should not be too hasty in entering into this crazy arrangement, and several more good reasons why he should turn aside from this folly before it is too late. Then mother Shirley Cole began shuffling through the pages of her leather bound purse size King James Bible, to present the scriptural constraints against such unholy unions. When she couldn't find any verse that particularly stated that polygamy was not allowed, she demanded that Larry consider the provisions found at Ephesians 5:31 and Mark 10:8 where in marriage the two become one flesh. To this Larry responded: "Mom. I know it's a weak argument, but when you see how much these two angels are alike, you'll see that they fit right into those scriptures. But, I have given my promise to marry them both, and your grandchildren will be so happy that I did." He was able to argue with them for the entire distance to the Remington place, but his folks seemed yet to be unmoved. His Mom wondered aloud to question why they had been hauled out all the way to California to participate in such a sham. Larry begged both his folks to say nothing of their negative sentiments, and try to promote interfamily peace in this awkward situation.

When they arrived at the Remington home, Larry was so proud and so very pleased to introduce for the first time his parents and his pair of fiancées, and was at first uneasy to introduce his folks to Stewart and Shimi Remington, for fear that Momma Remington might throw some kind of fit including her long list of words not heard in common Christian conversation. But, it was readily apparent that Momma Remington's sense of hospitality and cordiality so easily overcame her earlier bitterness as she immediately found camaraderie and mutual sentiments with Shirley Cole. These two started acting like they had been born joined at the hip like Siamese twins, laughing and chortling, chatting like long-lost buddies and puttering together in the kitchen making coffee and warming some pastries. Stewart Remington got into a long discussion of Republican politics with arch-conservative Richard Cole, and the snorts and guffaws echoed through the house. All Larry and the twins could do was watch as a miracle unfolded before their very eyes.

The ladies brought in the coffee and lemonade, along with some cupcakes and pastries, and the men stood to stretch and let the ladies do the serving. While standing there, Richard Cole leaned over and whispered to his baby boy "Larry. You hit the jackpot! God must love you a whole lot for Him to give you such a double blessing. These two chickies are the most beautiful girls I've ever seen. They are so perfect. They have really great moves, so graceful and charming. You are so lucky!" These comments led Larry to believe that his Dad no longer harbored any objections to his claiming the Remington twins for his bride(s).

When everyone was seated together in the living room, it was Shirley Cole that opened up the theme of their meeting, when she with an exuberant smile looked right at Teri and said "I understand that you girls are gonna marry my little boy! Well, congratulations for hooking the finest young man you could ever find, and I am certain that you will have with him a lifetime of joy. I am so proud of each of you, and can't wait to be there at your wedding."

Toni spoke up shyly to say "We thought you'd be upset about the circumstances, and we are a little bit embarrassed for anyone to know. Did Larry tell you that both of us are pregnant and that your little boy is gonna be a father in about seven months?" And to this Shirley Cole chirped: "Oh, yes. We know all about those little matters. So what? Nobody will know and nobody will care about a minor calendar flaw. You girls shouldn't let this bother you. You oughta focus on your wedding plans and have a wonderful celebration. By the way, when and where will the wedding take place?" These spontaneous comments convinced Larry that his mother had no further objections.

Shimi Remington seemed elated to take Larry's Mom to the girls' bedroom and show her the portraits of her son so prominently displayed over the bedsteads. Then Shimi sat down on one of the beds and invited Shirley to sit opposite her, and these new-found pals had a heart to heart talk. Shimi focused on the unusual close relationship the girls had with one another from the time of birth, and how the professionals said that they should never be separated, and how they never had a disagreement, and how their promises were like pure gold, and that she was sure that everything was gonna work out just fine. She added that she was terribly upset to find that her perfect little girls were in a family way, but had now almost worked through it. Shirley then told that she was not altogether comfortable with what appeared to her to be a polygamous marriage, illegal according to the law and not in conformity with her understanding of the scriptures, but that under the circumstances it appears that what has now been planned will somehow work out OK. There was no discussion at all about the traumatic events that had plagued the Remington family in past years, and all the talk centered on the hopes and expectations for sharing happy lives and particularly all about the upcoming weddings.

As Larry and his folks were leaving to go find them a motel for overnight nearer the LAX airport, they took note of a large portrait recently placed on the wall in the entry, sorta scuffed along the bottom but with a new gold frame, presenting a handsome young man posed with two lovely young ladies, all smiling confidently.

As they were zipping along the freeway west, Shirley Cole said "Larry. Those engagement rings are beautiful, but how can you afford even one set, let alone two? Those things must have cost a fortune!" to which he replied that he had to borrow the money, and will be making monthly payments for years to come.

CHAPTER 18

<u>PREPARATIONS</u>

With two weddings planned over less than a month to take place about 1800 miles between, the Coles had to get back to Springfield, get some work done and plan for travel. Shirley Cole was on the phone as soon as she got home, calling all the family to alert them to the Santa Ana fête, but sorta kept quiet about the other gathering planned elsewhere. She called sons Charley and Rick, only to find out that they had already talked with Larry as he asked both of them to take part in each nuptial event. Charley offered the opinion that Larry had gone off his rocker, while Rick gave a brief recitation about his baby brother being affected by evil California influences and that this whole thing was just crazy. However, Rick had met one or both of the girls (he didn't really know if it was one or both), and offered his further opinion that Larry was the most fortunate guy ever in the world to somehow latch on to such beautiful duplicates. Mother Shirley suggested that neither of them discuss the 'duplicates' with anyone, lest there be embarrassing inquiries and whispering about how that Cole family has been affected by ancient Ozarks customs. White lightnin' can cause disorientations.

Friday afternoon, Larry phoned to speak with Momma Remington, nervously and timidly to ask if it would be OK to take the girls out for dinner, adding that if a chaperone be necessary maybe she would like to ride along. Without bursting into a string of profane epithets reflecting on his character and calling down fire from Heaven, but still a little less than cordial, she informed him that the girls are at work today. She then barked "Why are you asking me? These girls are old enough to make their own arrangements. You can call them at work. And Larry, don't forget Monday and the portraits. We want you to show up with a chest full of medals or service ribbons or whatever it is you call 'em." To which the relieved inquirer mumbled "Yes, Ma'am."

Larry was then somehow inspired to phone Dad Remington at the dealership, knowing that he would there find a few further words of encouragement, and he was not disappointed. That fella soon to be his father-in-law seemed

elated that Larry would call, and he immediately launched into a pleasant
discussion of recent events saying "Larry, m'boy, you have really held up
well. I don't think my wife is through stomping your worthless hide, but
I'm sure you'll agree that she has softened a lot. She still seems to want you
nailed to the wall for your evil deeds, but she's really getting into euphoric
preparation for the weddings. These Mexicans love any kind of celebration.
I promised to give you a little better explanation about why you have had
to go it alone and silently accept your punishment and why it has been
better to have the girls stay back and away from all the blood splattering
and screaming. Larry, I know it takes two to tango. Or maybe in this case
it seems to have taken three to make for a real dilemma. But for so long as
Shimi can blame you with the naughtiness, she doesn't have to confront the
twins with their culpability or what she might see as her own fault for not
rearing them right. You surely have noticed that the girls don't have much
tolerance for screaming, and how they fall apart around hostility and angry
yelling. We have never raised our voices to yell at any of our kids. We've
never had to smack any of them. Four children can be fun to have around,
but they can be frustrating and irritating. Ya gotta just suck it up if you want
peace and light. My advice for your happy future is that you never raise
your voice to either of these girls, no matter what. If you want to be angry
and grouse about it, lock yourself in the bathroom and take a cold shower."
Larry the son-in-law-to-be thanked him for that advice, said that he really
had no particular reason for calling, and planned to phone the girls to see
if they would like to go out to dinner this evening. Stew Remington then
added "Larry, it is such a relief to have this matter resolved, and quite frankly
I want you to know I am so glad the girls found you!"

Larry phoned the twins at their separate dealerships, and they were giggly
with glee to hear that Mom and Dad had no objection to the three of them
going out for dinner. They departed from the Remington place about 6:00
O'clock that early evening, and opted to go over to Laguna Beach to a
romantic spot overlooking the ocean. With all the drama and distress of recent
days, the relief in having so much of the pressure off, and the delight shared
by these young ladies at having the matters resolved in such an unusual and
satisfying way, the ladies grabbed Larry and scrunched up as close as they
could as they walked into the fancy restaurant. The girls asked for a larger
table so that they could all three sit on one side, and so they did. Larry was
in a very good mood, a chatty mood. The girls were in a very good mood, a

very chatty mood. Larry's chatty mood was somehow displaced with girl talk, and all that girl talk was focused on weddings and preparations for weddings. They launched into one of their 'cheerful chatter' displays in simultaneous exchange of conversation, with Larry sitting right in the middle, enjoying all of it with amazement. The food came and these diners puttered over all of it, taking more than an hour to get as far with it as they were gonna get. The desserts came and they puttered likewise with that. When all was finished at the restaurant, they decided to go stroll on the beach, and as they did so those young ladies continued to hug Larry's arms. These lovely teenage fiancées talked about everything related to weddings. The one thing that did not pop into their conversations was the topic of the Honeymoon. When the girl talk slowed to a pace where Larry could interject the subject of Honeymoon, the girls just looked at each other and said "We'll worry about that later", whereupon they launched once again into the discussion of weddings.

Since the girls had dismissed any further discussion now of Honeymoon, Larry interposed an inquiry as to where the trio would actually live after the wedding(s). He said that he really didn't know how to handle this three-person arrangement, but then he had no personal experience with the two-person kind either. He added emphatically that he has suffered enough with the possibility that he might lose one or both of them, and that he wanted to be able to hold onto both of them in their own little nest where all his children would grow up together. Both the girls suggested that it seemed odd that Larry would think there might be a question on housing and raising a couple dozen kids in a common residence, adding that when they got back to the Remington house they would show him the answer. Larry was satisfied with that response for the moment, and quietly listened to the further prattle about weddings, as they strolled along the moonlit beach.

With weddings and receptions looming on the near horizon Larry suggested that they should do some practice waltzing and other kinds of current dance craze. The girls told him then that they had only the grammar school experience on the dance floor, and he responded to say that the three of them can sing and hum the words and music while they practiced on the beach and in the surf. And so they did. They whirled and twirled, spinning and prancing in the moonlight for the next couple of hours, and agreed that they ought to come again next week.

When they arrived back at the Remington place, they walked into the kitchen, found Momma Remington trifling about with baking some cookies, grabbed her by the arms and proclaimed "We want you to show Larry his new quarters!" With that, Momma smiled and blinked her eyes at Larry as she passed by him, reaching out to tug his sleeve, and pulled him to the long hall and to a place where Larry had never yet been. She opened the door leading to another large bedroom and said "You're gonna like this!" She and the girls were really pleased to show him all the details in that very nicely furnished place, with its massive walk-in closet, large bathroom with double sinks, huge tub and oversize shower, and ceiling-high wall to wall plate glass mirror over the nicely-lighted sink. This was larger and much nicer than any hotel room in town. Larry was overwhelmed, and told all three of the ladies that he had not expected anything like this. Momma assumed her most devilish smile, leaned over as though to make private conversation but speaking loud for all to hear "I forgot to tell you that you get to marry both my girls, but you can't take either of them away from my home. After the weddings you get to move in here." Larry started chortling, then almost laughing out loud, saying that he always thought that he'd be the man of his house, and that he would provide for the whole family in that house, but if he had to make concessions in order to gain the girls for his own, he could put up with just about any living arrangements. These things kept Larry amused for the rest of the next week.

On Monday morning early, Larry showed up at the Remington house all dressed up in his most impressive US Marine Corps officer dress blues uniform, just as his soon-to-be commanding officer had ordered. The girls were both dressed exactly alike, in light blue full-length sleeveless dresses that came down to about half-way of the calf, their hair brushed so nicely into his favorite style of ponytail. As he sat at the breakfast bar watching his twins scurry about, for the first time he noticed the difference in their hair, and had to ask if this difference was for the day or had he missed a distinguishing feature. He addressed his question to the girls but the answer came quickly from Momma "Surely, if you had been giving the girls the proper attention you would have noticed that Teri has wavy hair and Toni has more curly hair. Please make a note of that!" And he did.

As he sat patiently glancing casually about and nursing a cup of hot coffee, Momma Remington reached down behind the kitchen table, brought out a long cardboard box, and laid it on the counter in front of the handsome Marine, saying "My girls want their soldier-boy to look his best, and you can't look your best without this!" He opened the box to there discover a magnificent and most inspiring Mameluke sword, the official saber for commissioned officers of the US Marine Corps. It was beautiful, with bone covered handles and a shiny blade on which was engraved 'Lawrence E. Cole United States Marine Corps', and a very impressive scabbard with the regulation belt. This thing was not a cheap imitation. This was the real McCoy, with the serial numbers on the edge of the blade. Larry was flabbergasted, and in a sentimental gesture of gratitude he reached out to embrace Momma Remington, but she pulled away saying "Get your hands off me! Don't take liberties." The girls chuckled to see this awkward state of family affairs, and it was obvious the war was not yet over. A temporary truce maybe, perhaps an armistice, but not the end of the war. Larry stifled his snickers and accepted things just as they then were.

Momma Remington insisted on driving the crowd over to the photographer's studio in the family Mercedes sedan, and Larry jumped into the front passenger seat so that the girls could sit in the back as a pair. Momma fired up the engine, backed out of the driveway and with a look of contrived disgust she censured Larry openly "How is it that you can beg and plead for these lovely girls to marry you and you won't even sit by them?" Rather than to make for more contention, he responded "I can't thank you enough for that marvelous saber. How did you find one like that on short notice?" and from the rear seat one the twins said "She's had it for a long time!" Momma's face got red and she said nothing. Larry raised his eyebrows, put on one of those gaping accusatory smiles and turned to sorta face her as she was driving. She turned aside, pushed him away and said "Get away. I can't see the road."

When they got to the photographer's studio, Momma took over the whole show. The photographer had his standard way to seat the subjects, adjust the lights, primp the poses, and all that, but Momma had to have each girl's hair just faultless, the dress just right, the poses just perfect. She grabbed Larry by the shoulder, by the arm, shoving him this way and that, twisting his head, placing his hand just right on the saber handle, having him stand at attention with this regal posture and with that noble stance, with his hat on and with it stowed beneath his arm. White gloves on, then white gloves off. She had him pose alone for a few shots and with each girl in various poses.

What should have taken no more than an hour took about three hours. But Momma seemed so pleased when all was completed. On the way home she simply could not contain herself, and in keeping with the spirit of armistice she said "Larry, I am so proud of you. You are so handsome in your officer's dress uniform, and I had no idea that you had so many of those service ribbons almost covering your entire chest. With these pictures my grandchildren will see that their father was a great American hero!" Feeling brave, Larry asked "Does this mean that you forgive me?" She glanced his way and glowered "Absolutely not!"

As one might expect, with the romance(s) moving rapidly toward the first wedding, that's the prime topic of every dinner conversation at the Remington house. Larry was there with his twins at every opportunity, and even though Momma Remington kept up her relentless onslaught pounding him with insults and threats, he managed to smile through it all. When the calls started coming in from the invitees that received by mail their invitations containing a copy of the portrait of the happy couple, with all her friends gushing and pouring out accolades of admiration for that handsome young US Marine officer in that snappy uniform, and with that flashy saber alongside, Momma's diatribes seemed to wane in frequency and were becoming little digs and rude grunts. Momma would sometimes ask Larry what he would like for dinner tonight.

Then as Teri's wedding was near, she continued to spin and spin in joyous anticipation of her day. As you might expect, Toni was about out of control in a flood of vicarious thrill in sharing all the visits to the Wedding Gown place, choosing the proper veil, the best white shoes, the bouquet of flowers, the cosmetic details, all the refinements of ceremony, and whatever else. They brought sister Debbie in early to the game, and she put in her two cents worth on everything. In the evenings after a day of preparation with Debbie, in her absence the rest of the family would giggle and chuckle to hear what tasteless things Debbie had to suggest. Debbie and Toni were the only two bridesmaids participating in the ceremony. The two bridesmaid's gowns were to be just alike, and the accessories were to be matching just the same between them. Debbie's hair was about three inches shorter, but no matter, because Debbie's height was about four inches shorter. The Friday morning before Teri's Saturday wedding, Momma and the twins cornered Debbie and literally stripped her of all her bangles and beads, forbidding her to wear any of that junk at the wedding and she reluctantly agreed to let the wedding planners dictate the clothing and the manner in which it is to be worn, and to allow the recruited cosmetologist to design her eyes and eyebrows to match up with the decorum of the event. As you might expect, Debbie's husband was not welcome. But, then, Debbie had not actually seen him for many months, anyway. They got her all scrubbed up and dressed in a nice pantsuit by Friday noon, and she really looked great.

On that Friday afternoon before Teri's wedding the entire Cole family arrived. The only ones missing were Rick's two boys, and they had some sort of forgivable previous commitment that they couldn't get out of on short notice. Larry's folks stayed in his new room at the Remington residence, Charley and his family stayed in Debbie's old bedroom. Rick slept on the couch, and Larry was still in the officers' quarters on the base at MCAS El Toro.

There was a little wedding practice that Friday night, and this was the first time that Rick ever saw Debbie. This trip was the first time Charley and his family had ever been in California. After the wedding planner lady had finished with all her yelling and shoving people around, the wedding party went out for dinner. Another funny thing happened that nobody seemed to immediately notice: The first time that Debbie laid eyes on Rick Cole, she never again smoked any cigarettes, and shunned tobacco in any form. She had a half-empty pack of cigarettes in her purse, and when nobody was watching she dumped it in a convenient trash can.

After they had stripped Debbie of all her jewelry, she didn't even have left anything that looked like an engagement ring or wedding band. Rick showed more than a little interest, until someone mentioned that Debbie was married, and then he wondered why Debbie's husband had not shown up. Larry dismissed the inquiry, saying that it's a long story. This revelation was enough to stop Rick's serious flirtations, but by that time Debbie was warming to being treated like a treasure for the first time in years. She quietly asked Larry if his brother Rick was married, and Larry replied "No. He's a three-time loser and has sworn that he will never ever become involved with another woman." Well, there's nothing wrong with being civil and cordial with others, and when Rick was seated next to Debbie at the restaurant they amused one another famously with all the silly small talk. Toni noticed something about this small talk: Not once did Debbie say or do anything consistent with her temporarily abandoned lifestyle. Her conversation now tended to reflect standards of that little evangelical church she has been attending down in San Clemente.

On Teri's wedding day Larry showed up early at the Remington ranch, but he was told by a gruff mother-in-law-to-be that the groom should not see the bride at all before the ceremony on the wedding day, and to leave before he ruined everything. Larry was wearing his full blast of Marine officer's uniform, sorta lookin' like he was gonna lead the parade on New Year's Day. So Rick got all showered and shaved, and put on his black tuxedo rented from the local shop, and went with Larry into Santa Ana to have breakfast. Larry stowed his saber in the trunk of the car, lest he be arrested for openly carrying a weapon around. The wedding was scheduled for 2:00 that Saturday afternoon, and there was a lotta time to kill. Anyone passing by their restaurant booth must have been amused by the sight of The Grand Marshall and the Master of Ceremonies seated there playing with waffles and drinking massive amounts of coffee.

Meanwhile, back at the ranch, Momma Remington was obviously having the time of her life with this wedding idea, and everyone there just sat back and watched the show. That lady was bursting with joy as she primped and preened, tidied and groomed, painted and polished all three of her beautiful girls. Her eyes glistened; her face was shining with ecstasy and showed a smiling serenity. It was as though she had been planning this show all her life. Shirley Cole watched and glowed to see the preparation merriments.

As the family left the Remington place to travel the miles to the Catholic Church in Santa Ana, the car bearing Toni and Debbie pulled out just in front of the bride's carriage. The glowing bride was the last to leave, and her magnificent gown was so wide that she took up most of the rear seat by herself. As she settled in, clutching her bouquet, she said that she would feel so much more comfortable if Toni were with her. Knowing that this particular bride has a history of falling apart under stress, Dad Remington started blinking the headlights and honking the horn to stop that car in front of him. They told Toni to get back there and scrunch up in that rear seat with your sister. It's not all that far to the church.

There were about three hundred guests in attendance at Teri's wedding, and it was a grand affair. The beautiful bridal gown was magnificent, the bride was so beautiful, the bridesmaids so lovely, and everything went off so perfectly.

It was such a marvelous scene as she came down the aisle on the arm of her handsome father. When the father gave away the bride to the good-looking groom, Dad first kissed his little girl on the cheek, turned to present her hand to the waiting groom, and as he did so he winked at him and whispered "She's all yours!" The organist played so well, the priest said all the right things. The extremely handsome groom was so impressive in his officer's uniform with all the ribbons decorating his chest, his saber at his side, his best man and groomsman attired in those formal black tuxedo costumes. When the priest pronounced them man and wife someone in the audience yelled out "yaaay!" and a giggle rippled across the field of happy onlookers. The groom had a huge smile on his face as he pulled aside the veil to view his bride, and she was beaming so. He abandoned convention at this moment, kissed the bride on the forehead, then chucked her under the chin and said aloud for the entire congregation to easily hear "I love you so much, I just love you so much." And then he kissed her on the nose and finally on the lips. With this unique part of the ceremony finished, the bride grabbed him about the waist and gave him a huge hug, then stepped back, looked him in the eye and with her right index finger poked him in the shoulder saying out loud "I love you so much, just wait 'til I get you home!" and with that the audience broke into laughter and loud applause. The happy couple turned to bow to the congregation, and started to slowly saunter down the aisle as the organ played the recessional, but by the time they neared the exit door Teri was victoriously waving her bouquet in the air and almost skipping.

The reception was a catered affair. The cake was huge, and the cake cutting became quite a ceremony as they used the Mameluke saber to do the slicing. The newlyweds got a lot of wedding gifts. There was a five-piece orchestra at the end of a small dancing platform, and the bride danced with her father. The groom danced with his new mother-in-law and when he thought everybody was watching he leaned over and whispered something in her ear that caused her to giggle and roll her eyes. The groom danced with both of the bridesmaids, and as he was prancing about with Toni he whispered something that made her cackle out loud, and Toni seldom cackled out loud. Rick Cole and Debbie danced together almost every time the orchestra started up, and that was noticed by more than one of the observers. Stewart Remington seemed to enjoy spinning around with his wife, and they were the best waltzers on the floor. The reception lasted into the evening, but one by one the revelers drifted away. The three tuxedo-clad photographers captured everything on stills and video. The bride and groom drove away in the new Buick that the folks gave them for their wedding present.

Late that evening, the families were gathered at the Remington place, including Rick Cole and sisters Debbie and Toni. Charley Cole and his wife had put their kids to bed in Debbie's room, and everyone was sitting about the living room with all their shoes off of aching feet, ties loosened and jackets tossed aside, drinking coffee and happily reviewing all the really pleasant features that were part of the day's festivities. About midnight all were surprised to see the bride and groom coming through the front door. Somebody was bold enough to ask why they had not embarked on their Honeymoon, and Larry the groom said "Well, let's see who is here now. It looks like everyone here knows that there is another wedding scheduled for two weeks from now, and we just didn't feel right to be off on a Honeymoon trip that didn't have all its parts. This explanation should be enough to tell how we feel, and if not then you are at liberty to fill in the vacant spots as you please. Where's my coffee?" Teri and Toni cheerily pranced down the hall to change clothes, and returned in more comfortable garments to join in with all the family in happy merriment that lasted until about 3:00 AM. The sunrise found Larry still in his uniform collapsed on the couch with his feet up on the coffee table, fast asleep with his bride on one shoulder and her sister on the other. The first one to pass this scene was Momma Remington, and she quietly sat down in an overstuffed chair opposite the slumbering trio for about half an hour, and just watched them sleep. She jumped up, disappeared down the hall, then returned with her camera in hand, tip-toed over to stand in front of that coffee table and took a snapshot of the three of them sleeping there together. She sat down again, and got up to go into the kitchen only when someone else came passing by.

On the Following Tuesday afternoon, Teri went to the DMV and had her Driver's License name changed to 'Ximena Carillo Cole', as the Mexican lawyer had suggested. Then she took her marriage documents and her birth certificate from Mexico and had her Social Security Card changed to show her name as 'Ximena Carillo Cole', likewise her library card and her insurance papers. Larry took Teri to the Naval Dependents ID office in San Diego, along with her birth certificate and picture ID, the marriage license and whatever, and got her the Navy picture ID Dependents card issued to 'Ximena Carillo Cole'.

CHAPTER 19

MEXICAN MUSIC

On Sunday following the wedding, the household awakened mid-morning and commenced to stir about, as the extremely good mood boiling over from the previous day's celebration continued. Momma Remington and her buddy Shirley Cole were tossing the pots and pans around in the kitchen, the men were drinking coffee and gossiping like some Old Ladies' Garden Club, and the twins were humming happily as they set the table and puttered about at each place setting. Our hero the newlywed groom got all freshened up, put on his casual wear, and strolled into the middle of the activities. It was obvious that he was in great spirits. He grabbed the first one of his twins to pass by and she spanked his hand with a spatula, saying "Mr. Cole! Shame on you! You're a married man!" He did a quick check on the earlobes and said "Oh! It's you again. Did I mention how much I love you?"

As everyone was seated around the table for brunch, and considering that the twins had joined Larry to zonk out on the couch after the late night socializing, Toni piped up to say "When I woke up this morning I caught my fiancé sleeping with some other woman!" At least within the family it seemed that the unusual connubial bliss designs were already in place and accepted without further question, allowing for humorous reflections among them. What else would you recommend?

It was already too late to go to church this morning and too early to take the travelers to the airport for their late afternoon flights to the Midwest, so everyone sat around and drank coffee or lemonade, and talked about anything and everything. Eventually the men's conversation got around to flying jet propulsion aircraft, and Larry gave everyone a nice lecture on take-off and landing from the deck of a US Navy carrier, and that conversation got around to Larry's plans for his future military career, and he said that because of the then current political tides he had no immediate long term plans, adding that he hoped any day now to hear that he has been promoted to Captain. Charley's wife was the one to ask if Larry's war wounds were still bothering him, and whether those things were a current consideration. This was a topic that Larry had carefully avoided talking about in front of the twins, and he sorta glossed over it without really giving a direct answer. Unfortunately, both the twins heard the question and the nonresponsive answer. Later that evening, after everyone else had retired for the night, they renewed the inquiry, and peppered him with cross-examination. This was the first time they heard that Larry was still undergoing neurological evaluation for the damages to his spine. The injuries didn't seem to bother him at all in his exercise or ordinary physical navigation, and there was no pain. The problem that the military was so concerned with was his reaction time in the lower limbs, and that discussion was very important when it involves the control of a military aircraft in battle conditions where the mission and other human lives were dependent on the best maneuvering possible.

About mid-afternoon on this Sunday, Larry and the twins used the Chrysler van to haul Mom and Dad Cole out to LAX. Debbie volunteered to take Rick to LAX for an evening flight to Illinois. Charley and his wife wanted to stay over a few days and see Disneyland on Monday, Sea World on Tuesday, and the San Diego Zoo on Wednesday. Stewart Remington provided them with a new Chevrolet loaner car for travels. On Thursday morning the twins chauffeured them to LAX for their noon-time departure leaving for Arkansas.

Sunday late evening, the girls disappeared into their bathroom to prepare for sleepy-time, and Larry went to his new quarters to do the same. The twins were not willing to abandon discussion of the possibility that Larry might once again be flying in a war zone, and they agreed that everyone concerned would be better off if Larry were to have a career change that maybe put him in a car dealership zone. Those discussions were not yet so urgent as to handle the current pressing matter of their overnight sleeping zone. It would be insensitive and indiscreet for Toni to impose on her sister's temporarily exclusive prerogatives, and it would seem improper and imprudent for Teri to abandon poor Larry to snooze alone this evening. The two of them tiptoed quietly across the hall and tapped softly on Momma's bedroom door, and when she opened the door to greet her progeny, they told of the quandary and asked her advice. Her advice was to resolve the matter the best way they could, and let her know in the morning how it got settled. The girls tiptoed down the hall and into the front room, and there found Larry in his pajamas, sprawled on the couch with his feet shod in house shoes and propped up on the coffee table again. When he heard them whispering, he told them to come join him and get rested up for the coming day. There they were in the early morning, the newlywed husband with his bride cuddled up to him on the right side and her sister snuggled up on the other side. Sometime during the night someone had put a blanket over them.

That next morning the twins were still caught in that single track discussion over and over again of the wedding coming up in Mexico in less than two weeks. These two young ladies spoke Spanish very well, and on their many visits to that exotic place when they were younger oriented them to much of the culture and customs. However, they had very little knowledge of the wedding ceremony practices in that place. They were assured by the wedding planner in Santa Ana that there was no substantial difference when compared with the US. But Momma Remington brought up the question of whether or not Toni would want the ceremony in whole or in part to be in Spanish. One little problem: Larry had but one junior high semester in Spanish class, most of which he had completely forgotten in the past ten years, and could not yet speak Spanish well. But he knew how to say 'si' and that should be about all he needs to know. Fortunately, the priest in Mexico City was a member of the Carillo family and a graduate of the University of Notre Dame in Indiana, and could speak perfect English.

For some undisclosed reason Momma Remington delayed sending out the Spanish language wedding invitations to the families in Mexico. She did send the printed material and the portrait insert of Larry and Toni down in advance so that they could be mailed from Mexico City, including the very few that were sent to addresses in the US, mostly for Larry's family. In any event, those invitations went out to all the Carillo clan and such other guests as that family held dear, and in number those were about three times as many as were sent for the Santa Ana nuptials. Shimi Remington's cousin by name of 'Bibi' was handling all the wedding details in Mexico City, and with one phone call to her this Monday morning those summonses were in the mail.

Originally, Larry had scheduled this whole week off duty, but with the changes in Honeymoon plans he returned to base and was able to trade some time with a couple of other pilots, and just added the free days to his trip to Mexico in another couple of weeks. He left all the wedding planning up to the twins and their Mom, and in turn they entrusted most of the details to the Carillo family in Mexico. The wedding dress was no problem, since they decided to use the same bridal gown and bridesmaids costumes used in Santa Ana. The groom would wear the same frocks and saber worn in the previous ceremony, and everything would be the same except for the word 'si' substituted for the words 'I do'. Well, not exactly.

Both Teri and Toni resumed their work at their dealerships on Tuesday, to put in some time before they were to leave for Mexico, but there were the handy telephones on their desks in case they might need to make emergency calls to discuss details and refinements in the plans for the upcoming wedding of Toni. They kept those phone lines hot for the next ten days and chatted together and with their Mom every evening over that time. In turn, Momma Remington was on the phone almost constantly talking to her cousin Bibi, because cousin Bibi was an expert on Mexican weddings and festivities, and having her do all the preparations would guarantee a successful matrimonial event. They enlisted her to make so many decisions on the nuptials, the church, the receptions, the trappings of a grand Catholic Church wedding in Mexico City. With all the thoughts and talks exchanged, it would seem that all questions relating to the matter of Toni's wedding were thoroughly flogged.

Debbie went back to work at the Santa Ana dealership on Monday morning, looking very civilized without her regular pile of jewelry and face paint, wearing a nice pantsuit and brand-new sandals of current mode. So many of her fellow employees commented on her new look. Debbie beamed.

Very early Thursday morning before the Saturday wedding of Toni, the Cole family folks came in again from Illinois and Missouri, Arkansas and elsewhere, and the whole band of happy celebrants flew down together to Mexico City that Thursday noon on a chartered flight before the scheduled 2:00 PM Saturday wedding at one of the huge Catholic cathedrals in the Capitol City. Debbie came to fly down with them on that southbound flight, and you can bet that she showed up without the garish jewelry and face grease, and her garments were new and very conventional. Debbie really looked great. She somehow managed to finagle a seat on the plane right next to Rick Cole, and they giggled and twitched like silly teenagers all the way down south.

The Cole family was overwhelmed to see the reception that greeted them at the airport. There were four black limousines parked on the street awaiting their arrival, with a dozen or more motorcycle policemen to escort them to the place where they would stay, and that place was the swankiest hotel in the entire city. When they arrived at the hotel they were greeted at the curb by a dozen of the hotel staff in their servants' costumes, who grabbed the luggage and carried it in through a separate entrance. The Cole contingent marched into the lobby accompanied by the hotel manager, bypassed the registration desk and went directly to the elevators and on to their assigned suites. On arrival at their suites of rooms they were again greeted by two maids and two male attendants that were engaged to see to their every need. That evening they dined together with others of the Carillo family in a fairly large dining area set apart from the main dining room, and there were at least a dozen servants in marvelous formal attire that did everything imaginable to attend to their dining pleasure. About twenty of the Carillo family joined them there, and all were supremely genteel in manner and dress. As a courtesy to their guests, most all the Carillo's spoke English even among themselves and in Spanish to the servants. With assigned seating, wouldn't you know that Debbie somehow wangled a seat next to Rick Cole? At each place setting there was a glass of champagne and for those that chose to imbibe the servants kept the glasses full. After the dining, the host of the Carillo family stood to his feet, greeted the guests in flawless English and offered a toast to the betrothed couple. Well, you can imagine how this startled the teetotalers of the Cole clan, particularly Shirley Cole, but her loving son Rick just smiled and whispered "Go ahead Mom, take a sip, it won't get you pickled with just a little sip, and nobody will ever know." Well, everyone joyfully joined in the toast, actually for several rounds of toasting, and Mom Cole did not get tipsy. However, her husband told most of her friends around Springfield how Shirley Cole got plastered in Mexico, and was so schnockered she danced on the tables.

On Friday morning, after elaborate breakfasts served in their rooms, the black limousines showed up again to haul the Cole contingent around Mexico City on guided tours that lasted well into the afternoon. Debbie had seen it all before but she wanted to see it all again. Then they all took the required siesta, to rest up a while before those limousines again appeared to take them to one of the Carillo family homes south of town, for another grand dinner occasion. They arrived at a walled site with a huge motor driven double gate leading to a long paved driveway wide enough for cars to pass comfortably, and that long driveway took them to the massive front doors of a huge residence that looked more like it could be the Pope's palace in the Vatican. The massive green lawn took up many acres of ground around the buildings, and shrubbery was limited. Trees lined the walls that looked like they must be at least ten feet high all around and very inconspicuous were a number of armed guards with attack dogs patrolling. This was apparently not the home of Mexican peasants. It was the home of the uncle of Shimi Carillo Remington, and he personally welcomed the entourage at the massive entrance with the huge vaulted ceilings. He did not appear to be poor. Once again the Carillo family made a great impression.

While the twins were in California discussing the Mexico nuptials, Larry had not the slightest inkling that the wedding of Toni Carillo Remington might be a little different in comparison to the ceremonial in Santa Ana. Very different. Momma Remington had left it up to her family in Mexico to tend to details of Toni's wedding, and they did. They really did.

After that magnificent meal and all the toasting, there appeared a little old Mexican wedding planner lady to orient the wedding party on all the details they could expect at the nuptial celebration, and they really weren't vastly different from what they had dealt with two weeks ago, except for a couple of unique features. The first of these unusual particulars was the 'Padrinos de Arras' part of the ceremony in which there is provided a small box containing 13 coins, representing Christ and twelve disciples. The box and coins are blessed by the priest and handed to the groom, who in turn pours the coins into the hands of his bride to demonstrate his commitment to care for and support the bride, and by accepting those coins she is making her open commitment to care for him throughout their lives. The second feature was another ritual that can become part of the Mexican style wedding, in which there is a cord or jewel-encrusted rope, or as in this case simply an extra-long rosary, that they call the 'Lasso', which is ceremoniously placed about the necks of the bride and groom in figure-8 fashion as they exchange vows, representing union and protection in the marriage. For this wedding of Toni there was also a great difference in the size of the church and the number of guests in attendance. These Mexicans really do love romance and festive wedding revelries.

When the Patriarch of the Carillo clan sends an invitation it is more like a summons issuing from the Supreme Court, and though receiving that invitation is a great honor, and the right to attend is such a great privilege, the guys at the door check off the names, and anyone that is missing is remembered. They sent out a lot of invitations, and a whole lot of people showed up. The pile of gifts from folks they never even heard of was enough to fill the cargo hold of a passenger jet, and these were unusual and expensive gifts, beautiful gifts, very impressive gifts.

The pampering persons that prepared the bride were alerted in advance that this particular bride is very sentimental and prone to tears, so that heavy cosmetics would probably not be wise on her or her attendants. But these folks that do all the bride and bridesmaids polish are real professionals. All three of these Remington girls looked perfectly beautiful, and when they adroitly took over that magnificent center aisle the organist filled the sanctuary with the most dramatic and impressive music that echoed through the rafters in the utmost romantic way, and as those young ladies drifted majestically down the full length of that aisle they slowed on cue at the altar area where they met their assigned groomsman. Debbie was assigned guess who, and he gallantly extended his arm to further accompany her beyond the altars and to the place where the Maid of Honor and the one bridesmaid should stand. Charley Cole was the groomsman assigned to escort Maid of Honor Teri Cole to her place. That center aisle at this splendid cathedral was at least three times as long as the one in Santa Ana, and the vaulted ceilings seemed as though they were ten times higher, and the robed priests seemed so much more holy and probably in control of their own cathedrals somewhere in Heaven.

The bride wore the same bridal gown as Teri had worn in Santa Ana, but the bridal veil was selected by one of Shimi Remington's sisters, and that thing consisted of a jeweled crown and a flowing train of fine lace dragging behind. It was so wonderful.

The bride came slowly through the entry doors of the church sanctuary on the arm of her father, who was dressed in a tuxedo with a long grey mourning coat, very formal. They walked down that aisle as though they owned every inch of it. Toni must have been the most beautiful bride ever to grace that place, and she seemed to have an enchanting presence that charmed all that audience. Every eye was glued on her, and she surely was from then on their example of the perfect bride.

At the very first moment of her entry into that main sanctuary, Toni could see that all the way down at the end of that center aisle, way, way down there at the front of the church, standing with the best man and his groomsman opposite the waiting bridesmaid and Maid of Honor, there was this tall dark-haired gentleman dressed in that most impressive formal uniform of a commissioned officer of the United States Marine Corps, and even though she slowed to smile at folks of the congregation along the way as she kept pace with the leisurely and respectful rhythm of the Mexican style bridal entry march, she had her eyes essentially fixed on that handsome guy in that elaborate military uniform, and the closer she came to the altar space, the more she could not control her happy smile. As father and bride arrived at the holy altar area, the uniformed groom strode smartly over to where they were standing, and the commandingly attired father delivered the hand of that perfectly beautiful bride to that gentleman with the saber at his side, and with a broad smile saying aloud in Spanish *"Ella es tuyo ahora!"*, which in Spanish simply means "She's yours now!" whereupon the young officer extended his arm to escort the bride nearer to where the priest was standing so ceremonial in his holy robes, so solemn and serious. The priest had a young assistant also garbed in impressive robes and his job was to turn the pages of a large book that looked a lot like a big Bible. The priest looked familiar. He looked down at the pages of that book, then turned soberly and bent over and much nearer to Toni and whispered in English "Ain't this fun?"

This must have been the best wedding ever in that place. Including the ritual with the coins and the Lasso observance, as the priest completed the ceremony, he in Spanish suggested *"usted ahora puede besar a su novia"* which means in English "You may now kiss your bride." Then the handsome young man gracefully and dexterously lifted the veil and paused for a moment in a most dramatic way, then leaned over and kissed the bride on the forehead, stood back and looked into her beautiful dark brown eyes and said loud enough that the microphone picked it up so that the whole congregation could hear *"Te amo con todo me corazón"* which translates simply to "I love you with all my heart." Well, that's all it took to get Toni to blubbering, and as the tears rolled down her cheeks she buried her face into his shoulder and kept muttering "I love you so much. I am so happy! I am so happy!" Well, Larry is no fool. Larry couldn't pass up this opportunity to deliver some romantic entertainment to these sentimental Mexicans, and Larry knows that timing is everything. While his sobbing bride is proclaiming her love and happiness, Larry withdraws a small handkerchief from his pocket, and looks out over the smiling faces in the crowd, and wobbles his eyebrows as he nods his head, then takes the hanky and dabs away the tears of his bride. The congregation murmurs approval. Then that bridegroom notices that the

Maid of Honor has been somehow influenced to start her tears flowing. The bridegroom once again looks out over the crowd to seek their approval, then leans way over and dabs away the tears of that lovely Maid of Honor, then looks at the congregation and smiles, and there is at first a little applause and then a whole lot of applause as Larry dramatically replaces the hanky, then holds the bride's face cupped in his hands, leans over to kiss her on the nose, then to kiss away the tears, then a dramatic little kiss on her lips. The bride again buries her face in his shoulder and mutters *"Estoy tan feliz! Estoy tan feliz!"* meaning "I am so happy! I am so happy!" This caused the priest to giggle and try to suppress the snickering.

The bride and groom turned to salute the congregation, stood there for a moment as the audience again applauded, and the happy couple walked merrily down that aisle and through those big doors, followed triumphantly by the sniffling sentimental Maid of Honor and her new brother in law, and bridesmaid Debbie on the arm of Rick Cole.

There were more than five hundred guests at the great reception at one of the huge hotels just down the street, numerous toasts offered in English and in Spanish that the bride had to translate for her new husband, and everyone had a great time. The music was played by a Mariachi band, the dancing was traditional Mexican, and those clumsy Yanquis were not expected to keep up with any of it. The menu consisted of perfectly done steak and trimmings, and a lot of other things that only a Mexican could appreciate. There was beer and champagne on every table, plenty of each.

Among the guests was the President of Mexico, the Governors of two neighboring states, numerous public officials and a whole lot of rich guys and their marvelously appointed ladies. One would gather that the Carillo family was popular in Southern Mexico.

Debbie mostly stood around with her hand hanging on the elbow crook of the arm of the three-time loser, and finally she leaned over, pulled him by the ear down to where she could whisper "I feel so stupid. I am so dumb. I could have had all this, but I ran off to the cheapest wedding chapel in Las Vegas and married a thug." This was the first word from Debbie that even remotely suggested that she might not have a happy marriage. As Rick bent down to hear the whispered remarks of the relatively short-statured Debbie, he noticed up close the holes punched around the margins of her ear, and he was audacious enough to ask what caused those unusual scars. She paused as she looked up at him wistfully and said "Please don't ask. I promise I'll go somewhere and get that stuff removed so that nobody will notice."

The Mexicans use almost any excuse to have parties, and they celebrated Toni's wedding into the night. Even though the pace of Mexican music doesn't fit well with the dances that Larry and the twins were better able to perform, they did their best. Brother Rick couldn't dance well at all, but Debbie conscripted him to her tutelage and they managed to entertain themselves apart from the rest of the world. Mom and Dad Remington took notice of the attention showered on Debbie by the three-time-loser, and even more were pleased that she seemed to be chasing him. Whatever it takes to get rid of that thug. Debbie neglected to tell her parents that she had not seen hide nor hair of Mr. Verdugo for many months. Not even a phone call. The only way she could tell that he was still alive was by his frequent use of her credit card, on which she had to make payments, and the charges on that card at least told of his itinerary for cheap motels and gas charges in Arizona and Texas, and fortunately the card finally expired three months after he left. The last time she saw him she again protested his departure and again he gave her a black eye.

Then came the Newlyweds Cole Honeymoon.

CHAPTER 20

HONEYMOON

Anyone in their right mind could tell you that this outrageous marital arrangement that Larry Cole and the Remington twins got involved in is really stupid. There is no place in civilized Christian society that plural marriage is sanctioned, neither by law nor by social convention. Foolish doctrinal cavillation still leaves a residue of vapid confusion. Proponents of multi-spouse unions seem to be suffering from some sort of carnal perversion syndrome. How can it be possible that honorable people could imagine any circumstances to justify the practice, not even to provide security and identity to innocent children? Some have suggested that there should be assembled another convocation of enlightened clerics to issue their decree condemning such a lifestyle, and to confirm that all violators are bound for hell and a sinner's grave. Furthermore, those foolish people that engage in such practice should be forbidden from going on Honeymoons.

Well, be that as it may, Larry and his brides after careful consideration and confronted with the cruel harsh facts of life and gestational duration chose to take their chances. In their case it required a great confidence in Mexican lawyers and their perceptions of the frailty of American customs and justice. So, you know the story, and when you put all the pieces together you can imagine what their Honeymoon must have been like. Well, you don't really have to waste a lot of your time imagining all of it, because we actually know some few things.

Now for you guys that think having a couple of beautiful sisters to share at your leisure would really satisfy the lusts of the ordinary man, please consider that these girls were actually quite modest and virtuous, idealistic and of pristine Christian character, and seemed to radiate a precious innocence 'round about. They were bright, alert, intelligent, mature, confident and generally composed. Their plight of impending parturition was brought about by just a tiny, itty-bitty error in judgment imposed by spontaneous emotional forces beyond control. Compromise? It could happen to anybody. But these resulting circumstances should alert the practicing Christian to the pitfalls of compromise.

First of all is the question of whether these people should ever again show their guilty faces in public.

Then consider that children born of this crazy union will be exposed to social distortions and identity crisis. For instance comes the question: are you my brother or my cousin?

We must launch the rest of the story now with the question of just what sort of Honeymoon could one have when hauling about two remarkably beautiful young ladies that look exactly alike, both wearing very impressive diamond rings, and each of which is clinging to the arm of the man she loves. You know that two beauties like this will draw attention. Where would you take them for a Honeymoon? Best way to choose a place is to just ask them where they would want to go. It's good that you asked, because they had already figured it out: They had twelve days military leave to play with, allowing three days for travel, they had some nine days that they could split about four days in the Kingdom of Tonga and four days in Fiji, on those beautiful islands somewhere in the South Pacific. If you've never been to either of these exotic tropical paradise places, you really should have such a trip planned somewhere in the vaults of your mind. Start now to collect pop cans and bottles to get your refunds or take stuff in for recycling. Put away in hiding all the pennies and dimes.

Larry and his brides flew directly out of the Benito Juàrez Mexico City International Airport. There was an amusing family contingent to see them off. Stewart Remington was obviously much delighted and seemed unable to stop smiling. Momma Remington was so touched she couldn't stop crying and dabbing at her eyes, and boo-hooed incessantly as she hugged her two little newlywed daughters. She would have preferred to postpone the departure for a while, but there's no telling how long it would take to humor her for that while. Charley Cole and his wife had left their kids with relatives and felt sorta footloose about this whole thing, and Charley kept muttering something like "Wow! They don't do it like this in Arkansas". Mom and Dad Cole had wholly abandoned any negative feelings about the multiple bride stuff, and got to where they felt that their little baby boy probably could never be happy without the precious pair. Rick and Debbie were giggly about the entire wedding celebration and the whole unusual story that brought it all about. This married lady and the three-time-loser seemed oblivious to all the departure business as they amused one another with senseless prattle. There was no hand holding, no warm embrace, no little flirtation kisses, and they never even touched each other after they left the dance floor at the reception. They did not exchange spicy conversation or frisky remarks. However their giggle sharing might have appeared to others, everything was very respectful. Rick's Mom several times mentioned that she hadn't seen this son so happy for several years, but she lamented that he shouldn't be publicly flirting with a married woman. Larry's Dad was obviously amused by everything that had happened and seemed yet to be happening right before his very eyes, and was looking forward to telling all his wife's pals in Missouri about how Shirley got tanked-up in Mexico.

Larry Cole had traveled by commercial jetliner on several occasions and was accustomed to their relative size. The twins had many times traveled Aeronaves de Mexico on smaller planes. But now they are traveling over the ocean on a huge jet airliner. That's like comparing a Crosley to a fully loaded Tractor Trailer rig.

First destination: The Kingdom of Tonga. When Larry and his twins finally got settled into their seats, with him in the middle spot and a pretty girl hugging each of his arms and snuggling up with heads on each shoulder so affectionately, he looked to be very contented. While the plane was still parked at the loading ramp and the stewardess was closing the entry door, Toni reached into her carry-on purse and pulled out that extra-long string of rosary beads that was part of her wedding ceremony, and she leaned over to where Teri was seated near the window and placed one end of that rosary lasso around Teri's neck, then in a figure-8 she looped that triple-length garland about the neck of Larry the bridegroom person, then in another figure-8 she placed it about her own neck, and with a huge smile of contentment she fell back into her seat and closed her eyes A Mexican passing by to see this sentimental ritual would better understand the meaning, but Yanqui folks would just smile in ignorance.

As the plane taxied down the runway, it finally occurred to Larry the bridegroom person that he was a truly married man, and that these creatures clinging to him were his to keep. Feeling the plane accelerate he could sense the wheels leave the ground, surging forward into the clouds Larry sorta felt that this maneuver is symbolic of the future they would face together: up in the clouds. The whole wedding day adventure was so busy, busy, busy that the twins were justifiably exhausted, and when they turned off the cabin lights the soft vibration of the plane and the humming of those great jet engines lulled the ladies to sleep.

On the giant passenger jets, especially on flights over the ocean with all the many exotic Pacific Island destinations for the countless tourists and vacationers, it's quite a circus to observe all the people from distant lands with foreign languages and manners. In the quiet hours of such a trip, it can be a great source of amusement to simply watch your fellow passengers as they seem to perceive of themselves in their own little worlds. Some of them have the most outrageous wardrobes. While the twins were happily snoozing and lost in their dreams, Larry tried to get a glimpse of a few of these travelers, but the interior lights were dimmed and in that subdued light one couldn't really see clearly to distinguish features of those voyagers. But with the dawn those interior lights were turned on and with all the scurrying about in the aisles Larry could see better the yawning people and the drowsy facial expressions He spotted a very large gentleman tightly seated across the aisle, wearing extremely thick-lensed horn-rimmed glasses and a bushy moustache, who turned out to be a Turkish merchant on a business trip to the South Pacific to buy up some of the islanders' woven mats and such. He was dressed in tennis shorts that were tight about his thighs, displaying long black hairs on his milk-white heavy legs, and wearing white tennis shoes without laces. He kept admiring Larry's ladies out the corner of his eye, saying nothing. Larry noticed an elderly blind couple in the seats behind him, with a Chinese servant that helped them move about. These old folks were speaking German and their servant was incessantly rattling in what sounded like Mandarin Chinese. A group of about a half-dozen young people was speaking in Russian or Ukrainian, and all were wearing heavy coats. They seemed to be very happy and enjoying one another's company. Some Americans in tee-shirts were in another group, all wearing sunglasses and boisterously laughing at everything, playfully examining the breakfast fare being delivered by the stewardess. They seemed oblivious to presence of other passengers.

When the twins awakened the early morning sunlight filled the cabin as the Stewardesses were serving breakfast. Traffic back and forth to the lavatories was congested, and both girls thought they could go together into the tiny cubicle, but they found the accommodations to be too cramped, and decided that it would be OK to brush their hair and put on makeup while settled in at their assigned seats, so they vacated the restroom. Meanwhile, Larry had gone to freshen up at one of the washrooms aft, and when the girls got back to their seats they found the aisle blocked by the fairly large body of the Turkish gentleman and he seemed to be involved in some sort of disagreement with a lady scolding him in French as he seemed to be responding in Turkish or some other language not easily recognizable. The passengers seated around the area where the squabble was taking place were all greatly amused. The stewardess tried to intercede but apparently couldn't understand either one of them. After a few parting insults the lady shook her fist in the face of the Turk and left to make her way on down the aisle. Just a couple of minutes later the noises coming from further down on that aisle suggested that the French lady had chosen one of the toilets and was having difficulty convincing the occupant to vacate those premises, loudly screaming again in French, which the rest of the passengers found even more entertaining. Now, with Teri's past history of falling apart anytime hostilities erupt, you'd think that she would have had an episode at this time. Well, she did. But this was a giggling episode between these two young brides. You know, it happens to all of us at one time or another. Teri started giggling, then Toni started snickering, and they couldn't even stop long enough to draw a complete breath. Larry returns about this time and thinks the chuckling has something to do with breakfast or whatever. All this happens on the plane before they even land at Fua'amotu Tonga International Airport.

When Larry and his brides arrive in Tonga, it is a completely foreign tropical paradise. One of the good reasons to visit Tonga is the fact that they speak English there, in addition to their national Tongan Polynesian language. The Tongans are among the most hospitable folks in all the South Pacific. It is politically a monarchy, and there is a great respect for the King. Also, Tongan law strictly forbids importation of illicit drugs.

Larry did not get in on the entire squabble on the airplane, so he did not recognize all of the participants. In retrieving the luggage, he told the twins to watch for their suitcases on the other side of the baggage carousel, and he stood waiting to catch anything that they might miss. Unfortunately, he chose to stand right next to the French lady that seemed to have a penchant for confrontations. There was quite a crush of anxious passengers trying to drag their own luggage off the carousel, and the French lady got into a shouting match with a Tongan woman there in the crowd. The uniformed customs officers heard the noise and came to investigate. They escorted the belligerent French lady to the baggage examiners bench, and apparently those examiners found some sort of contraband wrapped in red and blue cellophane. While that Tongan woman was cheerfully looking on those uniformed officers hastily ushered the French lady away through the crowd and into another room.

The hotel where the Newlywed trio had their reservations was a few miles away, and they boarded a little taxi van along with a couple of other tourists to travel that short distance. These other people were British who had been to Tonga previously, and urged the Cole's to invest their time wisely to see it all. They had traveled no more than a few blocks when another van came through a blind intersection and hit the van in front of them broadside, but neither vehicle was moving very fast, so there was no harm to the passengers in either carriage. The passengers in one of those other vans were six revelers from Saudi-Arabia. Now, if you are acquainted with the customs of Saudi-Arabia you must know that drinking alcoholic beverages is disdained by Moslem custom there. However, these disobedient sheiks were on a holiday in a foreign place, and had tanked up on local booze and a lotta import stuff at their hotel, and they were on their way down to the beach to bask in the noonday sun. They had a large piece of luggage filled with more booze to further sustain them in event of sudden drought. The sheiks stumbled out of their van and started yelling accusatory insults at everybody. The other van was full of tipsy Swedish people that accepted the challenge and began to exchange insults, shaking their fists and tossing vulgar finger signs. When these contenders started physically flogging each other, the Tongan driver of Larry's van just shook his head and drove around the affray and on to their hotel, where the Honeymooners disembarked, leaving the British tourists the further use of the lorry to get to their destination. The British people were much amused and told Larry that almost this exact same thing had happened to them the last time they were in Tonga.

Larry and his brides got registered at the front desk of their hotel; the young steward helped them with a baggage cart and showed them to their suite. The girls disappeared immediately into the bathroom. The steward left and as the door closed behind him Larry went over to stand by the open sliding door onto the balcony. When the ladies exited the washroom, he motioned for them to come over his way, and as he smiled he took each one by the hand and said "When we get home you'll be expected to give your report, and your Mom and my Mom will want you to tattle on me. So now we gotta start this marriage off right, and that means we hafta stop right now and pray".

They all three joined hands and reverently bowed their heads together to seek the face of God. Larry started by honestly thanking God for all the miracles he has showered on these newlyweds, thanking Him for providing for all of them a genuine Christian love and commitment. He covered all the bases, offering worshipful praise for the mighty works of God, for salvation in Jesus Christ and the blessing of fellowship and family accord, with a special word of thanks for forgiveness of sin by whatever description, and right away at the very beginning of this marriage to ask that the Lord appoint his most reliable angels to take charge to protect all of them, particularly the little passengers still in gestation that they be perfect in every way, handsome and beautiful, bright little genius persons nurtured in admonition of God and his Majesty. Larry was about finished with his lengthy little prayer when he heard the community of snifflers holding his hands and muttering "amen" and he looked up to see both of them with tears of sentimental sincerity rolling down their cheeks.

Larry nodded at Teri and said "Your turn" and she took off into such beautiful prayer, with passion and purpose, asking the Lord to consider that He was doing business with folks that are caught up in the frailty of the human condition and whatever might have brought them to this point in this life that they were now placing everything in His hands and imploring Him to watch over all of them and guide them in all they do. Amen.

When Teri whispered her little "amen" Larry leaned over and smiled at Toni and said "Your turn" and Toni was well prepared for this initial nuptial prayer, as she launched into a fervent recital of all the miracles stacked up for them to this point in their joint lives, and was bold enough to ask for more. She petitioned for continuing mercies that endure forever, she asked for wisdom and direction for the coming days, she was bold in her expression of gratitude for this wonderfully perfect husband and even more audacious as to thank the Lord for giving her this marvelous precious sister to share life with. She prayed for her parents and for Larry's folks, and even sought the Lord's intervention into the disappointing world of sister Debbie. She nebulously requested divine guidance for Rick Cole that he might find a perfect companion and happiness all his days. She wanted to pray for her enemies but couldn't think of any on short notice, but she did ask for justice for all politicians. Amen.

This was yet early in the day and the newlywed trio opted to go for a romantic stroll along the beach, maybe take a dip in the surf, and generally bask in the warm southern sun of Tonga. Larry had with him a conventional blue colored swimsuit which he put on quickly and was ready to roll. On the other hand, his twins had brought several different kinds of swimsuits with them, and they went into the bathroom to choose which should be the beach garb for this day. Larry sat out on the little balcony awaiting the ladies, and could hear the childish giggling coming from behind that door, and he patiently waited, wearing his cool Polaroid sun glasses and sittin' in the sun. He heard them as they came up behind him and asked "Well?" He turned and was stunned by this vision of loveliness standing before him. He had seen one at a time in beach attire, but never had seen them in matching swimsuits. In keeping with their usual modesty, these were two piece suits but not of the string Bikini style. At first he was startled, then amazed as they merrily modeled their seashore fashions, strutting back and forth and turning about with that kinda look those models assume as they show off on the runways. Well, one might notice a whole lot of things at such a time, but under these circumstances what was most apparent to Larry was that these two young brides are truly beautiful. Each one had absolutely perfect legs, and marvelous features from the tips of the toes to the top of each head. He said the first thing to pop into his head: "What are you ladies gonna look like in just a few months?" which comment caused them to explode with laughter.

The Honeymooners felt such a great freedom, the bright and shining inauguration of a happy life together, and the lovely palm-strewn beaches of Tonga just added to that sense of togetherness. The three of them strolled casually out onto the shoreline, where they could see for some distance in either direction, and arbitrarily decided to go to the left, sauntering insouciantly on the sand and in the shallow surf, Larry holding Teri's hand on his right and Toni's hand on his left. They stopped beneath an isolated palm tree and sloshed a lotta sunscreen over themselves. As Teri was sloshing on the front Toni was sloshing on Larry's backside, and she said something about her being so proud of her US Marine Pilot, and Teri said something about how proud she was that he had chosen the two of them to spend his life with. Then in the shade of that tropical palm they had a three-way hugging session that lasted a long time, and Larry kept repeating how much he loved each of them and marveled at the entire spectrum of circumstances that brought them all together in this way, and how he was so proud of each and both of them.

They hiked further along down the beach and encountered a very large Tongan gentleman, very tall and very wide, with a most engaging amiable manner, as his pathway seemed to merge with theirs. He asked them what has brought them to this place, and they boldly told him they were on their Honeymoon. He reached down to take the left hand of each of the girls and asked if they were married to each other, and they laughed and said no that they were twin sisters. Then he looked at Larry and asked if he was married to these twin girls, and Larry smiled and said "Yes. It's a long story." The big man said "You don't owe me an explanation. I was told that you would be coming, and I am so happy to find you here." As they strolled casually along, Larry asked him if he was acquainted with God, and the man answered "I am pleased to inform you that I am a personal friend of the Lord Jesus Christ, and am anointed to preach the Word." He was delighted to hear Larry and the twins quote scriptures by heart and speak so freely of salvation and serving the Lord. They came to a large mound of sand, and the tall stranger said that he had to leave them now but would like to pray with them, and he did saying "Master, we know that You are the Creator and Ruler of the Universe, and that You are the source of all good fortune, and we thank You for Salvation in Jesus Christ and your promise that we may be with Him and in Your presence throughout eternity. We thank You for these marvelous young people that through Your grace managed to find one another. We do not understand all things but we do place all things in Your hands and ask that You save us and keep us always together until that day when all things are known. Until then we ask that You guard and keep these lovely young people and may they be blessings to one another and to all they meet, and that they together and each shall receive from You many blessings. We humbly ask these things in the name of Jesus Christ, Your only begotten son. Amen." and then he turned and with a wave of his hand he disappeared beyond that mound of sand. They had neglected to ask the man his name.

That evening as they sat at dinner, Larry asked the waiter if he knew of a very tall man, a very heavy man that walked along the beach. The waiter asked "Was he wearing a yellow sash over his shoulder?" And Larry then remembered that yellow sash and said so. The waiter said "You have met the King of Tonga. He comes along to walk the beach every few weeks or so. He is a very friendly person, and loves to talk with tourists." Teri said "Oh. We didn't have our cameras. That would have been a great picture for the album!"

This happy trio of Honeymooners had an absolutely perfect stay in Tonga, with warm days exploring the towns and beaches, evenings dining at the hotel and other really nice places in the Capitol City. In the twilights they would enjoy the Polynesian music and dancers, much like that of Hawaii. They would romantically stroll the warm sands hand in hand. Larry Cole was like most men, without enough erudite expressions, lacking the eloquence that a Princeton man should surely have for any situation, and found himself repeating that simple maxim that says 'I love you!' but in his case he had to alter that wording to more tenderly say "I love you and you!"

Four or five days are never enough to see all of Tonga and explore the historic sites. But as scheduled the newlywed trio hopped on the jet airliner flight to Fiji, and toured that island. For Fiji they had no hotel reservations. They checked most of their luggage at the airport in Nadi, rented a car and drove leisurely around the entire island, first on the Queen's Highway and then on the King's Highway, and even took a ferry ride out to and spent the night on one of the offshore islands where they went scuba diving to see all the beautiful multi-colored tropical fish.

They spent the night in the Capitol City of Suva and went to the old fish market where they leisurely strolled along the docks admiring the fishing boats in the harbor. They drove on up to the northern tip of the Viti Levu Island and spent another night there, and had dinner with a young Christian couple whose roots were in India. They were good friends with the DeWitt family in San Clemente. These folks spoke Hindi and excellent English, and the husband was a supervisor of a large sugar plantation. The trio got into Nadi in time to have a leisurely lunch and get right on the Airliner flight to the LAX airport where they were met by Dad and Mom Remington. The Momma Remington was so anxious to have her girls home again, she was as nervous as could be, and scolded Larry for keeping them away for so long. Twelve days?

The girls kept their Mom up for all hours telling every tiny tidbit about their glorious Honeymoon. Well, not every tiny tidbit, you understand. Such rejoicing. It was very obvious that these two young ladies were so very happy with their marriage. Momma was thrilled to hear everything, and she didn't even try to conceal her joy.

The following week, as instructed by the Mexican lawyer, Toni went to DMV and showed them all her documents from Mexico, and had them change her Driver's License name to 'Ximena Carillo Cole' and went likewise to have her Social Security Card changed accordingly, and had a new library card issued. Toni did not obtain any military dependent's ID. Toni changed her name on her health insurance, but did not add any names.

On a Friday evening the week after return from the Honeymoon, while the whole family is resting up after dinner in the living room, as everyone was watching, the twins gave Larry his new wedding bands: Two narrow platinum bands brazed together in such a way that it appeared to be a single ring with a groove all the way around the center of it. They both slipped it on his finger and he was never known to ever remove it. He asked which one was for which bride, and they told him they'd never tell because one should not be considered any closer to his heart than the other. At the next lull in the conversation, Toni reached under the coffee table and retrieved that nicely carved box of thirteen coins that was part of her Mexico City wedding ceremony. She poured the coins out on the table in front of all those onlookers, then carefully counted out six coins that she placed in the cupped hands of Larry's wife Teri, and then Larry's wife Toni scooped up six of the coins and held them in her hand as she replaced the thirteenth coin back into the box. While all this was being done she said not a word, and the rest of the folks just watched quietly. Then both Teri and Toni looked winsomely at Larry as they both poured all their coins back into the box. Whatever symbolism there might have been in this romantic little ceremony it was not explained at that time or at any later time. The little box of coins was placed on the mantel in the library and remains there to this day.

The following Sunday, Pastor DeWitt preached a very timely sermon on the topic of honor and trust, a feature of which touched on the duty of the husband to love and care for the wife and the duty of the wife to love and respect the husband, and how they are together one flesh, concluding that a happy marriage could only be achieved when each of the parties was comfortable and secure in really knowing their mate, and how conduct that arouses apprehensions and suspicions about sincerity and honor can quickly erode and destroy a trusting relationship. Larry recalled how his older brother had troubles with his first young bride that began with her demanding respect for her "privacy", and the way she would have her own little secrets, her own friends apart from her husband and his family, her isolated vault for keeping her own private mementoes and letters, tokens and souvenirs, and she would explode into tantrums and fits of rage when anyone uninvited would invade her space. When talking on the phone she would go into another room or speak in whispers, pushing others away from any place where they might overhear her personal conversations. This attitude made for a very uncomfortable connubial environment and that marriage failed. These things were matters of discussion at the Remington house that day and Larry simply informed everyone there that he had no claims of exclusive privacy, and that anyone in that household should feel free to search his pockets anytime and rummage through his car at whim. He said that he had no objections to anyone in the household opening his mail, no matter what the return address might be on the envelope. He boldly announced that he had no secrets now nor would he keep secrets in the future, and if anyone might be curious about anything all they had to do was ask, and emphasized that they should not be embarrassed or otherwise reluctant to ask.

CHAPTER 21

DAILY GRIND

Even though the time for formal Honeymooning was abbreviated, the aviator and his twins continued with their matrimonial bliss without lull or slackening the intensity. Their marital arrangement was unusual by all conventional social standards, but these two little ladies truly loved their man, and he loved them together. They worked everything out without jealousy or bias, and everyone seemed to be very concerned for the others. In further words they did not have feelings of apprehension or insecurity; there were no doubts or other misgivings.

Happiness can come in many dimensions, and can be described in words proportional to the intensity of the sensation, all the way from simple contentment, through delight, cheerfulness and glee, and on to elation, ecstasy and euphoria. Mature persons with adult reservation can be reduced to such silly childlike expression resultant of intensity of the bliss and overwhelming joy of a moment or continuing circumstance. That's what seemed to prevail in the Remington-Cole household when the euphoric teenage brides returned from that Honeymoon in the South Pacific, and that mood continued ad infinitum. Simply stated: everyone in the household was affected by the contagion of continuing joy. It became a very happy place. However, in presence of strangers or casual acquaintances the open display of these effusive practices were somewhat curtailed. For instance: during all the time that the Remington twins were working on their assignments at the dealerships, they were very businesslike, superficially cordial, but still reserved and somewhat socially withdrawn. They stayed that way until those portraits of Larry went up on the walls in front of their work desks. Actually, Teri's working manners seemed to change on that first Monday morning after she first met Lt. Larry, and it accelerated from there. But she had to make an affirmative effort to control her effervescence when that first portrait was nailed to her wall. Then came a couple of weeks of formal engagement before the wedding when she became giddy like a little girl. Then she nailed to that wall the picture of her hero standing alongside as she was smiling brightly in her wedding dress, and she could hardly contain her joy. Some few miles to the south the same story seemed to unfold for Toni, and she gushed with glee and dramatically displayed her delight as she would point to her favorite person images exhibited on her office wall, and everyone admired the handsome portraits from her Mexico City wedding. Well, in ordinary course of events all this romantic stuff oughta wear down so that things could get back to normal. No, no. By the time one might reasonably expect the newness to erode so to restore past humor the dimensions began to swell with the promise of parturition and that being an altogether different experience and circumstance that was of special delight to the guy that caused it. These pregnant persons seemed each day to demonstrate greater happiness.

Beginning that Monday morning after their return from the curtailed Honeymoon, these young newlyweds began the daily grind. There were other players on this stage. The girls' mother got what she wanted most, and that was simply that her twins would not be ripped away from her. The girls' father got what he wanted and that was peace in his home, including a continuing good will for his wife, and having his family intact where he could watch over them. The girls got what they wanted and that was to have each other and a man that loved them both and understood their peculiar symbiosis. Larry got what he wanted and that was his honor and integrity intact, and two really cute young ladies that worshiped him. Then into the mix comes the two squirming little babies that are yet in gestation, but the clock and calendar will inexorably bring about a time when all is revealed, and that really ain't all so bad.

In that first few days after their return home, Larry had to go on a four day flying event to Washington State. The girls took up their desks at the family car dealerships in Costa Mesa and Laguna Beach. Sister Debbie was at work at the family dealership in Santa Ana. In Costa Mesa Teri would spend quiet moments admiring that 8x11 portrait of herself in her wedding dress alongside her groom garbed in the Marine Corps officer's uniform with saber at his side. Very impressive. In Laguna Beach Toni proudly displayed that portrait of herself and her groom dressed in his snappy Marine Corps officer's uniform and with a Mameluke Saber at his side. Very impressive.

After all the preparation for and wedding of Teri, everything seemed to change for Debbie. At the family car dealership in Santa Ana, Debbie no longer came to work dressed in the questionable garments, and never could find her bag of bangles, baubles, jewelry and beads. It would be fair to say that Debbie had a renaissance in her appearance, and was surprised that so many folk were so bold as to comment on the improvement. She never wore false eyelashes again. She had a large portrait hanging over her desk showing the wedding party participants at the event in Mexico, in which Debbie was standing next to a very handsome dark haired gentleman in a tuxedo. Considering that Debbie was still married to an absentee thug off on an errand to get rich quick, it would be best for her picture to be innocently displayed with her sister's wedding party. And so began her daily grind.

The twins showed up for work in spite of the brief morning sickness and general blah. They went to church and raised some eyebrows when they both held hands with a guy that was married to one or more of them. They did not explain to anyone anything, even though to some it seemed rude that they did not respond to questions. No, it was impolite for folks to pry into the personal affairs of others, and those meddlesome questions should never have been asked in the first place, and the Holy Bible says that we should not gossip. In fact it seems that the Holy Bible admonitions come down hard on gossipers, and nothing said to attack outright the plural marriage, and very little that we can interpret as doctrine or policy against the practice, though there are many places in scripture that seem to suggest a more ideal arrangement would involve one man and just one woman, and there is the restriction against Deacon candidates that have more than the one wife. King Solomon was supposed to be a very wise man, but when you figure that his history included a whole lot of women, that might isolate his wisdom so that it is not universal. King David was one of God's favorites, and he had wives by the number. Do kings have special divine dispensation. Who knows?

Shirley Cole sent several pregnancy smocks out for her favorite twins. It seemed as though she became very comfortable with the whole scene but was particularly pleased with these two pregnancies. She began to phone more and more often, and every six weeks or so would get on an airliner to come and personally check on those precious passengers. Shirley Cole and Shimi Remington were becoming blathering old buddies. They loved to wander through the malls shopping for everything and nothing in particular, but they both were focused on those unborn blessings. Then they became preoccupied with expanding dimensions, and started making measurements with the tape measures and the weighing scales, much concerned when one of the waddling women would grow more than the other. They had the girls pose for snapshots from the time they returned from the Honeymoon(s) right up until delivery, catching a weekly pictorial proof of belly bulging development. When the family would gather around in the evening, these two grandmotherly ladies preferred to have the little ones as the topic of conversation, and everyone joined in to listen to heartbeats and watch the blips and feel the tummy ripples. The bassinettes were in place when the pregnancies were only about four months along.

The pregnant pair did have some nominal queasiness and nausea, but neither of them suffered greatly from morning sickness. Neither of them had any real back problems throughout the pregnancy duration. After the weddings they seemed to be very happy and so comfortable with marriage. Just as the grandmotherly persons were enjoying these gestations in their way, the twins were having their own joyfulness, and through the day they'd anticipate arrival of Larry to share their sentimentalities.

On the other hand, from the time they returned from the Honeymoon Larry liked to get in their new car and go to anywhere he could to show off his brides. These three actually made a remarkably beautiful trio as they strolled here and there holding hands or scrunched up together clutching arms. They were aware that they were being admired by others and it bothered them not at all. When the girls started really swelling up they began to proudly wear those smocks, making the same rounds at the malls, the county fairs, the Knott's Berry Farm, Disneyland all day Saturday. And when they got swollen up too much, they would go sit on the beach. Momma Remington had taken a snapshot of Larry sleeping in his uniform on the couch with one of the girls snuggled up on the left and the other on the right, all sound asleep, before they were all married. She managed to get another such snapshot of the three of them sleeping that way when the girls were nine months pregnant. That would make for a nice album collection, wouldn't it?

After the weddings, Larry would visit each of his brides at their separate places of employment, usually showing up at Teri's office and taking her to an early lunch. He'd leave there and head south to visit with Toni. Teri would be on the phone as soon as he left her shop to let Toni know he's on the way. Naturally, Toni would be all jittery with delight by the time Larry arrived, and they'd go have another lunch. These three continued these luncheon engagements for many months as the girls continued to swell up.

One evening, Larry brought a couple of boxes containing gifts for the bulging persons. Each box contained a new stethoscope for listening to fetal heartbeats. This added many joyful hours to the evening bliss. Larry the listener had heard the ladies talking about anticipated back pain discomforts as pregnancy moves along toward parturition, so he invested in a nice massaging machine with vibration pads to spoil the expectant mothers. He would mutter nice things to them as he rubbed back and shoulders, and in turn they would make cooing sounds to show their appreciation.

When the girls were really bulging, Larry took them to Lompoc to visit brother Reuben, and two very beautiful pregnant ladies that looked exactly alike caused quite a stir in the reception room. After the visiting hours were over, they drove down to Oxnard to see the relatives, and nobody there mentioned anything about anyone looking pregnant.

Several times during the gestation months, Larry would try to get his mother-in-law to forgive him for the misunderstandings between them. He would wait for a few encouraging signs before bringing up this topic. He was making monthly payments on those engagement and wedding rings, and Momma Remington would quietly take the money and say nothing, just give a nod. Sometimes the payment was by check, but usually in cash. Larry thought he'd embellish the payment with a little extra feature: On the way home from the MCAS El Toro he would stop by the florist's and buy a dozen roses, and go by the candy store and get a box of chocolates. When he'd hand her his monthly payment he would first hand her the bunch of flowers and she would grunt, then he'd give her the box of chocolates and she'd give another grumbling grunt, and then he'd give her the monthly payment, and she would grunt again, and with the final grunt he would ask "Will you forgive me now?" and she would scowl and say "Certainly not!". This went on for several months, each time with her refusing to forgive him, and then one time he handed her the money only, and she looked at him with a scowl, asking "Where are my flowers?" and he reached over on the sink to retrieve for her the box of one dozen long-stem red roses, and with a smile he handed them to her. She accepted the box, opened it up and said "I do love red roses!" then she looked him right in the eye and said "Where's my chocolates?" He reached over on the chair beneath the breakfast bar counter and pulled up the box of chocolates, handed them to her and asked "When are you gonna forgive me?" and she responded "Never!"

When the girls had really swollen up, their Mom wanted another group studio portrait of Larry standing with them as they gave a profile pose showing their protruding bellies. The resulting portrait was so very nicely done with perfect lighting and marvelous smiles of all three of them. That's another picture for the album, but Mom Remington had it framed and she put it on her bedroom wall. There was one other really great portrait, with Larry in his flight suit, holding his helmet under his arm, standing in front of his jet fighter-bomber out on the flight line tarmac, with Teri on his right and Toni on his left standing in a profile posture leaning up against their hero in such a way that showed both of those bulging bellies beneath the smocks.

The girls wanted to go sit on the beach on a warm Saturday afternoon, and Larry talked his mother-in-law into going with them. The bulging bellied brides were especially effervescent this day, giggling and wiggling, chortling and cackling, in such a happy mood. Momma was wearing a casual shorts outfit with a sleeveless shirt, and sat on a large towel with her sunglasses on as Larry went splashing in the surf with the expectant mothers holding his hands one on each side. Laughing and dancing in the water, they returned to where Momma was soakin' up the rays, and the happy mood of her girls seemed communicable as she was all smiles. As the girls were toweling off the beads of ocean water, Larry leaned over to ask his mother-in-law "Do you think your girls are happy?" to which she replied "They've never been so happy in all their lives!" and Larry asks "Do you think it has anything to do with those tiny creatures they carry in those bulges?" and she clucks "Oh. Yes. They are so pleased and so is everyone else in the family! These little ones will be such fun for all of us!" Seeing another opportunity to inquire Larry asks "Then maybe now you'll forgive me?" and she says "Not a chance!"

Momma Remington continued serious preparations for the arrival of her precious grandchildren, buying all sorts of stuff to welcome their arrival. She and Shirley Cole would march up and down the mall corridors looking for more clutter to fill the house. Bassinette blankets, baby cribs, pink and blue outfits, all the feeding equipment and little musical toys to hang over their beds. These little ones were more than welcome.

Momma Remington refused to forgive Larry for whatever, but she stopped calling him offensive names, and actually seemed to change her mind altogether about his being a hypocrite. When the family would all sit down to dinner she would ask Larry to turn thanks, and when he finished his little prayer of blessing over the food, Shimi the Granny-to-be would smile and say "Amen" Then she would occasionally pat him on the hand after a particularly touching little prayer.

Not long after the newlyweds returned from their Honeymoon, actually within a day or so after their return, they began their little community of prayer before bedtime, just the three of them. They would gather together and kneel beside the loveseat in Larry's quarters and each in turn offer their individual prayers to augment their common prayer session, touching on everything past and present, but always asking the Lord to send Guardian Angels to watch over the little ones then yet to be born. Then they added more prayers for everyone in the family, for Mom and Dad Remington, for Debbie and Reuben, for the relatives near and far and so on. They left the door open one evening, and Momma heard their session and all its content, and before you know it she was kneeling there with them and sharing the moment. There wasn't really enough room for four people around that little loveseat, so they decided to have their evening community of prayer out in the living room, and Stewart Remington was conscripted to participate, and he did. On those evenings when Debbie was staying over, she was sorta drafted to become part of their prayer meeting, and the whole household became a band of prayer warriors. This went on for a couple of months, and they began to have morning prayer meetings. They'd get stoked at the breakfast table, and when the men went off to work the ladies would continue on their own. The Remington family was so close many years ago, and with these prayer sessions seemed now closer than ever.

You can imagine that these circumstances and the events that brought these people to this point in their history would have a very maturing impact on the mind and spirit for each of them, and it did. But beyond the separate events there was the immeasurable influence of the prayer tradition that they adopted. That mantle of prayer added to the quality of spiritual life in this family, providing an environment conducive to their spiritual growth, strengthening the emotional bond among them as well as the separate spiritual determination of each member of this Christian clan. Observers might suggest that these people had become religious fanatics, silly Bible-thumpers, or just local loonies, but these folks basked and thrived in the ambient joy of that home.

In early December of that first year, as the expectant twins were starting to swell up a little, and as they were becoming better acquainted with Larry, it seemed that each tiny new discovery about his habits and idiosyncrasies were so amusing and so amazing. His presence in the household was an entirely novel and most delightful addition, and it seemed to cause such mirth and merriment with every fresh revelation. These young ladies didn't even know this interesting young man just a few months ago, and now he has become the centerpiece of their lives. It was on a Sunday morning when Larry's folks were in town, and the whole family was goin' to church in San Clemente, marching in from the parking lot to the front door of the sanctuary. Everyone of their troupe had already entered when Pastor DeWitt grabbed Larry's arm and pulled him aside to whisper "Sister Bowman is not able to be with us this morning, so could you play the piano for the congregational singing?" Larry nodded and replied "sure".

They had a couple of guys strumming their guitars as the congregation was in pre-service prayer, and as the pastor took up his post behind the pulpit, without any explanation to anyone, Larry left his pregnant pair sitting there with the family as he strode confidently up to the platform and settled himself upon the piano bench. Teri and Toni just stared at this maneuver, blankly turned to one another and then glanced over to where Debbie and her Mom were seated, and they all had the most astonished expressions on their faces. Shirley Cole immediately concluded that these folks were not aware that her baby boy could play the piano. Pastor DeWitt led the parishioners in an opening song of worship, then turned the service over to the song leader person for a bit of congregational singing. Larry knew all those songs by heart and just stroked those keys like a pro, without skipping a beat. As the musical pace seemed to warm up, they turned to an old Gospel Quartet favorite that speaks of flyin' away. That's all it took for Larry to explode with a sudden attack of 'happy feet', and he pounded those piano keys like Sister Bowman never had. Then followed spontaneous singing of fast-moving songs of worship as Larry really got that place rockin'. Mom Remington was shocked and amazed. Shirley Cole just smiled and glowed with pride. Teri leaned over and whispered to Toni "My husband can play the piano!", and Toni replied "My husband is the best piano player in the whole world!"

With this lively congregational singing and praising the Lord, the good Pastor DeWitt just sat back and enjoyed another "Pentecostal Breakdown", and everything just gravitated toward a Sunday morning musical convention without the sermon.

Maybe we should navigate away from our story at this point to enlighten the folks that are not acquainted with old time traditions prevalent among Pentecostal churches just a few decades ago. One of the most intriguing of these customs was known as the "Jericho March", which was an occasional spontaneous joyful demonstration among inspired saints, and could take place at almost any time during or after scheduled services. And then there was that occasion in earlier times known as the "Pentecostal Breakdown", which was simply an unplanned departure from the standard order of service, when the pastor might abandon his sermon notes and join in the session of singing and praise. The scheduled duration of services usually would then be extended for whatever time might be necessary to wholly vent the emotions according to leading of the Spirit.

Let's just say that once upon a time there was a little congregation that somehow acquired an old retired saloon building in Palm City, California, where the faithful would regularly gather for worship, evangelism and fellowship, rather than the imbibement of beverages. It was a ramshackle place with a leaky roof, a dirt-gravel parking lot out front, and slat-board wooden benches for parishioners to sit on and occasionally for the little kids to sleep on. This church had a small platform built up next to where the old bar was still located, two orange crates stacked one upon the other to serve as a pulpit, and an antiquated upright piano scrunched up against the wall, and that instrument was always totally out of tune. Most of the parishioners at this time were immigrants from Arkansas and Oklahoma, Tennessee and Alabama, mostly unsophisticated migrant farm workers and others from that social structure. For congregational singing there would be somebody banging on that piano and almost always there would be these four guys playing stringed instruments, including a banjo and a mandolin, a fiddle and a guitar. Actually, the five instruments together put out with some really great southern gospel sounds. Occasionally, an old drunken sot would wander in and stumble up to the bar to demand his booze. More than one of those inebriated sinners got holy hands laid on him to cast out the demon of rum. Needless to say, those song services at that little Palm City church were a real treat.

Well, that little Palm City church had several "amen corners" scattered about the congregation, and they sprinkled the pastor's sermons with their shouts of appreciative "Amen", "Glory" and "Hallelujah", along with other expressions of approval as the fiery preaching was delivered to saint and sinner alike. One of the most prominent of these amen people was a dynamic woman by name of Sister Gosnel. This marvelous Christian lady was not only imposing for her encouraging words of endorsement for the preachin', she was also the recognized anointed leader of the "Jericho March". She was kinda short and very plump, bein' almost as wide as she was tall. Sister Gosnel knew every word to everything in the "Songs of Praise" hymnal, and she had a strong clear voice very distinguishable during congregational singing.

Remembered well in the lore of that little Palm City church was a dark and stormy night long ago when the roof leaked and the parking lot was muddy, the piano playin' person was banging on such of those 88 keys as yet remained on that instrument and the string quartet was really workin' up that crowd. It started out while everyone was seated and singing some quick-tempo gospel song. Heard above all the crowd was the shrill voice of Sister Gosnel, as she was seated on the old wooden slat bench down front nearest the orange crates that served as altars in front of the "pulpit". Well, you could tell that Sister Gosnel was gettin' inspired as she lifted her eyes toward heaven and likewise lifted her right hand that was wavin' her hankie back and forth as the crowd lustily sang the words:

> *"Ho, my comrades, see the signal, waving in the sky!*
> *Reinforcements now appearing, Victory is nigh!*
> *Hold the fort for I am coming, Jesus signals still;*
> *Wave the answer back to Heaven, by thy grace we will!"*

Then she lifted both hands in a most worshipful way and started spinnin' that hankie around in circles. She stood to her feet and started to sway back and forth in pace with the happy gospel music. The guy with the banjo knew what was comin' next, and he got the attention of the piano person, as Sister Gosnel started to loudly sing

> *"We're marching to Zion! Beautiful, beautiful Zion!*
> *We're marching upward to Zion,*
> *that beautiful City of God"*

She then commenced to slowly tramp around those altar boxes with her arms joyfully thrust up toward heaven and her hankie spinnin'. After a few trips around the altars, she was joined by a number of other exultant saints as she led them in a jubilant parade up and down the aisles. As the number of marchers increased, Sister Gosnel was inspired to lead the troops out the back door and into the rain, around the muddy parking lot a few times, and everybody was singing about that great march to Zion. Then she led the completely soaked band of faithful followers back into the aisles of the church, down to the altars and again toward the very back of the sanctuary, and as the music seemed to slow down then likewise did Sister Gosnel. She was exhausted by the celebration, and chose to collapse on one of the benches at the back of the room where a little four-year old boy was trying to sleep, and that bench buckled and came crashing down to the floor, as did Sister Gosnel and that little boy.

Would you care to guess the name of that little boy?

Well, times have changed. Jericho Marches are a thing of the past, even though the Pentecostal Breakdowns pop up now and then. And it doesn't really matter whether you be Baptist or Nazarene, Adventist or C&MA, Presbyterian, Episcopalian or Catholic Charismatic, don't you just know that God must have planted a Gosnel somewhere in your church?

Is there a Gosnel in the house?

This disclosure about Larry's hitherto unknown skill on the claviature simplified the matter of selecting a proper Christmas gift for the new husband that year. When he arrived home on Christmas Eve he found that a credenza had been moved and a beautiful Baby Grand piano was there at the end of the library area. The family had never in the past done any Christmas singing together, but they spent a couple of hours then with dreaming of a White Christmas and Jingle Bells, and Silent Night and the Little Town of Bethlehem, and so many other songs of the season. Stewart Remington was heard many times to say that this was his best Christmas ever.

CHAPTER 22

FAMILY FEUD

By the minute, and the hour, and day after day, time slips by. With the passing of time comes the advent of event, and some events are dramatic but most are not. Some events of whatever duration are adventurous and momentous, worthy of storage in the vault of memories, and some occasions simply not worth remembering. Some unpleasant events are hard to forget.

Sister Debbie was still spending most of her time with her family, and bunked in her bedroom originally assigned many years ago. Without anyone saying anything to her they took note that she was staying in her room at the Remington house more than three weeks each month and seemed to seldom stay overnight at her own home. She would drive by her place each day after work, and if her husband King Pete was not around she'd go on to be with her family. Since her trip to Mexico to take part in Toni's wedding she had seen King Pete only three times, each for only a couple of days over the weekend, which would make a total of about six or seven days in about six months. He would phone her at work occasionally but never at her Dad's home. He refused to justify or explain his extended absences and told her he was 'gone on business' and that it was none of her business. On several more occasions when she pressed him for some further explanation she got thumped or shoved violently. She covered the resulting bruises with heavy cosmetics, but over the past six months or so she had not worn the heavy lipstick and eye shadow or thick facial grease. When Mr. Verdugo came home he got drunk and slept a lot. He no longer tried to hide his drug habit and would lay in a stupor on the couch. He smelled like he never took a bath anymore. In his pockets he carried large amounts of money, and in the glove compartment of his car he had hidden bundles of cash. He used to carry a loaded pistol under the floor mat of his car, but that item disappeared more than a year ago. The trunk of his car was always locked. He had developed an explosive temper and became violent too easy, and it was a relief when he went away and unpleasant when he returned. Without provocation he threatened many times to kill Debbie and her family, or have his gangster friends do it for him.

The twins continued to put on added dimensions while working for the family car dealerships in Costa Mesa and Laguna Beach, doing reconciliation of accounts, insurance confirmations and all the petty bookkeeping chores. But when they had only a few weeks to go in pregnancies as they each became swollen and were waddling around like whales on feet, they decided to take leave and stay home to await parturition. On one particular Monday morning the twins were with their Mom at home cleaning up the house after the men of the family had left for work. It was not yet 8:00 AM.

On the Friday before this particular day, Debbie had her car's transmission fail on the way to work, and it had to be towed in for repairs. She just took one of the dealership's loaner cars for temporary use, and was warned by a salesman that this old Ford loaner recently had some ignition trouble and might itself have to be towed. Deb had spent the weekend with the blimped twins and went back to her place on Sunday night, parking the car on the street in front so that if it had to be hauled in the tow truck could have easier access. On this particular Monday morning Debbie was still sleeping when she heard a couple of cars pull into her driveway, and she peeked out the window to see King Pete with three other men carrying something into the house. It was not very light outside but the sun would soon be shining.

Apparently, when King Pete didn't see Debbie's car in the driveway, he assumed that she was not at home, probably spending the night out at her folks' place. Verdugo and his three friends made several trips back and forth to their cars, carrying a number of packages through the front door and placing them in a neat stack along the wall. When they were finished with relocation of the packages, they raided the refrigerator and sat down in the front room to drink their beers and do some drugs. Their conversation was at first in happy speculation of the profits they were hoping for in selling the packages of 'grass' that were stacked nearby. Then they cheerfully passed around all their conclusions on the agreeable conquests of lady friends in one place or another, and King Pete took special delight in describing his recent successes with a number of love partners by name. His companions laughed and joked about these things. But then Mr. Verdugo began to crudely describe intimate details of his own wife and how his marriage to her was such a disappointment. Debbie was still in her nightgown, standing there in the dark and cringed to think that he would say such things. But King Pete was not finished with his conceited boasting, and he began to recount in horrible detail how he attacked and abused his wife's sister, how he beat her to a pulp and had his way with her unconscious body. Debbie was repulsed to hear this filthy account of the events of that October day, as she turned and went into her bedroom, grabbed the car keys from atop the dresser, then made a beeline for the kitchen and out the side door, running barefoot down the driveway and across the weed covered lawn area to the old Ford, fussed with the door but finally managed to throw it open and fire up that old clunk, and was gone as the dim early dawn was breaking.

King Pete happened to be looking through the front window and in the light of early dawn saw Debbie as she scurried across the sidewalk and into that old Ford and he immediately knew that she must have heard the conversations, and no tellin' where she might be headed. He told his companions to stop their party and get all this stuff back into their car and get out of town, because that woman might just be heading to call the cops. He then jumped into his car and squealed out of the driveway and the chase was on.

Debbie headed straight south to her Dad's place about twenty miles away, screeched to a stop in the driveway, and still dressed in her nightgown she ran into the kitchen through the side door, screaming all the way. Toni and her Mom were in the back bedroom tidying up, and heard the screaming. They then heard the tires screeching again as King Pete Verdugo pulled up behind where Debbie had parked, and Mom Remington immediately retrieved her double barreled shotgun that she had only a few days ago found in the garage where someone had moved it out from her closet.

Mr. Verdugo charged into the kitchen brandishing his razor sharp stiletto and demanding that Debbie return to his house. He charged at her but she moved quickly to the other side of the room, and as she passed he managed to swipe the tip of the knife blade across her back, opening up a bloody path through her nightgown. Teri started screaming hysterically as Verdugo shoved her aside; she dropped to her knees and he kicked her in her bulging abdomen. When he kicked her so harshly, to protect her belly she rolled up in a ball and scrunched into the corner of the kitchen cabinet, whereupon Mr. Verdugo kicked her very hard on her unprotected rump, then he went after Debbie again. He was crazy and uncontrollable as he scowled and shouted out vulgarities and profanities in Spanish and in English. Debbie cringed in the area between the cabinet and the kitchen island, and as King Pete raised his stiletto above her, Toni rushed into the room, so he smacked her on the side of the head with the back side of his other hand and sent her sailing onto the side of the kitchen island but missed her with a swipe toward her with his menacing stiletto. Momma Remington came then through the door about three feet away from the intruder and shoved that shotgun in his face and calmly said "Get on your knees or get a face full of buckshot!" Well, Mr. King Pete Verdugo got even more angry and loud, but he didn't want to test the lady's firepower, so instead of following her command he quickly darted out the door to his car and went squealing down the road. Toni excitedly asked her Mom why she didn't just shoot him, but Mom pointed the gun toward the ceiling and clicked both triggers, saying "I found my gun out in the garage, but I don't know where the shells are." Then Momma saw the blood smears on Debbie's nightgown, and said that she was gonna call the cops. Toni said it would be better to call Dad and Larry, and let them make the decision on whether or not they want publicity. Teri was still curled up in the corner hysterically sobbing. While Momma tended to her wounded Teri, Toni called her father and her husband to alert them to what had happened and asked them to come home right away. The wound on Debbie's back was superficial but probably needed medical attention anyway. The greater concern was for whatever damage might have been done to Teri and her little passenger from the stout kicks delivered by Mr. Verdugo.

Dad Remington and Larry arrived at about the same time, ran together into the house to find the four women trying to deal with the problems at least in part apparent. Dad was in his business suit and Larry was dressed in his military uniform with the khaki shirt and tie. Teri was still on the floor of the kitchen crying and fairly hysterical, and in her frequent shrieks she could hardly say anything understandable. Debbie had settled down some as her Mom was taking a cold damp towel to wipe away the blood from her back. Toni was becoming very upset with Teri's crying and unmanageable emotional disruption. Debbie was almost as bad as she described all that happened in that kitchen that morning and what she had overheard earlier, and was particularly upset by the crude way that King Pete Verdugo laughed and bragged to his companions in detail about his attack against Teri a couple of years ago. Dad Remington was calm at first but became more furious with each revelation.

As Debbie was telling the lurid tale, Larry went over and sat down on the floor next to Teri and tenderly lifted her into his arms and cuddled her lovingly, kissed her hand, kissed her neck, kissed the top of her head, kissed her on the nearest cheek, and rocked her back and forth until she seemed to be settling down. After a brief time, he tried to help her to her feet, but she started clinging to him and seemed to be suggesting that they might be safer behind that kitchen island. He picked her up and carried her in his arms into the living room and placed her on the couch. He whispered that he would be gone for a few minutes on a mission to be reconciled with a wrongdoer that he has not yet ever met.

Larry stood up and turned to his father-in-law and asked "Do you have a video camera handy?" Dad Remington replied to inform that he had several on a shelf in the closet. Retrieving a camera from the hall closet and testing the battery to see if the thing was actually working, the two of them got into the silver Mercedes to go visit Mr. Verdugo. Larry did the driving, and as they moved on down the highway toward Tustin and the Verdugo home, Larry mentioned that in all the time he was acquainted with the family he had never met Mr. Verdugo. Dad Remington said "He's easily recognized. He has long greasy black hair and a gold tooth here and a diamond studded tooth here." as he pointed to his own upper front teeth. As they drove along, memories boiled up in the mind of Stewart Remington and he was seething with anger and resentment for all the friction and discomfort that Verdugo had caused since he came into their lives, and he continued his mutterings and bitter mumblings the entire way to the Verdugo driveway. One would assume that Mr. Remington had a peculiar scorn for Mr. Verdugo.

When they parked the car in the driveway next to the front porch of the Verdugo place, Larry turned on the video camera, locked the trigger in the 'on' position, and placed the camera on the dashboard of the car in such a location that it was aimed directly at the entire porch and front door of the house. He told Dad Remington that he should not get out of the car for any reason, but just sit there, listen and observe.

Larry exited the car and walked casually to the front porch there and pushed the doorbell button. When there came no answer soon, he pushed the button a couple of more times, and then he gently knocked on the door itself with the knuckle of his right hand. The door swung open, Mr. Verdugo stood in the entranceway and angrily growled "Whatta you want?" Larry extended his hand as though to offer a handshake and said "I am Larry Cole and you know Stewart..." as he turned to point with his left hand at the place where

Stewart Remington was seated in the car. When he turned his head away, Mr. Verdugo did three things all at the same time. He started screaming profanities that surely must have been intended to hurt Larry's feelings. He raised his left arm as he scrunched up the fist that came crashing down onto the right side of Larry's neck. As he was screeching and pounding on Larry, Mr. Verdugo with his right hand reached behind his back and grabbed the razor sharp stiletto from his waistband scabbard and started poking that blade into Larry's back.

When that huge fist came bashing Larry on his neck, the blow was with such force as to buckle Larry's knees and he fell backward and off the step with his left leg. With that scary-looking knife Mr. Verdugo managed to slit through to the skin of the back near Larry's left shoulder. Larry grabbed the knife-wielding hand at about the wrist and as he pulled himself again to his full height he shoved that dagger away and upward with all his strength. Mr. Verdugo was very strong and would not let go of that knife, but the force of Larry's upward thrust caused that razor sharp blade to catch the scowling Mr. Verdugo in the flesh beneath his upper lip, and as that blade continued upward with such vigor it sliced through the lovely Fu Manchu moustache and both cheeks, then with such force that the blade continued through the cartilage of the nose and into the eyelid of the left eye in such a way as to leave the nose dangling with just a narrow piece of skin between the eyes holding it onto the head. Blood spurted everywhere. As Larry was trying to pull up to his full height, Mr. Verdugo continued to pound him with his left fist, and Larry with his right arm and fist let go a vicious blow to the lower left rib cage of his newly acquired acquaintance. Apparently because of the drugs recently introduced into his system, Mr. Verdugo was feeling no pain, and he stubbornly continued the affray. When he tried to claw Larry on the head with his open left hand, Larry met him palm to palm and they did a little wrestling dance that ended up with Larry pushing back the fingers of Mr. Verdugo's hand, and there was heard the happy little popping and snapping as those fingers shattered or the knuckles were displaced. Mr. Verdugo still was feeling no pain, and the damages to that left hand were not enough, and he continued to slap at Larry's head with that hand with the useless fingers. While this little operation was taking place with Mr. Verdugo's left side he continued to try to stab Larry in the back with that knife in his right hand, and did manage to slice open Larry's scalp on the back of his head.

The menace of that knife blade waving around needed immediate attention, and Mr. Verdugo managed to get loose his right arm and hand with the knife blade flashing and coming down, and aimed right at Larry's chest. Larry stepped back and caught that right arm with his left arm above and with his right hand he managed to grip the wrist, and with one swift crushing twist Mr. Verdugo's right arm snapped at about midway between his elbow and the wrist, and as his grip went instantly weak that shiny stiletto fell harmlessly into the nearby shrubbery. But Mr. Verdugo charged again with whatever weapons he had remaining, and that arsenal consisted of those harsh and harmful insulting words sheathed in profanity, the left arm where dangled the useless fingers of his hand, and two tremendously powerful legs. He snarled and cursed aloud and one could see those beautifully decorated teeth where the upper lip and moustache no longer covered them, so Larry grabbed a handful of Mr. Verdugo's handsome tresses, pulled the face around to where he could see the wild expression in the one remaining good eye, and Larry proceeded to rearrange the structures on Mr. Verdugo's face. With repeated hammer blows to both sides of the face, the zygomatic bones around Mr. Verdugo's eye sockets were both smashed to splinters. He absorbed a few very hard smacks to the side of his head and neck. But the worst skeletal damage done to Verdugo's head this day was to his lower jaw and the center line of his face below where his nose used to be. Larry found targets shining out of that sardonic smile, with a really nice uppercut that landed squarely on the chin, and then proceeded to pound repeatedly the jaw and entire face of his rude opponent. With one final smack the nose that was hanging by that slim piece of skin then became separated and went flying over and landed on the hood of the car nearby. All of the front teeth top and bottom were smashed and dislodged and went flying about. When Verdugo was running low on strength, he had one more weapon in his arsenal, and as both of these contenders stood facing one another on that porch, Verdugo with his arms hanging uselessly at his sides, let go with a crippling kick that landed on Larry's left hip just below the belt line, and it almost took him down. Before he could fully catch his balance there came another vicious kick to the side of his left knee, and this time Larry did go down. Oooh, that musta hurt bad! As Larry was scrambling to get to his feet, Mr. Verdugo the foot fighting person let go another swift kick aimed at Larry's head, and Larry the soccer star let go with a single mighty kick to the symphysis pubis that lifted Mr. Verdugo completely off the ground about six inches or more, and Verdugo's poorly aimed final kick was caught in midair so that Larry was able to move his bleeding left arm under the calf and grab the foot so that when he gave a mighty twist both bones of the lower leg snapped at about the midpoint between the knee and the ankle, and that leg buckled to where the toes were pointing backward and the leg bones there were at right angles to the rest of the leg. When this happened, Mr. Verdugo fell to the concrete porch and smacked the back of his head, real hard, and he began to groan. Apparently Mr. Verdugo was by then feeling a little pain.

Larry leaned over to say "As I was saying, I am pleased to meet you Mr. Verdugo, and I want to leave you with this message: You have until the end of this week to get out of town. If I find you anywhere in Orange County after that I'm gonna rip off what's left of your face, and break every bone in your body. You understand?" and Mr. Verdugo grunted something in response. Larry turned aside to return to the car, and as he did he saw Dad Remington with his arm waving out the passenger side window, pointing to the nose and moustache remains resting on the hood of the car. Larry picked up that ugly piece of flesh and returned to stand over the writhing body of King Pete Verdugo, and contemptuously placed the nose upside down on his face with the nostrils pointing up toward the eyebrows, and once again said "You have until Saturday night to get out of town!" and Mr. Verdugo grunted again. Larry glanced over to one side of the porch and saw some debris that needed to be taken sorta like a prize of war, so he picked up a few choice pieces and placed them in his blood-saturated shirt pocket. When Larry got into the driver seat, Stewart Remington looked at him then turned to look again at the bloodied body of King Pete Verdugo, and as Larry fired up the engine and backed out of the driveway, his father-in-law took the video camera off the dash to get one more bit of video of Mr. Verdugo laid out on the concrete all silent and still, and Stewart Remington was heard to chuckle "Heh, heh, heh!" Larry was bleeding and the blood was covering the driver seat from where Larry then modestly ruled the road all the way to the Remington house, as Dad Remington gleefully spouted comments like "To think that people pay good money to go to the fights, and I got to see this for free!" and "Wow. Your one kick lifted that punk off the ground!" and "Did you see that nose flyin'?" and he continued to rejoice that way all the distance to home.

The altercation on the porch that day lasted not more than one minute. When it was all over Mr. Verdugo looked like he had just barely escaped with his life from a local abattoir.

Knowing that the world is watching, each one of us that wants the respect of our neighbor, each of us that seeks enlightenment and spiritual excellence unto ourselves, pursuing the right and eschewing the wrong, examples to be admired for courage and noble deeds, should follow the well-known rules of geniality, written down in some obscure book at the Library of Congress, those rules that we should all apply to everyday life. If you just cannot make it soon to the library, consider the commandments following:

1. Thou shalt not with thine foot violently kick the unborn child of a US Marine.
2. Thou shalt not with thine foot violently kick the pregnant wife of a US Marine.
3. Thou shalt not with thine hand violently smite the pregnant wife of a US Marine.
4. Thou shalt not use provocative vulgar and profane language in the presence of a US Marine.
5. Thou shalt not with thine fist smite the neck of a US Marine.
6. Thou shalt not with thine blade stab a US Marine.
7. Thou shalt not with thine foot violently kick a US Marine.
8. Thou shalt not threaten violence to any US Marine.
9. Thou shalt not threaten to nor engage in violent exchange of fisticuffs with a US Marine.
10. Thou shalt not by rude words or nefarious deeds arouse the righteous indignation of a US Marine.

Consider also that Marine Corps Pilots love to see things flying. They seem to especially enjoy the spontaneous flight of noses festooned with Fu Manchu decorations.

Consider that Ivy League graduates seem to enjoy demonstrating the skills learned in bygone college days, and the Princeton soccer team boys love to show off their kicking expertise.

Oh, those mischievous Princeton boys, they're always looking to improve things their way. They don't seem to be content with how nature designs things, such as the structure of the human head, the skeleton and bones of the extremities. Smashing somebody's head and breaking various bones of the body might seem to civilized people to be taking things to extremes, but boys will be boys. Especially those cute Princeton boys.

When the returning heroes drove into the driveway, Toni and Debbie hurried out to meet them, and were aghast to see that Larry Cole was covered front and back with blood. The gore was oozing from the gaping open wound on his scalp; his shirt was smeared with blood front and back and on both sleeves; and the stab wound on his back was still pouring little streams of blood down onto his belt and pants. They couldn't understand why Dad Remington was so happy, and how could he be so jolly when Larry was so chopped up? Dad Remington said aloud "Wow. Ya shoulda been there. It was a great show. Toni girl you got yourself a real champ. You woulda been proud to see how he handled himself!" He went on with this praise as the girls sorta helped to prop up their champion all the way to and through the kitchen door, and on into the front room where Momma was comforting Teri who was still feeling discomforts in the lower abdomen.

Larry reached into his shirt pocket and pulled out those items he had picked up from among the debris on the Verdugo porch, and placed them on the coffee table in front of Momma Remington saying "Here are a few little souvenirs for your trophy collection." Momma chuckled to see several broken teeth and parts of teeth, along with an entire gold-clad tooth with the root intact, and another whole tooth with root intact having a blood covered diamond imbedded in the surface.

Larry looked terrible. The blood from the scalp wound was dried up on the side of his face, and all that blood splattered on him front and back, top to bottom. The skin on his knuckles was torn and shredded from their recent exercise and the sliced skin on his posterior looked dreadful. But he considered his wounds to be incidental to the more important matter of potential harm to Teri and her little unborn passenger. They as a group chose to phone their Mexican attorney in Santa Ana, and as they explained everything to him his first response was to tell them to make copies of that video, because this would be their last chance to do so before the cops impounded it and the camera that it was made on. He said to hold tight for a couple of minutes, and he would call right back. He did call back in about ten minutes to tell them that some neighbor saw the whole front porch squabble and called the cops, who then called in an ambulance to haul Mr. Verdugo away. The lady that took the call at the ambulance place said that the cops were amused with the placement of Mr. Verdugo's nose. They took Verdugo to Orange County Hospital Emergency. So, since Verdugo went to the county hospital, they should take Teri to Hoag Memorial in Newport Beach and if Larry's wounds are serious he should get sewed up there rather than to go to Balboa Naval Hospital all the way down in San Diego.

And so all six of them got in the car and drove quick as they could over toward Newport Beach at more than the posted highway speed. A wandering Highway Patrol car pulled up behind them with lights blinking, Larry motioned for the cop to pull up alongside, and all the blood on Larry's face told the tale, as Larry called out "Emergency! Hoag Memorial Emergency!" and the Mercedes got a siren screaming police escort all the way to the hospital.

The inquisitive cop held the door for everyone as they entered the building, Larry all covered with blood and anxiously propping up his big-bellied bride. When they got Teri into one of the emergency treatment places there, the cop calmly asked "What happened here?" Stewart Remington suggested that the CHP officer should call the Orange County Sheriff to send out an investigation team with a photographer, so that they can take a report. The cop turned to go out to his cruiser, and returned a few minutes later to inform that the crime investigation team was on its way. Then when the officer pressed his inquiry as to what had happened, Larry calmly said "Oh. It's just a family feud. I had a disagreement with my brother-in-law, and he has gone over to Orange County Hospital to get some Band-Aids and aspirin or something." The officer then contacted the Orange County Sheriff again to inquire if there was any report about a Mr. Pedro Verdugo. The OCSD Watch Commander came on the line and introduced himself, and told the officer that Mr. Verdugo is well known to them as a drug-dealing marijuana smuggler in LA and Orange County, now appears to be the victim of a vicious gang attack at his home, seems totally shattered and is in emergency now with broken bones and badly mangled body, and that his face is terribly shattered with lacerations and trauma. Looks like gang warfare.

At suggestion of the Mexican lawyer, Larry had the doctors stop the bleeding but leave all the mess to be shown to the investigation team from OCSD, so that their photographic record would be complete. Those pictures taken showed the open scalp wound and the dried up trail of blood that oozed down and over the ears and neck, the sliced up gashes on the back and arm, and a few abrasions where he got smacked on the face. The investigators took down a full report, and confiscated the video and camera as evidence. After seeing the video they went to the Verdugo home and recovered that knife from the shrubbery, and it matched the scabbard that Verdugo was wearing in his belt.

The OB-GYN doctor was a woman, fortunately, and she conducted a thorough examination of the injuries to Teri's tummy and rump, and felt that the blow to the abdomen would leave a large bruise beneath the rib cage, but that the little passenger was essentially unharmed. The huge bruise on her butt was already black and red, and the flesh was all swollen. Pictures were taken, modesty notwithstanding.

Larry waited until Teri was pronounced well, and then submitted to primary closures on his own wounds. Since he had an insurance card from Teri's employment to augment the military medical card, they called in the most expensive cosmetic surgery doctor in Orange County to do the honors in repairing the scalp and those two slicing wounds on his back and arm. It only took fifty-five stitches all told, and there would be almost no perceptible scarring. There was an amusing incident that took place at this point, when Larry mentioned that it was his wife that got kicked. Then Toni waddled in to check on Larry and introduced herself as his wife. The duty nurse asked if that was his wife, and he said yes. Very confusing.

Debbie's six inch scratch was not a puncture or penetration wound, and required no stitches. The nurse at Hoag Emergency washed it up and put a dressing on it and gave some topical salve to use on it as part of the healing process. Toni suffered not much more than the smack to her head, and did not require any sort of medical treatment.

They all left the hospital in early evening to go home. Stewart Remington was happily humming all the way.

When the whole family got home, they gathered in the living room to rest and recover. Larry was the only one with any real injuries to show for the day's adventures, and the bruises on his hip and leg were painful but any harm was negligible. Teri had the two bruising sites, but the bruising and swollen tissue on her rump was the most uncomfortable. Debbie was more concerned for the twins than for any of her little hurts.

They decided that Teri and Toni should not be seeing the copies of the video scenes, but Stewart Remington convinced his wife "Ya gotta see this! Ya gotta see this!" After she had seen it the first time, she thought that maybe Debbie might want to see what happened to King Pete in the moment of retribution, but while her father rejoiced and her mother was amused, Debbie was aghast. All three of them agreed that King Pete Verdugo finally got what he deserved. Shimi Remington placed the tooth remnant souvenirs in a small plastic box, and put it all away in a dresser drawer. Occasionally she would see that container and smile.

Toni was first to suggest that after the day's dispute resolution exercises maybe they should all join in a prayer of thanks that none of those present had suffered any life-threatening injuries or whatever. It was unusual for Stewart Remington to take the lead in this prayer stuff, but he had everyone bow their heads as he presented petitions of praise and adoration for the majesty of God and for His divine protection for the pregnant persons and their little unborn passengers, and for shielding Larry from the terrible harm that could have ensued from the encounter with the scoundrel so thoroughly dispatched in the altercation that day. He boldly offered thanks for Larry Cole and the unusual way that the Lord had brought him into the family. Momma Remington was heard to mutter a whispered 'amen' and 'amen'. Debbie was just a little more robust in offering an 'amen!'

During the week following the little spat with Mr. Verdugo, Larry noticed a twinge of intermittent pain in the small of his back and thought it to be merely a transitory strain resulting from the squabble. He had an appointment the week following with the medical experts at Balboa Naval Hospital and one of the doctors examining him asked if there were any sort of discomfort or numbness for Larry in that area of his spine, and Larry said "No."

CHAPTER 23

FRIENDLY PERSUASION

The investigation team from the Orange County Sheriff's Department had to wait two days before the medical people got King Pete Verdugo all sewn back together. They brought with them a shorthand reporter to take down everything that the victim Verdugo could get said.

Mr. Pedro Verdugo was so torn apart that he required a private room. He looked pitiful. His head was covered with bandages all around and only one eye was visible. The left eye was not repairable and had to be removed. His nose and the left eyelid had been successfully reattached but since it had become wholly detached there was some question whether or not the nerves would be functional, and the blood vessels might not carry enough oxygen to the injured tissues. His left hand looked like he must have been holding a fan when they put on the bandages. His right arm was in a sling, but his right hand was essentially uninjured. His right leg was in traction with pulleys suspended from the ceiling, and his right foot was resting on a block with some sort of restraint to keep it immobilized. Yes, Mr. Verdugo was surely a pathetic example of uncontrolled gang warfare.

Verdugo's broken jaw bones had to be set and wired together, with a spacer where most of the front upper and lower teeth were missing, but his tongue was loose and he managed through the agony to painfully render a full account about how Larry Cole and his several accomplices had without the least provocation pounced on him in the privacy of his own home, dragging him out onto his porch and pummeling him mercilessly, kicking him about his helpless little body and bashing his previously handsome face, stomping him while they held him down and was unable to protect himself from their violent onslaught. He identified Stewart Remington as one of the assailants, and he could not recognize the other five or six co-conspirators that reveled in his destruction, but surely their mug shots must be on the Post Office bulletin board.

They had his shorthand statement typed up within a couple of hours, and the investigators returned to have him read it and have it read to him, and then they had him sign it under oath with his good hand. As soon as he signed it Mr. Verdugo was told that a criminal complaint would be filed against him this afternoon for filing a false police report, and that 'warrant #1' would be issued calling for his arrest and prosecution.

Then they went on to inform Mr. Verdugo that they now have more than enough evidence and available testimony to convict him of burglary, assault and battery and forcible rape for the event now several years ago, and that as a feature of the felony criminal complaint against him there would be documents signed by the judge this afternoon calling for his immediate arrest and prosecution and that 'warrant #2' would be issued.

Then they went on to inform Mr. Verdugo that this afternoon there would be filed against him another felony criminal complaint charging assault, assault with a deadly weapon, assault with intent to cause great bodily harm, and attempted murder for stabbing his wife, and 'warrant #3' would be issued for his immediate arrest.

Then they went on to inform Mr. Verdugo that a further felony complaint would be filed against him this afternoon for assault, assault and battery, assault with a deadly weapon, assault with intent to commit great bodily harm, and assault with intent to commit murder in his quarrel with Larry Cole, and that 'warrant #4' would be issued calling for his immediate arrest.

Then came more unsettling news: Verdugo's house was under watch, and plainclothes officers had seen him and his three friends loading and unloading contraband, and they saw Verdugo speed away, but continued watching the three remaining accomplices re-load their car and tear off down the street, only to be stopped in Norwalk, in the County of Los Angeles, and those three good friends of Verdugo have been singing down at the Los Angeles County Jail, blaming Verdugo for everything. Looks like another warrant will be issued.

Hearing all this cheery news, one could hear Mr. Verdugo try to draw a deep breath, but his five broken ribs did not allow for deep breaths. The investigator in charge informed Mr. King Pete Verdugo that at the request of the Remington family this matter can be handled in another way. They told Verdugo that they were still gonna file all those criminal complaints and would have all those state-wide arrest warrants issued. They informed him that he had the right to have an attorney advise him on all the matters discussed, but if Mr. Verdugo would leave the State of California before next Saturday at midnight, they would hold all those warrants and not pursue him for prosecution, no extradition or anything like that, unless and until he returned to California. If he was found anywhere in California after next Saturday, he would spend the next fifty years of his life with free room and board at San Quentin or Folsom. King Pete just groaned.

On Thursday evening a uniformed officer of the Orange County Sheriff Civil Division came to visit the suffering Mr. Verdugo and brought some papers causing even more grief. He was served with annulment-divorce complaint and restraining orders, and was advised by the officer that there was a limited time within which to respond to the demands of the complaint, and that Verdugo ought to immediately retain an attorney.

The doctors at Orange County Hospital told Mr. Verdugo that he should not be moved for a few weeks, but that very next Friday at noon his family from Los Angeles came to pick him up and he checked himself out.

That Friday evening the California Highway Patrol reported that they had stopped the car in which Verdugo was in the rear seat all wound up like a mummy, on the eastbound Interstate 15 about the Zzyzx off-ramp, and that the car was later seen crossing the California-Nevada border before midnight. The car in which he was riding was that loaner car from the Remington dealership in Santa Ana.

Apparently the ride getting out of California was not all that comfortable, and King Pete Verdugo had to check into a hospital in Las Vegas. He used his medical insurance card that came with Debbie's employment at her Dad's auto dealership in Santa Ana. After staying most of the weekend and all day Monday as a guest there, he took a plane ride to Reno. The loaner car was found torched in the Nevada desert, sort of a parting insult to the Remington family, but it was covered by a blanket policy of insurance at the dealership.

Within a couple of days Verdugo checked into the hospital in Reno, again using that medical insurance card from Debbie's employment. He stayed there for about a week, and had to have some expensive plastic surgery to deal with his nose attachment problems and some bone work on his leg. Remington's were able at least in part to monitor his movements by watching where the medical insurance card was used. They thought that Verdugo would have to pay all the deductibles, but the dealership got stuck with most of those, too.

Verdugo left the hospital in Reno and went to some other place of refuge, where nobody knows. However, the insurance people informed that Mr. Verdugo had later used the insurance card again to get into the hospital in Dallas, Texas, for some sort of osteological repairs. He stayed in that hospital for another couple of weeks. Thereafter he visited a few specialists, but when ninety days had passed the insurance coverage was terminated.

Debbie's Mexican lawyer in Santa Ana was a real dandy. As soon as he could get a default entered on the annulment complaint that was filed and served, he got a hearing date and put the entire matter before the court. That lawyer was able to produce documentary evidence from the LA County Superior Court that indicated Mr. Pedro Verdugo was still married to a young lady in Bellflower, California, and that her petition for divorce filed six years earlier had never been pursued beyond original filing with the clerk. That's what happens or doesn't happen when the attorney doesn't get paid. Furthermore, the judge heard all that Debbie had to tell about the abuse and drug dealing, and the fact that Verdugo had not spent more than a few months in residence in all the time of the marriage. The judge made findings that the marriage was nul and void ab initio and granted Debbie an annulment, and then specifically restored her name to Ximena Debra Carillo Remington. There was no personal property worth squabbling over. Mom Remington was seated in the galleries, ready to testify if necessary. When the judge said "annulment granted" and banged his gavel on the desk Momma got up and clapped her hands together and yelled "Hooray". The judge leaned over and asked Debbie who that lady might be, and Debbie said "That's my Mom", and the judge lifted his hand and waved at her and said "Hi, Mom. Here's your little girl, and you can take her home now." Momma jumped up and down several times and waved happily at the judge. The judge's signature hit the line and that decree was effective immediately. Debbie walked out of that courtroom totally free of Mr. Verdugo. Both Dad and Mom Remington openly rejoiced. That very day Debbie took a copy of the annulment decree with her to the Department of Motor Vehicles and had them restore her name on her Driver's License as provided in the judge's order. Likewise with her Social Security card. Likewise with her library card. Likewise with all her insurance. She also had her telephone permanently disconnected at the Tustin place, and happily moved back home to be with her family permanently, or better make that semi-permanently.

On the Saturday evening after Verdugo left town, Debbie had Larry and her Dad go with her over to the house in Tustin, and found that it had been stripped bare, everything gone including the refrigerator, the lawnmower and light bulbs. Even all of Debbie's clothes and shoes were gone and the closets were totally bare. Most of her more recently acquired frocks and footwear were kept over at her Dad's house anyway. The Sheriff's office advised that Debbie should not be going back to that house, because there was the possibility that Mr. Verdugo's gangster friends might want to come calling some dark night. Stew Remington rented the place to the California Highway Patrol Watch Commander for the Orange County zone, whose wife was a uniformed officer with the Santa Ana Police Department. Momma Remington found her shotgun shells, and her 12 gauge Double Barrel Shotgun was loaded and within reach for uninvited night callers. They also placed a few loaded pistols around behind books and in closets, respecting the threat of reprisal from the cartels.

Nothing more was heard from or about Mr. King Pete Verdugo for a very long while.

However, 'Clarence Darrow II', Remington's criminal law attorney, did manage to acquire from the Orange County Hospital a copy of the medical report on the injuries suffered by Mr. Verdugo: "Parietal concussion with possibility of subdural hematoma; occipital trauma and concussion; massive structural damage to right and left zygomatic arches; separation of right and left temporomandibular joints; fractures of right and left side maxilla; fractures on right and left mandible, separated at the symphysis; five lower teeth fractured, two of which sheared at the gum line; seven upper teeth fractured, four actually missing completely; upper lip and entire nose completely severed; left eye completely destroyed; five ribs fractured lower left abdomen; both bones broken and displaced on the right forearm; four fingers broken or displaced at the knuckle on the left hand; tibia and fibula broken midway between the knee and ankle of the right leg, with total displacement and neurological damage; separation of the symphysis pubis, with apparent neurological damage to neighboring external organs; miscellaneous bruises and contusions. Repairs will require numerous medical specialists, including dental work and maxillofacial reconstruction, plastic surgery, major ophthalmological repairs, osteological specialists, urology reconstruction specialists, etc."

Stewart Remington read that report a couple of times in silence and was in an extremely good mood for the rest of the day.

CHAPTER 24

ARRIVALS

Teri Cole suffered no permanent injury from the kicking incident, just some large diameter bruises and a little swelling that swiftly faded, and the little passenger must have been protected by the padding afforded by a well packed womb. All during their gravidities the pregnant pair were pampered and spoiled in the best possible ways. The twins pampered each other and said all those encouraging things about prospects for each child to be of genius quality and beautiful beyond description. Then Momma soon to be Gramma was beside herself with anticipation glee, taking measurements daily, carefully checking the weight, watching the little tummy blips as the baby would kick, listening by the hour with the stethoscopes, and keeping charts for comparison. All results were by telephone reported to best buddy Shirley Cole in Springfield. Those telephone reports sometimes went on for hours.

Shirley Cole had heard about the little quarrel that her baby boy Larry had with some obscure former member of the family, and she just had to hear Larry's assurance that he had not gone out and started any more fights with the neighbors, and she had to hear the voices of Teri and Toni for reassurance that all was faring well with the little pouch persons. Then a few days later if not the following day, they had to go through it all over again. But day by day the calendar was moving along and the clock was ticking. Each pregnant person was bombarded by accolades from the man that caused it all, as he continued to tell them how pleased and proud he was, and how much he loved each one and anxiously awaited the time when he could count little pink fingers and toes.

Some pregnant ladies don't really gain too much weight. Some pregnant persons manage to move about without any problems right up until they break their water or start labor pains. Not so with Teri and Toni. They both managed to swell up like blimps, and they waddled as they walked. They did not waddle swiftly. They moved as though each shuffling step was a struggle, and from the side it appeared that the load up front could topple 'em over anytime. Toni was the worst, as she would stop, stand up as erect as she could, then place her hand on her hip as though she might tip over. Each of them could have benefited from a tummy bra. They would look at themselves in the mirror and giggle. They enjoyed every moment of these final days of their pregnancies, but were even more anxious to see what these little passengers actually looked like. The primipara people can become quite giddy. These parturient persons spent more and more time each day resting on the couch and chatting about anything and everything, and they were joined throughout the day by Mom Remington who was by this time really enjoying these final days. Momma warned them that they ought to be taking naps every day, to save their strength for coming events. The OB-GYN people estimated that Teri would deliver a week or more before Toni. And then Teri thought she felt labor pains.

A phone call to Springfield brought Shirley to the LAX airport, where she was met by Stewart Remington and transported immediately. But it was a false alarm. Everyone felt that the due date could be just any minute so Shirley Cole stayed on for the blessed event. One other silly thing: when Teri announced the onset of labor, Toni was sure that she felt something also. Neither of them actually started labor until Sunday night following, and all the family went with Teri to the hospital. Even Debbie was anxious and joined the crowd awaiting the arrival of the little one. Gramma Cole and Gramma Remington joined Toni in the delivery room with Teri to welcome Richard C. Cole V, and he had a shrub of dark brown hair to match that of his father. Shirley already had four grandchildren but this young fella was the first grandchild for the Remington family, and all the ladies went wild in that delivery room, stretching to see everything about this little blessing. They followed like a troop as the nurse went to show the little guy at the window where Larry Cole and Grampa Remington were waiting along with Debbie, and those three greeters just melted on the spot.

New father Larry Cole waited around the hospital until he could go see the new mother, and knowing that it would be an emotional moment he took Toni along with him. He greeted the new mother with a loving pat-pat and a little kiss, and said "Hi, Mommy!" and he could hear Toni behind him sniffling. Oh, this was a glorious moment. Grampa and Gramma Remington a few minutes later came in the door with Gramma Shirley and Debbie, and they had their cameras ready to record the whole event. Everybody was outrageously happy.

On the day for Teri and little Richy Cole to depart for home, Larry and Toni drove the Mercedes over to the hospital, got all the carry home stuff ready and in a bag, including the plastic drinking canister as a souvenir. The nurse loaded up Teri and her precious cargo in a wheelchair and pushed them out to the car, with Larry the happy new father walking along behind holding hands with Toni who with her own bulging belly was waddling along as fast as she could to keep up. Toni sat up front and the new mother sat in the rear cooing at the little infant guest. The car had hardly exited the parking lot when Toni and Teri looked at each other and started sniffling, then the tears began to flow. Larry tenderly asked why the tears and they told him they were oh so happy. Larry smiled.

The new father drove slowly all the way home, and upon arrival they were greeted by the grandparents standing almost on the curb, anxious to greet the newcomer. Oh, it was such a glorious day. They put the little sleeping bundle of joy on the bed and spent a half hour quietly watching him snooze. Shirley promised her husband she'd phone to let him know when the newcomer arrived safely at the house, and he wanted to hear the full report. Isn't it interesting how it would take an hour to describe hauling a little kid home and putting him to bed?

Well, Teri recovered quickly and was up and about in just a few days, soon taking long walks to burn off the accumulation of a few extra pounds. The entire house was so excited to have this little boy there to bless the place. Gramma Cole stayed on knowing that the second newcomer would be arriving in probably a week or so. She was not disappointed. Toni started labor pains late on the fifth day after Richy V arrived, and Debbie was chosen to stay with the precious little boy for a few hours while Teri and the rest of the troupe went with Larry to take Toni to the hospital. Toni's water broke in the car on the way over, labor was surprisingly brief, and she delivered within about an hour or so after arrival at the hospital. Teri and those grandmothers had to be in the delivery room when little Cindy Cole was born, and it caused the same celebration as there was less than a week before. These Grandparents were so thrilled to welcome her arrival. And when Toni was better able to welcome visitors, in marched Larry holding Teri's hand and so pleased for the divine gift of this precious little girl. As expected, these two sisters didn't wait for the trip home to commence their sentimental weeping session, and Teri hugged her sibling for a long while.

They left Toni to rest up, and went home for Teri to feed her little slurping machine. Larry decided to go back to the hospital to wait for Toni to wake up, and several hours later she did as Larry was standing there holding her hand and admiring her face. Toni was overjoyed to feed her little baby girl, as Larry the Daddy had his camera ready to record the event.

With essentially the same scenario, but in less time, Larry and Teri went over to the coast to pick up the new mother and all her stuff. Larry was holding Teri's hand as they followed the nurse pushing Toni in the wheelchair out to the car, and they were gone out the gate to slowly drive home. Upon arrival, the same joyous festivity with all the same rites and watching rituals.

That night Larry's suite was crowded, with bassinettes on both sides of the bed and the two new mothers curled up on his shoulders. Everyone was happy, oh so happy, at the Remington home.

The next morning, as Larry was lazily sitting on the couch drinking his coffee, Gramma Shimi Remington was happily humming as she came in carrying little bald-headed newborn Cindy, all wrapped up in a pink blanket with only her tiny moon shaped face showing. She was then just a coupla days old, with a totally expressionless countenance, her eyes were almost swollen shut and her face looked sunburned after the birthing experience. Her tiny little mouth was closed but the tip of her tongue was sticking out between her lips, though she seemed to be awake. Gramma Shimi admired her so, and mumbled something like "Oh, you beautiful little doll!" as she seated herself right next to Larry. He thought this might be the right time to once again ask "Will you forgive me now?" and Gramma Shimi turned and looked at him with a totally blank expression and asked "For what?" Larry seemed then to have a better memory than her and he said "Forgive me for causing you all this grief." Her face then assumed a quizzical appearance as she continued to look at him then at the little child she held and asked "Larry. Larry. Larry. Does this look like grief?" Then without his saying another word Gramma Shimi said "Larry. Don't you think she has my eyes?" and he looked again at that glum little moon shaped face and said "She is the most beautiful little girl in the entire world, and I think she looks just like you!" Gramma responds to say "Larry. I think you're right. This little treasure is the most beautiful girl in the world, and she is here because of you." About that time Teri comes in with little Richy V all wrapped up in his blue blanket but with his shock of brown hair sticking out, and he had that same bland expression on his face, including the tongue sticking out.

Teri sat down on the other side of Larry, and everyone admired those little gifts from God, and Gramma said "I feel so fulfilled. I feel so complete. I now know my mission in this life, and I can hold them in my arms. Larry, you are the best thing ever to have happened to this family!"

On the Christmas day several months following the arrival of the new Cole grandchildren, a courier pulled into the Cole Grandparents' driveway in Springfield, jumped out of the new silver-white Mercedes sedan he was driving, scurried up to the porch, and rang the doorbell. Richard Cole drowsily responded, opened the door to find the courier handing him an envelope. Then the courier disappeared across the lawn and sped off as passenger in a little red Ford truck. Dad Cole stood there holding the envelope for a few seconds when his wife came up and looked over his shoulder asking "What's up?" The envelope was addressed to 'Gramma and Grampa Cole' They opened the envelope and removed the Christmas card that simply said "Merry Christmas, Richy V and Cindy" Taped to the inside of the card were three keys that obviously fit the doors and ignition of the Mercedes in the driveway. On the front seat of that car were ownership and certificate of origin documents, and the Coles had a new car gift from their California grandchildren.

Reuben was still in prison and missed the excitement when his twin sisters gave birth to Richard C. Cole V and Cindy Cole, and he didn't get to change even one diaper. Then almost two years later he missed the arrival both on the very same day of nephews Stewart Miguel Cole and Charles Emanuel Cole also known as the twins. One further little comment about the second set of kids: Little Richy V and Cindy were celebrating their first birthday party, when Gramma Remington lamented that all her kids were born too far apart, and suggested for all to hear that Larry and his brides maybe ought to get started on another round of new babies. The wives then mentioned that they have been consulting their thermometers and schedules, and already knew just the right timing to have a couple more kids on about the same day. And they did. Stewart and Charley were born on the same day. Stewart looked like his father and mother both. Charley looked like his father and mother both. But Stewart and Charley did not look at all alike. They weighed the same, and as they grew up they were the same height and with the same dark brown hair and eyes, and everyone in the family referred to them as the 'twins', but they just did not look at all like one another.

The ladies tried a third time to arrange birthdates to coincide, but Teri was the only one then to get pregnant, and that was the last pregnancy either of the wives would have. When Teri had her third child, a little girl named Ximena Sarah Cole, she actually did look exactly like her Gramma Remington, and was spoiled accordingly. When she reached her full height it was about 5'3".

Someone asked the question about post-partum depression for either or both of these young mothers. It simply did not happen. Looking back to the earliest time of romance with Larry Cole, the strong spirit of genuine affection seemed to escalate and strengthen almost incrementally over time, and never faded or declined, so the tub full of love just kept churning and bubbling so that the resultant effervescent joy left no room for negativity of any kind. This was truly a dynamic interdependent situation. Teri was so happy to have the "Love of my life", and Toni was overjoyed to see that her sister was so pleased. Toni was so thrilled to have this guy as her answer to prayer, and Teri was ecstatic to see her sister so jubilant. Larry Cole was the centerpiece of their existence and they did everything they could to make him happy, and he constantly reminded them of how delighted he was to contemplate the arrival of these tiny creatures that made the slurping sounds. Add to this mix the unabashed euphoria of the rest of both families for the arrival of the little ones, and it caused both Teri and Toni to have a great sense of accomplishment in their mission of maternity. Each of these ladies radiated a contagious spirit of contentment and genuine joy.

We hasten to report what to some will cause annoyance, chagrin, jealousy, and a bitter sense that many of us are in some way cheated by the laws of genetic predisposition. More particularly we refer to the fact that these young mothers were slender before the onset of their pregnancies and without a whole lot of sweat and strain were again slender within just a short time after they ceased breast feeding several months later. They managed to slenderize after each subsequent delivery, and neither of them ever got chubby. However, please consider that us fat guys are jolly.

Another word about the popular rule that says 'spare the rod and spoil the child': When you have a household full of five squirming little kids, plus more visiting on frequent occasions, how do you maintain discipline? More particularly comes the question: 'How do you get these noisy brats to shut up?' and 'How do you get these messy little kids to be neat?' The simplest answer should be 'You don't!' But such a simple answer is not enough when you have neighbors nearby or guests that come to visit. It is much better to have good discipline and an orderly household, with well-behaved kids that can understand and respect parental instructions, and best if you can teach these things to children at the earliest times.

The Cole family had it a little easier than some. The children all tended to be more calm than most, but that doesn't mean they were silent. These kids were super-busy all the time. However, in the Cole household, the Gramma Remington had portraits all over the house showing Marine Captain Larry Cole in every one of his uniforms from camouflage up to dinner dress with all those medals and campaign ribbons on his chest, with a machine gun in his hands or a saber by his side, with battle helmet and field boots or officer's cap and shiny shoes, seated in the cockpit of a jet fighter-bomber or standing by the wing in his flight suit with helmet in hand. All these children were brought up from earliest age to respect the United States Marine Corps and all the troops from buck private to the Generals and everyone in between. When private Richy V was about three years old he got his first stripes, and every time he did something especially well he was rewarded with another campaign ribbon. Richy V worked himself all the way up to Gunnery Sergeant, and they gave him a swagger stick and case. When he spray-painted the side of Grampa's car, they had to punish him for his crimes, so they took away his swagger stick and demoted him one pay grade. That punishment was worse than any smack on the head or spank on the rump. It took another six weeks of good behavior to earn the restoration of his stripes and an extra four weeks at hard labor to earn the return of that swagger stick. For all you parents that might want to try this kind of discipline, you should be aware that you can find quite a few US and foreign military medals and campaign ribbons at about any thrift shop in your town.

Another good way to maintain discipline in the ranks is to have the children share in making the rules and developing a plan for order in the house. That way it cannot be said that an offender simply did not understand. The older kids should be enlisted to serve as guardians of the younger children.

When the little ones were almost a year old and walking around, the ladies started dressing them up in cute costumes and would take them to visits at the dealership offices. These costumes were clown suits, football hero uniforms, cheerleader getups, military camouflage regalia, Superman, Batman and Catwoman outfits, and other such adorable fashions. They did this for many years, and the novelty never did wear off.

CHAPTER 25

<u>CURRENT EVENTS</u>

About two weeks after the arrival of the two blessed events Lt. Larry Cole was assigned to take part in pick-up and delivery exercises of jet fighter planes onto Navy carriers off the coast of Washington. They would deliver new or recently refurbished planes to the ship and pick up those in need of repair or alteration of electronic equipment that could not be accomplished on board. This took about a week, and Larry was able to bring back one of the newest design jet fighter bombers to the MCAS El Toro base. When he docked and went inside he was told that the CO wanted to see him, so he pulled off the flight suit and ran over to the CO's desk to let the receptionist know that he was reporting. He sat down outside the inner office and relaxed, watching the foot traffic as several of his pilot friends passed by and a couple of them said "congratulations", and Larry thought they were referring to his recent upgrade to the new fighter bomber aircraft. He just smiled and offered a little courteous salute. After about a ten minute wait, he was invited into the inner office, the CO offered again a hearty "congratulations Captain Cole". Immediately Larry was flushed with sudden realization that he had been promoted, although he had not yet seen any confirming letter such as would ordinarily be the case. He took the handshake of the CO and simply said that he had not yet received that official written notice of promotion and the CO went behind his desk and plucked up a single page copy of that letter that was sent to Larry's official mailing address, which was the address of the Remington residence. "Thank you, sir, my original of that copy should be in my mailbox at home. Will this change any of my assignments?" and the CO told him that about all the difference between a Lieutenant and a Captain in the Marine Corps flying business is in the different decorations on the collar and a higher pay grade. "The work assignments are about the same." With that Larry saluted and thanked the CO then turned and left out the door, directly to check out, and he was soon driving home, thinking "It won't make a difference to the Marine Corps but it will make a huge difference when my ladies find out I'm a Captain, and my Mom and Dad will be glowing with pride."

When he got home he discovered balloons and paper decorations strewn about the yard and hanging down from the roofline, and taped to the walls in the entry and front room, with signs saying 'Congratulations to our Captain'. The girls had opened up that letter several days ago, and were bubbling with anticipation for him to come home so that they for the first time could hug and kiss a real live Captain of something. Gramma Remington had baked a cake, and made cookies and lemonade, and the girls had the babies all decorated with happy clothes, even though these little kids didn't yet show much interest in parties.

The 'Captain' novelty faded after a couple of weeks and everyone's attention again focused on those two little kids that had come to bless the family. Larry and his ladies went 'shopping' at the mall even though they had absolutely no thought of buying or examining any merchandise. All they wanted to do was parade those little rascals around in their strollers, as they sat with dull expressions not at all interested in being admired by anyone. Then it became obvious that Gramma Cole was gonna spend her life's savings on air fare on multiple visits to come and see her newest favorite grandchildren, just to make sure that they are growing up healthy and nice. When Debbie would come home from work, she would go directly in search of one or both of those little kids, and haul one or more around the house for the next hour. Stewart Remington would go to work late and come home early so that he could teach those kids the alphabet and the laws of physics. Everyone was having fun every day and so long as the kids were awake even into late evening, and then they'd all gather around and watch them sleep and sneeze occasionally. Life around the Remington house had changed a bunch.

Gramma Remington would often come into the breakfast area carrying one of the little treasures, and she'd be purring some little ditty as she made the rounds kissing everybody on the top of the head and having everyone kiss the little one atop the head.

Gramma Remington hired a professional photographer to take pictures of both girls holding their little ones and standing with their Captain in front of his jet fighter-bomber while in his flying suit. One of those poses she had made into posters to put up in her husband's office in Santa Ana and on the wall in the main hallway at home.

When the little children were about two months old a tragedy fell upon the Remington household. Stewart Remington had a serious heart attack and was rushed to the hospital. They shoved needles into his arms, masks over his nose, and scalpels into his chest. After they did their medical miracles they held him against his will for another week 'for observation' and some further treatments. When he had been there for several days, Larry came directly from the base to visit. Dad Remington told Larry that a couple of his doctors had come in to see him earlier, and had offered the advice to "take it easy" and the admonition to "let somebody else do the work" The doctors inquired of him if there might be some younger folks in the family that could take over most of his responsibilities, and Stewart told them that he "would think about it" Then he looked up at Larry and asked if maybe Larry "would think about it." Dad Remington went on to remind Larry that the only son in the Remington family has proven himself unreliable if not totally incapable of taking over the dealerships, and is still cooling his heels in prison, anyway, and unavailable to assume any responsibilities. He indicated that the only one he could trust and the only one he could turn to was Larry Cole. Larry said that all things considered he "would think about it".

When Larry got home a little while later, he called the girls together for a little discussion of their father's proposition, and asked what they would want him to do. He asked them to sleep on it and they could discuss it at length tomorrow. After dinner, Larry phoned his Dad in Springfield, who had already heard about the promotion to USMC Captain, and told him of the situation with Dad Remington and his request that Larry assume control of the Remington family businesses. Richard Cole told Larry that there was an even better way, and that was to pray about the matter, place the whole thing on the altar, and accept the Lord's leading. He told Larry that they would pray about it in Springfield, ask for unspoken prayer relief at the church, and see if the Lord would lead them to the more perfect way. And they did. Larry then called his girls together about mid-evening, and it was quite a sight to see them breast feeding their infants as they rocked back and forth on their separate rockers, and while the noisy slurping was going on they were intent on what Larry was tossing out for further consideration. Larry thought that the matter of leaving the Marine Corps was serious enough for all of them to pray and pray some more until the light shines through, and they can feel comfortable with one direction or another. Teri was first to ask "Why don't we just start praying right now, all three of us!" Toni chimed in to say that just claiming to be Christians is not enough, and they should do what Christians are supposed to do, and that requires some heavy submission to the Will of God. And so they did, and it was more than half an hour before they got out of there, and by the time they were through the little ones were fast asleep.

Larry reported back to Dad Remington that he and his girls were praying hard about the proposition, and that he had enlisted his folks to fast and pray, and for everyone affected to seek the Will of God. They kept this up for about a week. During that week Larry considered all his options, including that tiny itty-bitty fear locked up in the recesses of his mind about the possibility of bigamy or polygamy charges, even though the lawyers has assured him that it was not likely that he and the girls could ever be successfully prosecuted. Then it sorta worried him that even though there might not be a successful prosecution in criminal courts there could be some problems with the military justice system. Then Larry sorta got worried, anxious, concerned, nervous, troubled, vexed, and increasingly fretful, and when he told his father about how he was becoming more apprehensive about the military career being destroyed, his Dad said "Hasn't the Lord worked out this problem yet?"

Well, the answer soon came in the mail. Apparently the medical people at Balboa Naval Hospital had determined that as a result of the neurological damage to Larry's lower back from those Viet Cong bullets, his deteriorating condition was such that he was deemed unfit for further military service. He was placed on immediate extended leave and at the expiration of that period he was retired on full disability and his active military service terminated.

Now isn't it just like the military to promote a guy to some important sounding rank, give him some new decorations for his uniform, give him a raise in pay, and then put him out to pasture?

You'd think that Larry would be saddened by this turn of events, but he was elated to immediately phone Springfield to tell his Dad that the Lord had answered the prayers and kicked him out of the Marines. Then he laughingly explained that the Marine Corps had made up his mind for him and gave him a full disability retirement and a couple of months of paid leave and a service termination date. Actually, Larry felt relieved and was pleased to inform his ladies that their prayers had been answered. They confessed that they had separately prayed that Larry would never again fly aircraft in a war zone.

By the time this military retirement notice was received, Stewart Remington had been home from the hospital for a few weeks, now resting up around the house. Larry went to him privately, told him that the decision had been made and there would be no need to think any more about the proposition. Then he asked Dad Remington when they would want him to report for work at the dealerships, adding that tomorrow morning would be OK.

And that's how Lawrence E. Cole became the President of the master corporation that controlled a coupla dozen new car dealerships and used car outlets, while Stewart Remington remained as Chairman of the Board.

A coupla more days passed and Larry spent some time making casual conversation with his father-in-law, who kept repeating that Larry's decision to come on board was such a relief to him. Then in a more serious vein, Stewart Remington suggested that with his assuming authority over the businesses Larry would become more or less the master of the house, and there were some special responsibilities associated with that badge. He reminded Larry of his promise never to separate the twins, and now added that if anything happened to him that Larry would be responsible to care for the other ladies in the family, namely Debbie and her mother. And he was a bit more emphatic to suggest that Gramma Shimi Remington should never be separated from her twins, and those little grandchildren should grow up with hugs from this Gramma. Larry smiled and told Dad Remington that he had already made agreements with Teri and Toni to always have their mother live with them so that they can always keep an eye on her.

Maybe it was Dad Remington or Larry's brides, but someone must have revealed to Shimi Remington how Larry promised that she would always live with them so that they could all care for each other all the time. That evening, Larry is minding his own business and watching the TV network news when his mother-in-law comes in and plops herself down on his lap and throws her arms around his neck, and starts sniffling and shedding a few sentimental tears, and wouldn't say why. His brides crept up quietly to watch, as Larry shrugged his shoulders, grinned and sorta rolled his eyes and wiggled his eyebrows in a mischievous manner.

CHAPTER 26

ROMANCE

So many little adventures are happening around us all the time. Every individual spins in his or her own orbit, each with his or her own quests. Some adventures occur from beginning to end in just a brief moment, and some of those explorations are spread over a lifetime. When a person circulates in an individual track it often intersects other trails and joins in confluence with other travelers on the pathway of life. For instance: romance

Debbie Remington actually got her annulment from the thug shortly after the birth of Teri's baby boy. When Rick Cole heard about that annulment he felt a strong urge to go out to California and visit his newborn nephew, and that urgency was intensified when Toni had her little girl. Several weeks later when there was a three day weekend, he phoned on a Thursday night and suggested that it might be nice if someone at the Remington place could pick him up at the LAX airport on Friday evening. As fortune would have it Debbie was standing near when that call came, and she reluctantly set aside all the important things she otherwise had to do, sacrificing her valuable time to drive all that way to offer gratuitous taxi service to this visitor.

Debbie simmered and fretted all day long in anticipation of Rick's arrival. In fact, she had not felt so twittery since she was a teenager. Just a few weeks ago she had the plastic surgeon do some minor surface scratching to do away with those holes around her ears, and the resulting scabs had finally fallen off, leaving her with newly beautified auricles, and she was sure that the passenger flying in for the visit would notice and she would be proud. We have to recall how the three-time-loser showed a great interest in the then still-married young lady earlier, when he first met her prior to the wedding of Larry and Teri, and then as they sat together and chatted so happily on the plane down to Mexico City and thereafter at all the celebrations relating to the wedding of Larry and Toni, and folks there taking note of the way that the married lady seemed to be brazenly chasing the three-time-loser. Disgusting display, don't you agree?

On this visit to check out the newborn kiddies, it happened that Rick Cole's Mom had already arrived again several days earlier from Missouri, visiting La-La Land for a week or so to make sure that her newborn grandchildren were actually faring well in her absence, and she was pleased to hear that her elder son was coming in from Illinois also for a weekend visit. While Gramma Cole was rocking one of the little treasures early Thursday evening, Debbie struck up a casual conversation and trying not to show too much interest in son Rick, she managed to get in a few questions about the history of Richard C. Cole IV. When Gramma Shirley got started on her favorite subjects she could go on for hours. Each of her boys was a favorite subject. But as this doting mother went into detail about how perfect was her little boy Rick, it seemed that she made no mention at all of any flaws or shortcomings. Debbie wondered how he could be so perfect and still be a three-time-loser. Well Gramma Cole was well prepared to respond to that question. She said that the best way to find out just how perfect Rick Cole might be is to ask his former wife Sharon. Debbie thought about that idea for a while and concluded that as awkward as it might be, maybe she should chat with that former wife. But this is silly talk. Rick and Debbie are merely friends within a family identity, nothing more. Just dancing partners occasionally, nothing more. He was one of the people standing in the poster-size picture she had over her desk at work, and would occasionally point him out as being a dear member of the family, nothing more. But it would be well if she could talk to that former wife in Missouri.

Friday about noon, Debbie left work early to do some shopping at Nieman-Marcus or some such place, and she found the most perfect outfit to wear when she was to go pick up the visitor at LAX. It was an ensemble that fit just right, and just right meant that it was a modest garment that still showed off her excellent figure and in contrasting colors that blended well with her long dark hair and sorta Mexican features. She wore nice spiked heels of average height instead of Cuban heels that looked clumsy on relatively short girls. At 5'2"+ Debbie considered herself short. Her makeup was done just right. On this occasion little Debbie looked perfect. Debbie's appearance was that of a modest and prudent young lady.

At the appointed time and place, Debbie was patiently waiting alone near the passenger exit gate when Rick Cole came sauntering down the arrival corridor. When he spotted her he pulled out a camera and snapped a couple of pictures saying "I need these for our album" and he brashly added "Our kids will want to see what you looked like the night when we ran off and got married!" and she shook her head and said "No, sir. I ain't ever gonna get married again without my folks' consent!" to which he said "OK. Let's go ask 'em!" as he reached out to take her hand. Then Debbie glowed and beamed asking "Are you serious?" He looked at her with an impish grin and said "Well, I wish I could be, but you don't know me or anything about me, and I hope to get to know you a little better." To which she feigned her disgust and responded by snapping her fingers and muttering "Shucks! I thought you were serious!" He bent over and whispered "Well, until we get their consent, can I hold your hand and all that mushy stuff?" She noted "You are already holding my hand, and I wanna know what you mean by mushy stuff." He told her she deserved a demo, as he kissed the back of her hand, then abandoned the hand to place his arm around her waist, gave her a brief affectionate hug and invited her to accompany him to the luggage carousel. All this flirtatious badinage set a pattern of happy mood for the rest of the evening. The handsome young single man and the beautiful young single girl.

After gathering up the one piece of luggage, holding hands as they walked out to find Debbie's car parked in the LAX garage in some place that she had already forgotten, the two of them yakked about everything and nothing, and when they finally found the car they headed for the exit as Rick inquired whether or not Deb had yet had dinner, and asked if she knew how to find 'Belisle's' She said she was famished and that they'd be there in about forty minutes or so. Then Rick said "Y'wanna go ice skating? Larry says that he always enjoyed taking the twins out ice skating after munching at Belisle's." She told him that she wasn't dressed for skating, but if he was gonna be around for a couple of days, they could go somewhere to have him show his skills on ice. There was no time left for ice skating anyway, after they spent two hours puttering with their food and talking silly at Belisle's.

When later they finally got to the Remington place, they were still in a jubilant mood. Everybody was still up holding babies, and Rick was invited to take part in that merriment. Rick's Mom remarked it was nice that after so many years of goin' it alone he finally found a cute girlfriend. Rick turns to Debbie and asks "How about bein' my girlfriend?" and she says "How can we carry on a romance with you livin' two thousand miles away?" and he says "We can try!" and she says "OK!" Rick smiles and says "Really?"

And that's the way the serious romance of Rick and Debbie got started.

Rick had never seen Debbie's first husband, not even a picture. Rick had never seen Debbie in the lifestyle garments that she had been wearing for the past three years, and that means that he had never seen her wearing the provocative low-cut blouses and short-short skirts. Rick had never seen Debbie wearing those false eyelashes and black mesh stockings and garish Cuban heels. Rick had never seen Debbie with all her baubles, bangles and cheap jewelry, and those holes in her ears are now gone, scabs and all. But on the other hand, Debbie had never talked with the former wife of this three-time-loser.

As for any pictures of Mr. Verdugo, even though Stewart Remington gleefully suggested that he wanted to show the video again and again, both his wife and Rick's Mom begged him not to bring that stuff out. Debbie had already gathered up every one of the pictures she could find that showed her at any time during the past three years. She was worried that maybe somebody at the dealership might have taken some snapshots, but she'd just have to take her chances on that, and in case any such pictures might appear she conjured up in her mind a believable story about a Halloween party at the office.

Getting late, Rick and his Mom took the bedroom usually occupied by one of the twins, and in his apartment Larry once again had two bassinettes nearby, with Teri snoozing on one shoulder and Toni on the other. Larry and the twins continued the regular practice of praying together every night before bedtime, and this night they had an altar call like wow, and touched on every little thing they could think of that God should look into, and the one most important thing was this blossoming romance of Rick Cole and Debbie Remington. That romance appeared to them like it already was an answer to prayer.

On Saturday morning, the twins wanted to show everyone their culinary skills, so they prepared fried eggs, scrambled eggs, boiled eggs, poached eggs, omelets and sausage, plus some waffles. Gramma Shirley was at the sink counter fixing coffee and all the rest of the crowd was gathered around the breakfast table enjoying the bill of fare, when Gramma Remington comes prancing happily through the door, humming some pleasant little ditty, carrying tiny Cindy Cole and Cindy was totally unconcerned. Gramma made the rounds kissing everyone on the top of the head, and then inviting everyone to kiss little Cindy on the top of her little bald head. As she then sits down at the table she looks at Rick Cole and asks if he and his new girlfriend will be attending the event at the mall this morning. Rick says "What event?", and Gramma Remington replies to tell him that Larry and the twins get their little ones all dressed up and in the baby strollers to parade them around the mall "It's lotsa fun!" Naturally, Rick was stunned to hear that he might be so honored to participate in such a grand event, and he said he might attend if his new girlfriend would go along, as he turned toward Debbie with a questioning expression on his face. She blushed to hear that he might want her to join in, and she bashfully nodded her response, saying "I ain't got nuthin' else to do!" Phooey on pushin' the little kids around for strangers to admire, Rick sees another golden opportunity for holding hands with this cute chickie.

And so they did. Larry and the twins went strolling down the mall corridor with their kids. Rick and Debbie walked behind them but were totally engrossed in themselves. They passed one of those photography studios that specialize in the glamour poses, Debbie started beaming and tugging on Rick's arm, wanting to have a portrait that she could put up over her desk at the office, and another one that she could place above her bedstead. Rick would have to be totally stupid to think that Debbie's notions about this romance were born just yesterday.

Later that Saturday, Rick suggested that Debbie should go with him to the ice skating rink, so that they could practice their pair's skills in anticipation of Olympic trials. Unfortunately, they chose a rink in Fullerton that was jammed with little sixth grade kids learning how to work the ice. They were surrounded by youngsters doing their rumpsliding more than the two foot kind of gliding. The only redeeming part of this trip was when a couple of young men skated up to where Rick and Debbie were standing, one of them looked Rick right in the face and pointed toward Debbie saying "Sir, you do have excellent taste!" to which Rick with a huge smile responded "Yes. And I do so admire your extraordinary perception and incisive perspicacity!" The Olympians discussed how they ought to go for dinner at some outrageously overpriced restaurant, but Debbie suggested that they should be saving for their Honeymoon to Tahiti, and when Rick heard that he grinned, kissed the little girlfriend on the forehead and said "OK. I know just the place!" and they went to the Colonel's fried chicken shop and bought a big bucket of dead bird, then went over to the nearest parks & recreation picnic table and enjoyed the late afternoon sun. They stayed at that location well into the evening, sitting and strolling, smiling and carefree. Getting better acquainted.

When later they walked into the living room of the Remington home, everybody was sitting around gabbing, the babies were asleep in Larry's quarters, as usual everyone seemed so very content with life and living, and they all cheerily greeted the returning boyfriend and girlfriend pair. Dad Remington raised his hand and inquired for all to hear "Well, have you set a date yet?" to which Debbie responded "Dad. This guy moves slowly. He has kissed me on the left hand once, on the right hand twice and here on my forehead twice." Gramma Shirley giggled and pointed at her progeny saying "My little boy is a gentleman. He would never give a girl a serious kiss unless he was absolutely sure he was in love!" Debbie looked wistfully at her date and said "Well?" and he responded to say "Are you ready?" and as she nodded he leaned over and cupped her face in his hands and kissed her on the lips, then leaned back and said "Was that OK?", and she quietly looked at him for a few seconds and said "Let's try that again, if that's OK with you." As though oblivious to the crowd of onlookers, he kissed her again in that same romantic way, then stood looking at her with that quizzical expression, and she smiled and looked at him impishly saying "One more time!" After completing the one more time, she giggled and whispered "I think we're getting somewhere now. But, just to be sure would you mind doing that one more time?" And so he did, and the amused audience applauded. Debbie turned to address the group of spectators and said "In case you folks might want to know, I have never before been kissed like that. What's more I have never before ever had such a quivering thrill, and did you notice my knees shaking?" She turned and looked into the face of her skating partner and said "I hope you feel like I do!" grabbed him around the waist and buried her face into his chest, holding on tightly and mumbling something about being happy. Larry for the first time noticed that Debbie was sentimental like her sister Toni.

The next day, Sunday morning, Rick and Debbie rode to church with his Mom in the back seat of the Remington Mercedes, while Larry and his little family rode in their Buick. This was a very happy day for Gramma and Grampa Remington, to have their twins and Larry carrying their two most favorite grandchildren, and Debbie all scrunched up in lockstep with a handsome young man that they could really be proud of. Many of the folks at the church were aware of the unusual marriage of Larry and the twins, but nobody seemed to care enough to say anything about it. What was of interest this day was the handsome young fellow with Debbie, or the 'New Debbie' as some whispered among themselves. Pastor DeWitt made the announcements, and then mentioned that some time ago he had introduced a young man to the congregation, and that young man seems now to be a permanent fixture, and his mother Shirley Cole you met a few weeks ago. Now he wanted to introduce the older brother of Larry Cole, and asked for Rick Cole to stand and be welcomed. When he sat down as the applause faded, the pastor teasingly asked "Who is that young lady with you?" and he replied "She's my most precious person!" and Debbie smiled and her face got red, then she lifted her hand to say "He's my boyfriend!".

The whole gang went to Remington's place for lunch, which consisted mostly of cold-cut sandwiches and a couple of salads. Rick and Debbie took off in her car for nowhere in particular, but they ended up walking hand in hand along the beach and stomping barefoot in the surf. All of their conversation was light chit-chat, and it was noticeable to both of them that there was a prevailing pleasant mood not unlike that of a couple of teenagers doing the small talk. They didn't bother going back to the house, but just went to church that evening to hear Pastor DeWitt and his message on prophecy. The rest of the family did not show up. After church they went out to a local coffee shop with the Pastor and his wife, and chatted about anything and everything, nothing serious. They didn't get back to Remington's until almost midnight, but everyone was up waiting to visit with them some more. Dad Remington inquired of Debbie "Are you folks still doing the boyfriend and girlfriend thing?" and Debbie said "You bet. I'm gonna hold on tight!"

Debbie took Rick to LAX on Monday afternoon for his return flight to Illinois, and they sat around holding hands and bonking heads together for some time before the flight was called. They stood and faced each other, the short girl and the tall guy, and he took her face again in his hands and kissed her, and she grabbed him by the collar and gave him a more passionate smooch, saying "Please hurry back!"

Within a few days those portraits were ready for pickup. Debbie went to get them at 2:00 PM and by 2:20 the best solo pose of Rick went up over her desk. Another solo pose of Rick was tacked to the wall over her bed at home, and a fair size portrait of the two of them together ended up at home on the wall just inside the living room. She gave two portraits of the two of them together in different poses to Shirley Cole to take home with her, and sent the best of the portraits of the two of them together directly to Rick Cole along with the best of her solo poses. The romance of Rick and Debbie was moving along nicely.

Rick Cole came to visit at least three weekends each month for the next several months, especially if there happened to come a three-day weekend. Instead of settling down with the regimen, it seemed that Debbie was more and more excited in anticipation of those weekends. These two were acting like immature teenagers. The biggest difference was that teenagers would probably be a little more cautious and would not be so likely to want the whole world gawking at the romance as it matured. Then came the suggestion that for the upcoming three-day weekend Debbie might want to visit back East, meet Rick's two boys that lived in Missouri, and stay a few days with the rest of the Cole family.

And she did.

Debbie took off from work that Friday, got a flight out of LAX with a one-hour layover in Dallas, and Shirley Cole picked her up at the Springfield airport that afternoon at 4:30 PM CST. Debbie told how she was so nervous and anxious and didn't really know why. Shirley Cole told her that on Saturday morning at about 9:00 or so she would have her chance to cross-examine Rick's ex-wife Sharon and find out all about Rick's past flaws and failures. Rick drove in from Illinois, and arrived about 7:00 PM to take Debbie out to dinner at an exotic place in Ozark, Missouri called *'Lambert's Throwed Rolls'* where they serve all you can eat of whatever you want to order, and throw hot rolls to your table. If you ain't never been to Lambert's you ain't lived.

Debbie sacked out at the Cole family place in Springfield, but didn't get to bed until midnight. She sat up and talked with the family about everything Springfield, plus a lot about Branson. Shirley Cole had reservations for Debbie and her date at one of the shows in Branson for Saturday night.

Rick Cole's kids were named Andrew and Amos, names selected by and arbitrarily imposed by Sharon's folks. But rather than to have a couple of guys in the family by name of Amos 'n Andy, those boys were now better known as Billy and Spike. Billy was almost eight years old and Spike about a year younger. These two guys were the most perfect little gentlemen.

Shirley Cole got along well with Sharon in spite of the circumstances under which the marriage failed, when Sharon dumped Rick to run off with a man named Frank Shepherd, who was the principal of the school where she was a second grade teacher. She married Frank as soon as the divorce became final, and their little girl by name of Crissy was born a few months later. Sharon had been told in advance that Debbie wanted to meet her and the boys, and she did. As previously arranged, Frank and Rick went together to take the boys to Little League, leaving Debbie and Sharon to get to know one another. These baseball devotees were on their way out the door when Rick turned and said for everyone to hear "Sharon, Debbie wants to ask you some questions, and you should tell her anything she wants to know, plus anything you want to say that she might not want to know. OK?"

The four baseball fanatics had been gone for only a few minutes, the two ladies sat down on the couch as the little four-year old girl was running back and forth between the rooms. Sharon said "I talked with Rick's Mom about your coming to visit, and she asked me to just lay it all on the line. I'm just as nervous as you must be, but you might feel more comfortable if I just start, and you can interrupt me anytime you want. I'll tell you everything from the beginning." She went on to tell how she had known Rick from grade school, and had always been in love with him, and was so disappointed when he married someone else. Then when that early marriage failed, she was disappointed again when he married another girl. He never even noticed Sharon until college days, and she graduated a couple of years ahead of him. Rick and Sharon had the two children and then Sharon landed a job with the school system in Springfield. She got involved in a clandestine romance with another employee at the school. When Rick found out about it, he offered to forgive Sharon and live happily ever after. But Sharon dumped Rick and married that other guy, and he is the one she is married to now. When she filed for divorce from Rick her lawyer asked for everything hoping to get half, but Rick gave her the house and everything in it, the best car, and agreed to assume all the debts and pay alimony to her and generous child support. The alimony only lasted for so long as it took for Frank and Sharon to get officially married. The little girl Crissy was born, and that sorta brings the history up to date.

But then Sharon wanted Debbie to know a few extra things that might be of interest to Debbie. "I understand that you actually live in the same place with Larry Cole, and you've had a chance to see how he is. That's exactly the way Rick has always been, so kind and gentle, so thoughtful and affectionate. He and Frank discussed how the boys should be raised, and they agreed that Rick would always be 'Dad' or 'Daddy' and Frank would be 'Poppa'. You see this precious little Crissy running around here? Well, just wait and see what she does when Daddy and Poppa come home this afternoon. When she was about a year old Frank and I had to attend a teachers' convention up in Kansas City while Rick took the boys over to his folks' for the weekend. Our babysitter skipped out on us about ten minutes before Rick came for the boys, and when he heard that Crissy needed some supervision for the weekend he had us gather up all her stuff and he took her with him. When he brought her back on Sunday night she had several new outfits and a new car seat. Ever since then he has wanted to take her along with the boys for their scheduled and non-scheduled visitations. She has become 'Daddy's girl' and he just loves her so much."

Sharon looked mournful and said "I am so stupid. I must be the dumbest person in the whole State of Missouri. I once had the most wonderful and caring man, as perfect as a husband and father can be, and I discarded him. Please don't think I am unhappy with Frank. He is so good to me and such a good father to my boys. I am content to live out the rest of my life just as I am, but I now realize that I would have had a different life if I hadn't wandered."

Debbie sat there for a few minutes in silence, then asked "Tell me every flaw and failure about Rick Cole that you can think of!" and Sharon shook her head disconsolately and said "He doesn't have any flaws! He is probably the most perfect man you'll ever know. He never loses his temper. In all the time I've known him he has never raised his voice at me. We seldom ever had any disagreements. He is always pleasant and finds humor in everything. He never lets anyone know if he has a bad day. If you want my advice, you should go down on Monday morning and get your marriage license before someone comes to steal him away. But, according to Rick's Mom he has already decided that he wants only you. You must be the luckiest girl in the world."

These ladies sat and yakked for several hours, and then the baseball aficionados returned. When little Crissy spotted Rick she ran to him with her arms raised and yelled "Daddy! Daddy!" as he picked her up and tossed her around in the air. When he finally put her down, she turned to Frank and yelled "Poppa!"

and went through a similar scenario. Frank smiled and whispered to Debbie "You see who is most popular around here?"

Debbie and Rick went to see a show called 'The Baldknobbers' in Branson on Saturday night. On Sunday they attended early services at the Cole family's home church, and then went to a nice place for brunch with his folks. On Sunday evening they took in a performance of 'Presley's Country Jubilee' in Branson. Debbie got the distinct impression that Rick liked country music. If you're gonna be in Springfield, you really should try to get in all you can of the dozens of Broadway shows in Branson.

Debbie and Rick did not discuss anything about Deb's cross-examination of former wife Sharon.

Rick drove Debbie to the Springfield Airport about mid-afternoon on Monday, chatted with her until her flight was called, gave her the big hug and goodbye kiss, and she was gone off into the clouds. Rick drove directly home to Illinois.

About a month or so after Debbie returned from her Missouri visit, Richard and Shirley Cole came in from Missouri and Rick Cole flew in from Illinois. Debbie Remington was baptized in water at Pastor DeWitt's church in San Clemente.

That same Sunday evening after Debbie got baptized, all the Remington's and Larry's parents were sitting around sipping coffee and happily chatting about everything and nothing. Debbie was seated on the end of the couch, and Rick carried in a pot of fresh coffee. He placed the coffee on the table near Debbie, then turned to face Dad Remington and casually said "Mr. Remington, I would like to have your consent to marry Debbie." Hearing this, Debbie's face went blank, her mouth fell open, and she looked first at her Dad and then at Rick the inquiring one, then again at her Dad. Stewart Remington then winked at Debbie and said "Debbie, Rick here wants me to consent to your marrying him. Is that OK with you?" She said nothing but nodded her head in a gesture of approval. Dad Remington then looks at Rick and says "It looks like she wants me to say 'yes', so you do have my consent." Then kneeling down in front of her he first exchanged pleasant glances, then looked around the room at everyone present, and received approving smiles from all of them. Rick took her by the hand and simply said "Debbie. I love you. What do you think of me?" For the first time in many years, tears welled up in her eyes as she whispered "I love you more than words can say." and a voice came from the gallery of observers "A little louder, please. We can't hear you!"

Hearing all this Rick then asked "Will you marry me?" and her blubbering response was "Yes, oh yes!" Stewart Remington hears these words of endearment and inquires "Do you guys have a date in mind?" Debbie wistfully says "How about tomorrow?" Debbie's Momma says "Why don't we all go to Mexico City so Debbie can have someone in the family do the honors?" to which Debbie responds "No, Mom, I'm afraid I forfeited any nice big wedding several years ago. Anybody that's been married before shouldn't be wearing a beautiful white wedding gown. We can have us a little simple wedding right here in town." But Momma wobbles her index finger as part of her lecture and surges on with "You are mistaken young lady. I was there when the judge said that your marriage was 'void ab initio'. I looked that up and it means that other marriage never was. When the court granted you that annulment it meant that you have never been married. And since your marriage to Rick Cole will be your first time, you gotta have a really nice wedding. We can phone my cousin Bibi and ask her to plan just a little wedding, and we can invite a few of the family to come for just a tiny celebration and reception!"

Then Momma Remington really started feeling her oats, saying "If you kids will let me handle everything for a wedding in Mexico City, we'll pay for the whole enchilada. Rick, do you have the rings yet?" To which he responds "No. I thought I'd better ask her first. We can go down tomorrow to see a jeweler in Santa Ana and pick out something." Momma doesn't even try to conceal her excitement and says "If you'll let me pick out the rings, I'll pay for them!" On hearing this, Larry says "That's a better deal than I got!"

Hearing these exchanges between these people so close to everything, Debbie looks at Rick, and he smiles and shrugs his shoulders and says "We'll have to wait until school's out!" Instantly Debbie's eyes get big like saucers and her chin drops down as her mouth goes agape. She starts to get into the swing of things, recalling her sister's beautiful Mexico City wedding, all the pageantry, the smiling faces of all those happy Mexicans, all the reception celebrations and that huge mountain of a wedding cake, and suddenly the idea became so very appealing. She grinned and wrinkled her nose at every smiling face around the room and said "OK!" Then little Debbie the stalwart and mature young woman started sniffling and as the tears began to flow she said "I can't believe this is really happening!"

Three things ensued the following Monday morning: First, they went to the same jeweler where Momma Remington got those rings for her twins, so that she could make sure Debbie got about the same size glittery set of diamonds as her other girls, fancy enough to impress all the family in Mexico City, and she did. They went to the portrait studio again to have a picture made of the bride and groom for insertion into the wedding invitations. Then they called cousin Bibi in Mexico City to ask her to prepare for Debbie a tiny little wedding and an itty-bitty reception. Bibi exploded with glee. Nothing made Bibi happier than to be able to plan another family wedding. She told cousin Shimi that she already had in mind the most perfect wedding gown that would really be nice for Debbie, and asked for permission to order that wedding dress, the crown and veil. Debbie could come down for a couple of days to take care of any needed alterations. Debbie was tickled pink. A few days later Bibi phones to advise that maybe it would be a good idea for Rick and his groomsmen to come down for fittings for their simple wedding attire. So Debbie and her Mom went with Rick and his brothers down to Mexico City a week or so later, and that's the first time there was any hint that this wedding of Debbie was gonna be another whopper.

If a young lady knew that she was soon to be wed in a brief ceremony before a relatively small gathering of family and friends, there should be less anxiety about doing all the preparation for and execution of the plan. But once this whole project got rolling Debbie was incredibly anxious, overwhelmed at the immensity of the entire program. Her Mother was filled with massive amounts of real joy, overflowing with delight that her precious little Debbie was gonna marry such a perfect gentleman, such a handsome man. Mom Remington had been planning this wedding for Debbie since her little girl was in diapers, and now Debbie's world had turned around, and her Mom's world was becoming even more complete. Debbie's delight was contagious, and her twin sisters bridesmaids seemed to catch the flame as they shared her joy. But their Mother was the happiest of all of them.

It might seem unusual for the ex-wife to show up at a guy's wedding, but this was an unusual situation. Rick wanted his two boys to be there, and wherever those boys might go they would always want to take their little sister, and since these three kids were gonna go all the way to Mexico City then the whole family should go. So Frank and Sharon Shepherd made plans to be there. Hearing that little Crissy was gonna be available, Debbie wanted her to be the flower girl, and so she was. Give this a little thought: wouldn't it be great psychology to include this pretty little girl in such an event, knowing that the child will likely be part of your life for many years to come?

Just as with Toni's wedding not so long ago, for Debbie the family in Mexico put on a show to be remembered. The Remington's chartered an air carrier to haul everybody down to Mexico City from the Tijuana airport, and they had about ten vacant seats for the flight. Debbie phoned ex-wife Sharon to invite her and her household to ride down with the rest of the family, saving air fare for everyone. Sharon was delighted to hear the plan, but wanted to know how to explain this unusual arrangement if anyone asked. Debbie told her that they'd simply identify them as a part of Rick's family. Frank Shepherd thought he'd better clear this with Rick Cole, and got about the same answer. The Remington flight was welcomed at the Mexico City airport as before, with the black limousines and the entire spectacle, the swanky hotels and hosted dinner with all the trimmings and trappings. This whole scenario was one that they first encountered at Toni's wedding, so for most everyone it was old socks. But for the Shepherd family it was an amazing extravaganza.

The wedding dress that cousin Bibi picked out was so very beautiful, so elaborate. This one had a faux train that was detachable, and as did the veil fell down behind the bride dragging by about four or five feet in length. The full crown was covered in glittering stones. This wedding was not a simple little event. This was a celebration to rival anything Mexico City had yet seen, and this magnificent wedding gown was suitable for such an occasion.

The Mexico City Main Catholic Cathedral was so impressive, with its old turrets and vaulted ceilings, long aisles and all the things that one would expect in such a splendid sanctuary. The music was electrifying, to say the least. The place was packed from front to back and side to side with all those happy Mexicans. Ex-wife Sharon sat on one side of Shirley Cole and Shimi Remington sat on the other side, and all three of them were holding hands, watching intensely every tiny feature of the entire thrilling program, and they all cooed when little Crissy slowly passed by like a pro along that center aisle, moving in pace with the processional music. All of them gasped with delight as the twin bridesmaids passed separately with such excellent style and grace. Now, ya gotta appreciate that Stewart Remington is an old hand at marching with his daughters down that center aisle to give away the bride. But we have to imagine what thoughts must have gone through his mind that day, filtered through the heart and soul of this proud father, knowing that on his arm is his little baby girl that they thought might be lost, and now he's gonna give away this strikingly beautiful little bride to a man he greatly admired and fully appreciated. Stewart Remington had a huge radiant smile from ear to ear, glowing with pride as he marched slowly down that aisle, sparkling just a little less than Debbie herself. Again we emphasize that these Mexicans appreciate wedding ceremony pomp, and this presentation was equal to any. You can imagine the thoughts going through Debbie's mind, from the time she put on that magnificent gown just a while ago, from the moment she entered that center aisle, and with each measured step as she glided down that entire distance from the entry doors to the altar, there to meet her handsome groom. She was the star of the program, the centerpiece of everything to happen that day. This is what she once thought she had forfeited.

The Catholic Priest that officiated at these nuptial rites was a member of the Carillo family. In the best of Mexican traditions, they handed that Priest the lovely box of thirteen "arras" coins, which he blessed and handed to the groom, who in turn poured all those coins into the cupped hands of his bride, as she gushed and grinned. Then came the yugal lasso ritual with the triple-length rosary placed in the figure-8 fashion around the necks of the bride and groom, and both of them gushed and grinned.

When that officiating priest pronounced them husband and wife, Rick very dramatically kissed his bride, and those three ladies, Sharon, Shirley and Shimi, started crying altogether. Each one sniffling for their own individual and distinguishable reasons.

After the groom kissed his bride, the happy couple turned toward the audience and smiled. The congregation broke into applause and unabashed cheering as the newlyweds marched confidently down the aisle, followed by their entourage. Larry Cole the best man had on his arm his wife Teri, and Charley Cole had on his arm Larry's wife Toni, and nobody explained how it was that Teri and Toni didn't both grab their husband, but Ya' gotta follow the established protocol. The videos were terrific. The still photography was even better. On several of the still shots little Crissy was the centerpiece.

The reception was another grand affair, the tables heavy with great varieties of steak and seafood, and all the trimmings, the really great Mexican Mariachi music and dancing, the huge wedding cake and all the sweets, and Shirley Cole didn't dare to take a sip of anything for fear that what was left of her Springfield reputation might be lost. The pile of wedding presents had to be hauled to the airport in a large truck, and it filled the cargo hold of the chartered airplane. They had to wrestle with the customs people to get it all into the US.

When all the festivities were over for the bride and groom, they left on the great silver bird airliner, heading for Fiji where they spent about a week, and then on to Tahiti to stay another few days. Rick told that he stood on the beach in Fiji holding his bride in his arms for almost two hours while she kept saying over and over "I am so happy! I am so happy!" just as Larry has told many times that his sentimental bride Toni still does. Sisters can be very much alike. The newlyweds frolicked and splashed in the clear waters of the South Pacific and when for the first time Rick saw Debbie in her skimpy swimsuit he began to constantly remind her that she had the most perfect figure ever seen.

In the days before the wedding the Mexicans provided a couple of guided tours around Mexico City. After the wedding, Frank and Sharon Shepherd and the three kids wanted to go to Disneyland and some of the other vacationer sites around Southern California. Stew Remington loaned them a new Ford Station Wagon for all their travels, and Larry Cole drove them to the LAX airport when they left town about ten days later.

When Rick and Debbie returned from their Honeymoon the whole family drove in two station wagons down to the LAX airport to greet them on arrival. They skipped down the arrival corridor all tanned and happy. Debbie was not just happy, she was bubbly and babbly, bouncing and trembling with delight. She had never been this way before. She couldn't wait to start her story about each and every sight and site of their Honeymoon travels. When she got her sisters and her Mom off to where they could do all their girl talk, Debbie kept saying over and over how thrilled she was to be married to this most wonderful treasure, this perfect gentleman. Several times she boldly stated that she "Never imagined that love could be so wonderful!" When it seemed that she must surely have exhausted her stories, Debbie melted with joy to tell everyone about how things actually got started on their Honeymoon flight as they were taking off on the jet plane, as Rick leaned over and whispered "Let's get this started right. We ought to pray first thing, and let God know how much we appreciate His miracles shared with us!" Then Rick held Debbie's hands in his and cranked off the most lovely prayer as that jet plane was still climbing into the clouds, telling the Lord that their lives would from this moment be dedicated to His service, asking for divine guidance and protection, and for the Lord's blessing on all they do and wherever He leads them to go; thanking the Lord for the gift of love that He has showered on them, and acknowledging that it was by His grace that they found one another, and asking that by His grace He keep them always together. Amen and amen.

As a wedding present the Remington's sold the house in Tustin to the tenants, and bought a nice home for Rick and Debbie in Illinois, with title taken in the names of Richard C. Cole IV and Ximena Debra Carillo Cole. There was a whole lot of money left over to buy new furnishings. For Christmas that year they gave Rick and Debbie a new Mercedes convertible. It was obvious that the Remington's really did like Rick Cole.

About 14 months after the marriage of Rick and Debbie Cole, Gramma Remington and Shirley Cole were present in the delivery room in Illinois when Debbie gave birth to a little girl that they named Ximena Teresa Cole and they called her Teri, with dark brown eyes and dark brown hair, and she was a happy dancing child. A little more than a year after the arrival of the first girl a second child was born and she was named Ximena Antonia Cole. She was an extremely small child, with reddish brown eyes and flaming red hair, and they called her 'Cricket'. Cricket was a happy little girl and liked to sing for anyone and everyone, in English and in Spanish. In fact, she loved singing so much that you couldn't shut her up. They finally started leaving her in the church nursery during worship services, because she would spontaneously burst into song during the sermons.

After Debbie had the two kids, she gained about fifteen pounds and was semi-plump. When you're just 5'2" then fifteen pounds is a lot of extra weight. Her reading got blurred, so she had to have reading glasses, and then on to bifocals. Her hair turned grey a little early and she had to use coloring to maintain a near natural appearance. Husband Rick continued every day and sometimes several times each day to tell her how perfect she was.

As for the wedding pictures, they filled a really nice album with a complete copy for the Remington house and a duplicate album for Shirley Cole to keep open on her coffee table. The portrait of the bride and groom together in front of the altars, with the beautiful stained glass glistening behind them, was given a place of honor in the Remington parlor next to the similar portraits of the twin sisters' weddings, and likewise at the Colé house in Springfield. The portrait of Rick and Debbie standing before the altar with the whole group of wedding entourage included little Crissy posing so perfectly with such a pleasant smile right there in the middle, so they provided a copy of that item for the Shepherd household. Little Crissy insisted that such portrait be placed prominently on the wall of the library in that home, and as odd as it may seem to those of us that understand the rules of propriety, that portrait remains on that wall to this very day. Now give this some thought: When guests in that home ask about the portrait, how can it be explained?

CHAPTER 27

TEMPUS FUGIT

The passing of time. Time goes by and cannot be retrieved. Though time is transitory it is inextricably associated with events, and success or failure of those trials and tribulations, or fun and frolic, efforts that are constructive or destructive, triumphs and defeats, can be measured in degrees. Winning or losing can be measured by degrees, and some winning is counterbalanced by the cost of success. This is where we get the expression of 'Pyrrhic Victory'.

The passing of time. The aging process. As we move along in years the body weakens, the memory gets foggy, the wrinkles appear, the hair gets grey or disappears altogether, and we have to rely on past victories to rejoice in accomplishment. And then some folks have to live with recollection of defeats, and can find very little cause to rejoice. Victories can be great or small. Defeats can be great or small. Some victories are durational, the continuing effort rewarded by ultimate success or series of successes. Most personal defeats are minor, but some are catastrophic. Some defeats come in waves, redundantly disappointing. Where successes can be a joyful accumulation of satisfying accomplishments, a person should have the good sense to learn from early failures, so as to avoid accumulations of defeat. On the other hand, some people essentially never learn.

Time lounging in a prison can still be productive years. Some folks use their stretch to study for university degrees, some learn a trade, some learn to read and spell their own name. Some just watch the calendar and wait impatiently for their time of release. On the outside the world is still going on with its business: the new model years come out for all the cars and trucks; new electronic devices are innovative this week and out of date within another few months; clothing styles change drastically; politicians and their governments come and go; college and professional sporting teams win and lose; your relatives and acquaintances grow older; the Hollywood stars seem at first never to age because of skillful cosmetic surgery, then some of the females begin to look like cats. Prisoners lose contact with girlfriends and wives or maybe too often receive divorce papers. The jailbirds miss all the weddings and family celebrations; they miss the funerals of friends and family; they miss the joy of being there when newborns arrive. Reuben Remington missed three sisters' weddings in Santa Ana and Mexico City, but they would come to visit from time to time, and he did notice how marriage seemed to affect their dimensions and posture.

Reuben Remington spent a number of wasted years as a guest of the government. What good is it that he exhibited a great intellectual brilliance at an early age, and could have been a success at so many occupations? Reuben got greedy, and fell victim to his own lust for wealth and all that it could buy. Instead of using his idle prison time productively, all Reuben could think about were all the trappings of prosperity: he still craved the big home in the nicest neighborhood with fancy furnishings and the big swimming pool out back surrounded by acres of beautiful landscape; he wanted to be seen with the fancy expensive cars parked in the several garages; he wanted to mingle with the fast crowd of Hollywood moguls and the pretty starlets alongside.

Reuben had scored with phony corporate stocks. Reuben had scored big with the bond market on investment ventures that did not exist.

Reuben had scored on more than one Ponzi scheme. He had accumulated great wealth and all it could buy in a relatively brief period of time.

Reuben was an excellent accountant, and quite skilled in 'cooking the books', hiding things great and small in the financial records of a business or investment transaction. He could read financial reports and statements of various institutions and quickly ferret out the error. He could easily have become a successful accountant or attorney at law.

Then Reuben struck out with the US Securities & Exchange Commission and the US Justice Department. For his avarice and lust for great wealth he had turned to crime and had to pay for those crimes. Reuben seemed unconcerned for the shame and humiliation he caused for his family, but was greatly concerned for the impact his convictions might have on his future. The criminal courts not only put him in prison, there was also a huge fine levied such as Reuben could never pay in ten lifetimes. The Bankruptcy Court took everything that Reuben had to his name for distribution to his creditors. The civil courts granted decrees to various victims of Reuben's fraud, in judgments that could not be discharged in bankruptcy, for multiplied millions and millions of dollars, and there was no hope whatsoever that Reuben could ever honor those judgments. What's more, Reuben could never again in his lifetime have property anywhere in California that was entirely exempt from those unsatisfied civil judgments. These things should help a person to learn.

Reuben served his numbers of years in the United States Penitentiary at Lompoc, leading to an early parole for good behavior. Larry Cole and Dad Remington drove right to the front gates to pick him up. All he had with him as he passed through those ominous portals were the garments he wore and a bag full of items that altogether might be worth $20.00. On the way home they stopped in Oxnard to have lunch with the relatives, who greeted Reuben as though nothing had happened. Nothing was said about prison.

As the three of them were driving south toward the Remington place in Orange County, a distance of about 200 miles and a bit over 3 hours driving time, they had exchanges of idle chit-chat. Reuben mentioned that his Driver's License had expired; and suggested that he needed some new clothes; and hinted that he would need a job. Ah, but Dad Remington and Larry had already discussed the matter of having Reuben work for the dealerships. Dad turned and leaned toward the rear seat and said "Don't you worry about a job, son. We're getting you a job at one of the dealerships. But, since you have the criminal record, you don't qualify for a surety bond, so the only work we can offer you is maybe delivery preparation or maintenance engineer. The folks out in the paint and body shop always need unskilled labor to do the sanding and prep for the cars in for repair." To which Reuben inquired "What's delivery preparation?" and his Dad replies "That means washing cars." Reuben asks "What's a maintenance engineer?" and he is informed "That's what they call the janitor." Well, you can imagine how Reuben the Beverly Hills Playboy would respond to the suggestion that he soil his hands on menial tasks, and he further inquires "Well, Dad. Don't you have any work for me in management or supervision?" to which Dad hastens to inform that "You don't really have any experience selling new or used cars, and that's about all we do. It has taken Larry here several years to get acquainted with the industry, and he has an Ivy League college degree, and in this current economy we need experts to move units, and supervision of those expert salesmen requires someone they can respect for familiarity with the trade. The banks and other lenders would not want to deal with any manager without surety bond that has a track record for fraud." Reuben is learning fast.

All the family welcomed Reuben home. Debbie has come in from Illinois, visiting for a few weeks; she has her two little kids with her and is staying in her old room. Reuben gets to stay in the bedroom where one or the other of his twin sisters usually stays, and both the twins can bunk in Larry's apartment for a while. However, the bedroom where Reuben will have to stay has been suffering from alterations: the two beds once located there reduced to just one single bed. Along the wall are four little beds for four little children. Toni has her two kids. Teri has her two kids and is pregnant with her third now due in a month or two, and she is waddling around the house. Reuben is gonna have to share this bedroom with four little children until Debbie leaves in a few weeks to go home to Illinois. This is the first time that Reuben realizes how much noise six little squabblers can make when they are running around the house playing, and even worse to discover how much noise four little youngsters can make when they are supposed to be sleeping. Reuben soon learns that he hates little kids.

Parents and grandparents have altogether different perspective on what it takes to make a happy home. They seem to think that all that screaming and squealing around the house is music to the ears. They don't appear to notice all the crayon murals on the walls, all the flying kickballs, the loose marbles on the floors, peanut butter and jelly on the furniture, toys buried in the couch and overstuffed chairs, and all the pushing and pulling, running and sliding, chasing and wrestling, crying and accusing, and as boys will be boys they're apparently in training for the Olympic martial arts scuffling contests, and they do all this as they run in and out of the house, all through the day and into the night. After midnight the youngest ones take special delight in practicing duets and trios of incessant howling and bawling, and this is in the room where Reuben is trying to sleep. Reuben really hates little kids.

At the dinner table they have situated honored guest Reuben between little nephews Stewie and Charley, and directly across from Richy V. With unerring accuracy Richy V launches a spaghetti-sauce covered meatball that strikes Reuben in the face and then falls in his lap to stain the new pants he recently got from Nieman-Marcus. Reuben forces a diplomacy smile through the sauce and discreetly says nothing.

Several times over the next few weeks, when they knew nobody was watching, Stewie and Charley dumped their disgusting green peas and yucky broccoli onto Reuben's plate, and on at least a couple of occasions they stole Reuben's dessert.

Recall that Debbie's youngest is the darling little 'Cricket' who loves to dance and sing, jiggling and playing throughout her waking hours, and she has been this way since before she learned to walk. On this particular day she is still in diapers and with all the activity her Mommy has neglected to yet change that heavily-laden diaper. During the afternoon, as Reuben is lounging in the sun on the back porch, little red-haired Cricket comes crashing into his lounge chair and affectionately crawls up onto his lap. She has in her hand her recently acquired musical instrument that she is incessantly practicing. This is called a 'kazoo'. As little Cricket is whooozzing on the kazoo she is keeping cadence by bouncing her tiny little rump on Reuben's lap. Hearing her Mommy's beckoning call, she gives a big slobbery farewell kiss right on the mouth of Uncle Reuben, jumps down and trots away. Reuben looks down at his lap to discover that little Cricket has left a token of tribute smeared all over his only other new pair of trousers.

Little children get coughs and colds, and runny noses. This is so common that parents don't bother to equip those runny noses with masks and such. This is so common that in a household filled to the brim with little kids it is impossible to isolate the sneezers. Reuben fell victim to flying snot on a number of occasions.

Remington's had three TV sets around the house, but every time Reuben wanted to watch the news or some great drama, one or more of those grubby little kids was watching cartoons or their favorite commercials.

Reuben tripped over tricycles and panda bears. His feet slipped out from under him where one of the kids had emptied a bottle of shampoo onto the tiled bathroom floor. Reuben landed face first on the edge of the bathtub and had a large red welt swell up on his forehead.

Yes. Reuben discovered that he hated little children.

Reuben wondered why these responsible parents do not paddle some bantam rumps and smack these scamps up the side of the head, pull some hair, twist some ears and pinch some noses. These spoiled little brats need some firm discipline.

Reuben considers his options, and determines that he should petition his parole officer for permission to go back to his quiet quarters at Lompoc or leave California, or he must find somewhere in California to escape these little monsters. Somewhere in California should also be a location where he can have a cushy job and escape somehow the clutches of creditors.

Believe it or not, Reuben has a plan that will make everybody happy. Everyone that knows Reuben and his history would not believe anything he has to say, especially if it has anything to do with generating revenue, and definitely nobody in their right mind would be directly or indirectly involved in any of Reuben's money-making schemes. However, when this particular scheme is wholly disclosed, it at least has the tiniest bit of remote possibilities.

When in US Penitentiary Lompoc you can meet some very interesting people, both the inmates and their visitors. One particular prisoner had his 89-year old father come about twice each month to visit. The prisoner's name was Roman DiVincenzo III and his father was Roman DiVincenzo II, an immigrant from Italy, a widower whose wife died about a half century ago. Roman III had been convicted with his wife of smuggling parrots from South America, the judge gave him four years, and gave the wife straight probation. Roman III was enraged because the whole smuggling scheme was made up by his wife and her sister, and the sister didn't get charged with anything. Roman III took the rap for all of it. To make matters worse, within two weeks after Roman III landed in Lompoc he received from the Marshal the divorce papers from his wife's lawyer, and the court awarded her everything. Roman III was sixty-seven years old and suffering from emphysema of the worst kind, and was told he had but a short time to live. Roman III had served about all of his time and was scheduled for release a week or so after Reuben was freed. Roman III had no children and was the only child of Roman II. They had no close relatives anywhere in the US; they had no contacts with the family in Italy for the past half century, and believed most of that family had died in World War II. Roman II used to be an accordion maker when he lived in Italy, but had been in the wine-grape growing industry over the past fifty years since he came to America. No big producer, but still with about ninety acres of lush vineyards located near Napa, California, that had been essentially untended since Roman III got busted for the bird business. That grape growing place had a medium size older residence located on it, several barns and a wine-squeezing facility about two hundred yards away from the house, and an old unused gasoline service station located down on the highway, with a single pump that hadn't pumped anything for thirty or forty years. Reuben didn't think much about the DiVincenzo grape growing business until he began to weigh his options: tolerate these brats and wash cars and sweep floors, or maybe talk the DiVincenzo's into taking on a partner. Reuben tries to get in contact with Roman III but finds out that he was released from the joint recently. Reuben spends a little of his valuable time trying to get in touch with Roman III and finally reaches him at his Dad's place in Napa, and suggests that he might come up there for a nice visit sometime in the near future.

On his first day back in the Remington home, Reuben talked his Dad into lending him five hundred dollars. He used most of that money to buy some clothes, some fancy shoes, a few little personal items, and ended up with about fifteen dollars. Reuben has expensive tastes. A week or so later he comes to Dad and asks for another five hundred bucks, and Dad gives it to him. He spends a lot of time reading the want ads and whatever to find cushy employment that better suits his university education, but the only thing that showed up was a job selling chrome garbage disposers, and that did not appeal to him. Another week goes by, then Reuben asks for a new Mercedes Sports car, and Dad lets him have a loaner car from one of the dealerships, an old Ford sedan in fairly good condition, except the heater and air conditioning units are not working. He gets a new Driver's License, and decides to drive that old Ford north up Highway 101 to go visit his very close and dearly beloved friends the DiVincenzo's. Dad Remington pops for another five hundred bucks.

Reuben had been out of Lompoc for almost a month. Debbie and her kids had not yet left for return to their home in Illinois. On his last day back in the Remington home, Reuben was awakened very early in the morning by the reverberations of battle over there in the corner, where Gunnery Sergeant Richy V and his adjutant Corporal Cindy were engaged in field artillery maneuvers, hurling every missile in the toy box just to see if it would all bounce off the walls. Once again Reuben wondered why responsible parents would allow this commotion in the house. He covered his head with a pillow, but then those other two spoiled brats Stewie and Charley were pounding him with their own pillows. Reuben tried to ignore them but they intensified their attack and soon were both astraddle him, screaming and yelling about how Reuben should get up and make his bed. Hearing the early-morning commotion, Debbie's girls appear and noisily join in the affray. Is it too much to ask: Why don't the parents of these unruly little imps come and restore order?

Well, inasmuch as Reuben plans to leave this madhouse before noon today, it is now time to do the 'two birds with one stone' thing. Still in his pajamas, Reuben calls to Gunnery Sergeant Richy V and his adjutant to follow him out to the car. He opens the trunk of his car and starts lifting out a number of boxes large and small. He carries the largest box himself, but recruits the little kids to carry in several smaller boxes. They go into the front room and set the boxes down. Then Reuben tells all six of the kids that he will be gone over Christmas, so he wants them to open their presents now. When all but one of the boxes are opened and everything is set up Sergeant Richy V has a big bass drum, not an expensive drum, but a very noisy instrument, with a pair of big drum mallets. All six of the kids have smaller drums that they can carry around with shoulder straps, each conveniently equipped with a pair of drumsticks. There are four real tin bugles, cheap and noisy, with cords to hang them around the neck when not in immediate use. Should the bugles fail, each child has a brand new kazoo. Uncle Reuben gives the kids a little demonstration on how to do the drum and bugle corps march, tramping and tromping through every hallway and open room, stopping each time they pass the bass drum to give it a few 'bummm-bummm" smacks. Then Uncle Reuben takes two small boxes from his pockets, and turning to Richy V and Cindy he says that it will be their responsibility to lead the band. He opens the first box and takes out a shiny silver item that he tells is a 'Boson's Whistle'. He shows Richy V how it works, and while the happy leader-person is practicing the shrill sounds, Reuben hands to little Cindy another item, which he describes as the 'Referee Whistle', just like the one used by the guys at the football game. He tells her that she should blow real hard to get the best sounds for everyone to appreciate. The time is not yet 7:00 AM but Gunnery Sergeant Richy V is leading the band, loudly tooting his whistle and pounding the drum, followed by Cindy blowing that earsplitting Referee Whistle and banging on her drum, and they are closely followed by Charley and Stewie making their musical contributions, and there at the end of the meandering line of celebrators are Debbie's happy little girls. That long line of troops tooting the whistles and horns and banging the drums was still marching around the yard and in and out and through the entire house when Reuben drove out the driveway an hour or so later to head north. Reuben smiled all the way to Napa.

Reuben scores again.

When Gramma Remington finally got the marchers to suspend their musical crusade long enough to have breakfast, she promised that she and their mothers would join the corps with whatever instruments they might find available, and all could march together. And they did, with old pots and wooden spoons.

The one remaining box left unopened had a note on it saying: 'Do Not Open 'til Christmas!' This item was placed under the tree when they got all the decorations up, and on Christmas Morning they opened it to find a horse whip. Not a bull whip, but a small horse whip, sometimes called a quirt, also known as a riding whip or crop. It's a small compact horse whip with a short handle and a lash of braided leather, such as the jockeys use at the horse races. The card in the box simply said 'Merry Christmas' and signed by Reuben. There was no other card in the box or instructions on just when or how the quirt was to be applied, but to the parents and grandparents the message seemed to be clear and easily assumed. The message might be otherwise understood by little children.

The little kids asked what that thing might be and were told that it's something used with horses.

The children started happily jiggling and jumping and yelling "Yaaaay! Uncle Reuben is gonna get us a pony!"

Can it be said that Reuben scores again?

CHAPTER 28

HONORED GUEST

Reuben is warmly welcomed by the DiVincenzo's. Roman II is getting old and does not remember Reuben from anywhere. Reuben is assigned a small back bedroom, and is assured by Roman III that he is welcome to stay as long as he wants. Reuben looks the place over and decides that wine grapes are his destiny. The only vehicle on the whole vineyard ranch is a large truck with a wooden hopper on the back for grape gathering season.

Reuben had been there only a couple of days when Roman II has a heart attack, and luckily Reuben has his trusty Ford loaner car to use in rushing the heart patient to the hospital. Roman III rides along to comfort his suffering father. They arrive at the emergency room in plenty of time, they get the father stabilized, and he stays in the hospital for about a week. They discharge Roman II and Reuben hauls him home in the trusty Ford loaner car. The hospital and doctor expense is covered mostly by Medicare, but there is a fairly large co-pay amount that DiVincenzo's are required to contribute, but they don't have enough money.

Roman III and Reuben go back to the hospital to speak with the business office and make arrangements for monthly payments. While waiting and waiting and waiting some more there at the window Roman III starts coughing and coughing and the lady boss asks him to go outside and do his annoying coughing. Roman III can't stop coughing, and then starts coughing up blood, so Reuben says let's go and the hospital people can get the rest of their money the best way they can. They go back home.

Next day, the hospital phones with threats to call down fire from heaven to consume the DiVincenzo's if they don't pay up the balance due on the account, and likewise threatens to sue them and take away everything they own. Because Reuben loves the DiVincenzo's so much, he offers wise counsel suggesting that maybe they should put the legal title to their property in the name of a trusted friend before that nasty-tempered lady at the hospital can sue them and take 'em for all they're worth. Then Roman III suggests that since Dad DiVincenzo is dying of heart disease and Roman III is dying of emphysema, and since they have no heirs or even distant family, why don't they simply sell the whole place to a worthy friend for some nominal amount? Excellent idea! Now the question of where can they find such a friend? And how much would that friend have to come up with to seal the deal?

Well, fortuitously, Reuben offered to be the friend. Roman II continued to suffer with angina frequently. Roman III was coughing up more blood. The good friend suggested that maybe he could bamboozle his family out of $25,000.00, and with that amount the transaction could be completed, and maybe Reuben could some time later help them out by giving them more money out of the goodness of his heart. Sounds good. OK.

Reuben phoned Dad Remington and explained the deal. Both the Dad and Larry scoffed, knowing that nobody in their right mind would peddle a ninety acre tract of wine grape producing land for a measly Twenty-Five Grand. And even if it could be done, all of Reuben's creditors would grab everything to apply to his millions of dollars of non-dischargeable debt. However, somebody else could buy the place and let Reuben live there and maybe eke out an existence irrigating grapes and pruning annually.

Larry contacted one of the prime movers among the wine grape growers in the Napa County area to get some insider information on the DiVincenzo operations, and was told that for a number of years last past there had been what some might see as an ethnic conflict arising out of a failed business co-venture that Roman DiVincenzo II had been involved in with several Greek grape farmers in Napa County, and the participants in that dispute had been tossing insults at each other for a long while. Dad Remington knew a very influential lady lawyer in Sacramento who for many years had represented rice growers and wine grape people all over Northern California. Her name was Zenovia Paraskakis and she was a Greek that spoke the language. Larry had Attorney Paraskakis look into history and present status of ownership of the DiVincenzo vineyards. Her report came back to inform that the land had been in the name of Roman DiVincenzo II, in his name alone, for about fifty years, and the land was all free and clear of any debt, and worth a few tons of money, but that those disputes with neighboring farmers in that community could affect the wine grape growing operations on the DiVincenzo land. However, as she delved into the matter of those disputes she determined that all of those other squabblers were Greeks, and prone to saber-rattling as is common to their genre. She was able to get all these squabblers together at a meeting held in a back room of the Greek Orthodox Church with the local chief priest serving as moderator, and everything was worked out to satisfaction of all concerned. That does not mean that it was a tranquil spirit prevailing in those settlement sessions, it simply means that everyone there was shouting in Greek.

Larry asked Attorney Paraskakis how long it would take to form a California corporation and get it going so that it could take title to the acreage. Lawyer Paraskakis told him that she had an attorney from San Diego that did all of her corporation work, and his name was Allen Jan, and that the legal genius Attorney Jan could get a California stock corporation formed and operational by 4:00 PM that very day, including issuance of the Federal Identification Number, and stock could be issued almost immediately. And he did. The name chosen for the corporation was DiVincenzo Vineyards Corporation.

Escrow was opened with the Napa County office of a major Title Insurance Company, where their escrow department could handle everything and the deed could be filed in just a couple of days. All money consideration was to be via direct payment outside of escrow. Larry overnighted a $25,000.00 check payable to Reuben Remington and Roman DiVincenzo II. Reuben had the old man endorse the check and then took it to the Napa branch of one of the largest banks. For $25.00 cash out of his pocket he opened up a checking account in the name of R. Remington. He then opened a separate escrow trust account with that bank branch, the conditions of which were that Reuben would deposit the $25,000.00 check into that trust account, and the bank was to deposit all of that money into the 'R. Remington' checking account when another check for $25,000.00 might hit that account sometime in the next thirty days or in the alternative to hand over the $25,000.00 directly to Reuben Remington upon his demand. Then Reuben used the temporary checks issued for the new checking account and wrote a check payable to Roman DiVincenzo II for the full purchase price of $25,000.00 for the grape acreage, with legal title on the grant deed to show vested ownership in the DiVincenzo Vineyards Corporation. Then DiVincenzo's suggested that since they both were gonna die soon, and both wanted to be buried in their ancestral town's graveyard in Castelfidardo, Italy, they needed to get to New York so they could catch a flight to Italy. They thought it would be good to see some more of America along the way just this one more time, so they wanted to drive, but all they had to drive was that old truck. Reuben the trusted friend called Larry the benevolent brother-in-law and asked if it would be alright to lend that old Ford loaner car for the trip. Larry said OK. Reuben then convinced the DiVincenzo's that they should not be carrying a lot of cash as they travel cross-country, so they should wait until they get to New York and cash that $25G's check at the travel agency or somewhere like that. Generous Reuben the trusted one then called Larry the money source again to ask for another $1,000.00 to help DiVincenzo's to cover expenses of the trip while all this escrow business was pending. Larry sent $1,000.00 cash by overnight mail. Generous Reuben the trusted friend gave the DiVincenzo's half of the money out of the goodness of his heart, to cover expenses such as motels and gas stations along the way. OK.

The hospital collections department never did get any more money from the DiVincenzo family, nor did they ever receive another dime from Reuben to apply to their account.

DiVincenzo's packed up a few things to take with them, told Reuben he could have all their stuff left behind, and with a fond handshake of fellowship embrace, Roman II and Roman III took off across the country in that old Ford.

However, Reuben got a phone call two days later to inform of a DiVincenzo family disaster.

Ah, the beauty of the Rocky Mountains with all the flora and fauna, the majestic stone formations, the marvelous outcroppings, the wildflowers beside the roadways, the beautiful open freeways up and down the inclines, the highest roadway reaching up to about two miles above sea level, where the air is crisp and very thin. Some folks claim that they need an oxygen mask at the top. DiVincenzo's didn't have such an oxygen system as they were driving up over those highest mountains just west of Denver. Rather than to be viewing the lovely mountains the last thing that Dad DiVincenzo saw in this life was the murkiness inside of the Eisenhower Tunnel, as he grabbed his chest and died. He was really dead, no doubt about it. Roman III phoned to inform Reuben that it now looked like he'd have to cash that check so he could have the body embalmed and sent by air freight to New York City. Reuben urged caution, since Roman III is out on federal parole and had not cleared it with his parole officer before leaving California, and that check was made payable to Roman DiVincenzo II, and it might not be wise to sign a dead man's check or Roman III might find himself back in the Lompoc retirement center. Reuben suggested that it might be wiser to prop up Dad DiVincenzo in the rear seat of the old Ford and keep headin' east to New York City, where any one of those many Italian funeral directors would know just what to do to get those earthly remains sent to that cemetery in Castelfidardo, and those funeral directors probably won't care whose name is on that check. All that reasoning sounded good to Roman III, so he wisely folded that $25,000.00 check and placed it with the suitcase in the trunk of the car. Dad DiVincenzo had the back seat all to himself. It was right in the middle of a terribly hot summer and the Ford air conditioner was busted.

Roman III decided that the death of his only father deserved a proper ceremony before they set out on the long journey east, so he bought a case of wine and a case of beer for the traditional Italian *"Ceremonia di Morte Libagione"*, which is essentially a toast to honor the passing of the dearly departed. He pulled a few corks before he left town, and continued to drown himself in tears and beers for quite a few miles down the road, stopping at several isolated outposts to drain the tank. By evening he was really sauced, and by midnight he was a menace to have on the road. As he was careening along at excessive speed he came to an unknown and unexpected curve on the remote mountain road, Roman III and Roman II were both feeling no pain, and Roman III managed to drive the Ford loaner car over the side, launching that vehicle high into the air and landing with a crash and a full tank of gas. The ensuing blaze consumed both bodies beyond recognition, along with all their belongings including cash in their pockets and any checks they might have had in their luggage. The Colorado State Patrol was able to trace the car ownership to the Remington dealership, and Larry called to pass on the terrible news to Reuben, and his tender heart was touched to hear that the remains of the entire DiVincenzo family had already been partially cremated, and he determined that he would do what is right. He went down directly to the bank and pulled out in cold hard cash that $25,000.00 on deposit in escrow there, and said nothing about it then to Larry or Dad Remington, thinking "Why bother them?"

Reuben phoned the Colorado State Patrol, and they put him in touch with the funeral home where the badly burned DiVincenzo bodies were laid out in sad and lonely repose. Reuben advised the funeral people that the DiVincenzo's were paupers driving that old Ford from California to New York to see some Italians, and then from there planned to go to their ancestral home in Castelfidardo, Italy, and that's all he knew to tell them. The funeral guy wanted to know who was gonna pay for his excellent work, further advising that he could cremate the remains all the rest of the way for about $600.00 and send those remains in urns to Reuben in Napa for proper burial. Reuben said he did not want the responsibility but that he'd pop for $300.00 take it or leave it. The funeral man said if Reuben would make it $350.00 he'd send the urns full of ashes right away to anywhere he directed. OK. Reuben sent a money order for $350.00, with a note informing of what Reuben thought the birthdates must have been for both father and son, with instructions to finish incinerating the bodies and put the ashes in urns to be sent to the Cemetery in Castelfidardo, Italy.

And that's how Reuben dealt with his grief.

By the way: for $350.00 the urns are actually a couple of plastic garbage bags, each with a tag indicating name, birthdate and date of death. The DiVincenzo cremation ashes were placed in these two plastic bags and sent to the Castelfidardo Cemetery in Italy, together in one medium size cardboard carton, along with instructions but no return address.

The old Ford loaner car was covered by insurance, so the dealership incurred no great loss. For that matter, even if they never got a penny from the insurance, that old Ford was no great loss.

Larry Cole piled his wives and kids into the van and took a leisurely vacation trip up California Highway 1, and ended up in Napa at the newly acquired wine acreage. When they got there Reuben was just returning in the old wooden-side truck from his trip into San Francisco to sell some of the junk left at the house by DiVincenzo's. Larry inquired how much he managed to get for the junk, and Reuben replied by saying "Ah. Just a few bucks. All the stuff is old and pretty much worthless." The noisy little Cole kids went screaming all around the vineyard, tossing grapes at each other.

Larry agreed that the old house was worth investing a few bucks to repair, but suggested that if they fixed up the outside to make it look good the parole officer might want to know why Reuben is living high. Anyway, they agreed on an improvement plan that would really tidy up the interior and let the outside go. While in town Larry contacted the Grape Growers Association and arranged for professional pruning and cleaning up everything, and was informed that these particular grape vineyards were a very rare wine grape and would ordinarily bring a good price at harvest, but the vineyard had suffered much from lack of care over the past few years. Larry made arrangements for everything, and warned the Grape Growers Association man that the occupant of the property is just a hired hand and had no authority to say or do anything, "Call me directly for any instruction or whatever. All finances will be handled directly with me, and no money whatsoever is to be paid to Reuben Remington!" OK

Reuben needed another car. He rode in the front seat of the van all the way back to Southern California, sitting as far away from those kids as he could get. This time Remington's loaned him a fairly new Chevrolet. Reuben's heart was wounded by the lack of generosity. He bombed Larry for another $500.00 to cover expenses to get back to Napa.

Among the items left behind by the DiVincenzo's were an ancient organ and a number of old accordions. An antique dealer from Napa told that the organ was a very rare item and would bring about $50,000.00 at auction. The accordions were genuine Castelfidardo and in total worth about $75,000.00. That auction was in San Francisco and Reuben hauled these things there in the back of that old truck, sold them for even more than those estimates, and he had just returned home from the auction when Larry and his brides drove up for that first visit.

Reuben scores again.

Reuben did not like physical labor. He had a particular disdain for working out in the hot sun. However, he had to report to his federal parole officer, gave him his current address and the phone number left behind by the DiVincenzo's', and invited the parole officer to come see him do honest work, thinking that the parole officer would not travel all the way from LA to the Napa Valley just to check on one parolee. A couple of months later, Reuben got a call from the Federal Parole Office in nearby Santa Rosa, and the guy he talked with said they would that day be paying a courtesy visit on behalf of the assigned office in LA. Reuben went out to the barn, took down the old leather pants left to him by Roman III, along with the sweaty old shirt and the tight boots, and of course the well-worn leather hat and gloves, grabbed the little saw and the pruning shears, and headed for the grape vines down by the entrance to the driveway. Reuben was wearing that sweaty old leather hat and all the accoutrement of a grapevine pruner when the PO drove into the driveway and introduced himself. Reuben put down the tools, removed his glove from the right hand, wiped the sweat off his belabored brow, and shook the hand of the visitor. They stood there by the entry of the driveway talking for a while, then Reuben invited the guest to come on up to the house where he lived. The PO could see from the looks of the ramshackle buildings that Reuben was in poverty barely existing, living the humble life of the grape pruning person. Reuben informed the PO that he did not own anything, just worked for the DiVincenzo Vineyards Corporation that owns everything on site, they paid him in cash for the seasonal work he does, and he gets free rent for the house over there. Reuben invited the PO in at least three times, but they never did make it into the house. The information was taken down on a report sheet, the PO bade him farewell, and the last thing the PO saw of Reuben that day was down by the end of the driveway where Reuben returned to his labor pruning the grape vines. Reuben waved that old leather hat in the air with his left hand and waved his saw in the air with his right hand, and apparently became immediately engrossed in his work. As soon as the PO's car disappeared around the curve, Reuben went into the house to squeeze some grape juice.

All things considered, you'd have to say Reuben scores again.

Larry had all the mail for the DiVincenzo operations forwarded to him in Santa Ana. Remington's paid Reuben considerably more in cash than any field hand could earn. The first year working the grapes brought in a substantial amount, and the leftover beyond operations and paying Reuben was placed in a separate account that he could not reach. The second season was a whopper for the DiVincenzo Vineyards Corporation, but they paid Reuben about what they paid the year before, and put the rest in the bank. The neighboring vineyards did not do so well for a couple of years, which made the DiVincenzo harvest more valuable. They were able to buy up neighboring vineries for a fraction of their real value, and DiVincenzo Vineyards became a major winegrower in Napa County.

Reuben scores again.

CHAPTER 29

SERIOUS FLIRTATIONS

Reuben lived happily on that Napa county land, and got more accustomed to driving a Chevrolet. He circulated among the upper crust, and met a wealthy old fellow by name of Luces E. Dilbeck that lived in a huge castle up on the rim of the valley, who had only one heir, a childless divorcee daughter by name of Gladys, who was almost a dozen years older than Reuben. Gladys was not ugly, but she was dumpy at about forty pounds overweight, and she peroxided her short hair to look more young and sexy. This old Dilbeck guy musta been a multi-billionaire, maybe even a zillionaire, but he appreciated Reuben's appearance of frugality which he discerned from seeing that Reuben drove a Chevrolet. The old guy had graduated from the University of Southern California back in the dark ages, and was very pleased and greatly impressed to hear that Reuben was also a USC graduate. Now, recall that Reuben had spent all those college days at USC, but Reuben had not attended even one USC football game during that time, had not attended even one basketball game or any other kind of sports gathering over all those years, and was not in the least interested in half-naked girls swinging their pom-poms. Reuben spent his time devising schemes for making money, and all his social contacts were with others of like mind. Believe it or not, Reuben had never bothered to memorize the words to the USC Fight Song. He knew the tune because they blast that all over the campus night and day. When the old rich fella tossed Reuben a big smile and started singing *"Fight on, for ol' SC...."* Reuben had to feign some sort of distraction, and immediately marked it down in his mind to do some research. That next week Reuben visited the Napa County Library, hauled down a book of reference, found the page that had that USC Fight Song, slyly ripped out the whole page and folded it for placement in his pocket, handed the book to the librarian, and beat a hasty exit. He memorized that very brief little ditty.

When next Reuben visited the Dilbeck castle, Gladys greeted him first and then Dad Dilbeck came onto the scene, whereupon Reuben moved over and stood next to him with his right arm over the shoulder of the old man and looked so gallantly up toward the sky and began to sing *"Fight on, for ol' SC, our men fight on to victory! Our Alma Mater dear, looks up to you. Fight on and win for ol' SC! Fight on to victory! Fight on!"* At the end of that first verse, the old man seemed to be content with it, but Reuben waved his left hand toward the sky, tossed his head back, and sang the verse again as the old fella joined in, and then they did it again, at the end of that third rendition Reuben dabbed at his eyes and suggested that it was so touching to have comrades share such a moment of reflection.

Dad Dilbeck is no fool. When Reuben first started to court Gladys he had investigators provide a full report on just who he was and what he was, and when he had read that report he said nothing about it to his daughter or to Reuben. Before asking Gladys to marry him, Reuben went privately to Dad Dilbeck and just let it all hang out. He told him about his business problems and the crimes he was convicted of and of his years in federal prison, and provided a capsule history of his family. Then he told Mr. Dilbeck that he'd like to have his consent to marry Gladys, and suggesting that he would understand if the past history negated any prospects for such marriage. Dad Dilbeck smiled and told Reuben how he appreciated his decency in making the disclosure and felt that it was a display of honest respect for the Dilbeck's, then he told Reuben "Sure!" and wanted to know if they had yet set a date. Reuben responded to say that he had not yet seriously discussed marriage with Gladys, preferring to first get approval from her Dad. Having now gained that consent from her Dad Reuben then asked Gladys and things accelerated from there. Reuben phoned Larry to let him know that he was engaged. Larry did not wait for Reuben to ask for money but quickly offered that there was plenty of cash in the vineyard corporation's coffers to pay for a very impressive set of rings.

Reuben scores again.

Naturally, considering the prospects of inheriting the castle and all the wealth, Reuben would fall in love. However, this older woman had one terrible flaw: she was a born-again Evangelical Christian who was in church every time the doors were open. Reuben courted her seriously, but she threatened to cut off the romance if Reuben could not repent of his sins and get baptized, and he did. So with permission of her Dad and his PO they got married. Instead of the happy newlyweds living in the little home on the DiVincenzo Vineyards place, Reuben would move in with the bride and her father up there in the castle, where there were maids and butlers, chauffeurs and gardeners. The new bride imposed on her Dad to buy her a new car for their wedding present.

Larry and his brood, Rick and Debbie and their kids, and Mom and Dad Remington all showed up for the wedding of Reuben and Gladys at that little church in Napa. They had a very nice reception later at the castle, a number of Napa County upper crust millionaires showed up bringing expensive wedding gifts, and after the rice got thrown the happy Honeymooners Reuben and Gladys drove away in their brand new sparkling white Bentley convertible. The Coles and the Remington's were amazed.

Reuben has scored again.

On the way home from the wedding of Reuben and Gladys the family decided to stop in Oxnard for a little visit with Shimi Remington's cousin that they had been visiting all through the years of Reuben's confinement at the Lompoc Federal Corrections Center. The cousin's name was Bartolomeo Vazquez, and was the son of one of Shimi's uncles. The Vazquez family had an old car that had quit running, and Stew Remington thought he'd be generous to the relatives of his beloved bride. The next week they sent one of their employees to take a fairly new Chevrolet up to give to Bartolomeo just as a gift.

The following week Larry and his little family were on their way up Highway 1 and stopped off again to visit with the Vazquez family, to make sure that they had registered the Chevrolet in the Vasquez names, and they had already done so. However, Bartolomeo admitted that he had some misgivings about going to DMV, because he had no Driver's License and had no Social Security Number, and had no car insurance. He shrugged his shoulders and said that he and his wife had come to California more than thirty years ago from Guatemala but had never bothered to get any sort of legal papers to stay. What he was saying was that he and his wife were illegal immigrants. Larry thought nothing of this, but later asked his Mother-in-Law if she knew her cousin was in the US illegally. She said that was impossible because her cousin was born in Los Angeles and had lived in Oxnard all his life and that none of her relatives were from Guatemala. They contacted the family in Mexico City to get the address of cousin Bartolomeo Vazquez, and found that he was living about six blocks away from the folks that the Remington's had been visiting for many years. Well, how many guys do you know by name of 'Bartolomeo'?

Shimi giggled and muttered "I thought he looked kinda tall to be the cousin I remembered!"

Stew Remington called his Mexican lawyer in Santa Ana and had him do all the paperwork to get the second 'Bartolomeo Vazquez' and his wife those 'Resident Alien' cards so that they would be legal. Last word heard was that Bartolomeo Vazquez now has his Driver's License and a Social Security Number., and with his wife wants to eventually become US citizens.

Meanwhile, the saga of Reuben and Gladys continued to churn with many incidental features. These two lovers were in church every Sunday morning for weekly worship among the saints, every Sunday night for evangelism and after-service fellowship, and every Wednesday night prayer meeting and Bible Study. Reuben began to enjoy the new chums met at the church and at church functions, and one of them invited Reuben to go with him to the regular Saturday morning prayer breakfast of 'The Gideons'. Soon, Reuben was a card-carrying member of the Gideons and was pressed into service handing out Bibles at schools and colleges around the Napa County area. Reuben began to chirp like a real Bible-thumper, and his manner over a brief time became fairly evangelical. Instead of the somber and sober scheming manner he had shown most all of his adult life, Reuben became very pleasant and amiable in just about any and every social situation. It was unmistakable: Reuben the scammer had truly become Reuben the disciple of Christ.

Reuben had been married to Gladys for less than a year when she came down with some dread disabling disease. Now we don't really know whether or not Reuben was protecting his own meal ticket, but he seemed to really rise to the occasion. Gladys actually had to spend several days in the hospital, but the doctors told her that she would likely fare as well at home. At the castle, Reuben attended Gladys morning, noon and night. Dad Dilbeck offered to bring in a nurse, but Reuben declined, saying "She is my responsibility and I want to care for her myself!" and he did. He bought a couple of electric massage devices and would rub her back and legs for hours, and would massage her feet for as long as she asked. They had a cosmetologist come in and do manicures and pedicures, and Reuben watched closely to see how it should be done. He then took special delight in doing her fingernails and toenails, in such a tender and loving way. Gladys would watch him as he happily tended to her every need, each whim, whatever made her feel better and happy. For at least two months Gladys couldn't keep anything on her stomach, and whatever she tried to eat she would toss up all over her gown and the bedclothes. Reuben would happily help her into clean garments and would change the sheets and such. After about three months of restorative convalescence, Gladys was not really fully recovered but was in a much better mood. As Reuben was fluffing her pillow one evening, she took him by the hand and soberly said "Reuben. I love you, and I want you to know how much I appreciate how well you have taken care of me." He very dramatically kissed her on the hand and assured his bride that he would always be devoted to her.

Reuben was greatly concerned for Gladys, and in the quiet hours as she was sleeping he began serious intercessory prayer. Now this serious continuing prayer stuff was altogether new to Reuben, who was more accustomed to the brief mutterings preceding the meals, but because of the sincerity of his concerns it seemed the natural thing to do when nothing else really worked. Gladys would be sound asleep as Reuben in a muffled voice prayed that God would send ministering angels to chase away the hurts and harms that had been a plague to her body. He would stand over her by the hour, holding her hand and in the dim light just watching her sleep, all the while praying that God would reach down deep in His bag of miracles and send one to Gladys. These prayer sessions had the incidental effect of maturing Reuben's own heart and soul, as he became more of a spiritual giant.

Gladys awakened one morning feeling bright and cheery, and without even the slightest hint of any lingering sickness. She looked over just beyond the foot of her bed, and there in an overstuffed chair sat the slumbering form of her husband Reuben, clutching his King James Bible. She happily tossed her feet over the side of her bed and went quietly over to where Reuben was snoozing, kissed him on the forehead and stood back to watch as he awakened. When the cobwebs cleared, Reuben for the first time noticed that Gladys had lost a whole lot of weight. She must have lost about fifty pounds, and now had a slender frame. He stood up right in front of her, reached out and placed his arms about her and kissed her so romantically, then said "Come with me." As he tugged her over to stand in front of a large full-length mirror and said "Gladys, you are just perfect!" She said "Oh, see how my hair has grown out, and it's so grey!" Reuben smiled and said how much better she looked with the longer hair, and if she is not happy with grey, then let's try a darker tone to match her beautiful brown eyes.

Gladys pranced around like a teenager, feeling great. They drove down to the local drug store and bought some hair coloring, and Reuben took special delight in applying it to her longer hair, and she looked stunning. They had to go to the mall and buy her a whole new wardrobe. Reuben was very proud of the result, and wanted to go right away and have some portraits made to distribute to his relatives. Now, for those portraits they chose to enlist one of those glamour photographers that have talented cosmetologists well-trained to prepare the subjects for the shoot. They primped this lady up like she never imagined she could ever look, and they did even more magic on Reuben, so that the end result on those many poses for pictures had them looking like professional models or movie stars. The portraits were terrific.

Luces Dilbeck muttered over and over how much he appreciated the way Reuben had taken care of Gladys in her hour of need.

It seemed that there was an unusual result of all this prayer that Reuben was sending up to the throne of God. To Reuben it just seemed that Gladys was touched by the unseen Healing Hand, but there was more, much more. That's the way it is so often when you commune with God. True, it is the squeaky wheel that gets the grease, and there is the primary pressing problem being addressed in the prayerful petitions. But that principal concern becomes transitory as the simple act of intercessory prayer has the incidental and even more important effect of purging the heart and promoting a very durable spiritual excellence. There was a very subtle but discernible change taking place with Reuben, and it influenced his entire life. It even changed the expression on his face, and he appeared always to be relaxed, smiling and serene, gentle and calm, pleasant and always in an agreeable mood. Once he was set upon this path, he seemed to be walking up the King's Highway, where the load gets lighter and the way gets brighter. Reuben never wavered from this course, never faltered or did any backsliding. Reuben and Gladys were a great team, just as happy as clams, two peas in a very pleasant pod.

Dad Dilbeck asked Gladys and Reuben to sit with him for a while, as he wanted to make them a proposition. Simply stated, Dad wanted Reuben to take over all the businesses, since Dad was getting old and has not made any arrangements for transitions otherwise. Reuben said that he would be pleased to act as the Chief Executive Officer, so long as he would not be touching anyone's money. Gladys could be the corporation president and Dad could continue as chairman of the board. Agreed.

Well, Dad Dilbeck was amazed to see how quickly Reuben integrated and absorbed all the essentials of so many business operations, particularly in analyzing financial data. If anyone was imminently qualified to review financials on any corporate enterprise, it would be Reuben.

Reuben was told that the same two accounting firms from the San Francisco Bay Area had been faithfully handling all the financials for Dad Dilbeck for more than a dozen years. He trusted them with everything. It did not take Reuben more than one week to gather all the indicting information and present it to Dad Dilbeck to prove that his trusted accounting servants had been skimming millions out of the Dilbeck Empire during all those years of faithful service. Dad Dilbeck didn't want to believe all this, but Reuben showed him the irrefutable facts of embezzlement and pilferage. Dad Dilbeck asked Reuben what should be done. Reuben just said "Do you want me to handle it for you?" Upon confirmation of his authority, Reuben phoned Larry Cole and asked him to fly up to San Francisco to do exactly nothing but keep quiet.

Reuben arranged for the six senior accountants from the two accounting firms to meet with him in one of the Dilbeck offices in San Francisco down by the Bay, for a private conference. Reuben walked in with Larry, who was all dressed up like a banker in sunglasses, wearing a black Fedora Hat and a black overcoat. Reuben took his place at the head of the table and brought the meeting to order. He did not introduce Larry, who stood sullen and silent in the background with his hand in his overcoat pocket, and did not remove that black hat or those sunglasses. Adding to the drama, Larry continuously twiddled with a toothpick slowly wobbling from between his sneering lips.

Reuben calmly said "Gentlemen, we have conducted an internal audit of the financials for the past dozen years, and have discovered a number of irregularities. You all know what I am talking about, and I am not here to argue with you or negotiate anything. I will make you an offer, and you have twenty minutes to consult among yourselves as to whether or not you want to accept that offer. There will be no discussion of compromise. You take it or leave it. If you have not accepted the offer within that twenty minute time frame, the offer is to be considered withdrawn. This is the offer: we will accept your cashier's check in the sum of One Hundred Million Dollars, to be paid within thirty days of this date, as a full and final settlement of all claims between the Dilbeck companies and your firms, and nothing more will be said of it to anyone. We will leave you here now to discuss the matter among yourselves." With that, Reuben motions to the silent sentinel in the black Fedora and they quietly leave the room without saying more, closing the door behind them.

The six accountants are horrified, and their faces turn ashen white as sheets. They give no thought to the fact that this room could be bugged and all their exchanges of conversation might be recorded. Reuben and Larry are listening on the equipment in a neighboring room as everything is being taped. These six guys were in a panic, wondering how their crimes were ever discovered. They had so carefully planned and executed each and every bit of thievery, covering their tracks down to the very last detail. These conspirators had already checked out Reuben when he first came onto the scene, and they now knew that he had spent years in the penitentiary, probably the fall guy for the Mafia. One of the most disarming features about this Remington guy was his genial style that mysteriously added to his confident manner. Who is that sinister guy in the black overcoat? Why does he keep his hand in his pocket? When these schemers started their skimming, what they didn't count on was that the real expert in cookin' the books might somehow show up.

The spokesman for this group of thieves was one John Bosch, the chief honcho at the larger of these two accounting firms. He was a CPA, but he was also one of the sharpest and most cunning trial attorneys in all the Bay Area, highly respected for his forensic skills and social standing. His wife Cecilia was from one of the oldest and most influential families in San Francisco, whose roots went back in California history for about a hundred years before California became a US State. Bosch wore the most expensive garments, highly polished wing-tip shoes, a classic Errol Flynn moustache, and always displayed an arrogant confidence in dealing with anyone and everyone. He had great political influence, and even the trial judges of San Francisco feared his powers of persuasion in Sacramento. Bosch was the first then to say that there was no alternative but to surrender to Reuben's demands, but still suggesting that maybe he could work out some sort of compromise rather than to simply fork over a hundred million bucks.

Reuben waited about eighteen minutes before returning to the room to confront the guilty parties. They were yet as a group apprehensive, but their leader calmly suggested that there was no way that they owed any Hundred Million Bucks to Dilbeck companies, and indicated that they might be receptive to a much smaller figure. Then as the clock was running they inquired "Who is your friend here?" pointing at Larry the soundless sentry, and Reuben calmly informs them "Gentlemen. It doesn't really matter what his name is, but I will tell you that he could be your worst nightmare."

Reuben then looked at his watch and glumly said "Gentlemen. Your twenty minutes has expired, and our offer to you is now withdrawn. However, I will now make you one more offer, and you have another twenty minutes to accept that offer or it is deemed withdrawn. When that offer is withdrawn there will be no further offers, and you will have to accept the consequences. We will not deal anymore with any of you or any of your attorneys. You are the authors of your own grief. You are the architects of your fate. The offer is in two parts. First: We will accept your cashier's check in the sum of One Hundred Fifty Million Dollars, to be paid within thirty days of this date, as a full and final settlement of all money claims between the Dilbeck companies and your firms, and nothing more will be said of it to anyone. The second part of the offer involves the office building down near the wharf, where the Bosch Accounting people occupy the entire fifth floor. The full purchase price for that building was paid every cent by the Dilbeck companies, and the legal title was taken by a corporation wholly owned and controlled by John and Cecilia Bosch. An escrow has been opened at the Chicago Title office down the street from here, and a deed has been prepared for transfer of unencumbered legal title on that property to the Dilbeck Properties Corporation, and that deed must be duly signed, notarized and properly recorded within thirty days of this date. Furthermore, the Bosch Accounting operations are to vacate that fifth floor space within those thirty days, leaving behind all desks and chairs as well as other furnishings, including the art work on the walls, and the entire area left in a neat and clean condition. You have been collecting rents on that building for the past decade, including rental money paid to you by several Dilbeck companies. You can keep that money as though it be included in the One Hundred Fifty Million Dollars, but the legal title is to be transferred by Grant Deed to Dilbeck. We will leave you now for you to discuss the matter among yourselves, and will return in eighteen minutes." Reuben quietly exits through the door, and Larry stays behind for about ten seconds with a terribly sinister look on his face, looking into the eyes of each and every one of those frightened embezzlers, never taking his hand out of that overcoat pocket.

In the other room, Reuben and Larry are greatly amused to overhear the frightened skimmers as they further discussed the more recent offer for fifty percent more than the offer they let pass by. They were sure that the guy in the black overcoat was a Mafia hit man. These guys knew they were in trouble one way or the other, but Bosch insisted that there was really no alternative, advising all of them to agree to pay the new demands. It would still be cheaper and quieter, and a whole lot safer. The one of them that stood to lose the most would be John Bosch if all the facts were disclosed to the public, and his air of confidence quickly eroded as his manner became more timorous. He repeatedly urged the group to accept the new terms, and to close the deal as quickly and as quietly as possible.

When Reuben walked calmly back into the room, Larry the hit man in sunglasses sauntered in just a little slower and took up his position over near the wall, with his hand in his overcoat pocket and not the least hint of a smile on his face. Reuben was silent. John Bosch simply said "You'll have your cashier's check for One Hundred Fifty Million Dollars within ten days, payable to Dilbeck Industries, and that deed will be signed this afternoon." Reuben then said that the check is to be delivered by courier to the address of this building, to the attention of Reuben Remington, then adding "If you don't have that check in my hands before the thirty days expires, the hammer will fall."

Then Reuben coolly added "You folks have in your possession the financial records for Dilbeck companies, and even though I have already acquired some copies, we now want you to deliver to this office within two weeks all remaining records. If you withhold or destroy any records, you will cause me to become very angry, and I will deal with you in a most painful way."

Once again, now without the least hint of a smile, with a bland resolute expression on his face, Reuben turned and silently left the room, as Larry the sinister sentinel once again stayed behind for just those few seconds to look into the face of each and every one of those guilty guys, then he dramatically turned and left through the door, closing it behind him. Reuben and Larry went out for some pizza, and then Reuben took Larry to the airport for his return flight to Southern California.

The cashier's check for One Hundred Fifty Million Dollars was delivered to that office as promised, as well as the records demanded. The Chicago Title people provided a copy of the deed as recorded, the original of that recorded deed came by mail a week or so later, and those accounting folks quietly left the building as required. John Bosch still acting as the spokesman for the group of malefactors phoned to ask Reuben if they shouldn't memorialize their agreement in writing. Reuben simply said "Would you really want anything in writing to fall into the hands of the State Board of Accountancy or the California State Bar?" The anxious reply "No. I guess not. Your word is good enough for me!"

Reuben inquired at the bank to make sure the cashier's check was good. When he took that check to Dad Dilbeck and showed him the huge amount involved, Mr. Dilbeck almost fainted, saying that he had no idea that such an amount could have been skimmed off his accounts. Gladys was seated there, looking so pretty, so svelte, so cute, as she scrunched up a nice smile for her husband and said "I'm so proud of you." Dad Dilbeck endorsed the reverse side of the check and handed it back to Reuben saying "This belongs to you for a job well done." Reuben gallantly pushed away the check and told his father-in-law that this little expedition was all part of his commitment to Gladys and her family, and not done for any sort of gain to himself. So Dad hands the check to Gladys and says "Sweetheart, you put this money wherever you want. Obviously I didn't miss any part of it for the past dozen years, and I won't miss it now. I am so proud of you for choosing such a marvelous husband!"

Reuben scores again.

Whatever happened to the $150,000,000.00?

Gladys and Reuben recruited that lady lawyer in Sacramento to get together with the attorneys for all those creditors that had unsatisfied judgment claims in Reuben's bankruptcy, and all those judgments were wholly settled. There were a number of individuals that lost money in Reuben's schemes that never filed suit or made any sort of claim in the bankruptcy, and the statute of limitations had run on those debts years ago. But Gladys and Reuben went to each of them and paid back all their losses plus 10%. It was embarrassing to face those folks that he had cheated, but he dealt humbly with each one, and in at least one instance dealt directly with the widow of one investor that lost a substantial part of his retirement savings in one of Reuben's schemes. He paid her an extra 20%.

After Gladys and Reuben had made things right with all those creditors, they went to the Office of the US Attorney in L.A. and made arrangements to have the fines imposed against Reuben reduced down enough so that whatever remained of the money satisfied that judgment, and Gladys and Reuben were left with nothing more from that Hundred and Fifty Million bucks. It was a great day when all these matters were finally finished.

Reuben and Gladys took a trip to Italy, and visited the Castelfidardo Cemetery where the remains of father and son DiVincenzo were located in an unmarked repository at the end of a long stone wall, with just a small cellophane-covered handwritten memorial on a wooden stick to mark the place of their final repose. Reuben had the cemetery officials move the ashes into a pair of expensive matched carved stone urns and those urns were then placed in an impressive medium-size private family mausoleum with iron bar gates, located in the best part of the cemetery park, with a very impressive carved granite memorial stone above the closed entry, showing the names of father and son as the only two occupants and indicating their proper dates of birth and death. Reuben paid for it all. The Catholic Church in town had a respectful funeral ceremony when the DiVincenzo ashes were relocated to that place of rest.

When Gladys and Reuben were visiting their relatives in Southern California, Reuben sat with Larry on the back porch swing, and tried to bring up for explanation that $25,000.00 he pocketed on the DiVincenzo transactions involving the vineyards, and all about the sale of the musical instruments from the DiVincenzo home. Larry said that he had heard about that money matter directly from the bank people a long time ago, and the receipts from the auctioneers had been forwarded directly to him in Santa Ana when the mailing address was changed, adding that further discussion is not required.

After all was said and done, it appeared that Reuben had actually scored again, over and over. Not by enrichment of his pocketbook, but in the immeasurable gain in self-respect and clear conscience.

And there was yet another little change in the heart of Reuben Remington:

A Mexican lady by name of Silvia Gomez with the proper resident alien status and green card in hand has legally worked for Dilbeck's for a number of years, doing miscellaneous household chores and such. She is a widow, and has adult children living in the Los Angeles area. Silvia is a born-again Christian of the Pentecostal persuasion. She stays in a small apartment over one of the Dilbeck garages, and is always available on call at all times, and was on excellent terms with Gladys. They would often have coffee in the mornings and chat about all sorts of things. On one particular morning Silvia was emotionally upset about a personal family matter, and Gladys was able to pry out the details of a very sensitive situation. Silvia has a son in LA involved in a romance a few years ago with a young undocumented alien girl from Southern Mexico, resulting in a pregnancy that produced identical twin girls. The young mother abandoned the little ones to go back to Mexico and only recently was found. She has married another young man and they together do not want anything to do with the two children who are now twenty months old, just about four months shy of their second birthday. Silvia's son was renting a small apartment from Silvia's older brother in East LA, and that brother's wife has been taking care of the children ever since they were born, but now has personal problems that impinge on her ability to care for small children. Meanwhile, Silvia's son has plans to soon marry another young lady and she refuses to have anything to do with the offspring of his earlier relationship. The parents of these little ones are now discussing the surrender of the children to the LA County Social Services for adoption. Silvia is terribly distressed that her grandchildren might be adopted by strangers. She produced a snapshot picture of the children taken about two months ago. Gladys was pleasantly surprised to see two beautifully perfect children and wondered what hidden genetic or other flaw might there be that neither parent would want these tiny treasures. Gladys took Silvia and that photograph immediately to the front room of the mansion where Dad Dilbeck and Reuben were plotting out some involved business plan. As briefly as possible she explained to them the situation with these two beautiful baby girls. The men glanced at each other quietly, and Reuben calmly looked at Gladys and said "Well, Honey, if you promise to learn how to speak Spanish, then it will be OK with me." Gladys touched Reuben on the hand tenderly and just looked him right in the eye, then inquired "Sweetheart. What will be OK? I haven't said what I want to do. Are you telling me that maybe you might want me to be a Mommie?" Reuben grinned sheepishly.

Well, Reuben and Gladys left within the hour to drive down to LA to see about these two little girls. Silvia got on the phone and gleefully made all the practical arrangements. Gladys got one look at these lovely lassies and just came unglued. Reuben watched as Gladys twittered and gushed and acted like a teenager in love. To make the story as brief as possible, let's just say that Reuben and Gladys showed up unannounced at the Remington/Cole residence in Orange County a few hours later to introduce these beautiful young baby girls and see what might be the reaction of the rest of the family to the suggestion that Gladys was soon to be chirping Spanish for these kids. Needless to say, Gramma Remington exploded with joy, sat on the floor and grabbed both of those little kids and hugged them for such a long time, and was much amused to hear that these tiny treasures had been immersed in the Spanish language since they were born. When she finally let them loose, they both made a bee-line over to where Reuben was sitting, and each one grabbed a leg and hugged Reuben in such a loving way. Gramma Remington looked at Gladys and Reuben and grinned to say "Are they really gonna be ours to keep?"

That evening Gramma Remington, Teri and Toni went with Gladys down to the shopping mall and bought dozens of new outfits for the twin treasures, along with shoes and all that stuff. As the family was just sittin' around that first evening after the shoppers returned home, everybody took part in choosing names for the priceless pair of precious permanent guests, and as you might expect they determined that each should have the first name 'Ximena'. The one child then was named 'Ximena Carmen Remington' and the other named 'Ximena Carla Remington', and the court orders entered some time later altered their birth certificates accordingly.

About a week later Reuben had his attorneys file the necessary documents for formal adoption of these kids, the natural parents signed off on the arrangements, and Gladys started seriously to study how to speak Spanish.

And that's how Reuben became a Daddy.

Reuben scores again.

These twin treasures were tiny little ladies, very healthy but still scrawny, and their small size just added to their charm. They were such adorable creatures, busy and into everything, happily clambering over the furniture, searching through every drawer and closet, laughing and squealing like little piglets as they chased through the halls of the Dilbeck Castle. Being a "Grampa" was an entirely new and unexpected experience for Dad Dilbeck, and he held up so very well under that mantle. The children were such fun to watch as they seemed to take over the whole house. Their most impressive talent was the way they seemed to know how to handle Reuben. He was enchanted with these cute kiddies. He was under their spell. He was putty in their hands. When they would together hug his legs and look adoringly up at him, or scramble into his lap and snuggle and hug him around the neck or kiss his hands, Reuben melted.

Reuben and Gladys fixed up a bedroom adjoining theirs for the kids, and had two nice rocking chairs there for coaxing their little kiddies to sleep. Once they got them snoozing in their beds, they would quietly stand there watching over them sometimes for hours. Just watching them sleep.

The casual observer would conclude that Reuben loved little kids.

The Dilbeck Castle had a number of servants and domestic retainers, groundskeepers and general maintenance persons, several of which lived on site in small apartments or houses strewn around the estate, and all of them were very much amused with the new family members. But the most pleased of all was Silvia Gomez, and she was so delighted that Reuben and Gladys introduced her to the children as "Gramma", and she thrilled in that honor for the rest of her days.

Reuben and Gladys began traveling back and forth to Southern California to visit frequently with the relatives. They enjoyed the unusual ambience of love and joy in that Cole-Remington household, and were honest enough to actually ask Larry and the others there to give them parenting instructions so that the precious manner of the Cole kids might somehow rub off onto their own little twins. Larry was so bold as to tell them that they simply encouraged a rich diet of spiritual commitment and regular prayers. Reuben and Gladys would take part in those family prayer sessions each evening with Larry and the family, and their little ladies would respectfully bow their heads and clasp their hands together, close their eyes, and when they thought nobody was watching they'd peek to surreptitiously watch everything. But as those little girls grew older and shared in the prayers with their parents, and absorbed all those Christian teachings and Bible stories, they became little evangelists quoting scripture and spreading the Gospel their way.

Reuben and Gladys were consistent in their personal and family commitment in spiritual matters, and never wavered. Those precious twins were dedicated in church before the entire congregation and were brought up in the nurture and admonition of the Lord. They memorized their scriptures and spouted them at every opportunity, sang all the Christian kiddies songs when they were so young, and would offer testimony of salvation in the Lord Jesus Christ without reluctance when they got older.

Reuben was a happy man.

CHAPTER 30

CONTROVERSY

After his misfortunes in California, King Pete Verdugo made it to Las Vegas, Nevada, where he was forced by circumstances to have medical treatments at the hospital there, using his medical insurance card from his wife's employment with the Remington auto dealerships. Against medical advice he left that place and went by air to Reno, Nevada, where he used that insurance card again to gain admission to another hospital to get his nose attachment problems worked on again and enlist the services of an orthopedic specialist in sports medicine that could deal with his badly broken leg that was in a condition much like that of the skiers that smack into trees and rock formations on the mountainsides of the Sierra Range. After a few weeks in Reno, he left to go to Dallas, Texas. He managed to get some expert facial repairs from an eminent cosmetic surgery specialist there. After the annulment judgment was entered terminating the marriage with Debbie Remington, his name was removed from the insurance coverage, but according to the rules he had a period of time to take up the insurance on his own, but he never did. Stewart Remington monitored Verdugo's movements by watching the record of such charges, but when there was no more insurance there were no more charges, and Mr. King Pete Verdugo seemed then to disappear into the mist.

About a year had passed since anyone heard anything of the whereabouts of King Pete Verdugo. Then one day a call came from Remington's lawyer in Santa Ana who told of a recent conversation with the investigation people at the County Sheriff's Office, telling an interesting tale of more bad luck for Mr. Verdugo.

Apparently, Verdugo was able to walk again fairly well without crutches or cane, but because of his leaving against medical advice at two hospitals where the broken leg bones were being treated, he had further complications so that he ended up with his right leg about an inch shorter than the left, and the neurological damage relating to the break caused some problem with flexing the foot, so that the overall result with that leg was a perceptible limp.

Mr. Verdugo was involved in drug trafficking and smuggling vast amounts of illegal drugs and marijuana into California and Arizona for many years. He continued that business deep in the heart of Texas, and did a lot of work along the border with Mexico. He was with three cohorts, one of which was his own brother, making a midnight delivery to several undercover agents and got into a gunfight. The four of them bolted for their car parked a short distance beyond, but his loving companions were able to sprint quickly to that vehicle and race away. Verdugo with the gimpy leg was unable to sprint anywhere and was easily captured. His three friends made it to another vehicle parked about six miles from there, but it was on a watch by the State Troopers and County Sheriff. All three of those loving companions of King Pete Verdugo were killed in the shootout. King Pete was the only one of the three that the prosecutor could burn, so he did. Take these things into consideration: Three people were dead under the felony murder rule in Texas, which under the law of the parties made it look kinda bad for King Pete Verdugo. He looked atrocious, with scarred face and that black patch over his left eye, his long black hair and Fu Manchu moustache, the gimpy leg, all together made him look more like a cold-blooded pirate. King Pete displayed a callous and surly manner in court, glaring with his good eye at the prosecutor and the judge. He was lucky he didn't get shot on the spot. The judge merrily gave him a long, long sentence.

And so, King Pete Verdugo ended up in that lovely retirement home known as Huntsville State Prison, also affectionately branded as the Walls Unit, one of the most violent places in all the State of Texas.

State Prison is not like County Jail. It's not like those prissy little reform schools where do-gooders are constantly pushing for more TV time and naughty magazines for the young folks that simply must be salvaged for the good of humanity. Huntsville State Prison is not like those fluffy little bed and board revolving door rehabilitation recreation centers up north. Texas don't take no guff off nobody. Huntsville staff persons are the most highly trained personnel in the corrections industry, and they have to be that way to deal with some of the meanest hard-core criminals in the world. Huntsville is not a pleasant place. Consider that the uniformed officers that patrol the halls and walls of Huntsville for eight hours each day must for that block of time from their lives be surrounded by the prison experience, where they share the dreadful exclusion from society, where the environment is supercharged with the threat of violence that could explode at any moment from any and all directions. The great difference is that the guards and other corrections people get to go home after their shift, and they have otherwise the right to come and go as they please. It takes a peculiar kind of person to take on that kind of occupation, and some of those corrections people have to be at least as mean and intemperate as the folks that they are sent in there to guard and control.

A person can actually adjust to incarceration. Long term prisoners often become 'institutionalized' and find the regimentation and order of prison life to be more comforting than the discomforting fear of life 'on the outside'. Times and circumstances constantly change, and what the world looks like now can be so altered and thus much more threatening with the passing of years of time. Predictability adds to a feeling of security. Acquaintances become like family, and many relationships compliment that adage that there might be 'honor among thieves'.

On the other hand, some convicts never adjust. They live every minute of every day saturated with bitterness, waiting for that moment when they can somehow impose retribution on those that they perceive responsible for their predicament of prison, yearning for vengeance, longing for reprisal, hoping someday to somehow find a way to retaliate for their pain and misery. As a long term guest of the governor a man gets a lotta time to think about past wrongs he has suffered, distant wars and personal conflicts greater and lesser. When one cannot in freedom seek out an old foe for face to face bouts governed by Queensberry rules, he has to do what he can do, and that includes stabbing that old adversary in the back in other ways.

And so it was that Larry Cole had to deal with an old enemy.

It had been about three years since Larry Cole had rearranged the face of King Pete Verdugo. Larry was at work in his corporate office in Southern California about mid-morning when an investigator from the County Sheriff's Department came with an assistant DA to talk about some charges being made against him for polygamy and related causes. Larry told them that he had a local attorney that had worked with him on such questions several years ago, and that attorney was authorized to discuss the matter at any length and to provide whatever documentary evidence as might be required. He offered them the use of his telephone to call that lawyer, and after some telephone discussion that Larry was not wholly privy to, the investigator thanked the lawyer and promised that sometime before the end of the next week they could get together. The visit then at Larry's office was otherwise cordial, and the visitors assured Larry Cole that the matter could and would be worked out to everyone's satisfaction, and that Larry should not be at this time greatly concerned.

Apparently the seething sentiments of Huntsville Inmate Pedro Verdugo had boiled over. He talked with a number of fellow prisoners about his passion to affect retribution against his tormentor Larry Cole, the man that wrecked his life. One of those prisoners who did not have all the information in his hands came up with the bright idea that a simple act of tattle-tale complaining to the law enforcement people in California ought to do the trick. It appeared to Verdugo's Chief Counsel on the Inmate Board of Jailhouse Lawyers none of whom ever passed the bar or ever went to law school that this guy Larry Cole has broken the rules of the great State of California, and should pay for his high crimes and misdemeanors.

Unfortunately for Mr. Verdugo the Mexican lawyer in Santa Ana was well prepared to blunt the spears of the polygamy accusation. He provided all the documentation relating to the marriage of Larry Cole, and augmented that with a showing of the video of the flying nose incident, and convinced the Sheriff and DA that Mr. Verdugo just wants to recruit the California justice system to finish for him the fight that resulted in his being chased permanently out of California. A quick review of the DA's records of the case persuaded them that they simply did not want to do Verdugo's dirty work. A letter emanated from the office of the District Attorney informing Larry Cole that after review of the matter there would be no prosecution against him for bigamy or polygamy, and the matter is deemed closed.

Several more years went by, and Mr. Verdugo just sat in his cell and fumed over the whole matter, and could not let it rest. He became more and more bitter. He thought he'd try just one more time to impose revenge on Larry Cole and the Remington family. King Pete Verdugo found out that there had been an election and a new no-nonsense District Attorney had been sworn into that office. What's more, the old Sheriff had retired after many long years of distinguished service, and the new Sheriff after three unsuccessful campaigns against the old Sheriff had now won the election to this office under a banner that claimed he had no tolerance for wrongdoing by former public servants and promised to weed out to expose all their wrongdoing within his jurisdiction.

Another letter was sent by Mr. Verdugo, addressed to the then current newly elected Sheriff, but this time it was a typewritten work, with more precise language in a more sophisticated style, a touch of class, a bit of eloquence, charging the former Sheriff with taking a payoff under the table from the Remington family to cover up the charge of polygamy against Larry Cole. In that same letter was the charge that there had been a conspiracy between Remington's and the now departed District Attorney to just ignore the polygamy charges in exchange for a substantial contribution to the DA's political reelection campaign committee. The new Sheriff and the new DA relished the thoughts of stomping on the carcasses of their former political opponents.

Once again, Larry Cole received visitors from the Sheriff and Prosecutor's office and went through the same scenario as before, but now comforted by the written assurance of former administrations that the matter was wholly concluded and with the reassurance that it would not be resurrected. Ah, but this time there was the added charge that there had been a criminal conspiracy in the earlier discharge of the complaints. These new administrations are honor-bound to further pursue the matter, to determine if surely the former conclusion itself was a result of criminal acts. Larry dialed his Mexican lawyer and handed the phone to the investigator seated at his desk. The angry shouts could be heard coming from the other end of the line. When the investigator hung up the phone, he looked at Larry and said "You have a tiger for an attorney!" The investigators told Larry that they would further discuss this matter with his lawyer, who promised to provide greater documentary evidence in support of defense against Mr. Verdugo's charges, and would get back to him.

The DA was serious enough about the matter to actually dispatch an investigator and shorthand reporter to Huntsville Prison to get a proper statement from the person that seemed to know so much about everything. Apparently, even Mr. Verdugo had to admit that he had absolutely no percipient witness testimony or anything to offer that would lead to any evidence beyond what Remington's lawyer had already provided. The DA even sent an Hispanic investigator to Mexico City to gather whatever evidence could there be located, but what was found was duplicative of and further confirmed the materials that had already been provided by the Mexican lawyer in Santa Ana. After about four months, another letter was sent addressed to that Mexican lawyer, referencing proposed criminal charges to be brought against Lawrence Emmet Cole for various criminal acts including bigamy, polygamy, bribery of a public official, conspiracy to commit bribery, and a whole list of criminal charges. The letter was accompanied by a written agreement signed by the current District Attorney himself, signed by the present-day Sheriff himself, signed by a Deputy Attorney General of the State of California, signed by the Mexican lawyer for Lawrence Emmet Cole, and countersigned by a Judge of the Superior Court of California, in which all of the proposed charges are wholly dismissed with prejudice and cannot be ever again filed or otherwise dealt with directly or indirectly by any trial court in the State of California, and with the further order that the entire record is sealed and not available for public viewing, and all the individual lawyers involved in the case, including the attorneys for the former DA and the retired Sheriff, are specifically enjoined from discussing directly or indirectly any feature of the case or cases with any third party. The letter that accompanied the copy of that stipulation and court order was on the stationery of the District Attorney and was simply a one-liner saying "The attached stipulation and order speaks for itself. Have a nice day!" One would have to conclude that the Mexican lawyer was indeed a real tiger.

Larry took the letter home and showed it to Stewart Remington, who smiled. They agreed that they would not show the letter to the twins or to Gramma Remington. No sense disturbing them with this kind of stuff.

CHAPTER 31

REPENTANCE

"Wisdom too often never comes, and so one ought not to reject it merely because it comes late." Famous words of wisdom by Supreme Court Justice Felix Frankfurter.

Growing old is better than the alternative. But living each day with a burden of guilt and oppressive conscience can make growing old a very uncomfortable existence. Circumstances can be such that apologies for past wrongs are perceived as further harm. It might be true that it is better to leave sleeping dogs lie, but the troubled sleep of the oppressor over a period of time can cause tremendous mental, emotional and spiritual agony. It does seem strange how a word of forgiveness can alter a man's spirit, bring about the dawn of a new day, giving hope and release. Well, you might ask, why shouldn't the bad guy be punished? Well, when is the punishment enough? On the other hand, perhaps we might consider the wisdom of William Shakespeare, writing in 'The Merchant of Venice', where it is said of mercy: "it blesses him that gives and him that takes" and "It is an attribute of God Himself."

King Pete Verdugo was put away at Huntsville Prison for a long while. He was a troublemaker from the day of his arrival. He was a tremendously strong fellow, though he walked with a limp. He considered himself to be a handsome man at one time, but now his face was terribly scarred, he was missing his left eye and wore a black patch over the vacant space, and he tried to hide his ugliness with long dark hair and a black beard that covered the sides of his face, but that was soon shorn. He scowled and growled at almost anything and anyone, and had a terrible temper. He had his band of admirers that were alienated with him from others in the prison, but they turned on him one day, attacking him with makeshift 'shanks', and one of those blades penetrated to sever the spinal cord in such a way that King Pete Verdugo was paralyzed from the waist down, and was forced into a wheelchair. His existence from that time was further isolated, and he stewed in his own memories and thoughts, with constantly churning anger and resentment.

But there came a fresh face to Huntsville. They recruited a new chaplain that took an interest in King Pete, and patiently counseled with him, seemed to understand his problems, and that chaplain became Mr. Verdugo's best if not only friend. King Pete started to go to the chapel services, took account of the miserable lives of the other prisoners, and somehow a spark of wisdom was working in his mind, and from that spark sprang a spiritual revelation, and with that revelation soon followed a spiritual regeneration, the new birth as Mr. King Pete Verdugo accepted The King of Kings, and Pete realized that 'King Pete' was not king of anything. That Pete Verdugo who always thought only of himself first and last and everything in between met the Alpha and Omega, and it was a new beginning for Pedro Verdugo. Some might say that he came to God only as a last resort. Well, where else would you suggest he might go? Why, this is just a jailhouse religion, nothing more. When you have no other religion, might this be better than nothing? That 'jailhouse religion' usually refers to someone that claims a great change by way of religion in hopes of garnering some special treatment and maybe a release based on great changes that make a person a better citizen. Pete Verdugo had no hope of gaining any special treatment, no hope of ever getting out of Huntsville alive, no hope of release.

Pete Verdugo had a lotta time on his hands. He was so much less mobile, always restricted to a wheelchair or on a couch or mattress. He was able to tend to his own personal needs but not much more than that. What he was able to do with that one remaining good eye was to read. He didn't care for mystery novels and other conjured whodunits and products of sick minds. Pete Verdugo became a Bible Student. He obtained some Bible Study materials, concordances and religious literature. He wasn't prejudiced about where the materials came from, and by study of the scriptures and history of events he was able to discern the right from the otherwise. For several years he studied, night and day. He took an active part in the chapel presentations, and was a counseling resource for a whole lot of Huntsville inmates. Many of those prisoners served their time and left much better than when they arrived because of the influence of Pete Verdugo.

But there was unfinished business that troubled Pete Verdugo. He really had no way to address the wrongs that he had done to harm the Remington family. He readily confessed that it was the single most troubling thing on his conscience, the one thing that burned his thoughts continually. He once spoke of this matter when it was his turn to preach in the prison chapel. His topic was 'mercy'; 'forgiveness' was the premise of his sermon, and he confessed that the one thing that oppressed his spirit night and day was the lack of forgiveness from those he had wronged. He wanted the Remington's to forgive him, but he didn't know of any way that he could be so bold as to ask them to somehow forgive what he had done to wreck their lives, to destroy their family, to disturb their peace. In his mind he felt certain that it would be too much to ask for forgiveness. Guilty, guilty, guilty!

A number of years had passed since Pete Verdugo left California; several years since he made malicious retribution efforts to attack Larry Cole and the Remington family. One December day, as Larry Cole was opening the mail at his Santa Ana office, he came upon an envelope showing the return address as Huntsville, Texas. The letter inside was from one of the chaplains at the prison. The message indicated right off that it concerned a prisoner by name of Pedro Verdugo, and went on to say that Inmate Verdugo was confined to a wheelchair since a squabble with other inmates left him paralyzed from the waist down. The letter then went on to describe how Verdugo had undergone a marvelous salvation experience a few years ago, had become the best Bible teacher and counselor in Huntsville, but was yet troubled by his inability to honorably approach the Remington family to beg their forgiveness. The prison records show outstanding warrants in California, and Larry Cole was identified as a complaining witness in one of those matters. The chaplain contacted the Orange County DA's office to get Larry's address. Then the chaplain asked for an unusual favor from Larry, if maybe he could find it in his heart to drop a line to Pete Verdugo and just say "all is forgiven!", and it would make a tremendous difference in Verdugo's life.

About a week later, Pedro Verdugo was seated in his wheelchair at the medical clinic of Huntsville Prison, when he received an envelope in the US mail with a return address showing it was from L.E. Cole at a Post Office address in Santa Ana, California, and inside was a money order for $250.00 payable to 'Pedro Verdugo' on which it showed the remitter to be 'Larry Cole', folded up in a plain piece of letter size paper on which was scribbled "Merry Christmas. Don't spend this all in one place." and it was signed "Larry Cole" Mr. Pedro Verdugo exploded, as he waved that money order around over his head and kept yelling "Praise the Lord" and "Forgiven! Forgiven! Forgiven!" The money was not the important thing but the message was clear and convincing: ***Forgiven!***

Within a few days, Larry Cole received from Pedro Verdugo the most humble and appreciative letter thanking him for the money, but thanking him mostly for the gesture that he interpreted to mean that at least as to $250.00 worth he is forgiven. He explained that there was in his heart a morbid fear that if he offered any sort of apology or explanation it would seem so shallow and meaningless, simply arousing ugly old memories that would do much more harm than good. Verdugo went so far as to say that when he received that envelope with the name and return address in Santa Ana he was almost afraid to open it for fear that it might tell him to poke himself in his good eye or something like that, but when he saw that cheery greeting and the money order he just knew he had been forgiven, and that was a very important thing. He added that he was able to look at the world in an altogether different light, and to tell everyone he comes in contact with every day that he has been pardoned for his sins by the Lord Jesus Christ and forgiven by the ones he wronged the most.

A couple of weeks later, Pedro Verdugo received another envelope with the Santa Ana postmark and inside found another money order from Larry Cole, but this time for $500.00 folded into a letter size sheet of paper, where was scribbled "Happy New Year. Right you are. Here's another $500.00 worth. Larry Cole" and beneath the signature was drawn a happy face with a huge smile. About six months later came another money order for $500.00 accompanied by another note "Just to let you know we are thinking of you. Larry Cole". At irregular intervals, usually about six months apart, Pete Verdugo would receive another money order for $500.00 and a brief note of cheer. In return, Larry would receive things like the bulletin for the Bible Study Class with the instructor named 'Pedro Verdugo' and occasionally a copy of the chapel program where Pedro Verdugo was bringing the message.

Then there came a letter from Pedro Verdugo, first thanking again for the kindness shown to him, and secondly to ask a question that might best be kept a secret. He wanted to know about Debbie and what her life has become, just to know that she is safe and happy.

Within a couple of days, a large manila envelope arrived for Pedro Verdugo, in which was an 8x10 portrait surrounded by a green cardboard frame, showing four people: a man and a woman with two young girls. Debbie was easy to recognize, although so very much changed from how she appeared years ago. With the picture came a brief handwritten note saying "Debbie and her husband Rick, and their two girls. The older girl is named 'Teresa' and the younger girl we call 'Cricket'. Teresa loves to dance. Cricket is very slight in stature and has bright red hair, and she will dance and sing all day. Both girls are always happy."

The exchange of brief messages and the sending of money orders went on for a number of years, until Larry Cole received a medium sized cardboard box with another letter from the Huntsville Prison Chaplain, saying:

"I regret to send bad news, but I must inform you that this past month our Brother Pedro Verdugo passed away. He died of natural causes.

"Before Brother Pete died he asked me to dispose of his personal items. Two particular items he requested be placed in his hands as he lay in his coffin, and we did as he asked. He wanted to have that portrait with the green border showing the man and woman with two young girls, the younger girl having red hair, to be buried with him in his left hand, and his Pulpit Preaching King James Bible in his right hand. Most all of his Bible study materials he gave away when he knew his time of departure was near, but the pictures from his wall are included in the things sent here. The three items he wanted you to have in particular were his Concordance and his personal study King James Bible, and a portrait of Pete made by another prisoner, with Pete wearing a glass eye borrowed from a fellow inmate. Please note the inscription on the front flyleaf of the Bible. You will be pleased to know that most of the money you have sent him over the years was used to obtain Bible Study materials for Huntsville inmates that could not afford the purchase price. There is also a check in the amount of $27.00 made out to 'Larry Cole' which was the balance remaining in his prisoner's account, and since you were the source of that money it is now returned to you. You might be interested to know that you were the only person on his mailing list. His parents died several years ago and his brother died in a shootout with the police on the night Pete was arrested on the charges that brought him to Huntsville. You might also be amused to know that several years ago Brother Pete preached a great sermon in which he said that Larry Cole had saved his life. Then he went on to tell that the two of you had a scuffle in which his leg was broken, so that he had a bad limp. Because of that limp he was unable to run from the police as his three accomplices made it to their car and drove off leaving him behind. Those three guys were killed in a shootout with the State Troopers not more than fifteen minutes later. Thank you for being so kind and generous to Brother Pedro Verdugo. You added a great deal of joy to his life."

And then there was a PS:

"Enclosed you will find a snapshot I took of Pedro Verdugo in his coffin, clutching his Holy Bible and that picture of the four people, and I wanted you to see the pleasant expression on his face. It appears that our Brother Pedro Verdugo is at peace."

Larry found a number of pictures in the box, a couple of snapshots of family members, and several snapshots of Debbie, and that portrait of Pete Verdugo with a glass eye, his face clean shaven and with ordinary length hair, smiling and kinda handsome holding his Bible close to his heart. The Concordance was obviously well used and worn. Then he pulled out the Bible and casually turned to the front flyleaf where was written: 'Happy Birthday to King Pete Verdugo. Love, Debbie' and dated the first year of their marriage.

Every single page of that well-worn Bible had some underlining or highlighting of verses, and scribbled notes in the margins. There were between the pages a couple of chapel bulletins where his name was featured as a speaker or teacher, along with a half dozen letters from discharged prisoners telling 'Bro. Pete' how much his ministry had changed their lives, thanking him for his leading them to the Lord and teaching them how to forgive and how to be forgiven.

God can use anyone.

CHAPTER 32

FINE WINE AND OLD CHEESE

They say that the best wine is the oldest wine, and that aging just makes good cheese better. That same rule applies in the human condition, but where some fear the accumulation of years, where some fear the loss of youth, the cosmetic surgery business flourishes. Wrinkles and years used to be cause for respect, used to bring reverence for the wisdom wrought of years, and confidence in grandpa's guidance.

With the passing of time one gets a much better perspective of events in the distant past, and upon detached reflection many regrets are born. How many times have you regretted that you gave priority to some stupid transitory attraction and passed up the opportunity to spend a little quality time with a relative or friend now passed away? Those worthless priorities seem so trivial now. Grampa and Gramma are gone. We can no longer tap into their wisdom. We can no longer share with them a moment of honest love and the lingering joy that kind of love can give. The only remaining point of contact is a cold headstone. Photographs are really great ways to jog the memories but the best kind of memoirs are of the warm touch of a wrinkled hand and the sound of a voice now stilled.

On the other hand, isn't it interesting that some of our worst mistakes can result in the most rewarding results? Isn't it interesting that some circumstance once viewed as abject failure is now seen as the greatest success? Isn't it interesting when that cranky old mother-in-law becomes your best friend? Or, better yet, isn't it very interesting when your daughter marries the worst deadbeat in town and he gets elected to congress?

The scriptures instruct us to fear not. Several places in the Holy Bible cover the subject of fear. A truly great Baptist preacher once observed how it seemed to him that worry was an effective weapon, because some of the things he feared the most, those things that caused the greatest amount of worry, simply never happened. That should be proof enough that worry really works. Then that same Baptist minister suggested that if anything is worth worrying about it is worth praying about, and we know that prayer changes things.

The Bible specifically says that we should pray without ceasing. The Bible specifically says that we should not worry at all. Fear not! Fear not!

Larry Cole and his twins lived very ordinary lives, and over the years there was very seldom anyone to ask anything about the extra wife. Early on in the marriage, after the first two children were born, Larry took his then five member family to his hometown of Springfield, Missouri, returned to the church of his youth, and renewed acquaintance with so many of his old classmates. For a while he would introduce his twins as "This is my wife Teri, and this is her sister Toni" then with the next introduction say "This is my wife Toni and this is her sister Teri." But he tired of the disparity and simply said that "these ladies are my most favorite persons, my wife Teri and my wife Toni." About the only response he got was a whispered "Wow. She is beautiful!"

One of the local church pastors in Missouri asked Larry if he had become an advocate of plural marriage, and Larry quickly replied to say "absolutely not". That pastor further inquired just what sort of advice Larry might have for anyone contemplating such an arrangement, and Larry respectfully informed him that he never gives marriage counseling advice to anyone, and suggesting that anyone contemplating marriage should consult the scriptures and through prayer to enlist the leading of the Holy Spirit. Larry felt that any marriage counseling advice from third parties would be impacted by their own human experience and personal prejudice. Many individuals have a personal opinion about other people's marriage choices, and Paul the Apostle seems to have expressed his sentiments in I Timothy with constraints for Deacons, and in his ministry to the Corinthians to encourage celibacy for believers to enable them to better dedicate themselves to serving the Lord. That inquisitive pastor chose then to ask Teri and Toni what their position was in this discussion, and they together responded to say that they felt it was silly to debate the matter, since it is so obviously sinful for a married man to seek romance outside his marriage.

The five Cole children lived their lives just like all the rest of the kids in their neighborhood. They had the same innocuous life experiences, with all the little bumps and bruises, the mumps, chicken pox and that kind of stuff and all of them suffered with piano lessons. All five of the Cole kids went to Catholic school. It seemed that nobody ever asked them about any of the personal lives of the Cole family. Really, now, they were just ordinary people.

Five-year-olds Richy V and Cindy Cole marched confidently into their kindergarten experience, and all the other little kiddies seemed to blend nicely with their pleasant personalities. There was one little boy named Elton Strong that took a shine to Cindy, and from the time he first laid eyes on her he initiated his flirtations. He was at first content to quietly admire, but at first opportunity he grabbed Cindy and gave her a big hug, then a quick kiss on the cheek. For his outburst of passion he was rewarded by a big fist in the face delivered by Richy V and the blood dripped out of an injured nose, and both boys got sent to the principal's office. Elton thereafter conducted his amorous campaign from a distance, and all Cindy would do was scowl and frown in return. When the kids were about twelve years old, Cindy was standing with a crowd of Hispanic girls chatting in Spanish as Elton bravely came up from behind and whispered some romantic notion in her ear, whereupon Cindy whirled around and smacked him right in the face so that once again his nose was dripping a fountain of blood. Cindy strode away a few paces, turned and shook her fist at him and with a scowl yelled for all to hear "Stop bothering me or you're gonna need a transfusion". The crowd laughed and howled and Elton was humiliated. Richy V and Cindy attended school in Mexico City during their junior year in high school, and returned to their California classes for the senior year. The very first day of their return was the day that Elton Strong commenced again his campaign to win the affections of Cindy Cole, but now the young lady noticed that Mr. Strong had grown much taller and so very handsome, but she still maintained her totally negative attitude toward his crusade. Cindy was in the crowd of spectators at a soccer tournament, Elton was on the team, the game was in its last few seconds, two players moving full speed collided near the end zone, and both hit the ground. The one player got up and staggered away, but Elton Strong remained down motionless and still. The referee signaled for the bench to come render aid. Cindy sprinted out of the crowd of spectators and was first to reach the lifeless form of Mr. Strong, as she knelt down beside him and took his head in her arms. With tears in her eyes she began to pray aloud that God might send ministering angels to touch the waning life of Elton Strong, reminding God that Elton was such a wonderful person, such a deserving servant, such a marvelous Christian, such a precious spirit and in need of divine intervention. While Cindy was imploring the Lord, Elton opened one eye to see what was goin' on, then at a lull in the prayer action he inquired "Does this mean that you're gonna start likin' me?" Cindy looked down in horror, dropped the wounded head to the ground, and shrieked *"You big phony! You're not hurt!"* She jumped to her feet and with her fists clutched down at her side she stomped and scurried off the field, whereupon the wounded one propped himself up on one elbow and called out "Wait! Don't leave me here to die! Are you comin' back? Shall I wait? Are you gonna come to my funeral?" Cindy kept trudging away, but did turn to shake her fist at the wounded one and barked *"You're disgusting!"*. The crowd cheered.

Larry Cole's family was a praying family. They had regular bedtime prayer sessions, and everyone would take part in turn, without reluctance, because that's just the way it was. When the kids left the nest, they were expected to take part in those prayer sessions upon their return.

Larry Cole grew older, his hair turned grey, but his physique was yet as muscular and trim as the day he graduated from Princeton. He has infrequent discomfort from where that Viet Cong bullet tore up his lower back, and occasionally uses a walking cane, but he is not crippled in the classic sense in that none of his pains really restrict his movements. Teri and Toni chopped off those lovely ponytails when their kids became teenagers, and you'd never know they had grey hair, because they put coloring on at regular intervals. These twins are physically still the most beautiful ladies; both still have their youthful slim figures at weight of less than 120 pounds each. Larry's wives never stopped loving him, and never stopped hugging him and smothering him with kisses every day. This is what their brood was exposed to during all their childhood, and you know this had to influence their choices and behavior in their own lives. Larry's children were all successful. The Coles had grandchildren, and then came great-grandchildren, and as of the last word we heard, more great-grandchildren were on the way. Over all the many years of his unusual marriage there were only a few times when the awkward question of plural marriage came up, and two of those questions were when the Sheriff and DA conducted their investigations. Larry became less and less concerned that somebody was gonna ask again the question so challenging to answer. It helped tremendously to assuage the apprehensions when he received that word from his Mexican lawyer that a Judge's order had been entered finally disposing of the legal issues.

Conversations within a family might be much different in comparison with more public recitals. For instance: Larry might in a family context refer to his ladies as 'wives' (plural), but in public or social situations he would only refer to his 'wife' and to his 'marriage'. Teri felt that she had a husband, and Toni felt that she had a husband. Neither of them felt that there was any sort of sharing of a husband. When referring to the husband or to the marriage neither Teri nor Toni used descriptive words that suggested any sharing of a husband. All agreed that since Richy V and Cindy were born so close together in time they should be 'twins', quickly informing inquirers that they were 'not identical twins'. When Charley and Stewie were both born on the same day, they likewise became 'twins' and likewise with the admonition that they were 'not identical twins'. Larry and the family became so very popular among the several churches they attended around Orange County, including the Catholic churches and schools where the kids attended. It was generally known that Larry was 'married' to both of the twin ladies and you know that there must have been a lot of gossip. But these social and marital questions simply never did come out openly, and neither Larry nor anyone else in the family was required to address this intimate topic.

The Remington Auto Group in Orange County was part of several business associations, and those folks would have social events from time to time to gather for dinner and a little music, and maybe some dancing for those that would care to participate. At one of these programs, while seated with Teri and Toni, Larry asked if one of them would like to prance around on the dance floor with him, and Toni was so delighted to stand and say "Me first!". While they were spinning about on the dance floor a handsome young attendee approached Teri and asked if she would dance with him. Her reply was simply "I only dance with my husband!" The young man seated himself across from her and said "Your husband doesn't appear to be around to object, and he will never know anyway." About that time, Larry and Toni came spinning by and stopped to greet the newcomer, at which time Teri said "This is my husband!", and both the girls were then seated as Larry introduced himself and shook hands with the handsome intruder, who then leaned over to speak to Toni and ask "May I have this dance?" and her reply was to decline and add "I only dance with my husband", and the young man asked "Where is your husband?", and Toni smiled real big and pointed at Larry still seated nearby. The guy then looked at Larry and silently pointed first at Teri and then at Toni, and Larry nodded his head in the affirmative. The fella chortled and as he departed he looked back at Larry and said "You must be the luckiest guy in town!"

The Remington Group moved all general administration activities to a separate office where they had no autos and only office staff. Larry was the youngest person there, and none of his employees at that office were under sixty years of age. Larry's office had a double-door entry, and he had both doors removed so that anyone passing by could see whoever was in that room and whatever they might be doing. The room was brightly lighted, and the switch for these lights was an extra item on the wall nearest the main entry, some distance away. He had pictures mounted all over his walls, showing his family in Missouri, his brother and family from Illinois, his brother and family from Arkansas, his brother-in-law from Northern California along with his wife and kids, and all five of Larry's kids alone and with their mothers and grandparents. He was especially proud to display portraits of the weddings in Santa Ana and Mexico City. There were only two topics regularly discussed in that office: (1) new and used cars and automobile sales administration and (2) Larry's family. There was no hanky-panky and not the least appearance of impropriety nor any dark place where that stuff could happen in that office.

When Larry's three sons were all in high school, Grampa Stewart Remington was really getting along in years. He quietly called the boys together, and under pretense of his concern that he might topple over and die of old age just any day, he wanted his journey on earth to be complete, and being complete required of him that he disclose to the boys some family secrets that nobody else would ever be likely to share. Then being sworn to secrecy, they huddled in the back room with Grampa as he pulled out an old video player and a copy of the videotape in the 'flying nose' incident. He simply could not contain his glee as the eyes of these young men were focused on the screen to see blow by blow how it all happened, and why their Dad had that scar on his scalp. Grampa did not share any of the underlying circumstances, but he chuckled to himself to hear the exclamations of the boys and their request to play it all over again. The only explanation they heard from Grampa was that the whole thing was just a neighborhood quarrel.

After many years of marriage, Larry Cole's firstborn son Captain Richard C. Cole V was nearing retirement from the US Navy as a Chaplain assigned to the 3rd Marines, and another son was still yet a career USMC Master Gunnery Sergeant; and two of Larry's grandchildren were still serving with the United States Marines and one had unexplainably ended up as a Petty Officer in the US Navy. His oldest daughter married a Pentecostal pastor; and three of his grandchildren ended up in pulpit ministry; and so much otherwise to demonstrate that this family had good sound Christian rearing that continues on and on. But there was an amusing event that brought into focus the validity of it all.

Get the scenario:

Gramma Shimi Remington is still living, now in her nineties. She has always been part of the home where Larry Cole is the 'Master of the House'. All four of her children are living honorable Christian lives. She is constantly praising the Lord, and at all times seeking to do something to please God. She has been an anonymous source of benevolence to most of the Christian colleges around Southern California.

Toni Cole and Teri Cole have pristine Christian character, well beloved by all their children and grandchildren and now by their great-grandchildren, and they have never once said or done anything to betray any immoral feature in their makeup. They spend more time in prayer individually and in concert, and with all their progeny, and can quote more scripture than any recent seminary graduate.

The children and grandchildren of Teri Cole and Toni Cole worship them at all times and at every opportunity they hug them and squeeze them and pour accolades of love and affection on them. They are the very picture of successful parenting. All of the Cole children and grandchildren are truly bilingual, speaking and reading Spanish as easily as English, and all of them love to visit the families in Mexico City.

Teri Cole and Toni Cole are the most perfect wives and homemakers. They don't spend a lot of time watching television or listening to the radio, but they do have their favorite broadcast preachers. The have been married to Larry Cole for about 45 years and still act like newlyweds. They tease him constantly with tickles and pinches, and spend most of their time in the evenings sitting on his lap and leaning their heads on his shoulders. They have never had a dispute between themselves and have never once ever shown any anger or hostility toward husband Larry. The home where Larry Cole thinks he's the boss is a sanctuary of peace and love, and a place of resort for all the kids and their kids and their kids. This home is a happy place and it has always been a happy place. Kids and grandchildren come so often at the same time for various occasions that they had to build a large garage addition with three extra bedrooms and an apartment for longer-term guests. The backyard is still a huge playground with slides and rings and such. On the other side of the garage is a tennis court. There is no room to park any cars in this garage because of the bodybuilding and exercise equipment located there.

After the five Cole children were older, and that means when Sarah the youngest was about ten years old, both Teri and Toni took all the courses for real estate sales license, and a few years later they obtained California real estate broker's licenses. They did manage to sell some real estate, but they mostly were in the business of acquiring property for bargain prices, and just accumulating equity. Their banker friends unloaded some apartments on them for a pittance and that property was occupied by rent subsidy people that didn't take very good care of their facilities. Then they took on a couple of other distressed apartments just a few blocks away. They recruited some professional property managers, and actually turned a profit on all units, with a very low vacancy rate. With the appreciation of property values during the late '70's they amassed quite a strong financial statement for their private corporation that held all the titles. They had to have office space and simply moved into the area next to Larry's Remington Group office, and when that building came up for sale, they acquired it also. Meanwhile, the Remington Group new and used car businesses scattered around Southern California flourished and grew.

The Cole family had given substantial financial assistance to a little independent church in Tustin, California, and would occasionally visit there. When they began to visit more often then more of their children and adult grandchildren would attend. In all there were about seventy-five individuals attending regularly that were directly or indirectly identified with the family of Larry Cole.

That little church of about 225 parishioners had a fine pastor by name of Reverend Dale Peters, who was one of those guys that every church is looking for to provide pastoral and pulpit leadership. He was young enough to be trusted by the young people who could identify with his relative youth and vitality, and still old enough that the rest of the congregation could respect his maturity, his excellent education and knowledge of the scriptures and great leadership experience. One of his most valuable assets is his wife, Gail, who is the granddaughter of Rev. Charles Augustus Bell, that renowned tent revival evangelist from the early twentieth century. She is really good-lookin', always interested in the adult ladies Bible Study groups, always taking part in the teenage girls activities, great for counseling the young people with their endless chain of problems, and she could actually take over the pulpit on occasion to present some very impressive sermons on a Sunday morning. But there can be problems to erupt from having such top-notch leadership, because such superior guidance cannot be easily duplicated when that pastoral team moves on to other callings, and that's what happened with that little Tustin church. Pastor Peters' wife's parents lived in Arizona, and were getting along in years, needing some family to come and care. There was a local church there in Kingman that needed a pastor, so they recruited Brother Peters to come take over that pulpit. He gave the little church in Tustin notice that he would be soon leaving, so the Church Board began the search for a new leader, and as part of that search they consulted with the District Superintendent of one of the major denominations very active in Orange County.

Thus there came on a temporary trial basis the good Reverend J. Arlington Perkins, a young man about 30 years of age, a graduate of a fine Bible College located south of Dallas, Texas, who was the grandson of a prominent pastor at a great church in Arkansas. The family of Brother J. Arlington Perkins had a genetic predisposition toward morbid obesity, and this Pastor of average height was very wide. He wore heavy horn-rimmed glasses, and spoke with a strong southern drawl. His sermons were delivered with a gasping kind of frantic oratory, breathing heavily as he loudly cast hell-fire and brimstone onto the consciences of sinners that surely must have been herded into the church by divine powers to receive salvation from the inspiring sermons of Reverend J. Arlington Perkins.

Now, being a responsible leader, the good Pastor Perkins enlisted one of the older ladies in the church to be his source of information as he needed to know all about the individuals and families within the congregation. It's always good to know who and what you're dealing with when you start pounding the pulpit and crushing sin in the human condition. That nice old lady informed Pastor Perkins of the gross sinfulness rampant in the Cole family. "Why,

Pastor did you know that the Cole fella has two wives? Did you know that they just walk around here actin' like they own the place? Everbody knows they been livin' in sin all these years and have all them childern that just think they're legal born. Pastor, you oughta do sumthin' about this sin in the camp! You oughta throw them wicked people outa this church. The Lord cain't bless this church or your leadership until you deal with this immoral behavior, and as one of God's chosen leaders once said 'We must excise this cancer from the body of Christ', and it's up to you Pastor Perkins to clean up this mess!"

Now comes the next Sunday morning. Larry Cole brings Teri and Toni and their aging mother Gramma Shimi Remington to church in the van. They unload the aluminum walking assistance frame that Gramma Remington refers to as her 'cruiser', and they all move toward the front door of the church. About halfway there, maybe about twenty feet from the door, they are joined by a couple of teenage boys, two of Gramma's favorite great-grandsons that walk beside her and help to steady her as she shuffles along. Right behind them is Larry Cole and clinging to his right arm is wife Teri Cole and clinging even more tightly to his left arm is wife Toni Cole, and all of these arriving parishioners are smiling and happy as clams.

As the Cole entourage entered the main sanctuary of the church they had traveled only about fifteen feet on a shuffling gait toward their usual seats down near the altar area. Gramma Remington and her two great-grandsons managed to get by, but then Larry and the twins were met by Pastor Perkins rushing up to stand in the middle of the aisle and blocking their way. He was obviously very agitated, carrying a large Bible in his left arm clasping that Holy Book close to his chest, and as Pastor Perkins had his right hand thrust up with his index finger pointing toward the rafters, apparently directing his screaming at the Cole wives, saying "Stop! Ye Whores of Babylon. Ye shall not enter in! Ye shall not defile the House of God! Yay, the Lord sayeth ye shall not enter in! The Lord sayeth 'depart ye workers of inequity, ye lovers of Satan', ye that practice that life that is evil in the sight of God. Get thee hence! Out! Out! Yay. So sayeth the Lord!" Larry and the twins looked at each other, then quietly turned and walked out the entry doors.

When Shimi Remington heard the bombastic delivery of castigating oratory from the pompous Pastor Perkins, she stopped and looked around and immediately was confronted by the wide backside of the good Pastor. She turned her cruiser about without assistance, slammed the frame into the rump of Pastor Perkins, then reached up with her fist and popped him in the his ample posterior and said "Get outa the way! You stupid jerk!", and as the pious Pastor sorta moved aside about a half step between the pews, the irate and impatient old lady shoved him again and said "You must be the dumbest screwball in all the world!" as she followed her family out the doors and away. However, as she shuffled along she gathered a long train of others following her toward the exit, mostly grandchildren and other families intermarried with the Cole descendants. Maybe about seventy-five persons or a little more of family, but then a whole lot more that well knew the Remington history and their faithfulness in attendance and their financial assistance when the church needed it most. Near the end of that line of quiet exodus was a young man carrying a small child, and as he passed by the imperious Pastor Perkins he leaned over and said "You have just made the biggest mistake of your life!"

The Cole van led a long line of cars leaving the parking lot of that little church, and they all gathered at the City Park near downtown. One of the Cole family was just a teenager but intent on someday entering the ministry, and he was appointed to deliver a sermon on whatever subject came to mind. His delivery without notes was on the topic of 'The Grace of God', heavily strewn with memorized quotations from the Bible. They sent a couple of youngsters off to buy some pizza and fried chicken, and a lotta cases of soda pop, simply made a grand picnic of the occasion, and it lasted most of the afternoon. The little kids had swings and slides and revolving apparatuses to keep them amused and the older kids got together in groups to talk teener stuff. The old folks just relaxed on the grass or nearby benches and talked about politics and the economy. Nothing much was mentioned any more that day of the eviction from church.

As though one block of people, all the folks that thought of themselves as evictees ended up at a couple of other local churches the next Sunday morning, and the Coles drove all the way up to San Bernardino to visit a Hispanic church where their grandson was part of the Youth Ministries program.

About two weeks after the great 'eviction' Larry was hard at work selling Chevrolets and Buicks and whatever, and took a phone call as he was seated behind his office desk. It was the pious Pastor J. Arlington Perkins. Reverend Perkins told Larry that he had been in touch with the Throne of God, and as he virtually sweated as it were drops of blood in fervent prayer, he had heard the audible voice of God, instructing him to make peace with the Cole family, and that God had instructed Brother Perkins to deliver a message to Larry Cole to get rid of one of those wives and get himself back into church. Larry inquired of the good Pastor "Did the Lord tell you which one of the wives has to go?" and the good Reverend replied "Well, just use your own judgment. Keep the one you like the best and send the other one packin' and then you can live for God!" Larry thanked the good Reverend for his Saintly Spirit demonstrated in the matter, and said "Goodbye!" Larry snickered and chortled for the rest of the afternoon.

Well, when the crowds did not return to church over the next couple of Sundays, the Reverend J. Arlington Perkins again phoned Larry Cole to further discuss the matter of delinquency of the Cole family from Sunday services. More particularly did Pastor Perkins say "Now Brother Cole, I been talkin' to the Lord again, and he has expressed some concern for your soul, 'cuz you ain't been comin' to church as you should. The Lord has revealed to me that if you don't want to dump one of them wives, it'd be OK if you bring 'em both to church, but one of 'em is gonna hafta sit on the back row." And Larry inquires "Did the Lord indicate which one oughta sit on the back row?" and the Reverend Perkins says "Well, the Lord didn't say. But I'm sure it'd be alright if you just choose whichever one is the better Christian to sit up front with you, and the one that is more of the sinner can sit in back!" And Larry says "Well, Pastor, I thank you for your righteous guidance. Goodbye." This little sermonette and personal testimony about a two-way conversation with God was so very amusing that it left Larry shaking his head, and he cackled and guffawed about it for the rest of the day.

The throngs continued to bypass that little church, and the good Pastor J. Arlington Perkins phoned again to solicit Larry Cole for his return to meetings. This time the Reverend Perkins said "Brother Cole, me'n the Lord we been talkin' about the church and all the faithful folks that the Lord is wantin' to bless, and He has laid it on my heart once again to invite you and your family to come on back, and the Lord will forgive you for all your bad choices and just tolerate them two wives until He can get 'em on the right track!" Then Larry asked the good Pastor Perkins about how the finances are going at the church. Pastor Perkins said "Well, Brother Cole, to be honest with you we are a'hurtin'. Since you folks left you ain't been payin' no tithes nor offerin's to the church and with no money comin' in we cain't make payroll, and the mortgage payment is a month overdue. Could you find it in your heart to help God out of this crisis?" Larry told the good Pastor Perkins "Reverend Perkins, may I suggest that you take a few minutes aside from your busy schedule this afternoon and go to your favorite title insurance company and get what in California is known as a 'property profile' on the church property. You will find that the property consists of three parcels. The church sanctuary is in the middle of two parcels that make up the parking lots. The two parking lots are owned in the name of those 'Whores of Babylon' that you publicly insulted, and the mortgage on the sanctuary parcel is owned by those same ladies. If you will check the finances of the church for the past few years, you will find that the greater part of all the missionary giving has been donated by these 'Whores of Babylon'. They have given more in the offering plates than anyone else in the congregation. After you publicly disrespected them and boldly dismissed them from the aisles of the church I don't think you'll ever be able to charm them into returning to sit under your ministry." To this the Pastor Perkins responded "Well, dear Brother Cole. How about you? Cain't you find it in your heart to invest some money in the Kingdom of God? This church cain't even pay little bills this month." And to this heartrending news Larry responded "Pastor Dear, I have bad news for you. I am just a volunteer here. I am just a freeloader. I do not own any real property. I do not own any personal property. I do not own any corporate stocks or bonds nor any other kind of business investment. I do not have a car of my own. I am a genuine pauper and receive a military disability retirement pension each month. This place where I work gives me an expense account and a credit card. I don't even get a paycheck. The home where I live is owned by those 'Whores of Babylon'. The businesses I am involved with are all controlled by a corporation, and that corporation has five persons on the board of directors, and the majority there consists of the 'Whores of Babylon' family that you tossed out of their church. If you have any church employees that are suffering for lack of payroll, you should tell them to contact Teri Cole and she will arrange to help them out, maybe give 'em office jobs or some sort of handout. Goodbye!"

Well, as fortune would have it, that certain denomination that introduced Reverend J. Arlington Perkins to ministry in Southern California had its 'District Council Convention' about the time of this last phone call between Larry Cole and Pastor Perkins. The happy and noisy convention attendees were entertaining some proposed legislation submitted by the Chairman, and Pastor

Perkins leaned over to ask local advice from one of the other pastors voting on the measure. After the ballots were collected Pastor Perkins extended the hand of fellowship to that other pastor standing nearby and introduced himself. That other pastor was Rev. Elton Strong who was a pulpit minister in Los Angeles, and he told Pastor Perkins that he had heard so much about him and his leadership. Feeling flattered by his fame, Pastor Perkins inquired of Bro. Strong where it might be that he heard of the Perkins Personae, and he said "From my Mother-in-Law", and Pastor Perkins further inquired what that Mother-in-Law's name might be, and Pastor Strong says "Her name is Toni Cole, and she is one of the 'Whores of Babylon' that you kicked out of the church!" *Whooops!*

Strange as it might seem, this little Perkins blunder didn't cause much humiliation or suffering, but seemed to have an immediate further ameliorative effect, and thereafter Larry Cole could chuckle and snicker about this whole polygamy thing, and he never again gave it much thought.

That little independent church got a much better new pastor, and the church received documents that transferred to the church corporation the legal title to those three parcels of land and improvements, parking lots and sanctuary, entirely free of debt.

Our God is still in control. In the human condition nothing can happen except it be by consent of God.

CHAPTER 33

EULOGY

Among the most notable American heroes of our time, Stanford E. Linzey, Jr., ranks along with the greatest and most highly revered. He was a hero of World War II, and was actually a Navy intraship radioman on the USS Yorktown, and had to be retrieved from the oil covered waters of the Pacific when that mighty warship went down in the Battle of Midway. He survived that conflict and the Battle of the Coral Sea one month previously. After the war he was discharged and thereafter studied for the ministry. He founded a local church in El Cajon, California, and that church is still in business this very day. He carried his studies far beyond that of the average Bible student, obtaining a list of advanced degrees that are very impressive. He gave up his church and accepted a commission with the military, being the first individual from his denomination to serve as a chaplain in the regular US Navy. Most notable of his many achievements would have to be his career as a Navy Chaplain from which he later retired after more than twenty years of dedicated service. The United States Marines Corps gets its chaplains from the Navy, and at various times during his career Captain Stan Linzey served with the 1st and 3rd Marine Divisions, as well as other units.

Captain Linzey was a supremely popular evangelical preacher. He was in demand to preside over funerals for Christians with some ties to the US Marines, but would be called on so often to speak over the caskets of men and women he did not know, had never met, and didn't really know of their spiritual condition in this life. And then there were funerals for folks that he knew were atheists or otherwise lost. For those of us that were privileged to attend a few of those unique funerals, let us say that each was a very unusual and inspiring event. Chaplain Linzey would deliver the most impressive oratory, the most stirring and persuasive spoken words and the most dramatic gestures and passages. He could stand perfectly still and freeze an audience. His voice could be so intense, somber and sober. His facial expressions alone were so communicative. His gaze could be so penetrating. He used all these skills to impress the audience about the importance of living for and serving

Jesus Christ. There is no way to adequately describe the moving experience to be present when Captain Stan Linzey was presiding at the funeral for a US Marine.

When Chaplain Linzey was to officiate at a funeral for a US Marine, let's say for a young man killed in the Vietnam hostilities, he would give instruction for placement of the US flag nearby behind the pulpit. That flag would be set over to his stage right a couple of feet behind and at about five feet away from the pulpit, and that banner would always be an important part of the funeral message. Chaplain Linzey would usually be seated quietly on the front row over to stage left with his legs folded and hat on his lap until he was called to the pulpit. When so called, he would stand alert and tall, place his hat upon his head, walk confidently up onto the platform, stand silently for several seconds at full attention in front of the US Flag, then salute the flag for about five or six seconds, then move over to stand in front of the pulpit. He would then dramatically remove his cap and place it upside down on the table of the pulpit, and without any expression on his somber face he would step back about one pace with his hands down at his side, and look around the room. By this time he has the full attention of everyone in the place, including the funeral directors that would otherwise be preoccupied with whatever. Then the expression on his face would suddenly change to a confident half-smile, and he'd stride up to the pulpit and grip it on each side, waiting dramatically for a few seconds as again he glanced about the room.

Most of his funeral message would be designed to meet needs of the actual situation, particularly as it relates to the hereafter and the eternal consequence of the life of the one who had just died. There are usually some Marines or former Marines present to bid farewell to a fallen comrade. If Brother Linzey knew that no Marines were present, he would at least infer their presence by word and application. At that point the funeral seems to become much more like the average eulogy and delivering a few words of praise for the recently departed. There would always be some recital of a bit of the history of the United States Marine Corps and the part that the deceased might have played in peacetime or war, and in the process to reveal his or her importance for the benefit of the family and friends. But especially if that young person had fallen in battle or other service for his country, Chaplain Linzey would become very passionate in a most vibrant and emotional manner, moving one or the other of his arms with his hands palm up or palm down depending on the words to accompany the thought, leaning forward slightly bowing at the waist, his eyes moving over the audience as though to peer into the souls of everyone within the sound of his voice, so to inform all that this departed special person might have some special place in the eternal order.

He then would wax eloquent, tilt his head a little and gaze over the heads of the congregation, and without referring to any notes, in a very somber and reflective way slowly say something like this:

"One of the most touching memories I have of the Second World War are the white gravestones, row after row, thousands upon thousands of markers on the resting places of brave young men. I have stood in the morning light on the bluffs overlooking the graves of fine American Soldiers, Sailors, Marines and Airmen who gave that ultimate sacrifice in the invasion of Normandy, and I've walked between the rows to read the names of those noble heroes beneath the crosses and stars marking their place of repose. Time has not eroded the respect for these martyrs, nor has the passing of time washed away our memory of what they gave in exchange for our freedom. It is emotionally overwhelming to touch the cold white stone markers, to read the names carved into them, and to know that they died for freedom. Our freedom.

"There are a number of places around the world that stand out in our memory of ultimate sacrifice. I have stood on the high ground overlooking the beaches of Iwo Jima in the quiet of evening between sunset and the dark of night, and in the distance can be seen the shadow of Mount Suribachi, where young marines raised the American flag now in pictures and statues well recalled. Just below where I then stood was the original gravesite of more than eleven hundred young men identified with the United States Marines 3rd Division. It was quiet as I lingered there for some time, only to imagine the noise of war that was the last sound heard by those brave Marines. Among them were fathers, sons, brothers, uncles that were greatly loved by wives and mothers, families and friends. I imagined the stench of battle, the many bodies littering the beaches. The US Navy warships gathered beyond the horizon, the landing craft moving men and equipment onto the beachhead, the explosion of Japanese ordnance on the beach site and aimed at the arriving and departing transport vessels. Fright and fear must have been everywhere, but so was Semper Fi.

"The scriptures tell us of a great resurrection day, which the angel will announce with a blast from his trumpet, and there will be a great shout as the graves open to surrender the saints who will rise, then to gather at the pearly gates of that great New Jerusalem. Well, the version told by the Marine Corps Chaplain probably does not exactly conform to the actual wording of Holy Writ, but there has been the suggestion that at the graveyard of US Marines that trumpet will sound 'reveille' and that shout will be 'Semper Fi', and rather than to float around in the air like aimless vapors, those sainted Marines will confidently march together in one proud and orderly troupe to present themselves to the keeper of the gates of that city. But they shall not enter the regular pearly gates, as there will be a special access just a little ways down from the main entrance, with portals reserved exclusively for US Marines. You can imagine how grand it will be, with precious stone and tall doors beneath a magnificent portico over which there will be in solid gold letters the words 'Semper Fi'. There will be no sounds of battle or the groans of the wounded and dying. There will be no stench of death or the foul smell of gunpowder and exploding mortars. There will be the sweet fragrance of a divine presence, and the welcoming committee of many angels will strum their harps and sing about some places called Halls of Montezuma and Shores of Tripoli, and surely will there be heard the reverberant echoes of 'Semper Fi'. Can you imagine the magnificent welcoming celebration beside the Crystal Sea? Maybe so, maybe not, but it's a good thought."

Chaplain Linzey would somehow always weave into his eulogy the message of salvation in Jesus Christ, even in those funerals for atheists and declared agnostics. Many of those otherwise somber funerals erupted into altar calls and prayer meetings. He calmly proclaimed that such was his mission for which he was called, and he was not the least reluctant to offer the plan of salvation at any time or place. Many responded. Seldom was there any criticism from anyone in this regard.

The last words of Chaplain Linzey's presentation from the pulpit for funeral of a departed US Marine were always 'Semper Fi!'

Then he would quietly replace his cap to his head, and standing tall and erect would make a military turn to face the American flag, standing silent for several seconds just gazing at the flag, then snap off a military salute and hold it for about five seconds. Then he would turn and look over the audience, and that congregation would by then be almost to a man in tears and sentimental reflection. He would in silence take the time to try to make eye contact with everyone that would look at him, then he would dramatically touch the brim of his cap and adjust it comfortably, step down from the platform and stride over to a place in front of the marines that are actually in the audience usually located over to his right, or even if he had to create a phantom battalion there, if they were uniformed Marines they would by this time be standing at attention whether on command or spontaneously and as Chaplain Linzey would stand then at attention, he would turn to salute the flag-draped casket.

Chaplain Linzey might then turn to the Marines, smile and raise his fist and yell "Oooo Raaah!" and usually every Marine in the building would respond loud enough to shake the walls "Ooooh Raaah!" Then Brother Linzey would remove his cap and go into the audience to stand with the lowest ranking Marine he could find, as the remainder of the service continued. Most preachers that deliver the funeral sermon will stand with the funeral directors or the family to shake hands and greet the mourners moving by the casket, but Chaplain Stan Linzey would always stand with the Marines. That's part of Semper Fi.

Ooooh Raaah!

Semper Fi. There are recitals in scripture to confirm for the saints the same admonitions urging commitment to the mission. One of them is found at Proverbs 3:5-6, where it says "Trust in the Lord with all your heart; and lean not unto your own understanding. In all your ways acknowledge Him, and He shall direct your paths." And in Isaiah 26:3 we find the promise that God will keep him in perfect peace whose mind is stayed upon the Lord. These recitals are commands and promises to guide the Christian in his daily walk. It's another declaration of 'Semper Fi'.

Go ye therefore unto all the world and tell everyone about ***Semper Fi!***

FAIT ACCOMPLI

That which is recited here is simply a tale about how ordinary people can be caught up in the most ridiculous situations. These things do occur and often are without conventional remedy. When such misfortunes happen to others we too often impose on them what we are taught is the most effective or otherwise acceptable therapy. Actually, some of these human foibles require miracles to rescue victims of what are perceived as shameful circumstances, and society imposes an even more disgraceful cure. Occasionally, some unforeseen remedy seems to fall out of the sky and we fail to see it as the miracle that we hoped would come. The truth is that many of us could tell of our own little miracles, but some miracles seem to go unnoticed.

FIN

****

DISCLAIMER

DEAR READER, AS YOU GO THROUGH THIS LITTLE EPISTLE, YOU ARE AT LIBERTY TO USE YOUR COMMON SENSE. A PERSON OF EVEN LIMITED INTELLIGENCE WILL EASILY RECOGNIZE THAT THE SOCIAL EVENTS PORTRAYED IN THIS RECITAL ARE SO OUTRAGEOUS, SO RIDICULOUS, SO FAR-FETCHED, AS TO PRIMA FACIE BETRAY ITS ORIGINS IN FANCY AND FOLLY, THE PRODUCT OF AN IRRATIONAL MIND, A SILLY ROMANTIC AUTHOR OF QUESTIONABLE PERSPICACITY. IT SHOULD BE OBVIOUS TO THE KNOWLEDGEABLE OBSERVER THAT THESE WANTON CONCOCTIONS OF INCREDIBLE FANCY ARE BEYOND REASON, WITHOUT RATIONAL ASSOCIATION. THE INTELLIGENT READER FILLED WITH THIS WORLD'S WISDOM WILL SURELY SAY HOW SILLY IT WOULD BE TO BELIEVE THAT ANY OF THESE EVENTS ACTUALLY HAPPENED. THE CHARACTERS AND NAMES HEREIN WILL BE RECOGNIZED BY THE MAN OF THE WORLD AS FICTITIOUS, AND ANY SIMILARITY TO THE NAME, CHARACTER AND HISTORY OF ANY PERSON, LIVING OR DEAD, WILL BE BY SUCH INTELLIGENT READER SEEN AS ENTIRELY COINCIDENTAL AND UNINTENTIONAL. PLEASE AUGMENT THESE DISCLAIMER WORDS WITH THE ADMONITIONS OF THE ANCIENT ONE WHO ADVISED THAT HOPE DEFERRED MAKES THE HEART SICK, BUT WHEN THE DESIRE IS FULFILLED, IT IS A TREE OF LIFE. THERE IS THAT WHICH IS BETTER THAN RUBIES OR PEARLS, YAY MUCH BETTER THAN SILVER OR GOLD. THE KEY TO UNDERSTANDING THE FOREGOING ADMONITIONS CAN BE FOUND IN ANCIENT WRIT AS WELL AS WITHIN THE STORY ITSELF.

IN MEMORIAM

CAPTAIN STANFORD E. LINZEY, JR. CHC USN, 3rd USMC (Ret/Dec)

We shall meet again. Yes, we shall soon meet again.